DESTINY

THE SKY JEWEL LEGACY

GREGORY HEAL

ACKNOWLEDGMENTS

To my wife and daughter.
You keep me dreaming.

DESTINY

Book 3 of The Sky Jewel Legacy

By
Gregory Heal

CHAPTER ONE

Jennifer Lancaster stood steps away from the hut in which her distant ancestor, Genevieve Lancaster, rested. Countless stars dotted the deep velvet sky above Camelore, the floating island that was sanctuary to the last remaining Lightseekers of the Sorcery Guild. Yet several hours from dawn, the night air was deathly still and brisk, making Jen feel like time had stopped since she and her group had fled the Eye of the Sahara, where they had witnessed the destruction of the Halostone and sudden demise of Lord Ferox, the demonic sorcerer who sought to subjugate the eleven known realms.

Not eleven, Jen thought, still reeling from the revelation. *Twelve.*

And there, in that previously undiscovered realm, had rested the Halostone for over fifteen hundred years.

Now that her adrenaline was subsiding, Jen's hands were beginning to cramp up; she'd been balling her fists to prevent them from shaking. She kept squeezing though, digging her fingernails into her palm for fear that tears would start once she began to relax. Not out of sadness, but relief. Relief that the war into which Jen had been thrown was finally over—one that had lasted for over a thousand years and cost the lives of several generations of sorcerers.

Jen stared unblinkingly at the wooden door, her dry eyes

screaming for her to blink. She refused, unable to stop reliving the events from earlier that evening. She still couldn't quite believe how quickly it had all ended. No one could have expected that the Halostone had been holding both Ferox *and* Genevieve, preserving their duel that had gone down in infamy as the Great Battle.

And, in a heartbeat, it was over.

In between the crackling sparks and blinding lights of the deafening crescendo, Genevieve's final spell had successfully engulfed Lord Ferox, eviscerating the sinister sorcerer entirely and leaving only a tattered, dark-green robe to flutter aimlessly along the arid battlefield that was once home to the fabled—but very much real—lost kingdom of Atlantis.

Lord Ferox had finally been defeated.

So why did Jen feel like something was . . . off?

She knew that Malcolm was still at large, having escaped on the back of his wyvern dragon, Volcanor, seconds after Ferox had been defeated. She knew he had to be found before he caused any more damage. But that wasn't the feeling that she couldn't shake. She shook the thought from her head with a self-deprecating snicker, finally allowing herself to blink. She was probably just overly tired, she mused. After all, her nexus was still recovering from the blackout she'd sustained seconds after helping her father, Charles Lancaster, raise the entire city of Atlantis into the sky.

A chill crawled across her bare shoulders. She wrapped her arms across her chest, resting her fingers on each shoulder. She traced the slight indentations of both lines of scar tissue that had been left by her first encounter with Volcanor when that hellish dragon picked her up by its talons, like a hungry eagle snatching a salmon that had been swimming too close to the water's surface. As if it were yesterday, she vividly remembered being lifted high into the air, the searing pain of the dragon's grip quickly turning her shoulders numb as nerve connections were severed. She would have sustained irreparable damage if not for her nexus. It activated the moltic spell and formed an exoskeleton around her, which allowed Jen to slip from Volcanor's grip and the gruesome fate that would have awaited her had she made it back to wherever Ferox would have taken her.

Thankfully, her shoulders had healed quickly—even regaining normal feeling—though they remained scarred. Shortly after, Jen had tried to hide them out of embarrassment, but she now viewed them as marks of bravery, a reminder of one of the many things from which she had survived during her brief but intense time as an omnimancer-in-training as she helped stop a centuries-long war. A war which, due to Jen's efforts and that of those around her, from its ashes had finally released her distant relative. The one who, fifteen hundred years ago, had sacrificed herself so that Lord Ferox's evil would never have the slightest chance to infect all eleven—*Twelve,* Jen amended—realms like a deadly plague.

With the knowledge that Genevieve didn't in fact die in her last stand but was merely trapped in the Halostone with Ferox, questions of all sorts had started to stack in Jen's mind. She hoped she could remember them all by the time Genevieve awoke and was deemed ready to be seen.

Still deep in thought, Jen traced the doorframe with her eyes when she felt a warm hand rest atop her own. She didn't have to look around to know that it was her uncle, Victor Huxley.

"Do you Lancasters even sleep?"

Victor's voice was strong yet gentle. He gave her hand a barely noticeable squeeze.

Jen smiled and turned toward him. "Apparently only when we get knocked out," she joked. "Charles is awake, too?"

"That father of yours insisted on relieving me from my watch. He's with Cindergray now," Victor said. He blinked slowly, showing his fatigue.

Jen's smile vanished. "How is the Grand Mystra?"

Victor rolled his lips inward until his mouth was a thin line. He shook his head and let his hand slide from hers. "He regained consciousness about ten minutes into my shift, screaming and writhing around like something was eating him from the inside. I never thought I'd see the Grand Mystra like this, Jenny." His eyes were distant, elsewhere.

"It's hard to watch," Jen agreed. She remembered seeing Cindergray rolling on the desert sand, trapped by one of her father's spells moments after Genevieve's spell had decimated Ferox. He was screaming *"Mother!"* over and over again, until Charles knocked him out with a second spell.

Another shattering revelation that was difficult for Jen to believe: Grand Mystra Cindergray was actually Philip Lancaster II, the only son of Genevieve and Philip Lancaster—the latter of whom had fallen and took the mantle of Lord Ferox.

Thinking aloud, Jen said, "So if the Grand Mystra is actually Philip II, then—"

"That," Victor interrupted, seeming to know exactly where Jen was going, "is something I too am very interested in learning." He straightened, reaching his full height as he gazed into the night sky. "Though it remains to be seen how cooperative he'll be now that we all know his true identity." He looked down, back at Jen. "And his intentions."

"I have . . . *so many questions*," Jen breathed, breaking away from Victor's gaze to stare at the hut's door. She'd been staring at it, willing it to open, for so long that she could now effortlessly retrace all of its knots and grains if it came down to it. Feeling her bottom lip start to quiver, she bit it in the hopes of distracting herself with the pressure from her teeth. When that didn't work, she cleared her throat and said, "After everyone went to bed, I felt . . . *pulled* to her." She nodded in the direction of Genevieve as if able to see her through the petrified wooden door. She slid her hand from her shoulder to wrap it around her family ring, the Ring of Lancaster, but she only felt her collarbone, reminded that it was drawn back to Genevieve almost the instant she'd been released from the Halostone.

"Makes sense. You both share the same blood," Victor said, acknowledging her feelings. "I can't quite believe Genevieve has survived . . . but she's safe now, and not going anywhere." He took a deep breath and stuck his thumbs in his belt loops. "I'm sure you'll get your chance to speak with her once she awakens."

"You're right," Jen said after a few seconds. Scratching her head, she squinted up at Victor. "Is it weird that I'm expecting something bad to happen?"

He chuckled through his nostrils. "You're not used to peace and quiet, Jenny. Ever since Malcolm revealed who he really was and attacked you on Earth, you've been either on the run from him or leading an expedition to be the first to collect all the Mysti-Crystals. Which"—Victor jutted a thumb in the direction of the helioarch, Camelore's grand ceremonial chambers and the temporary holding place of the five MystiCrystals—"I'd say you've accomplished." He gave a lopsided smile. "So, no . . . no, it's not weird to be thinking that."

"Hearing you say that helps. But just a little bit." She threw a wink at him.

"Hey, that's what uncles are for," Victor replied lightly. He draped an arm around her, and together they walked in the direction of her hut.

Under the crisp moonlight and twinkling constellations, they walked across the compound in silence, passing by huts ranging from fully intact to charred remnants (thanks to Malcolm's ambush, complete with a small army of golem soldiers). The ones that were salvageable were already in the process of being rebuilt. Jocelyn and Resolved "Rez" Hephalon—her mother and friend, respectively—had started repairing those specific huts after they had volunteered to stay behind to tend to Rez's father. Sterling Hephalon had been gravely injured by Malcolm in the waning minutes of his ambush before he left to track down the AniCrystal (which had led Jen and the others to travel back to Atlantis to warn its queen and people of the impending attack on their seemingly untouchable hidden city).

As Jen silently gave thanks that her hut wasn't terribly affected, she was pleasantly surprised at how much progress Jocelyn and Rez had made in such a short amount of time. The work was far from over, though, as she and Victor saw as they

5

traversed the debris-strewn barracks area: there were extra cot sheets, rough burlap sacks, and other large pieces of fabric being used as makeshift doors, roofing, and walls in the interim.

Right as Victor was about to reach for her door handle, Jen rolled into his chest and embraced him tightly.

"Oh-ho, hey . . ." Victor whispered as he wrapped his arms around his niece.

Jen prolonged the hug until she was able to control her emotions. With everything that had happened, she couldn't measure how grateful she was for Victor, Charles, and her friends. "You've no idea how much you mean to me, Vic," she said as she pulled away.

Did Victor's eyes have a little extra moonlight sparkle?

He sniffled. "Well, whatever amount that is, double it and you'll get how proud I am of you, Jenny. Everything you've been able to overcome and accomplish in such a short—not to mention intense," he said with a chuckle, "amount of time . . . it's truly astounding."

He affectionately squeezed her arm before turning back to the hut and pulling the door open, slowly revealing the darkened interior. Therein lay the sleeping form of Jen's best friend, Mirabelle "Mira" Amian, in the hammock across the room from her own.

"You deserve a good night's rest. We'll talk more in the morning," Victor added, but much quieter so as not to stir Mira.

"Who will take the watch after Charles?"

"His better half," Victor said, referring to Jocelyn. "Now . . . *go to sleep.*" He playfully prodded her inside.

"All right, all right." Jen chuckled lightly, putting her hands up in mock surrender while trying not to wake Mira as she stepped deeper into the hut. She took a few more steps before stopping and looking back at her uncle. "Thanks, Vic. For everything."

"I'm always here for you," he said before closing the door, leaving Jen in the dark stillness with Mira's deep breathing.

Wiping away a tear, Jen looked at her best friend, her sleeping form softly silhouetted by the silver moonlight shining through a crack in the drawn, opaque shades. Her chest rose and fell in deep, rhythmic cycles; Jen desperately wanted to experience that kind of sleep herself. She slid off her boots and curled up in her hammock, not bothering to change out of her clothes. She wondered if Gavin was still awake, maybe flipping through Merlin's journal in his hut (which also had only sustained minimal damage since it was near the barrack's outer perimeter). He'd taken the journal back with him after they'd returned to Camelore and put the MystiCrystals in the helioarch. He'd said there were more passages after the ones that had helped them decipher the locations of the MystiCrystals, and admitted he found a sense of serenity when reading the coded text that only he, the Light Bringer, could decipher.

Jen scoffed to herself. Gavin sure did love bringing up that he was the *only* person able to read the journal. Jen rolled to her other side in an attempt to get more comfortable, opening herself up to Sleep's warm embrace, but something in her gut made her toss and turn. Scowling, she sat back up and let her toes dangle inches from the ground. She silently rocked, trying to ascertain why that lingering sense of paranoia wouldn't leave.

After a few minutes, Jen knew that she wouldn't be able to fall asleep without clearing her mind. So, having an idea, she slid her boots back on and quietly exited the hut. A few more minutes passed before she crept back in, holding something that glistened prismatically from the silver moonlight, and slid into her hammock's rocking cradle. Her paranoia eventually lessened enough to welcome the long-awaited fatigue, and when it came, it hit her like one of Hephalon's forging hammers. Before Jen could realize it, she was wrapped in one of the deepest sleeps she'd ever experienced.

Not even the slight rumbles emanating from deep underneath the Pentarena, the main training area on Camelore, stirred the young omnimancer . . .

CHAPTER TWO

Through the invisibarrier wall of the Cube—a small underground extension of the Pentarena—Charles Lancaster watched a man in deep emotional and physical turmoil. A man who, for years, convinced everyone that he was Aldred Cindergray, the Grand Mystra of the Sorcery Guild. In reality, he was Philip Lancaster II, son of legendary mystra Genevieve Lancaster, born in the sixth century CE . . . and Charles's distant ancestor.

How Cindergray managed to stay alive for this long, Charles had no other ideas except for that Cindergray must have mastered the forbidden proxichronomancic spell that delayed aging. Each of the five Mancy planes had its own proximancic spells—certain spells that were deemed forbidden, mostly because failure to successfully execute them meant instant and agonizing death to the recipient. Even to attempt conjuring such spells required complete mastery over that specific Mancy plane and one's own nexus. Historically, the only sorcerers who could stand even a remote chance of achieving such remarkable and deadly feats were mystras of each Mancy plane . . . and omnimancers.

Of which Cindergray revealed himself to be only hours ago.

It was written into legend that Philip II had become so obsessed with his final quest of finding the Halostone that he had died in his pursuit, leaving behind both a wife and an infant daughter. That legend was now debunked, for Philip hadn't perished during that quest, as evidenced by Charles guarding him at the current moment. Philip must have trained for years—nay, *decades*—to finally reach a point where he had felt comfortable enough to try conjuring the forbidden chronomancy spell. Sadly, while he had successfully prolonged his own life, he had allowed his wife and daughter to grow old and eventually pass on, never knowing what had become of him.

The skin around Charles's eyes went taut as he examined the man to whom he had given all of his trust and loyalty. Cindergray seemed to be a shell of his former self, frail and erratic instead of stalwart and composed, as he paced around the small confines of the Cube like a feral Bengal tiger. The only light that reached this far beneath Camelore's surface came from the thick roots of the Arbor Sacré, the mystical tree responsible for Camelore's suspended state above Earth. Its colorful ribbons of light passed over Cindergray as he continued to stagger inside the Cube, trying to exert his Mancy powers in fruitless attempts to escape. Within the Cube, however, each spell was completely nullified.

The Cube was created by the Camelore Twenty-Four nearly fifteen hundred years ago. Those last remaining sorcerers of the Dark Purge thought it wise to have a place specifically designed for deep meditation as the Sorcery Guild was being rebuilt (the headquarters' location having been decided as Azumar). Fueled by the roots of the Arbor Sacré, this subterranean section of the Pentarena was mostly invisible, save for the rainbow-lit lines delineating the corners and sides of the Cube, and simulated a vacuum for all of the five Mancy planes, neutralizing one's ability to tap into their nexus should they find themself inside. The Camelore Twenty-Four had thought it necessary for sorcerers to never forget their humanity and respect for the powers that were bestowed upon them. Spending time in the Cube ensured that they remained humble and grounded.

Now, it was being used as a prison for one of the most deceptive sorcerers to ever live.

Charles remained motionless as his eyes tracked Cindergray,

listening to his muted, hoarse yells and exasperated grunts as the old man rammed his shoulders and threw his fists at the Cube's walls. The Grand Mystra had been rendered powerless. It almost made Charles smile.

Almost.

The thought that had stopped him from grinning was the realization that Cindergray could have been the mole in the Sorcery Guild, not Simone Chen . . . which would mean that this man was the reason for Charles's amnesia and Jocelyn's death and eventual resurrection as a vampire. Charles ground his teeth so hard that his ears rang. He wasn't certain whether or not Cindergray was the actual mastermind behind Lord Draconex's trap on Ocuul those twenty years ago, but he was now determined to find out. Relaxing his jaw muscles, Charles drew in a long breath through his nose, refocusing as he tapped into the meditative powers of telemancy. He crossed his arms and rooted his feet on the densely packed soil.

That small movement alerted Cindergray. The Grand Mystra turned his head in Charles's direction and trained his eyes on the younger omnimancer. With surprising spryness, Cindergray charged at him, only to be abruptly stopped by the Cube's invisi-barrier wall.

Charles didn't even blink at Cindergray's attempted assault; instead, he continued glaring at his former chronomancy mystra with a look of aggravation and pity, the former being a little more prevalent than the latter. Cindergray sucked in ragged gasps of air as his chest heaved up and down. His eyes trembled, not focusing on anything in particular, as he screamed *"Mother!"* several times, before Charles finally reached his wits' end.

"No one can hear you." Charles enunciated each word loudly and slowly. The striated muscles in his forearms rolled underneath his skin as he wrestled with how to temper the pent-up contempt he felt building up inside. He dug his heels into the well-trodden dirt floor that had once felt the boots of mystras long-passed, powerful sorcerers who had most surely taught

Cindergray—*Philip*, they would have known him as Philip, his actual, given name—back when he was just a boy.

The old man's eyes flicked back to Charles, his posture suddenly becoming rigid. Incoherent whispers babbled from his lips as he grabbed his head with shaking hands, hunched over, a man gone insane. His breathing slowly calmed and he fell silent. Cindergray drew himself up to his full height, dropped his arms to his sides, and faced Charles, now with a different air about him. His eyes, now stable and piercing, seemed to be trying to burn a hole in Charles's very soul.

"No one can keep me from my mother," Cindergray said, eerily in control of his emotions. His chin dropped a touch.

Charles felt a chill frost the base of his spine, which he managed to suppress with the slightest of shoulder rolls. "Look at where you are. I beg to differ."

Cindergray's left eye twitched before he shrugged, his eyes still trained on Charles. "I've found myself in worse predicaments."

That comment triggered something deep inside Charles. His mind brought him back to the night of the explosion on Ocuul. The night that he and his wife, Jocelyn, had together planned to oust the Sorcery Guild's mole, only to instead find themselves in a trap. For the next twenty years he'd been a prisoner in his own mind, force-fed lies that Jocelyn had died as a result of the explosion.

Charles sneered. "I think I've got you beat."

"You don't want to know what I've been through, Charles . . . what I've had to do," Cindergray breathed.

Hold back. It's not worth it, Charles told himself. *Hold—*

"Don't try to justify what you did to Jocelyn and me."

He leaned forward, but his feet remained planted, his grip on telemancy now an afterthought, his meditative state shattered. Almost immediately Charles regretted not holding back, and silently berated himself for not being more in control of his emotions.

"And what exactly are you accusing me of, Charles?"

11

Cindergray said, squinting as if trying to locate Charles through a dense fog.

Charles's breathing became shallow. He bit the inside of his cheek to prevent himself from blurting out the first thing that came to his mind.

To Hell with it.

"You know damn well what," he growled.

The Grand Mystra snickered, cavalierly pulling taut the creases of his robe. "No sense in keeping up any last remaining pretenses." He clasped his hands in front of him. "*I* was the one who ordered Draconex to follow you and Jocelyn to Ocuul after you had claimed you deciphered the Halostone's location."

Cindergray's emotionless admission tore at Charles's guts like a starving lion. But that feeling quickly morphed into searing, heart-wrenching pain. He let his hands drop to his sides, fighting against the tunnel vision that threatened to throw him into darkness.

So it's true . . . The mole wasn't Chen.

He took a step forward, suddenly unable to catch his breath. With tear-streaked eyes he looked at Cindergray, arms crossed and shoulders set squarely forward. How could the Grand Mystra of the Sorcery Guild knowingly put a fellow sorcerer in harm's way?

"Does the Sorcerer's Oath mean nothing to you?" Charles said. His throat hurt from its sudden dryness. He could hear his heart throbbing as vertigo fought to take over and send his senses whirling. He took another step closer to the Cube so he wouldn't collapse, but once he started he couldn't stop: he staggered forward until he collided with the invisibarrier.

Now it was Cindergray's turn not to flinch. He stood resolute as he said, "Finding the Halostone to save my mother had always taken priority over the contrived, hollow intentions of the Sorcery Guild."

Charles rolled onto his back and slid down the Cube's outer wall until he came to a rest on the ground, staring blankly at the pulsating roots of the Arbor Sacré. He had put his entire faith into

Cindergray and the Sorcery Guild when, in reality, it was just as corrupt as the Dark Watcher tribe, the very sorcerers who wanted nothing more than to resurrect Lord Ferox and allow him to rule every realm. What made it worse, though, was that the one who was at the top of the Guild wore an altruistic, disarming façade, and Charles had bought it, had put all his faith into such a man. Reeling, Charles realized he had no way to pinpoint when the corruption could have possibly started.

"Even if it meant sacrificing my progeny," Cindergray continued. He had moved right up to Charles's ear, so that his whisper was menacingly loud, cutting through him like a freshly sharpened longsword.

Charles let out all the air in his lungs with one withered breath as he reached into his nexus and activated terramancy. Columns of air shot from his palms, pushing him off the ground and spinning him back around to face Cindergray. He then switched to animancy and, with the strength of a silverback gorilla, slammed his fist into the invisibarrier. Camelore shook ever so slightly.

"You took two decades from me!"

Cindergray slowly stood back up from where he was kneeling. "I had to."

Charles ignored him, continuing, "You killed Jocelyn!" He let a warm tear streak down his cheek. "You let Draconex turn her into a vampire!"

"I . . . *had* . . . to," Cindergray repeated.

Charles slammed his other fist against the Cube, his brute power again shaking the very core of Camelore. "No, you *didn't!*"

"Draconex was about to reveal my involvement on both sides of the war. That would have unraveled everything I had spent centuries planting and letting take root. Charles," Cindergray said, cocking his head slightly, "you would have done the same to save Jennifer."

That was when his pain finally gave way to anger. "How *dare* you infer that!" Charles slammed the Cube again, this time with both closed fists. "I would never compromise others for my selfish gain. I am *nothing* like you!"

Again, a tremor.

KRCKK!

Charles was seeing red and barely noticed the stress he was putting on the integrity of the Cube. When he pulled his closed fist away from the transparent wall, a hairline crack remained.

"Au contraire. You are, Charles." Cindergray gave him a knowing smile. "More than you would ever think possible. Or care to admit." His eyes glinted as if gazing into the future.

Charles pushed himself from the Cube and—did Cindergray step closer to the invisibarrier?—summoned astromancy, turning his arms into the hardest mineral found in the universe: lonsdaleite. His arms shimmered in dichroic translucence as with all his might he swung at the Cube, wanting nothing more than to crush Cindergray.

KRRAACKKKK!

Charles's ears rang as the invisibarrier stopped his wild, uncontrolled punch, but his strike landed exactly where he had made the first small crack in the wall.

Before Charles fully realized what he had done, a migraine formed in his frontal lobe and his vision spiraled into Stygian darkness.

CHAPTER THREE

Genevieve Lancaster wasn't asleep . . . and she wasn't Genevieve Lancaster.

Even though the form lying inside the dark hut, listening to the hushed tones of two strangers outside, did indeed belong to Genevieve Lancaster, she was not currently in control. Instead, her husband, Philip Lancaster I, the one a great many dead sorcerers had once called Lord Ferox, was possessing her body.

And in full control.

It had all happened so quickly. Back on Earth, next to the archaic and mysterious Stonehenge, Ferox had been chipping away at Genevieve's barrier spells, weakening her to the point where he could then cast a finishing blow and be the most powerful sorcerer in existence. That was when he'd caught sight of the Halostone, its geodic crystals of purple and gold shimmering in the night as it arced through the air, tossed by Gwendolyn Lancaster, between him and Genevieve. As it had completed its arc just above their currents of colorful spells, he noticed Genevieve redirect one of her hands and track the Halostone. Ferox hadn't had enough time to conjure a counterattack before Genevieve lanced a spell directly at the stone, from which it augmented into a blinding, electrifying surge that hurtled straight toward him.

The only thing he could do was yell.

Ferox had felt his instincts kick in as his nexus had burnt up every last bit of its reserves in a last-ditch attempt to protect him from the massive energy spell that was rolling his way. In that rash effort of self-preservation, he must have bonded with Genevieve's containment spell and inadvertently carried his soul into his wife's body while he left his own unprotected. Ferox had never experienced that level of pure power or heightened awareness before. Nor did he ever think it possible.

Back in the present, his new ears twitched, picking up the retreating footfalls of the two strangers. Then, finally, silence. Ferox expected the eerie, melodic whispers of the ShadowCrystal to bubble up and echo in his mind, but no such thing happened. Rightly so: the ShadowCrystal was gone. To where, he hadn't a clue. His only company now was infinite silence and his own thoughts.

In a body that was not his.

Slowly, Ferox pushed himself up until he was sitting. His wife was still wearing the elegant purple velvet gown, hand-stitched by her mother. A band of gold ran through silver borders of ornate Celtic design along the trim of her gown, accentuating her sharp collarbone and soft, curved shoulders. Those stunning colors, also present in an eloquent sash that lay flatteringly around her small waist, contrasted beautifully against the rich purple color of the gown's fabric. The minimal tears and burn holes from their duel revealed smooth, undamaged skin, and he peered over knees covered in more fabric to see her golden-silk-heeled shoes embroidered with small pearls. He raised his new, slender hands and flexed the fingers, noticing the Ring of Lancaster on the right ring finger. He angled it so he could look upon its central shield, depicting the writhing form of the first dragon tamed by the Lancaster Clan before two clashing longswords.

Then came the tremors of withdrawal.

Even though Ferox noticed a clarity of mind since being separated from the ShadowCrystal, its absence overshadowed that clearheadedness and instead began taking a toll on his soul. Ferox had merged so completely with the ShadowCrystal that his abrupt separation from it left him craving its intoxicating qualities like an opium addict. The tremors which had begun in his hands now traveled throughout Genevieve's entire body. Bracing himself, Ferox grabbed the edge of the cot, digging in with the long fingernails he now controlled, puncturing deep into the fabric.

With the withdrawals then came vertigo. His senses swimming in an endless vortex of nauseating dizziness, Ferox succumbed to its intensity and fell back onto the cot. Groaning, he covered his feminine porcelain face with his delicate hands. The smell of his wife's perfume triggered memories which briefly caused the shaking to subside. A normal person would feel a sense of warmth, of comfort, at the smell of a loved one, but Ferox was far from normal. What he felt instead for Genevieve Lancaster, the woman who was once the love of his life, was indignant contempt. Loathsome tears ran down smooth cheeks as Ferox grimaced, simultaneously wrestling with the pain of his withdrawals and the suffering Genevieve had put him through—the same suffering that had led him to obsessively seek out ways to artificially turn himself into an omnimancer. Ways that were deemed by the Guild to be unnatural and unholy.

His breath caught in his chest, and Ferox let the feminine hands hover above the face he controlled, rotating them slowly as he realized that his wife was an omnimancer . . . and he was in *her* body. An idea formed in his mind as he struggled to employ certain meditative breathing exercises he'd learned back when he was a paladin. As badly as he wanted to be with the ShadowCrystal, he needed to first think clearly so he could concoct an escape plan and then reunite with it.

Ferox pushed himself back into a sitting position. The vertigo was still present but not as debilitating as seconds before. He decided to tap into his nexus to properly recenter himself. Ferox closed his eyes and tried to establish a connection, but the feeling that he wasn't in his own body made it difficult to pinpoint his own nexus. He was quickly distracted as half of his mind was still trying to process the potent, foreign sensations of having his essence thrown into a different body.

Time had seemed to stretch and contract simultaneously. The instant that Ferox was in her mind and colliding with her nexus, he had been able to sense Genevieve's abilities as an omnimancer, feeling its radiant beams of power as if he were standing inches from a roaring wildfire. He could never have imagined the amount of vibrant, limitless power his wife had at her disposal.

He was too preoccupied to fully register a slight rumble below his wife's feet.

O how shortsighted and naïve he'd been, Ferox realized, in wanting to turn *himself* into an omnimancer by possessing all the MystiCrystals. He had never taken it one step further and entertained the thought of possessing an *actual* omnimancer so he could access and control the rarefied power in its purest form.

Brushing off another faint vibration beneath him, he opened his eyes with new fervor and scanned the dark interior of the room. Ferox didn't know where he was or who had brought him here, but he did know one thing: his captors thought that he was Genevieve, the savior of the Sorcery Guild and that of the eleven realms. Capitalizing on that assumption, he relinquished his search for his own nexus and, closing his eyes once more, lustfully tried to find Genevieve's instead. Maybe it would be easier to find and access animancy, his inherent plane, since he was in the body of a powerful omnimancer.

Well-manicured eyebrows raised in surprise at how quickly Ferox found Genevieve's nexus but were then once more furrowed in concentration as he tried—and failed—to *access* it. All he felt was a cold void, like a burnt-out, wind-chilled stack of brittle wood the morning after a fire.

Ferox let out an impatient grunt. He squeezed his eyelids tightly together and winced, trying harder to locate a Mancy plane—*any* Mancy plane—to tap into.

Animancy? Unresponsive.

Telemancy? No.

Chronomancy? No.

Terramancy? Dead.

Astromancy? Nothing.

Like flipping through a thick tome that had no writing in it, he couldn't glean an ounce of power from her nexus. Frustrated, he let a harsh exhale slip from her lips. Ferox was completely powerless.

He scoffed. "Ironic."

He heard Genevieve's voice as his own, briefly distracting him before he regained composure. Thankfully the tremors and vertigo did not return. He then focused on continuing his search for his own nexus, but dread quickly wrapped its tendrils tight around his mind. Could his nexus have stayed with his body and been destroyed with it? He couldn't feel that familiarity anywhere inside the body he was currently occupying . . . only the dormant and impenetrable nexus of Genevieve Lancaster.

Each breath he took became shallower and quicker as it dawned on him that his nexus was most likely forever gone and that his wife had locked shut her own. Even though Ferox was in control of her body, Genevieve still held domain over its intangible core. She was responsible for cutting Ferox off from not only her nexus but from his natural Mancy plane of animancy.

Rage boiled deep inside. He still underestimated his wife's power. His churning ire prevented him from feeling any admiration for the woman he once had loved so deeply.

He'd gone from one prison to another.

He clenched his jaw tightly as he balled his hands, clumping the velvety fabric of the gown he was stuck wearing in the process. The only thing that distracted him from laying waste to the room was the unwelcome sound of shuffling feet from just outside his hut's door.

With his rage briefly corked, he stood. The motion was too quick, and he felt his legs start to give as he inadvertently taunted the vertigo to return. In an effort to not collapse, Ferox stumbled forward, getting caught in the flowing gown he wore. Cursing, he managed to stabilize himself just as the door swung open to flood the hut's small interior with moonlight and reveal an old man in a regal Guild tunic, formal but with new embellishments. Layers of ivory-colored silk emblazoned with golden borders flowed around his body, giving the wearer the air of a grand mystra. Moonlight reflected off of long, wiry strands of white hair that cascaded down his head and over his eyes before it picked back up in a thick waterfall of a beard.

"M-Mother?" whispered the man.

Ferox could only see a silhouette, but as he squinted in the darkness he vaguely recollected hearing that voice shortly after being released from the Halostone. If this man thought Genevieve was his mother, then he must be . . .

My son.

"Philip?" Ferox said in Genevieve's voice.

The man rushed at him with outstretched arms, and before he could blink, Ferox was wrapped in an embrace.

"You remember," Philip sighed.

As Philip held him, Ferox thought for a quick second. If this man—who couldn't be younger than eighty-five—was his son, then . . . how long had he been imprisoned in the Halostone? He felt a slight tug deep inside. Genevieve was trying to regain control of her body.

No, not your turn, my lovely.

Ferox softly pried his new body away from the old man so he could get a better look at his son now that moonlight was drenching the inside of the thatched hut. He flashed a smile and cupped Philip's face with a hand. "How could I ever forget my boy?"

Philip leaned into what he thought was his mother's hand and sighed. "They would never prevent me from getting to you."

Ferox's mind was working overtime. He pulled his hand away and asked, "Can you tell me where I am?"

"Camelore."

Ferox's shock made his spine go rigid as if he'd been struck by lightning. Camelore . . . yes, the hidden fortress that the First Five —the original omnimancer clans—had created to prevent their extinction by his hands, the hands of a man they had labeled as a leper . . . an outcast . . . because he had started asking questions and begun dabbling in the more *experimental* forms and functions of animancy—and, shortly thereafter, the other Mancy planes once he discovered the ShadowCrystal.

Hadn't they known that by ostracizing him, they'd only furthered Ferox's disdain for sorcerer-kind and fanned the flames of his desire to watch their precious Guild crumble? They—along with Genevieve—had become delusionally trapped in their own dogma, causing them to act as if they were gods.

O, grovel on a genuflected knee to the almighty omnimancers and pray they don't cast you away!

Ferox had planned to humble those self-proclaimed titans and save the eleven realms from their grip of inevitable destruction and stagnation. And he would have succeeded, too, had it not been for, of all people, his *wife* and *sister-in-law*, Genevieve and Gwendolyn Lancaster.

"Mother?" Philip whispered, pulling Ferox out of his memory's vortex.

"I-I'm fine." Ferox put a soft smile on his wife's face, which immediately placated Philip.

"After centuries of searching," his son said, "I've finally found you." Philip grabbed both of Ferox's hands, holding them tightly and focusing on them.

Philip—his only son—had been obsessed, Ferox realized. The man before him seemed to have devoted his entire life to searching for him. The smile that he had put on his wife's face faded as he remembered whose body he was in. His own body had been atomized by Genevieve's last spell, and he was wearing his wife. *She* was the person who his son had been searching for. *She* was who he cared about.

Philip hadn't yet mentioned his own father—the person after whom he was named.

His contempt began to show in the thinning of his lips just as his ears picked up steady gusts of batted air from outside the hut. What followed was the sound of gravel sliding under hooves. Ferox looked over his son's shoulder to catch movement of a large wing through the open doorway.

"Don't be alarmed," Philip breathed as he released Ferox's hands and looked over his shoulder. "That's Soter, my pegasus. I summoned him so we could make our escape." As Philip reached again for his hands, Ferox pulled them toward his chest.

Philip froze, a look of confusion on his face. "Mother . . . ?"

Since it was revealed that he was on Camelore, Ferox wanted to stay, but he convinced himself that he would find his way back. Thinking on his feet, he said, "Not before we collect the Mysti-Crystals."

Philip's eyes darted across his face before he replied, "Yes, too true. Now that they've all finally been found, it is our duty to ensure their safety." He waved her toward him. "Come, Mother. We must get them before they notice I've escaped."

Ferox extended a hand, allowing Philip to take it and lead him outside toward the enormous pegasus. Ferox instinctively tried searching for the familiar energy pulses of the MystiCrystals, but to no surprise he felt nothing.

Philip stopped at the side of his pegasus and looked at Ferox. "Is everything all right, Mother?" He was reacting to the wince that had lined Ferox's new face.

"I'm still very weak from the duel." He shook his head, feeling long curls brush against his neck and shoulders. "My nexus isn't responding. I . . . the crystals—do you know where they might be?"

Philip smiled through his white beard and nodded. "I managed to pry the location from Charles's mind before escaping. They're safely inside the helioarch."

Ah, so one of my captors is named Charles . . .

Philip pointed at a large, circular building several hundred yards away. It looked to be a hallowed place of some kind. It towered over every other structure in the vicinity, showing looping buttresses spaced around the exterior as it curved into a dome at its peak.

"Come," Philip implored as he mounted Soter.

Once both of them were atop the giant pegasus, his son commanded it to take them closer to the helioarch. He was sliding off of Soter even before its hooves touched down, sprinting into the helioarch. As Ferox waited for his son to return, a newfound jealousy bubbled up from deep in his soul. Not because Philip could sense the MystiCrystals, but because he was also a natural-born omnimancer.

Just like his mother, Ferox silently fumed.

Ferox fought the urge to dismount Soter and burn Camelore to the ground. But then, what damage could he actually inflict? As long as he remained in Genevieve's body, she would hold hostage her nexus and the power of each Mancy plane. If Ferox couldn't find a way to overpower her—and soon—he would need to find another host. Quick footfalls to his left caused his gaze to lock onto Philip, who slid out of the helioarch's double-door entranceway.

A new host . . . one who was also an omnimancer and willing to give Ferox control over their immensely powerful nexus . . .

A mischievous smile formed at the edges of the soft, heart-shaped face he puppetted as Philip jumped back onto Soter. The pegasus whinnied softly as it rebalanced under the addition of more weight.

"Sorry, boy," Philip said as he twisted around, handing a satchel with a long strap to Ferox. "All five accounted for," he said to the person who he thought was Genevieve. He turned forward and commanded his steed to fly.

As the silver-maned pegasus lifted off into the night on strong wings, Ferox opened the satchel to reveal the five MystiCrystals. They clinked against one another as he tugged at the lip of the satchel to get a better view of their spoils, letting himself revisit the moments when he had struck down each omnimancer clan leader in his path to obtain all five MystiCrystals.

The clans that were unlucky enough to be graced by his presence first had little to no time to prepare for his vengeful onslaught. As word quickly spread to the remaining First Five clans, they had done their best to fortify their strongholds and protect their designated MystiCrystals, but not even those revered omnimancers could stop Lord Ferox's momentum and his wielding of the proximancic spells—especially when paired with the ShadowCrystal and his own insatiable desire for domination.

A sickening smile spread across those full lips as he remembered his nexus spiking in power with the addition of one MystiCrystal after another to his collection, the heap of smoldering corpses belonging to the untouchable omnimancer clans—the Scymarths, Dwins, Castleberrys, and Goldammers—growing in his wake.

Until he found himself facing off against the last living clan leader. The keeper of the TeleCrystal—the very person he'd once fallen in love with and had taken her last name when he married into her omnimancer clan: Genevieve Lancaster.

By the time Ferox had worked through every other omnimancer clan and tracked her down, she'd had time to form a coalition of sorcerers around her clan and the TeleCrystal. But this had proved to be nothing but a small hindrance. With conceited ease, Ferox had systematically destroyed the inferior ranks of the Sorcery Guild before locking onto and mercilessly disposing of Genevieve's relatives and obtaining the final MystiCrystal. He wanted to save his lovely wife's demise for last.

His hubris would lead to his eventual downfall, as he now realized that Gwendolyn had still been alive. Dying but not dead, just enough life left to toss the Halostone into the air, giving Genevieve the final assist to cast the containment spell that would trap him inside the Halostone and therefore prevent him from completing his Dark Purge before he then set his sights on the subjugating the remaining ten realms.

Now he was given a second chance to complete what he knew was owed to him. There was much work to be done first, though. Ferox continued to plot as he closed the satchel back up. The crisp night air tingled his barren shoulders.

"Where are we going, Philip?" Ferox put on a tone of meek intrigue.

His son stayed focused on what was ahead, but his voice was easily heard above the wind. "A place where I can explain everything."

CHAPTER FOUR

Malcolm couldn't explain what just happened.

Under the xanthic, phosphorescent light tubes that flickered, well past their expiration date, he knelt in the dead center of the Pit, the underground dueling ring on Azumar, mindlessly sifting clumpy, coarse sand through his fingers. Panting from his intense but short-lived outburst of pent-up rage that destroyed the Pit's corroded doors, he mulled over the unexpected turn of events that led him to the spot where he had become Lord Draconex's apprentice nearly a decade before.

Malcolm should be at the right hand of Lord Ferox right now, watching in awe as the eleven realms bent to his new master's ruthless will; instead he was alone yet again, forced to retreat with his proverbial tail between his legs. Surprisingly, the voices of the ShadowCrystal held their tongues (or whatever they had that helped them speak). He looked down at the shard of the Shadow-Crystal that was in his gauntlet; it hadn't pulsed its bruised-purple hue since Lord Ferox died in that fiery nimbus of spells moments after being released from the Halostone.

Letting out a ragged breath, Malcolm scanned the section of the ring before him. It hadn't changed much in the last ten years since his fateful confrontation as a tenderfoot with his then-master, Victor Huxley. That night from long ago had culminated in his forsaking Victor and his teachings and leaving with Lord Draconex to start anew as a Dark Watcher initiate. The thought made Malcolm snicker—the irony was delicious, considering that he had managed to kill Draconex before Victor.

Killing Victor . . . another thing he still aimed to do.

Malcolm's brow furrowed in disgust as he took in the plexiglass partitions that were heavily smudged with sweat, scuffed with sand, and caked with dried blood. Immediately behind him and as a direct result of his own actions, the thick, dense metal doors of the Pit barely hung on by their hinges, warped and dented in ways that made them more like abstract art sculptures than barriers of entry.

Instead of returning to Feralot, the Dark Watcher stronghold on Nyzanth, Malcolm decided to go to the Pit on Azumar. He needed closure from what he had encountered after he charged into the MystiCrystal's portal on the Richat Structure. His mind was like a broken record, forcing him to relive his experience on repeat.

And he finally admitted to himself that he was terrified.

Malcolm looked down at his chest and placed a hand below his sternum where he'd been stabbed by Gavin all those years ago here in the Pit. Except the one who guided the blade into Malcolm's abdomen wasn't Gavin, nor was that place really the Pit. It was like a visceral nightmare. He could still feel the sharp pang, as if a blade had actually punctured his skin, wreaking havoc on his innards and causing blood to pour out of his midsection like a busted sand hourglass.

Everything had felt so . . . *real* . . . while Malcolm was in that other realm, which made it difficult for him to believe that he was experiencing anything but reality. But it had to be a trick of his mind or he had to have been transported to a completely new realm. Otherwise, Malcolm would surely be dead.

Dying had never bothered him before, but what had changed his perspective was witnessing Lord Ferox—a man whom Malcolm thought too powerful to destroy—get atomized in seconds. It reminded him, none too subtly, of his own mortality, and that not even the most powerful of omnimancers can escape death.

Malcolm just needed to cheat death long enough to achieve his destiny, which he hoped would not stray far from the plan that Ferox would have unleashed upon the eleven realms if he had lived.

But that didn't change the fact that he was alone . . . again.

No one would be swooping in to pick him up, dust him off, and point him in the right direction. He had to do it all on his own. Even though a slight uneasiness crawled up his spine with that sobering realization, at least his heart was still beating. A rush of anticipation quickly charged his nerves that were once numb, firing neurons in his brain that assisted him in forming his next move. Malcolm needed to be several steps ahead of Jen and the others if he planned to succeed.

Jen . . .

Her streak of luck was about to end.

With a smirk firmly etched into his face, Malcolm slammed his open hands on the sand in front of him. He clawed as much of it as he could into his palms and squeezed as tightly as he could—so tightly that his forearms felt like they were going to burst. He felt a satisfying heat all along his fingers and palms, and when he looked down, the sand in his hands, thanks to his powers of terramancy, had formed into rough, transparent balls of super-heated, pressurized glass.

The ruby set into his Mancy totem ring (the one he scavenged from the cold, dead corpse of Lord Draconex) was roaring with a self-contained fury of red-orange flame as he fanned his nexus awake. Throwing caution to the wind, Malcolm whipped one of the glass balls at the Pit's ceiling, shattering the light tube directly above him. A shower of broken glass and sparks danced around him as the space dimmed by at least a third. He slowly stood up, tossing the other glass ball in his left hand as he chose his next target. As he brought his arm behind him for the wind up, he felt a familiar buzz radiate from his right wrist. Almost immediately, he heard the inhuman voices of the ShadowCrystal return, a million talking in unison.

He is coming . . .

Malcolm froze and let the ball slip from his weakening grasp as he looked down at the center of his gauntlet that housed his ShadowCrystal shard. His connection with the crystal was so strong that he didn't even have to ask who they were referring to.

Lord Ferox was coming. How was that possible?

Malcolm's neck twitched as the crystal reawakened, sending forked veins of purple across his skin: up his arm, over his chest, under the skin of his neck. He could feel its power inside him like worms digging through moist soil.

Don't be fooled. The shell is different.

His eyes rolled at their enigmatic warning. His brow tensed as he attempted to decipher what it meant while he willed his feet to move.

The second glass ball, forgotten on the sandy ground, showed an inverted image of Malcolm heading toward the gaping hole of the Pit's entranceway with gliding, purposeful strides reminiscent of those of his late master.

CHAPTER FIVE

Jen awoke to commotion outside of her hut. Not sure what time it was, she rolled to the right to check the clock, which tipped her hammock too far to one side. She jerked in the opposite direction to prevent herself from falling out of her swinging bed, which sent the item she'd been holding while asleep clattering to the floor. Jen let out a gasp and, without a modicum of grace, fell out of the hammock reaching for it.

As Jen stood from the floor, Mira sprung up from her own hammock, hair tousled. "What's going on?" her friend said. She slid from her hammock with her usual grace, despite the noisy, unexpected awakening.

"I—I don't know," Jen said, pulling her mid-length curls into a ponytail after discreetly sticking the item in her back pocket. She followed Mira out the door and caught sight of Victor and Jocelyn striding quickly toward the Pentarena.

Jen slid around Mira and ran toward Victor. "What's going on?" She could feel unease and tension radiating from both her uncle and mother.

Victor held up a hand as he increased his pace. "Jenny, stay here." The usual warmth was currently devoid from his tone.

Jen faltered but still continued onward. "Is everything all right?"

"Honey, please listen to your uncle." Jocelyn spoke with more understanding, but she too increased her speed as she followed Victor.

Victor didn't turn back to look at Jen, so she reluctantly came to a halt and watched as they rushed toward the Pentarena. At its center, the Arbor Sacré continued radiating its brilliant dance of colors amidst the stark backdrop of the night sky.

The skin around Jen's ears tightened as from behind she heard a heavy flutter of burlap. She turned to see Mira helping Mystra Sterling Hephalon slowly limp out of the makeshift convalescence hut, his armor on and his weapons fastened to hooks and mounts all around his body like he was about to go into battle. Her heart pulled her toward him and her feet obeyed. She hadn't seen Hephalon since she'd left to save Atlantis. He was now standing on his own, Mira still remaining close by his side, but his face— the parts that weren't covered by a full salty-ginger beard—was sallow and his eyes drained. Jen fought the urge to yell out his name and bowl into him with a hug; his burly, seventy-seven-inch frame looked like it could be toppled by a soft breeze. Still, her heart swelled: he looked much better than the state Malcolm had left him in.

"Hey," Jen said instead, once she made it over to the man who'd forged her totem charm bracelet.

"Oh, not you, too," Hephalon groaned. "Please, don't pity me, lass. I have heaps of that stuff already." He smiled weakly and opened his left arm for a hug.

Jen smiled back and wrapped her arms softly around his side. "You look much better, but what are you doing with all your gear on?" She pulled away and noticed Gavin making his way to them, pulling a shirt over his toned chest.

"You can thank the healing concoctions courtesy of Charles. They've really been doing the trick." Hephalon flexed his muscles underneath his armor, barely concealing a grimace; it was clear that he was still in need of rest. "Wearing my armaments makes me feel like I'm doing better." He smiled faintly before changing the subject. "What's all the ruckus out here, then,

31

eh?" Hephalon squinted over her shoulder at the Pentarena in the distance.

"Yeah, is everything okay?" Gavin said, only a few steps away. He stopped next to Mira, yawning into his fist while rubbing his girlfriend's lower back with his other hand.

Jen shook her head. "I'm not sure. Vic was pretty adamant that I stay here."

Hephalon let out a ragged breath. "Well, y'know, if I were in my usual tip-top shape, I'd already be over there right next to him." He winked at Jen. "But, alas, I cannot, so why don't you take my place, lass?"

Jen rubbed his arm and looked at Mira and Gavin. Before she could ask, her best friend said, "Don't worry, I'll look after him."

"And you're probably the only one who Vic can't stay angry at," Gavin said with an envious chuckle.

"Thank you," Jen said as she side-hopped into a sprint. She reached into her nexus, easily finding animancy, and was instantly bestowed the celerity of a cheetah born under the harsh, unrelenting sun of the Serengeti.

Her feet were moving so fast beneath her that she felt as though she were gliding toward the entrance to the Pentarena, the transparent stadium at the center of which grew the Arbor Sacré, the immense, mystical tree that kept the entire island suspended in Earth's stratosphere. She decelerated a few yards away and put on an air of stealth, her footsteps the whispers of windswept leaves. With how Victor was acting, she knew the chances were low that he would overlook her disobedience, even armed with the excuse of Hephalon telling her to come in his place.

Brilliant hues of every visible color of the known rainbow flowed up and down the Arbor Sacré, lighting its trunk and branches in rivulets of magical light that rolled over the dark interior of the Pentarena. Jen spotted, right next to the tree's massive trunk, the opened hatch that led to the Cube. Her heart rate seemed to double with every step as she crept closer to the darkness-filled hatch. Muffled voices, tense and firm, increased in volume from deep within Camelore.

Jen hesitated at the hatch's lip, her shoulders taut. A voice in her head insisted, *Turn back!*, but she dispelled it and quietly descended, taking one step at a time. Slowly, she sank deeper and deeper into the belly of the floating island. As the steps spiraled downward, her dread grew and grew. Were they talking to Grand Mystra Cindergray or her father? Why were their voices so clipped and worried?

At the end of the winding flight of steps came flickering yellow light, splayed across the floor. She continued around the bend and then stopped a few steps from the floor of the secret chamber, where she peeked around the curved wall until she could see Victor. He was hunched over, one hand shaking the supine form of her father while the other held a floating bright ball of flame. Jocelyn stood off to the side, hands covering her mouth and head slightly shaking in worry.

"Charles! Hey, *Charles!*" Victor said as he switched his grip from the man's shoulder to his jaw. "Come on, man. Snap out of it!"

Jen wanted to yell her father's name, too, but her throat clamped up. Her body was telling her that she wasn't supposed to even be there—and then her heart stopped when her eyes fell on the empty Cube, its closest invisibarrier wall showing a barely noticeable, shattered hole . . .

And no Grand Mystra Aldred Cindergray inside.

With a jerk, Jen looked warily over her shoulder, as if Cindergray was hovering behind her this whole time. Seeing nothing except the fading, spiral steps back toward the open hatch, she brought her full attention back to the catatonic form of Charles. His eyes were glassy and stared straight through Victor. Jocelyn fell to her knees beside him and stroked his forehead and cheek.

Jen's heart wanted to clear the last few remaining steps and rush to her father's aid, but her brain warned her that this would only distract Victor and Jocelyn from their attempts at reviving Charles. She had no clue what spell he was under or how harmful it may be. Biting her top lip, Jen turned away and rested her back on the curved wall, her eyes sewn shut as she prayed for her father to be okay as she tried to reach him through telemancy. Victor and Jocelyn's pleadings were snuffed out as she fell into her nexus.

Jen felt as though she were traveling at the speed of light as she activated the remaining Mancy planes like candles strewn about a dark room. Some responded to her touch immediately, while others took more effort to light.

With the calm hand of meditation trying its best to settle her nerves, Jen lilted through the infinitesimal void that was her nexus, not allowing herself to spiral with hypothetical scenarios. After what could have been mere seconds or several minutes, her spirits buoyed when she sensed the familiar comfort of Charles's nexus, a ship that was currently set adrift on the placid surface of a windless sea. For Jen to help him at all, she needed to identify what was wrong with him and which plane Cindergray could have used to incapacitate her father. Her heart plummeted when she realized, after cycling through each plane, that the spell controlling Charles had traces of them all.

Her concentration began to crumble. She felt herself pulled from her meditation, and all her mortal senses rushed back into her like she'd just been splashed with ice-cold water. She gasped.

"Jennifer, what are you doing here?" Victor was at her side, grabbing her arm.

The last time she'd heard him say her full name was back when they first met, moments after he'd rescued her from Malcolm's attack on the night of her twenty-first birthday.

Tears welled up on her lower eyelids as she stared at Victor, a hard-etched look of stunned disappointment and momentary frustration lining his features—one that reminded Jen of her traumatic time in that place to which she had been sent by the Mysti-Crystals' portal where she had found the Halostone; the Victor from that . . . realm? . . . had given her a similar look. Jen froze, unable to make any noise as his steel-blue eyes darted across her face, waiting for her answer. A second, sharper gasp finally escaped her lips; reflexively she tried to escape from his grip.

In her struggles, Jen noticed Victor seeming to realize something, his body language immediately changed. His eyes became gentler, his mouth opened a touch, and he let her go. Jen, unprepared for him to relinquish his grip so quickly, lost her balance and hit her back on the hard-packed dirt of the step she'd been on.

More unwelcome memories of her time in that unknown realm flashed in her mind's eye like lightning strikes, coming often and only aggravating her anxiety further. Her tailbone throbbed as she clambered back up, shuffling backward until her shoulder blades felt the inside wall of the stairwell. She remembered running the Chimera Course again, overcoming every obstacle that the fallen members of the Elder Synod threw at her and, waiting for her at the finish line, an open path to the Halostone . . . until Victor had appeared.

And he had mercilessly choked the life out of her.

"Jenny," Victor said, breaking her out of her memory spiral.

Reflexively, Jen threw her hands up over her face, even though she knew the Victor who had hurt her in the other realm was not the same man standing in front of her now: uncle, mentor, terramancy mystra, and friend. But as much as she fought it, her brain still struggled to distinguish between the two.

Jen blinked, shaking her head, as if that would jostle out all those bad memories so they would never return; but she wasn't that naïve anymore. Still on the ground, she looked down at her mother at the base of the stairwell, wearing a different kind of worry on her features.

"I'm sorry, honey. I didn't want you to see your father like this," Jocelyn said.

Jen glanced back up at Victor, whose expression and posture hadn't changed since he'd let her go. His hands were raised, showing open palms, almost as if an outlaw had told him to reach for the sky before robbing him of any fine jewelry and money. She abandoned all thoughts of convincing them that Hephalon had given her his place and blurted out, "I couldn't stay back there and do nothing."

"You're right," Victor admitted after a few seconds of silence. "I should've explained more instead of just shutting you out."

Jocelyn had reached her by this point and extended her arms. Jen smiled and took them, surprised at the strength her mother possessed as she lifted her upright. She guessed that came with being a vampire. Jen dusted herself off, waiting for Victor, who seemed to have more to say.

"But," he went on, "like your mother, I didn't want to have you see him like this. Not if I could break the spell he's under first . . . whatever that might be."

Jen stepped closer to Victor and rested her hands on his arms, allowing him to relax and drop his arms to his sides. She smiled warmly and the look they shared evaporated all tension and discomfort between them.

"He's not just under one spell," she told him. She stole a glance back down at Charles; he hadn't moved a hair's length. "But several. One from every Mancy plane."

Jocelyn gasped, looking between Jen and Victor.

Jen looked back at Victor and saw his eyes widen. She thought she heard a curse escape with his breath. It looked as though the life had been drained from his face. His eyes stared down at Charles.

"That's why I could sense a terramancy spell but couldn't even come close to connecting with it . . ." Victor's voice trailed off, his visage flicking between looks of shock and nervousness as he placed a hand over his mouth in thought.

"Could it be the forbidden proxiomnimancic spell?" Jocelyn said.

Victor's eyebrows raised slightly, his eyes first trained on Jocelyn before jumping to Jen. In them were endless whirlpools of worry, swirling between the blues and grays of his irises.

"There are *forbidden* spells?" Jen asked.

Victor nodded solemnly. "Every plane has one . . . but the rarest and most fatal of them all belongs to the omnimancy plane." He shifted his weight nervously, wringing his hands as he looked downward at Charles. "No sorcerer alive has witnessed the effects of the proxiomnimancic spell. We've only heard it passed down as a cautionary tale . . ."

Cold seeped into Jen's bones; her face went hot, her breath becoming short. There was a real possibility that, if they couldn't break this forbidden spell, Charles would never awaken . . . or worse. She winced as she tried to swallow, her mouth and throat depleted of saliva. Neither Victor nor Jocelyn had to tell Jen where this conversation was heading. She bit the inside of her cheek and set her shoulders.

"Let me try."

"Honey, wait," Jocelyn said, gliding closer to her and Victor.

"Whoa, now, hold on." Victor's response only made Jen more defensive.

"I'm an omnimancer. You have to let me try," Jen pleaded, tears threatening to trickle down her face. "Unless . . ."

As if on cue, all three tensed as the same thought occurred to them: Genevieve Lancaster was the most powerful omnimancer— and she was now, impossibly, currently alive and mere steps away, sleeping in one of Camelore's huts. *She* could help save Charles.

Jen said her ancestor's name, and Victor nodded. "Someone should stay with Charles," he said as he put a boot on the step above.

Jocelyn didn't even hesitate. "I will."

Victor nodded and motioned for Jen to follow as he bounded back up the steps, quickly climbing back into the atrium of the Pentarena.

As they rushed side by side back to the barracks, Jen's mind worked overtime. Her subconscious was putting things together, finally asking a question that made her stride falter: If he escaped, where would Cindergray go first?

Victor urged Jen to keep up, which she eventually did by summoning animancy. With the speed of an antelope, she caught back up to Victor's side, all the while dreading what they would —or wouldn't—find when the door to Genevieve's hut was thrown open.

Gavin was leaning on the outside wall of Hephalon's convalescence hut, now with Merlin's journal, flipping through the last third of the leatherbound book. He looked in Jen's direction and closed the thick tome, pushing himself from the hut as his brow creased in worry. Jen held up a hand, hoping he would hold off on following them. He, along with every other person on Camelore, would be afforded an update in due time; but first she hoped with all her heart that Genevieve was still inside her hut, soundly asleep.

Jen wasn't half the omnimancer Genevieve was said to have been, so of course she wasn't the ideal choice to assume the responsibility of curing Charles from the proxiomnimancic spell, but in the event that Jen was the only choice, she was prepared to do everything, including stretching the limits of her nexus, so she could see her father conscious and free once again.

Loose gravel crunched under their boots as they slowed their pace, now only a few steps from the door of the hut that held Genevieve. Without pause, Victor threw open the door, allowing moonlight to drench the space in soft silver. Jen's eyes scanned the room in a fraction of a second before her heart became an anchor, digging a trench of dread into her stomach.

Genevieve was nowhere to be seen.

Jen's eyes flicked to Victor. He was standing in front of her, his cloak billowing back toward his feet as he stood motionless, his shoulders rigid. Something inside Jen stopped her from giving her uncle the reassurance of a gentle hand on his shoulder. She didn't need to use telemancy to know that he was lost in thought, forcing himself to adapt to this unforeseen—and disastrous—development.

"He took her," Victor whispered, his shoulders finally slumping, giving Jen the resolve to reach out toward him.

She walked up so that she was to his right and laid a hand on his shoulder when he drew in a harsh breath. "We'll find her." She let a few seconds pass, then said, "But Charles needs us now."

Victor moved his head an inch in her direction, the pupil of his right eye trained on her, the rich amber flecks in its iris sparkling in the moonlight. "You're right," he said, exhaling and letting his eyelids fall.

Jen smiled grimly as a shadow fell over them and part of the room. Both she and Victor turned to see Gavin's figure just outside the door frame. "Guys," Gavin said, his voice taut and low, "the MystiCrystals are gone."

Jen tensed for what felt like the millionth time that night, unconsciously reaching for the item she'd retrieved before falling asleep . . . the item that was now in her back pocket.

The TeleCrystal.

* * *

Growing up back on Earth, her mom, Beth, used to tell her that bad things happen in threes. Now, Jen could not think of three worse things to happen than finding Charles incapacitated by the dangerous proxiomnimancic spell, Genevieve Lancaster abducted by Grand Mystra Cindergray, and the MystiCrystals stolen.

Well, every MystiCrystal except the TeleCrystal.

At the time the idea had come to her on a whim, but Jen was now extremely grateful that she'd taken one of the MystiCrystals and swapped it with a replica that she'd conjured out of thin air with a cloaking spell. She'd taken it as a contingency should the MystiCrystals for whatever reason fall into the wrong hands again.

And that reason had arrived with Cindergray's escape.

Despite the triple flogging of bad news, Jen was able to keep some positivity after disclosing to Victor and Gavin what she had done. Back at the Richat Structure, she'd witnessed firsthand what the MystiCrystals were capable of when their powers were combined: a shaft of light that electrified the air, one that stood as a portal to an unknown twelfth realm of which not even the Elder Synod had been aware.

And unknown meant dangerous.

Jen hadn't a single clue how that place had been kept a secret for as long as it had, nor why to her it had looked like the courtyard of the Elder Synod atop Watercress Castle. (She wondered what the twelfth realm had looked like to Cindergray . . .)

A chill ran down her spine just at the thought of that staggering amount of power being used for anything other than good.

Everyone was awake and had made their way into the helioarch by the time Jen and Gavin levitated Charles through its open double doors. They chose to rest him atop the lacquered roundtable on a makeshift bed of Lightseeker robes (the ones that had hung over each of the table's twenty-five chairs). The chairs had been pushed to the perimeter of the room so everyone could stand right up to the edge of the table. At the opposite side of where Jen and Gavin stood was Hephalon. Next to the burly terramancy metallurgist was his son, Rez, his fiery curly hair still tousled from being abruptly awoken only minutes before. Gavin squeezed Jen's arm and grimaced in sympathy, leaving his place next to her to stand by Mira. She was biting her lip and nervously stroking her braid as she focused on the spellbound omnimancer, finally breaking out of her intense thoughts as Gavin slipped a strong arm around her back and held her close.

Jen and Mira made eye contact and shared a brief moment of nervous positivity before Jen decided to stand next to her mother. Jocelyn was standing alone, rigid. When Jen embraced her, she relaxed slightly but remained rather tense as she stared desperately into her husband's open but unfocused eyes. Jen chewed at the inside of her cheek and glanced at Richard and Beth Smith— the adoptive parents who had raised her for twenty-one years— holding each other near the back wall. Both stared pensively at the man who'd given them a baby to raise as their own all those years ago. Her younger brother, Tyler, remained asleep in their hut. How they managed to not wake him, Jen didn't know, though she was glad that he wasn't here; he was too young to see this.

The lanterns resting on the ornate sconces that evenly dotted the inside perimeter of the helioarch slowly dimmed as the starry velvet night sky welcomed dawn, lightening its once deep purple coloring to a calming azure blue. The sun was not yet at an angle to cast the light mural onto the table.

But the feeling in the ceremonial chambers was all but calming.

Victor, for instance, looked as though he had aged considerably in the length of time it had taken Jen and Gavin to transport Charles from beneath the Pentarena into the helioarch. He had since closed the chamber's doors and was standing at the table's closest edge. He placed his open hands, each index and ring finger adorned with his totem rings, on the curved edge of the table as he looked around.

"I think I speak for all of us when I say that this was the last thing that could have been expected. Even though Lord Ferox is now vanquished, it has come to our attention that not only is Charles stricken by the proxiomnimancic spell, but Genevieve is missing, presumably abducted by . . . by *Cindergray*." His tone quickly became biting and contemptuous when he said the Grand Mystra's self-anointed name, and he composed himself before continuing. "Also missing are the MystiCrystals. We still have the TeleCrystal in our possession thanks to Jen's quick thinking"— Victor gestured to Jen, who placed the TeleCrystal in front of her on the table—"so their combined power, fortunately, cannot currently be summoned. Have faith that we will get through this. We have to."

He said those last three words quieter, as if trying to convince himself.

"I need every one of you to focus on what needs to be done first and foremost, which is freeing Charles from the spell that Cindergray placed on him," Victor continued, looking at everyone in turn until he stopped at Jen. His eyes were unwavering yet plaintive as they shimmered from the torches' diminishing flickers of light, dawn lightening the dark sky above.

With a clenched jaw, Jen nodded once, not breaking her uncle's gaze. She would do whatever it took to get Charles out from under this terrifying spell, and Victor knew that. He broke their stare, looking down at his hands, and took a deep breath.

"In the annals of the Sorcery Guild, there has been no written account of the proxiomnimancic spell actually being used. It has

41

only been mentioned as a cautionary tale—a what-if exercise should an omnimancer ever conjure a spell from every Mancy plane at once with the express purpose of inflicting harm." Victor's eyes rose from his hands and fixed on Charles in the center of the table. "Charles . . ." He cleared his throat as his chin quivered. He was fighting to get words out. "My friend." He reached forward and covered Charles's right hand with his own.

Jocelyn held Jen a bit tighter as her heart rate doubled. Her heart seemed to have every intention of exploding out of her chest as she witnessed Victor choking back sobs. Scanning the room, she saw the same look of desolation mixed with sadness etched on everyone else's face. Jen knew it well because she also felt it. How could she not, and how could she blame anyone else for feeling that crippling weight? They'd managed to find themselves in a new devastating situation just hours after the previous one seemed to finally be finished.

But even in darkness a light can grow—as long as there's hope and resilience.

Jen needed to personify that light now.

She rubbed her mother's back before letting go. She stepped closer to the beveled lip of the varnished roundtable and primed herself by swallowing (even though her mouth had dried up minutes before in anticipation).

"I know I've only been studying the Mancy planes for a few months, but I've had great mystras who have taught me so much in such little time."

She threw appreciative glances at Mira, Gavin, and finally Victor. Jen waited for him to look her way before continuing.

"I also know that I still have a long way to go in each plane, but my father needs our help. He's a prisoner in his own body, and I honestly don't know what will happen the longer he remains under this spell."

Jen felt Jocelyn rest a hand on her shoulder and squeeze. Victor had pulled away from Charles and was intently listening to her every word.

"I know that Genevieve is the clear choice to be the omnimancer who should break this spell, but we've been robbed of the luxury of having her with us." Jen scoffed. "Frankly, many luxuries have been taken from us since the Dark Watchers' ambush at Watercress Castle. But guess what? We didn't need them. We didn't need them because we banded together and never gave up until we found ways to overcome every obstacle that had been put before us."

Jen felt her voice growing stronger, more confident; her heart rate was steady. She didn't let herself become too aware of this though, because she knew that if she did, she'd start to overthink. Instead, she let it flow through her, almost like a sixth Mancy plane activating in her nexus.

"I have an idea, and I'm asking you all to just hear me out." Jen made her way over to Victor's side and purposefully bumped into him, which elicited a small smirk from her uncle. Jen smiled, glad to see some brevity return to his countenance, slight as it may be. It was still there; that's what mattered.

"When I first sensed the proxiomnimancic spell, it reminded me of a very complicated and sensitive combination lock. Instead of having numbers in each dial wheel, *this* lock uses different power levels from each Mancy plane."

She paused to see if anyone wanted to say anything. No one spoke up. They were giving her the floor.

Jen tucked a stray black curl behind an ear before she continued. "I know I'm definitely not adept enough in any of the five Mancy planes to break this complex spell by myself." She looked to Victor at her side, then down at her totem bracelet hanging on her right wrist. "I alone can't keep each Mancy plane open long enough to supply each lock with the required power it needs to be unlocked."

Jen briefly thought back to when she and Charles had raised the lost kingdom of Atlantis into the sky, how he'd guided her through that traumatic process. *He* was the one who helped her commune with all of the Mancy planes. *He* was the one who gave her the confidence to open herself up to each plane as she used her nexus as a funnel. He was her guide, and she trusted him implicitly. Jen scanned Charles from head to foot. He was physically only inches away, but miles seemed to separate their souls. Jen didn't want to risk hurting her father any more by attempting this monumental task alone.

She bit the inside of her cheek, collecting her thoughts as she gazed up at the helioarch itself, a gorgeous framework that was still considered a marvel of metallurgy centuries after the Camelore Twenty-Four had constructed it. Jen let herself take in its beauty as she mentally prepared for what, realizing in that moment, she was destined to do. Bits of azure morning sky could be seen through the ornately stenciled depictions that stretched across its entire length, designed to cast murals of light and shadow on the roundtable as the sun traveled across the sky. The first half of the arch depicted historical events that had already occurred: the creation of the MystiCrystals; King Arthur pulling Excalibur from an anvil atop a stone. The last half portrayed a prophecy currently coming to pass: the discovery of the Lightbringer's identity and some enormous battle, which Jen had initially assumed was the ambush at Watercress Castle, but now she was not so sure. Jen couldn't forget the sense of awe that had come over her when Victor had first shown her the helioarch, as he had explained its purpose and importance to the Sorcery Guild's work across the eleven realms.

Jen forced herself to return to the present, knowing how much weight her next words would carry. "So what I'm saying is . . ." She stopped, feeling Victor's hand rest on her left shoulder. She looked over at him and touched his hand with the tips of her fingers. "I need all of you to help me free my father."

Jen reflexively looked at Richard, the one who had raised her for practically her entire life. Her *dad*.

His soft brown eyes showed the pride and confidence he had in her. That galvanized Jen, making her posture a little straighter. She then smiled at her mom, who was still hugging her dad. Her parents.

Mira's voice pulled her gaze to the other side of the chamber: "You don't need to convince *me*, girl."

Her friend unlatched her bullwhip totem and laid the long, coiled braid on the table. Gavin almost immediately slid his orb pendant off his necklace and put it inside his girlfriend's whip so it wouldn't roll away.

T-TOK TOKK. Hephalon's brass knuckles were the third totem to be laid on the table. Next was a pair of earrings belonging to her mother, Jocelyn, followed by Rez's totem, a metallic playing card. The love she felt grew with each totem laid on the table, reaching its peak when she felt Victor retract his arm from her shoulder and four brushed silver rings floated into her peripherals, landing gently on the table as if guided by invisible hands.

"Tell us what you need from us," Victor said.

CHAPTER SIX

Ferox was at his wit's end.

Aside from getting used to maneuvering his wife's much smaller and weaker body Ferox now controlled, the gown he was stuck wearing was catching on loose rubble beneath his feet, causing him to stumble—and even, a few unfortunate times, fall —on increasingly bigger and sharper debris as he followed his son, Philip II, who, on the ride to the realm of Azumar, briefed him on exactly how long he'd been trapped in the Halostone. His son had also told him about his vow to find the Halostone, never relinquishing his belief that Genevieve had actually been sucked into the Halostone along with Ferox—a vow that would cause him to dedicate years upon decades to mastering the proxichrono-mancic spell of age prolongation (the closest any sorcerer could get to immortality).

Cold, dark clouds were beginning to grasp at the clear blue sky in the west, the placid water of a nearby lake reflecting its gray tones and melancholy appearance. The telltale signs of a storm, no doubt. A brisk breeze swirled around Ferox as he navigated a minefield of rubble; it was as if the pieces of metal and shards of stone were hungry hands, clawing at his gown as it brushed softly over the uneven terrain.

Ferox cursed under his breath as a splintered metal girder

sliced into the left side of his gown. He tumbled to his knees, the abrupt downward motion knocking the satchel that held the five MystiCrystals from its secure place across his bare shoulder and falling down to catch on his hips. Philip turned around with the same alarm he'd shown after the first several times Ferox took to the ground, pausing his current explanation of how he had become the Grand Mystra of the entire Sorcery Guild under the alias of Aldred Cindergray.

Blowing strands of long, obsidian curls from his eyes, Ferox pulled the strap over his head so he wasn't encumbered by the satchel any longer and sat down. Using the massive rip in the fabric, he tore a fair bit of the gown away, revealing his wife's smooth shins and delicate ankles. He then stood back up with his son's help as his pegasus, Soter, stood patiently at Philip's side. At least the tripping hazard of a flowing gown was no more.

Curse his wife for holding all of her nexus's powers under lock and key, forcing Ferox to follow his son like a sheep rather than lead Philip into a new era under his leadership.

"How do women get around in these?" Ferox bit out in a coarse tone, dusting himself off and swiping at the satchel's strap. He found his son's eyes trained on him, confused, as he quickly remembered whose body he was in. He coughed as he pulled the strap back on his shoulder, stammering, ". . . In—in devastation like this!"

His higher-pitched voice echoed across the ruins of the leveled castle, startling several carrion birds that squawked in response. Those flying skeletons took to the skies as he raised his hands outward, motioning to the remains of what Philip had told him had been the headquarters of the Sorcery Guild.

There came a muffled thunderclap in the distance. Ferox looked to the sky to see the band of gray clouds rolling over more of the sky, threatening to blot out the yellow orb that was this realm's sun. Soter huffed, shaking its large head and neck; in worry or impatience, Ferox couldn't tell.

"It's okay, boy," Philip said as he stroked his pegasus's mane. "We'll let you graze here soon enough." He patted it twice as he looked around solemnly. "It's such a shame to see a tangible representation of centuries of growth and tradition now become a permanent resident of the past . . ." He looked at Ferox and waved him to follow. "But it was a means to an end." He smiled wanly at the person he thought was his mother.

Once Philip found a meager swatch of lightly charred grass by the main drawbridge entrance to let Soter graze, he led Ferox to the southwestern part of the destroyed castle. Some stone walls were still erect—clearly far enough away from whatever blast that had taken out the epicenter of the building—to show what had once been well-built hallways and corridors; now all that was left of them were uneven stacks of rectangular-cut, grayish-ivory stone blocks that at any second might crumble to the ground. Philip stopped before a gaping hole that seemed to have once been a doorway; it was blackened from the heat and power from another spell's explosion, but Ferox was able to make out a section or two of the filigreed doorframe that were untouched.

Philip offered his hand to Ferox before he carefully stepped around pieces of splintered wood from the remains of double doors that belonged to a chamber befitting a headmaster of a once-great school of sorcery. Surprisingly, not much else was out of place as they made their way to an immaculately carved mahogany desk. Behind it was an ornate stained-glass window depicting the crests of the five Mancy planes; the omnimancy crest was predominantly set in the center, making Ferox both sneer and salivate at the same time. A brief crackling flash awakened the colors of the stained glass, momentarily washing the room in a kaleidoscope of color. Ferox counted not even two seconds before a thunderclap responded to that strike of lightning, reverberating around them in the enclosed chambers. The storm was at its strongest just above the ruins of this castle.

"The sunsets through that windowpane were indeed miraculous," Philip said, his eyes glazed with reminiscence. He sighed, then continued around to the opposite side of the desk. He opened a drawer and took out a gold signet ring. Smiling, Philip spread the fingers on his right hand, slid the ring onto his pinkie finger, then made a fist as though to let the ring settle.

Ferox caught sight of a hole in the floor behind Philip and stepped around to get a better viewpoint. The hole was an opening to a spiral staircase that led down, presumably, to the bowels of the castle.

"We're almost there," Philip said as he began descending the stone staircase. The slight pitter-patter of raindrops streaked across the stained-glass window as Ferox silently followed.

Wherever he's taking me, it'd better be worth all this mystery and time lost . . .

The cramped echoes of their footfalls bounced haphazardly around them as they stepped deeper and deeper into a part of the castle that never saw the light of day. A nip from stagnant, cold air tickled Ferox's naked shoulders as the stairs leveled out.

After turning down a few more passageways, they stopped in front of a stand that held a wheel which reached the middle of Philip's chest. Behind it was another gaping hole, this time in a nondescript brick wall, the dust of the blasted mortar still seeming to hang in the air.

His son brought his hands in front of him and paused. "You're going to want to hold on, Mother," Philip said, motioning for Ferox to stand abreast of him.

Ferox felt the now-familiar tug of Genevieve deep inside trying to assert control again.

"*Clockwise*, this time," Philip muttered.

Ferox grabbed his son's left arm a little too tight as he internally fought with his wife's presence. Philip didn't react much save for his bicep flexing as a result of Ferox's strong grip.

Philip then stuck the face of his signet ring into the central depression on the wheel and twisted his fist to the right.

There was a slight rumble, like cogs in a massive clock had begun turning for the first time in a long while, and both he and Philip started *sinking* into the floor as if it were starving quicksand. The liquified floor rolled up over Ferox's bare shins as it tightly covered his small waist and slim upper torso, giving him a quick bout of claustrophobia. He clamped his eyes shut as the floor covered his face, but that sensation left just as quickly as it had arrived.

When his eyes opened, he was in a new place: a smaller chamber with shelves of old tomes and time-worn scrolls lining the walls. Soft, warm light—not from fire but something irritatingly bright and completely foreign to him—contained in glass housings set in the walls drenched the enclosed space. A large banquet table was pushed up against the only barren wall on the far side of the room; on it were artifacts Ferox had only ever heard about in legend.

But what caught his eye wasn't any one of those fabled artifacts on the table; instead, on a section of the far wall next to the table, a particular sword found hanging in a scabbard adorned in gold and gemstones.

A sword wielded by a man who had once stood in Ferox's way, trying to halt his quest in collecting all of the MystiCrystals: Excalibur. The mark of a warrior to defend the weak and bring justice to the corrupt.

Ferox snickered. Such pompous actions of a self-proclaimed "savior" of England.

Look who's still standing, Arthur.

"Yes, your friend's legendary sword," Philip said, brushing past Ferox, just as the memories of his last encounter with King Arthur were also brushed away like spindly cobwebs in the corner of a house.

His son paid no heed to the items on the table as he reached with both hands and slid Excalibur out of its scabbard, orienting it horizontally so that one palm held the hilt while the other made direct contact with the cold, perfect, naked blade of the legendary sword. Its hilt gleamed a crisp gold, its cross guard extending over a blade hammered a thousand and one times as the sheets of steel became inseparable from each other. Black filigreed etchings covered the lower half of the blade and artistically transitioned into a fine central crease that traveled up to its sharp point.

"This, along with everything in my personal Sacrarium"—

Philip nodded first toward the banquet table, then at the other three walls of this secret room—"is what I have discovered while searching for those MystiCrystals."

His eyes fell to the satchel resting on Ferox's right hip.

Ferox took a protective step back as he placed his delicate hands over the satchel's flap.

Philip grimaced. "I know this is a lot to take in, Mother. I—" His head cocked upward. "Soter . . ." Philip spun around and resheathed Excalibur. "Something is spooking the pegasus." He rushed up to Ferox and held his shoulders firmly but not painfully. "Stay here, please. Wait for me to return."

Ferox followed his son with his eyes as he slid his signet ring into the wheel again and rose up into the ceiling, which accepted his body like he was a hot knife going through butter. Soon enough, Ferox was alone . . . except for an incessant, dull *buzzing* sound. Furrowing his wife's slender eyebrows, he strutted over to one of the light fixtures and tapped it with a well-manicured fingernail. The glass tube that emitted this confusing, new kind of magic flickered, but still issued that annoying buzz. He stepped back and looked at it, wondering what futuristic advancement it was as he lifted a hand to scratch his cheek.

The instant he touched skin, he felt the sharp tip of a fingernail slide across and *into* his cheek, immediately giving way to a line of fiery pain. His hand shot out to his side, and he looked down at it in shock. He couldn't relax that arm.

Genevieve's soul was fighting to regain control.

"*I'm* in charge, not *you*!" he bit out through clenched teeth as he grabbed the stiff arm with his other hand. He could feel his wife doing everything she could to assert herself as he wrestled to move his arm's now-aching muscles.

Finally, as if Genevieve had expended all her energy, the arm relaxed, allowing Ferox to hug it to his chest and shake out the ache from the hyper-tensed muscles. Wincing, he looked around until he saw Excalibur again. Slowly, licking his lips in anticipation, he walked closer.

As he had begun the Dark Purge, Ferox had wanted nothing

more than to defeat Arthur Pendragon and claim the sword he'd wielded as his own. He'd often fantasized about using it to squash any and all whom he deemed an enemy of his new state, his new realm, his new *reality*.

And now there was nothing, no one, to stop Ferox from taking the sword for himself.

With bated breath, he reached out with a slightly trembling hand, palm open and ready to wield the most powerful sword known to man. The instant skin touched hilt, a pain that made Ferox think his skin was being flayed from the bones in his fingers and palms forced him to pull his hand away almost immediately, as if he'd been scorched from an errant splash of boiling water from a pot.

He cursed, staring at the sword, his hand throbbing. Merlin had probably laid a spell on it for Ferox in case he'd ever come across it without the rightful king as its steward.

With abject contempt written across his wife's uncharacteristically harsh face, Ferox decided that he would not be denied any longer. He shrugged the satchel's strap off of his shoulder and tossed it on an open section of the banquet table. He lifted its bottom so its contents could roll out, and a new shock made his stomach muscles clench. He waved a hand over the MystiCrystals on the table, feeling their uneven, rigid bodies roll over his palm as he counted out only four, not five. He looked inside the satchel and rummaged around, making sure the last crystal wasn't stuck in one of the bag's folded corners.

It's gone. He returned to look at the four on the table and confirmed which one was missing. *The TeleCrysal is gone.*

The idea to access the Mancy planes through the combined powers of the MystiCrystals was dashed like waves against a rocky cliffside. He was as useless as any other non-sorcerer.

Ferox ground his wife's teeth, trying to contain the bitter anger churning under the guise of Genevieve Lancaster. Ringing pervaded every nook and cranny of his skull as his breathing became more forceful and audible until not even his iron self-control could contain his frustration. Unleashing a high-pitched scream, Ferox swatted MystiCrystals with the back of his hand, sending them clattering to the ground; their dense, crystalline bodies bounced and rolled at odd angles as they spread all around the chamber—much like how they had separated during the last fleeting seconds of the Great Battle as Genevieve bested him, her husband.

Ferox needed all of the MystiCrystals if his plan was going to work.

In a huff, he tossed the empty satchel across the room without an ounce of care and tried again for Excalibur, hoping that the pain would subside if he could just hold it for a second. He recoiled even more drastically than the first attempt, shaking his hand so feverishly that all the blood rushed to the tips of his fingers. He cursed again, a caged animal, unable to do anything except pace around the confined space.

Ferox would have to speed up his plans and go after his son. He needed to shed his wife's body and get inside an omnimancer whom he could trick long enough to gain access to their nexus.

Curling his lips into a snarl, he twisted his long, thin neck and stared up at the area of the ceiling into which his son had disappeared.

CHAPTER SEVEN

It was only a matter of time before they tracked me down . . .

Cindergray felt lighter as he walked up the spiral staircase leading into his office chambers. He could finally dispense with the alias he'd assumed and be known once more as Philip Lancaster II. Omnimancer and son of Genevieve Lancaster.

He moved stealthily through the soaked ruins of Watercress Castle's main level, careful to not call any attention to himself . . . for the time being, at least. No one knew about the Sacrarium's second chamber, so his mother would be safe inside until he returned once he took care of this latest development. The only family that mattered to him was his mother, and since she was now free from the Halostone, not even Charles or Jennifer would be shown an ounce of mercy should they try to take her away from him again.

Thunder rumbled hungrily across the mottled gray sky, giving way to a downpour. He pressed his back to the last-standing part of the southwestern hallway that opened up into what had been the main atrium of the castle, not caring that his cloak and robes were beginning to gain the cold weight of rain. He activated animancy and channeled the extremely sensitive hearing of the greater wax moth, allowing him to hear Soter's wet huffing and urgent neighing in the distance. Sidestepping a few more meters,

Philip stole a glance in the direction of Watercress's destroyed main entrance gate and drawbridge. His pegasus was high in the air, trying to find an opening to dive-bomb an intruder. Its light-gray wings sloughed off the rain in sheets as it remained airborne above . . .

Malcolm?!

Philip froze, half relieved that it wasn't Jennifer or any combination of the others (they should have their hands full dealing with the proxiomnimancic spell he'd cast on Charles), half curious why the boy was even on Azumar.

No matter. Philip would dispose of him in short order. Intent on getting back to his mother as quickly as possible, he pulled out his pocket-watch totem and waited for the hands and gears to glow an iridescent silver-white, imbued with the rising power of his nexus. He breathed in deeply as he sensed the countless raindrops splattering on and around him with the help of terramancy, fortified his skeleton with astromancy, and, flipping back to animancy, felt Soter's agitation rise.

A pulse reverberated through his body as a blast exploded inches to his right, connecting with the stone wall he'd been up against and splintering the centuries-old architecture like it was the husk of a rotted tree. Philip tucked into a side-roll, extending his body out into a defensive stance as he came out of it. Alert, he held the primed totem in his right hand, his left providing the support to help aim any and all spells that he had every intention of lancing with deadly accuracy at Malcolm . . . but the boy had vanished.

And he couldn't sense Soter anymore . . .

A whisper sliced through the air, emanating from every direction as Philip was pushed by an unseen hand out into the open and toppled onto the marble floor, slick with fallen rain. His left shoulder took the brunt of the fall, but any ounce of pain he would have felt was allayed by the astromancy spell he'd fortified his body with. He pushed himself up, but hesitated when he glimpsed his downed pegasus out of the corner of his eye. Soter was still as a statue, looking like a discarded plastic toy; its body was frozen in a dynamic pose: its wings in mid-flap, legs outstretched at different intervals, glassy eyes locked on a target that was no longer there.

Philip began to see red. Grunting, he pushed himself all the way up as his peripherals caught a bright purple light growing alarmingly in intensity. Finally landing a successful block, he spun around to see Malcolm speeding toward him.

He was like a deadly shadow unencumbered by the thick cords of rain, practically hopping from one side of the castle to the other with amazing celerity as he closed the distance between them. The old man gritted his teeth and unleashed a salvo of chronomancy spells at the boy, hoping one of them would connect and freeze him just like what Malcolm had done to Soter. But Malcolm was a millisecond quicker. Philip's eyes slitted as he caught a pinprick of dark-purple light emanating from the boy's wrist. Whenever a spell would come a hair's breadth away from Malcolm, it would flash amethyst and the spell would either sail harmlessly over the boy or slightly alter its course. Philip's barrage was not hindering his progress in any way.

Philip found himself backpedaling, trying to keep a healthy amount of space between him and Malcolm. He held on to his totem firmly and dropped his other hand, his fingers curling into a fist. The square-cut marble slabs beneath Malcolm's feet liquified, engulfing his boots to the ankles. Almost immediately, the ground cracked as he stepped out of the holes as if they were dried sand, and he continued closer. Now Philip could see his close-cropped hair matted to his head; the rain made inverted peaks in his bangs as it flowed into several rivulets that streamed down his face.

The closer Malcolm got to Philip, the more he realized that Malcolm didn't look like the boy he'd briefly fought at the Sesquimillennial Jubilee massacre after he'd given Jennifer the order to take the ChronoCrystal and Merlin's journal to further fuel the centuries-old war of finding the Halostone. In the years Draconex had taken control of the Dark Watchers and apprenticed Malcolm, Philip had made sure to keep his meetings with

Draconex clandestine so neither side would be tipped off at his duplicitous involvement in the war. As the years went on, he had heard about Malcolm's growing tendencies through his master. Now, standing across a battlefield that was once an imposing, glorious castle, the boy seemed . . . stronger, jaded, and more determined.

Malcolm, it seemed, was no longer a boy.

The sharp scar across Malcolm's face was more prevalent when wet; it shined as lightning flashed overhead, and veins of dark purple pulsed across his throat and over his jawline. His eyes were black, soulless pits.

Philip didn't waste any more time. He rushed at his much younger opponent, hoping to close the distance first and catch Malcolm off guard before he cast his next terramancy spell. Almost as if expecting this change in tactic, Malcolm spun around the spell that would have liquified his eyeballs and lunged toward Philip. In a desperate effort to evade the attack, Philip channeled animancy and chose to gain the leg strength of a red kangaroo. Belying his advanced age, Philip flipped over Malcolm, clearing his head effortlessly and with meters to spare. He landed spryly several meters away, back toward the hallway that led to his office.

Malcolm—along with several eerie, disembodied voices— yelled as he spun around. Unsettled, Philip looked around for anything to use as a projectile; luckily, they were fighting in a scrapyard. He pointed his pocket-watch totem at a pile of loose rubble near Soter, and every piece down to the smallest pebble lifted off the ground. Philip strained as he brought the mass of stone and brick in between him and Malcolm. Thin waterfalls cascaded off the rough mound, and just as he was about to unleash a rockslide overhead, he noticed Malcolm focus on something behind him.

He looked over his shoulder and saw his mother, out in the open and unprotected.

"Mother . . ." he gasped, releasing his hold on the debris. How did she find her way out of the Sacrarium? The pile of stone, brick, and metal crashed harmlessly to the ground as he faced Malcolm again, horror etched all over his face.

A cold chill that didn't come from the rain blasted down his spine as Malcolm trained Draconex's totem ring on Genevieve, its fiery-red ruby already pulsating with the growing power of an unreleased spell.

"YOU!" Malcolm said, his voice carrying over the thunderclaps and the heavy splatter of rain on marble.

Philip didn't see the spell emanate from Malcolm's ring; he was already sprinting toward his mother, waving at her to get down. But she just stood there, watching what would fatally strike her in mere seconds. Philip could see the spell's sickly yellow color reflected in the standing water on the ground as it traveled with alarming speed to its target. He was only a few steps away from her when he realized he wouldn't be able to get to her in time, so in the span of a heartbeat, he jumped sideways in front of the spell, pulling telemancy to the front of his nexus. The forcefield that he'd created a moment before impact connected with the yellow streak of magic, protecting him enough, but the blast was so great that it sent him flying into his mother.

Philip slammed into Genevieve's side and they both went down to the ground. His lungs burned, devoid of air from the harsh impact of the spell. Spluttering to regain oxygen, he remained on the ground and reached his hand out. Keeping his hold on telemancy, Philip conjured another forcefield, this one larger, covering both him and his mother as he crawled over to her. She was on her side, deathly still and curled up in the fetal position.

Several spells of different colors splattered on the curved invisible forcefield like thrown paint, only to dissipate almost immediately after impact. Philip knew that with every blast his protection spell would weaken. He needed to get her to safety, and fast.

"Mother . . ."

Philip turned her toward him. Her jaw was slack and her eyes fluttered open.

"I-I'm fading, my Philip," she said weakly.

Philip propped her head up and wrapped an arm around her waist. "We need to get you out of here."

Genevieve winced. "No . . . I'm not going to make it."

Philip looked at the forcefield he'd created. Malcolm had stopped his onslaught of spells and was walking in their direction, his head tilted slightly, his gait quickening. He brought his tear-blotted eyes back to his mother, swallowing with a tight throat. "I can heal you, I can—"

"My body is fine, my darling," she breathed. "It's my life force that is waning."

Philip held her stiffly, blinking in abject shock. He quickly diverted his thoughts to an alternative plan. "Well, then, I can—"

"No, Philip, you're not hearing me," his mother said. Her neck drooped deeper over his arm. "You need to conjure the proxianimancic spell to save me."

Philip stammered, not sure what to say, or how to think. He hadn't attempted that forbidden spell in ages . . .

"It's the only way. A little will propel my nexus to take over," she added after a brief pause.

Philip didn't need to look behind him to know that Malcolm had made it to the edge of his forcefield. He could sense him.

"Mother, I—"

"You've spent centuries bending each Mancy plane to your will, mastering the proxichronomancic spell." Genevieve feebly lifted a hand and cupped his chin. "I have complete faith in your control over the proxianimancic spell . . . my dear, dear boy."

Stunned at the request and eyes burning, Philip stared down at his dying mother as she begged for his help.

For him. Her only son.

Muffled collisions as a result of large debris being thrown at the forcefield reverberated around him as he took her hand off of his chin and held it.

Philip would do anything for his mother . . .

He slowly closed his eyes and reached into his nexus and tapped into animancy. Everything except him and Genevieve fell away as if they had been transported to a remote island and were the only living souls for thousands of miles, mother and son.

Philip allowed his grip on animancy to strengthen inside his nexus until he could almost touch his own life force. Keeping that pathway open, he synced up his heartbeat with his mother's (which was extremely fast, like a rabbit's) and quickly located her own life force. He paused, briefly confirming that her nexus was dormant. He realized just then how much damage his mother had sustained whilst trapped inside the Halostone for the past fifteen hundred years. A mix of pity and determination spurred him onward, reaching out to guide her toward his nexus as if he were a lighthouse casting its beam to a boat lost in dark, choppy waters.

But then Philip sensed something else in his mother's life force, and he was instantly overcome with a chilling sense of unrecognizable danger. His nexus was wide open, sending the proxianimancic spell into the void that held both his mother and him, and his senses were heightened.

Something was wrong . . . terribly wrong . . .

The life force Philip had mistaken as his mother's was something completely different. And malicious.

Like a pouncing lioness, this unknown presence latched onto his spell and traveled back toward his nexus, darkening it like spilled ink across a tablecloth. Philip was sent spinning into a vortex in his own mind as he tried to repel this new force. He now knew something had attached itself to his mother—something to which he had opened himself up; something pure evil.

And it was about to access his nexus.

Like trying to wrestle a kite in a windstorm, he used all his mental power to reverse the proxianimancic spell and reject whatever was connected to his life force.

He prayed he wasn't too late.

The evil force didn't seem to be affected . . . at first. Though as he felt his nexus accommodate his late change, the malicious presence slowed in its advancement until it reversed course and shot back out in an instant.

Synapses fired, lighting up his mind much like the lightning strikes dancing around Watercress Castle, as Philip was thrown out of his nexus and back into the physical world.

It hurt to move his eyes, and blinking felt like someone was pushing them into his skull, but after a few hard-fought blinks, his vision cleared. He looked down and was holding nothing but air. His mother was no longer in his arms. He jerked backward, turning to look at where he'd last seen Malcolm for fear that he'd taken her.

But the boy, too, was gone without a trace.

Philip heard shuffling off to his left and saw his mother a few meters away. Her legs were shaking as she tried to stand. Relief washed over Philip as he reached out to her, but how she reacted made him falter. His mother gazed upon him with a look of utter confusion. She seemed to have no clue who he was . . . or where she was. She pointed the Ring of Lancaster at the ground at her feet and, before Philip could utter a single word or move a single muscle, a mist fell over his mother and she vanished.

Philip was alone once again. He stayed there until the rain had relented, bringing in a calmness that sucked all the warmth from his being and left him devoid of hope.

CHAPTER EIGHT

The sun was now at just the right angle so that its rays streamed through the first stencil set in the helioarch, casting a crisp, abstract illustration of the creation of the MystiCrystals onto the surface of the roundtable. On the easternmost part of the table, streaks the width of needles curled and coiled from a swirling orb of differing opacities, giving the illusion that there was a three-dimensional supernova in the act of exploding. Abstract versions of the five MystiCrystals were spread out, circling the blast, letting the eye connect the dots to form a mosaic of light that resembled a star.

Jen's adoptive parents were outside keeping Tyler occupied as the remaining six sorcerers sat evenly spaced around the large roundtable. Gavin, of course, sat in the Light Bringer's chair, and counterclockwise from him sat Rez, Hephalon, Jocelyn, Jen, Victor, and Mira. Jen had chosen the chair closest to where she'd been standing when she'd proposed her plan to break the spell that was over Charles; before her, the TeleCrystal hadn't moved from where she'd set it.

Jen was finishing up explaining the finishing touches of her plan: "Now, since this spell is like a combination lock, we need to open the 'locks' in a sequence, one at a time, steadily increasing our energy inputs until it's full, and hold it there. I'll jump in last and work on the chronomancy lock." She let a haggard breath out. "Hopefully that can pull Charles out of the proxiomnimancic spell."

Jen's gaze fell on her father. The longer she stared at Charles, the less familiar he looked. It was a weird feeling, akin to attending an open-casket funeral for a loved one. His eyes remained shut and his cheeks were slightly sunken, devoid of that indescribable way he moved his face: his comforting smirk, pensive grimace, focused scowl. Jen didn't know why, but whenever he did any of those movements, she knew that everything would be all right and he wouldn't be going anywhere. She blinked as it dawned on her that she was now the one who needed to give everyone around her that same comforting feeling.

Jen looked at Victor. "We'll start with terramancy."

Victor nodded, absentmindedly running his thumbs across each of the totem rings on both his hands. "Ready," he said in a determined tone.

Jen closed her eyes and fell into her nexus. The black void caught her like a heavy blanket and she let it surround her while she activated each Mancy plane. Selecting terramancy first, she kept the other four planes on standby. She reached out into the void and located Victor's nexus. It shone like a high-grade flashlight bobbing around in a dark, subterranean cave.

Jen began guiding Victor to Charles's dormant nexus, which had remained as directionless and untethered as when she had first felt it back in the Pentarena. She wondered if Charles was even aware of what was happening.

Making sure Victor's presence was still close by, Jen pinpointed the part of the spell that had the strongest sensation of terramancy and alerted her uncle. She felt Victor's aura immediately clamp onto it. Without wasting any time, Victor channeled his masterful command of terramancy and began supplying that section with his own energy. Confident that Victor had it under control, Jen brought herself back into the physical world. She wanted to be as efficient as possible; she knew that once the levels of each plane were reached, continual effort was needed for them to remain stabilized so the entire spell could be broken. And Jen knew from firsthand experience that not a single sorcerer had limitless reserves stored in their nexus.

Time was of the essence.

Trying to think as pragmatically as possible, she next sought out the Mancy plane that seemed the closest to terramancy. Gavin was more than ready and, in short order, he had attached his nexus to the spell and was siphoning his energy into the astromancy "lock."

Next, Jen brought in Mira to take care of the animancy lock, followed by Rez with his strong connection to telemancy. Jocelyn desperately wanted to help (since she'd been a telemancer well before her resurrection as a vampire), but she hadn't used that plane in so long and didn't want to risk jeopardizing the entire operation. She chose to monitor each sorcerer, available if extra help were to be needed.

Victor had already reached the required level of the terramancy lock and was steadily holding it; same with Gavin at the astromancy lock. Mira was about halfway done and showing excellent stamina, considering the constant energy that was required; Rez was right behind her, uncharacteristically silent and deep in focus.

Jen wanted to do one last thing before she latched on to the spell's chronomancy lock. She pulled out of her nexus, again returning her presence to the helioarch. The ceremonial chamber was quiet; the four sorcerers helping Jen were in a meditative state, their totems glowing as they exerted energy from their nexi into the complex proxiomnimancic spell. Jen glanced at all of them in turn before holding her gaze on Hephalon. He was sitting next to his son, resting a meaty hand on Rez's forearm, giving him all his attention. Jen smiled and was pulled away when her ears picked up a sigh to her left. Jocelyn was staring intently at Charles. She was as still and as white as a marble statue in her chair, but the look on her face lent even more gravity to the situation . . . and Jen's ability to hold her own with the chronomancy lock, the last obstacle between her and freeing Charles from Cindergray's spell.

Jen sighed too. She was the only sorcerer who had any chance at breaking it. As fate would have it, this plane was the last of the five that Jen needed to master—and, ironically, Cindergray had volunteered to be her mystra. That definitely wasn't going to happen.

Back when Jen and Charles had raised Atlantis into the sky, she'd been able to tap into the chronomancy plane with her father's help. She could still access it, but she wasn't sure if she had enough control over chronomancy to provide the last section of the spell with enough energy for this to work . . .

Then Jocelyn looked at Jen and her doubts immediately melted away. She was going to succeed. She had to.

Here we go . . .

It was hard for Jen to end the touching moment with her mother, but she didn't want to keep Victor and her friends waiting a second more. She let her eyelids drape over her eyes as she drew in a deep breath and dropped back into her nexus. Like retracing her own footprints in a field of fallen snow, Jen found her way back to Charles's nexus, the proxiomnimancic spell hovering directly above like a deadly thundercloud.

Victor and her friends had all been able to reach the power levels of their assigned "locks" and were currently keeping the levels stable while Jen identified the final, untouched lock and tapped into chronomancy.

Almost like witnessing the first sparks erupt from a dry pile of kindling, Jen felt her chronomancy sputter to life. Scared to lose her meager grip, Jen slowly let her nexus welcome this unfamiliar energy. With every breath, she could feel time speed up and slow down. Thin waves of red undulated in her mind's eye as time seemed to slow; blue waves appeared as Time accelerated. They shifted back and forth and in every direction as Jen fought to regain the normal speed of time. She was glad this wasn't happening in the physical world; otherwise she'd vomit from vertigo.

Everyone was counting on her. That knowledge alone pushed her to overcome imposter syndrome that had crept up inside of her. Galvanized, she stabilized her nexus and established a firm connection with the lock like opposite poles of a magnet. Surprise flooded her mind, but she quickly calmed herself, focusing on the next step of creating a funnel to direct her nexus's chronomancy energy. The lock slowly accepted her nexus's energy at first, giving her a sensation akin to butterflies in her stomach.

It's actually working!

Jen was beginning to provide more energy into the lock when a flash of light overtook her senses. Her connection with the lock remained stable, but the flash was so unexpected that her focus started to crack. The lock threatened to reject her energy. Another flash appeared, not as bright this time; an afterimage of an enormous, scaly dragon appeared, coiled like a serpent as it soared through the sky.

Wait, is that . . . Fuzanglong?!

Another flash assaulted her, and another, in quick succession, bringing with it a vision of Charles on a floating slab, no color left in his face. The sinking feeling of death accompanied this vision, distracting Jen even more. Her connection to the chronomancy lock was hanging on by a thin thread when a third vision—one that involved her—knocked her reeling.

In the midst of an out-of-body experience, Jen saw herself levitating in the epicenter of a turbulent storm, her eyes as black as coal. Gale-force winds whipped her black curls all around, her hands reminiscent of claws as purple-black lightning crackled along her fingertips.

No . . .

In an instant, everything went from stable to erratic. Her focus shattered into too many pieces to rebuild, the chronomancy lock rejected her touch, and, instead of closing back up, it started releasing not only the energy Jen had been supplying, but its own. Panicking, Jen tried to latch back on, but the torrent of energy was too strong. It was like trying to swim up a rushing waterfall with only her arms. Eventually her nexus's connection was severed so abruptly that she found herself in mid-scream back in the physical world. She jerked so hard that she gave herself whiplash and toppled her chair over, slamming into the helioarch's floor.

Jen was numb. Her body was convulsing—she couldn't control herself, but as her mortal senses started to return, she realized she was being shaken by Jocelyn. Her mother sounded miles away and deep underwater as Jen was rolled onto her back. The sky above was a blob of light blue, and she could just make out a thin line in the sky that slowly coalesced into the helioarch.

"Jennifer! Jennifer Mintaka!" her mother was shouting, Hephalon now by her side.

Jen rolled her neck muscles and groaned, trying to sit up. Hephalon righted her chair while Jocelyn helped her back onto it. As her line of sight came over the lip of the roundtable, Jen saw her friends, one by one, come out of their meditative states, their totems dimming and eventually glowing no more.

Jen grabbed the table for balance, her nerves fried and limbs shaking involuntarily. Her mind was still processing the visions she'd had, what each one had made her feel. Victor was shaking his head groggily, Mira leaning her head against a palm, Rez blinking as though a harsh light had been shined in his eyes, and Gavin wearing a grimace as he slowly stood up.

"What happened, Jen?" Jocelyn whispered in her ear.

Jen trained her eyes on Charles and haphazardly brought herself back into her nexus. In not even a second, her nexus returned her to the omnimancy spell. Every plane was dormant and unresponsive to her touch except for the chronomancy lock. It was hemorrhaging energy, and Jen couldn't stem its flow as she tried to reconnect with the lock. She could feel her father's vitals slowing down with the release of this energy, and then without warning the spell sent her recoiling away.

Jen was back in the helioarch before she knew what had hit her. She caught the last vestiges of energized light leaving her totem bracelet, now hanging limp on her wrist. Nearly everyone was standing, some moving to get closer to Jen.

"The spell . . . it isn't accepting my touch," Gavin said. The astromancer cupped his hands around his orb totem, trying to get his nexus to reach Charles and the spell.

Before Jen could attempt to explain, a dark streak blotted out the sun, and an image of Fuzanglong flashed in her mind again.

"We're too high in the atmosphere to get clouds . . ." Victor thought aloud, using his hand as a visor as he looked upward.

A second image of the serpentine dragon assaulted her mind; she knew what needed to happen. She pushed off the table and ran out of the helioarch, almost in as much shock as the people she'd left behind. She felt like at any moment her legs would lock up, still a bit shaky, but she risked it anyway. She had to. In the distance, she saw her foster parents sitting on a grassy knoll while Tyler played with Skarmor.

"SKAR!"

Jen whistled and the griffin's eagle eyes dilated immediately. He took off in her direction, leaving a bewildered Tyler in his wake. Jen banked slightly to the left so she could run up next to Skarmor. He was stretching his mighty wings, preparing for a quick takeoff as he bounded closer. Jen's feet left the ground and she deftly fell on Skarmor's back—he didn't even have to slow down or alter his course—as he left Camelore behind.

Jen surveyed the skies to her left with no sign of Fuzanglong, but when she turned to her right, the serpentine dragon soared up from under Camelore, much closer than before, reminding her how gigantic he truly was.

She urged Skarmor to fly higher despite his cautious *caws!* of protest (she was lucky to have a creature so trusting and loyal). As Skarmor ascended, Fuzanglong circled them. Jen could feel the massive gusts of wind that his scaly body was creating as Skarmor fought to fly straight. After a few more seconds (Jen wanted there to be a fair distance between her and Camelore, just in case) she patted Skarmor's side and whispered in his ear. He slowed until he came to a stop, flapping his wings and holding a stable altitude.

Fuzanglong twisted around to face Jen and Skarmor, magically suspended in the air, his two long, yellow whiskers rippling.

You are a Lancaster, he boomed. His words were loud and clear, but his mouth didn't move.

Jen was not afraid, despite her last run-in with the dragon when he tried to level Atlantis and steal the MystiCrystals. She felt, if anything, more determined.

"Yes," she called over the wind.

The dragon's scales shimmered in the direct sunlight as his body slowly slithered in the air. His tail whipped around almost involuntarily as he stretched and retracted claws that could slice you open just from looking at them too long.

You look like her, Fuzanglong said. *Like Gwendolyn.*

Jen's heartbeat pitter-pattered in her chest. He knew Genevieve's younger sister?

Instead she asked, "Why did you try to destroy Atlantis?"

Fuzanglong's eyes roamed her face intently, but before he could respond, Victor called out her name from below. The dragon looked downward, moving his writhing body to get a better vantage point.

Jen couldn't explain it, but she knew that Fuzanglong meant no harm. Maybe he could shed some light on her visions.

"Vic! It's okay." She held out a disarming hand.

Her uncle brought his equivolian steed, Kuirhan, to the same altitude as Skarmor before he brandished his glowing totem rings, ready for anything. "I find that hard to believe." He looked out of the corner of his eye at Jen. "What happened back there? You rushed out without an explanation."

"I know . . . I'm sorry, it's just—" Jen took in a breath and slowly let it out as she forced herself to gather her thoughts. "I had these visions. Horrible visions. And the instant we all saw Fuzanglong in the sky, I knew I needed to go to him. It's hard to explain."

A reckoning is coming, Fuzanglong said.

Jen glanced at the dragon, still several meters away. Her throat tightened, thinking back to her last vision, with her fully merged with the ShadowCrystal and its dark energy, black eyes and all.

"So those visions I had . . ."

Jen couldn't bring herself to finish the question.

Show what is most likely to pass.

Jen looked off to the side, relieved. "So they could be changed?"

The future is always shifting, Fuzanglong said enigmatically.

She could still save her father then. And prevent herself from slipping into darkness.

Victor guided Kuirhan closer to Jen and Skarmor, his body language now less primed for battle and more hesitantly curious to learn more about Fuzanglong's intentions.

The divine dragon broke the silence.

For millennia, I have made this world my playground, amassing treasures that far exceed the wealth of your mortal kings and queens. I've watched their armies war over the meager scraps I left behind. I didn't care about humans—in fact, I enjoyed watching you fight—until I came across Gwendolyn Lancaster. She was . . . different.

Jen shared a look with Victor, who seemed just as surprised as her.

We first met in a cave that I was using as one of my pathways to my dimension, Empyyr.

Something in the back of Jen's mind fell into place, making her ask: "Is that where I found the Halostone?"

The dragon closed his eyes in affirmation.

After Gwendolyn watched her sister sacrifice herself and trap the dark sorcerer in the Halostone, with her final breaths she called on me to ensure that that very stone would be protected. I brought it to Empyyr knowing that my home hadn't yet been discovered by humans or any of the other realms' inhabitants.

But over the centuries since my last encounter with my friend, the promise I made to her had faded and my insatiable fondness for treasure resurfaced. It wasn't until recently that I was foolishly manipulated by a fallen sorcerer.

"Malcolm," Jen breathed. It was all starting to make sense.

If that is the name he goes by. He has reminded me why I have had limited involvement with your kind. It is clear that I have meddled one too many times in your affairs. For that, I apologize.

With a *woosh* he glided beneath Skarmor and Kuirhan, leaving Jen unresolved. She still needed to know if there was any way Fuzanglong could help her so that her visions wouldn't come true.

"Fuzanglong, wait! *Please!*" she called out as she turned Skarmor around to face the retreating dragon.

He was farther away than she'd realized, but still he paused.

I only came to you with this explanation as a courtesy to Gwendolyn's memory and the bond we shared. Fuzanglong did not turn around to face her, though his voice carried as clear as if he hadn't added any distance between them. *I am bound to no more.*

"The visions I had . . ." Jen hesitated. She wasn't sure if she was ready for Victor to hear about them. She let out a tired breath before she picked back up, "I need to prevent them from coming true."

Fuzanglong's long body rolled, turning his mountainous mass around to face Jen again. She fought the urge to flinch and rein in Skarmor. He stopped less than a meter from her and extended his whiskers. She froze as they touched each side of her head, her senses rushing to display a new vision, one with a white stag standing tall atop a rocky bluff, its sleek, shiny coat rippling in a lazy wind that blew in a star-flecked blanket of a dusky sky.

Fuzanglong's voice then invaded her mind: *Change will present itself to you, at which time an irreversible decision will have to be made. Take heed.*

The vision elongated and faded to white as Jen was pulled back to the here and now. Her sight returned and with it, no view of Fuzanglong. The only one who remained near her was Victor. He floated beside her, emanating concern as he gripped Kuirhan's reins with one hand and placed the other supportively on her shoulder.

"Jenny, are you okay? What was that all about?"

Jen continued to stare ahead, where Fuzanglong had been only moments before, processing her latest exposure to another vision. She leaned forward and laid her head and chest on Skarmor's back.

"You wouldn't believe me if I told you."

CHAPTER NINE

Ferox had been *inside* Genevieve?

As Volcanor hurtled through the rumbling Azumarian skies, Malcolm finally understood what the ShadowCrystal had meant when it had said that Lord Ferox's shell was different. The rain was letting up, but it was still stinging his face as his dragon covered scores of meters in mere seconds.

What began as a duel to the death with Cindergray, the Grand Mystra of the Sorcery Guild—and, apparently, the only son of Genevieve Lancaster and Lord Ferox—had quickly turned into a chase to follow Ferox's jettisoned life force after he had been released from Genevieve. Malcolm's surprise only doubled when the ShadowCrystal said it was able to track the fleeing life force since it had once been intertwined with Lord Ferox.

Malcolm hadn't a clue where the ShadowCrystal was leading him, but he couldn't contain the newfound hope that had begun to surge in his chest. Lord Ferox had actually survived—and Malcolm would be the first to pledge his loyalty and watch as a new order was ushered in to each and every realm . . .

Wispy, gray smoke erupted from Volcanor's snout with each forceful flap of its venous wings as it carried Malcolm over the soggy, muted hills. His body tingled in anticipation of finally interacting with the one sorcerer he'd grown to idolize during his training as a Dark Watcher.

The ShadowCrystal's murmurings were getting louder and louder with every passing second: *The harbinger of darkness is close by—he lives—the realms will all be—no one left standing—*

Intense hatred and lust overcame Malcolm, but these weren't his own emotions. He looked down at his wrist gauntlet, which housed the ShadowCrystal shard. It throbbed purple as it continued to pump its magic—and desires—into his veins and mind. His body's internal temperature rose and his heartbeat thundered in his ears, interrupting the crystal's disembodied voices, which seemed to be fighting over each other to be heard. His breathing became more forceful as he fought to concentrate; the voices were causing him to tip on the brink of going mad.

"Stop . . ." Malcolm said between shallow breaths. He dug his nails into Volcanor's scales as he winced.

The voices only grew louder.

"Stop!"

He only picked up more of the crystal's ramblings as its murmurs overlapped, crackling in his ears. Fighting with all his might to suppress the growing control of the ShadowCrystal within his own body, Malcom pressed harder into his dragon's back, tapping into his nascent plane, terramancy, as he repeated his command a third time, so loud that his vocal cords ached.

"STOP!"

The pressure of his terramancy-enhanced fingernails cracked the wyvern dragon's scales like brittle candy. Volcanor groaned in pain and tried to buck Malcolm off its back. The ShadowCrystal finally relented and fell silent, but Malcolm now had a new problem. Adrenaline surged through his system as he slid down Volcanor's left side. What stopped him from tumbling off was his hands finding the sturdy base of the dragon's left wing. Feet dangling in heavy boots, Malcolm looked down and saw only a shiny brown-green blur, making him hold on even tighter. At least the rain had subsided. He swallowed hard as he tried to pull himself back up, but his armor and dense cloak were making it extremely difficult.

Volcanor clumsily adjusted to the abrupt imbalance of weight and roared with clear agitation. It chomped at Malcolm, bringing its bristly, horned head as far around to its side as it could go.

Malcolm knew he was losing control over Volcanor. He needed to calm his dragon. With no other option springing to mind, he entered his nexus and reluctantly searched for the ShadowCrystal so he could merge with its unnatural connection to telemancy. He could barely feel the ShadowCrystal's energy in the void, its essence like a monster peeking through a cracked-open closet door. Malcolm coaxed it out as he released his access to terramancy and asked the crystal to help him tap into telemancy.

His forearms burned as his grip on Volcanor started to weaken, forcing Malcolm to merge with the crystal expeditiously. Almost instantly he felt the vaguely familiar but foreign sensation of telemancy erupt in his nexus. He pulled himself back into the physical world just as he lost hold of Volcanor's wing with his right hand. Dangling by only his left, his tendons burning with the extra effort, Malcolm lifted his free hand and shot a spell out of his totem ring straight at Volcanor's head. The spell crackled along its brimstone scales and seemed to seep into the burnt, lava-red hide below, instantly calming the ferocious beast.

Malcolm couldn't even catch his breath in relief before a gust of wind caught his thick cloak and tugged his left hand free, sending him into a freefall hundreds of meters above what had now turned into a rocky landscape. In his tailspin, he tried to touch the dragon's primitive mind and command it to catch him before he collided with the harsh, unforgiving terrain. Malcolm calculated the odds of him surviving the impact as a dark blur swooped beneath him. He landed roughly on Volcanor's spine as the dragon arced in the air. Malcolm strained to hang on as the wyvern dragon looped high in the air before planing out into a controlled descent with long, steady flaps.

Malcolm realized he'd been holding his breath since he had lost his grip on Volcanor, so he sharply inhaled as the dragon touched down on its massive clawed feet. Silently cursing the ShadowCrystal, he shook his head and looked at where Volcanor had landed.

The cave where he'd killed Lord Draconex. Almost ironic.

Taking a few minutes to compose himself, Malcolm finally, cautiously, stepped into the mouth of the cave. Volcanor waited obediently outside. The gloomy weather prevented the flat afternoon light from entering too far into the cave, and so, as the eerie voices in his head awoke once more, he used the large ruby that was inlaid in his totem ring to light the way. Awash in crimson light, the cave looked like the inside of a giant snake's esophagus. His boots crunched on ash and splinters of rock from the battle he'd waged not too long ago, each step a memory of a spell he'd cast at Diaema, a kick he'd whipped at Charles, a vile sneer he'd thrown at Victor when his former mystra came in atop his griffin, tilting the advantage away from Malcolm and Draconex as he quickly rescued both Charles and Diaema from what Malcolm would have ensured was a brutal, tortured fate.

The cave curved to the left, and even before the light could reach down the rocky tunnel, he heard it: weak, raspy, erratic breaths.

Belonging to Lord Draconex, his late master.

There he is . . . the ShadowCrystal's voices crawled inside Malcolm's skull.

The light from his ring splashed over the back of Draconex's corpse, still pinned to the cave wall by the quartz spear Malcolm had thrown into his neck. His eyes widened seeing the head and arms of his late master twitch as his body fought to take in air through a heavily damaged esophagus.

It seemed Lord Ferox's soul had found a new host.

Malcolm's adrenaline spiked again as he walked up to his vanquished master. Slowly, Draconex's face came into view as he knelt in the same spot from which he'd watched the life leave his master's eyes. Eyes that were open and cloudy as beneath them the mouth gaped open, struggling to coax in needed oxygen.

76

Remove the spear, murmured the ShadowCrystal. *We can heal him . . .*

Malcolm clenched his jaw and reached toward his master's throat—but hesitated. The revulsion he felt toward Draconex made him pause.

Quickly, boy! He doesn't have much time.

Malcolm glowered in contempt. He thought he had proven himself enough to not be called a *boy* ever again. He looked down at his hands, which shook slightly with indecision. The freedom he'd felt after vanquishing Draconex had been intoxicating, allowing him to decide the future of the Dark Watcher tribe. He didn't want to jeopardize that, especially since he had just become the undisputed commander. But he wasn't saving Draconex, he reminded himself; that horrid master was long gone. Ferox was now laying claim over his late master's withered body, but only if Malcolm chose to help him.

It would be nice to have Lord Ferox indebted to him . . .

His master's skeletal hands now futilely swiped at his own throat. Malcolm noticed missing pieces of skin from his fingers and palms. Cave rodents had surely made quick work of any unprotected flesh on his decomposing corpse.

An impatient yell from the thousand disembodied voices inside his head made Malcolm flinch and settle on a decision. He slid closer to the butt of the quartz spear and, with both hands gripping the end, pried the tip from the cave wall.

A wet gurgle escaped Draconex's mouth and throat as the body was jerked to the side, but its new host seemed too preoccupied with getting enough air to care about the abrupt pull. Malcolm repositioned and pressed his shoulder into the corpse's side and began to extract the spear from his late master's neck, leaning into the body as he did so. In less than a couple of seconds, the spear was free from the pale throat, slick with fresh jugular blood. Looking at the spear, Malcolm couldn't help but twist his face into a look of disgust as the body of his late master slumped to the ground.

Cover the wound! Now!

77

Malcolm tossed the spear aside and twisted around to face Draconex's body. He quickly covered both openings with his hands and immediately felt a warm trickle of energy flow through his limbs. Eyes wide in awe, he watched as the sallow skin around his hands faintly illuminated. The body suddenly jolted and then went rigid, startling Malcolm, but not enough to release his hold on the corpse's throat. He thought he heard the soft deluge of rain starting up again, but it was instead a soft wheeze from Draconex's body, which transitioned into an open-throated gasp. The eyes lost their cloudiness and the body lurched into a sitting position, pushing away from Malcolm's hold.

Lord Ferox was now completely in control of his late master's body.

Malcolm didn't know what to say or do. He'd been fantasizing about the day he'd meet Lord Ferox, the destined ruler of the eleven realms, but now that he found himself in front of the dark lord, dressed in Draconex's skin, he couldn't formulate any words. The head of his late master slowly turned to his side, showing a macabre profile of a reanimated corpse in the light of Malcolm's still-powered totem ring. It was a weird, terrifying sight to behold—but it was one that left him in pure awe.

Lord Ferox was indeed the savior of the eleven realms, Malcolm realized, for he could not be silenced, not even after his mortal body had been destroyed. And for Ferox to fulfill the prophecy in no other vessel than the body of Draconex . . . oh, how Malcolm's stomach turned over at the irony as he gazed upon his late master's sunken cheeks and raised, curved facial scar (in the same place as Malcolm's own) once more, a face that Malcolm thought he'd rid himself of once and for all.

As he ground his teeth at the cruel twist of fate, he could almost glimpse the very soul of Lord Ferox clawing his way out of the abyss of Draconex's glassy, dead eyes. Malcolm swallowed, remaining still as those eyes took on a different glint and locked on him. A shadow thrust itself at Malcolm and, before he could process what that was, his windpipe was being clamped shut in a clammy, leathery vise grip.

"Who-o-o are you-u-u?" Lord Ferox wheezed. He still sounded like Draconex, but also not.

It was Malcolm's turn to wheeze: "I just . . . saved you . . ." He fought to get those three words out as he pointed to the bloody spear lying on the ground a few feet away.

Ferox didn't look at where Malcolm pointed, instead staring hungrily at the ShadowCrystal shard inset in his wrist gauntlet.

"Where did you get . . . *this*?" Ferox asked. His control over a new set of vocal cords was getting stronger.

He released Malcolm's throat and went for the gauntlet. That was when Malcolm found the courage to spin away from Ferox, gasping for air and clutching his throat. They were probably a meter apart; not much space in this cramped cave, but already better than before (for Malcolm's sake).

"That's *mine*."

Ferox lunged at Malcolm, but he collapsed to the rocky ground, his arms and legs splayed out like he had just fallen on slick ice. The dark lord made a sound that was a cross between an irate yell and a wail and brought his hands to his chest to push up off the cave floor when he noticed his decaying hands and paused.

"You are in the body of a recently deceased sorcerer once called Draconex," Malcolm said after his throat had stopped convulsing. He hated how shaky his voice had become. "One whom I had slain."

He slowly stood back up, body rigid and ready to fight, and cast his ring's crimson light on Ferox, who was still prone, inspecting his hands. Malcolm could hear the ShadowCrystal screaming in his head, but somehow it wasn't distracting him from what he wanted to say.

"I am not your enemy. Indeed, I command an army of devout sorcerers, all of whom vowed to resurrect and serve you, Lord Ferox, as you bring about the prophecy of realm unity."

Malcolm saluted, holding his left fist out in front of him, and touched his right fist to the inside part of his left elbow.

Ferox slowly picked himself up and paused in a kneeling position, one hand pressed on the ground for stability. "Why did you kill this . . . Draconex?"

Malcolm thought to tell him the truth, but he didn't want to impress upon Ferox that he was disloyal and prone to killing his masters. "He was getting in the way of your arrival."

Ferox grunted as he slowly stood up, and before Malcolm knew it, Ferox was atop him.

"Give me my ShadowCrystal!" he rabidly growled as he clawed at Malcolm's gauntlet, a few blows purposefully aimed to spin his head right off his neck. Malcolm brought his left arm up to protect his face as he tried to flip Ferox onto his back and gain the upper hand.

Malcolm's ears were ringing from a nasty blow to the back of the head when Ferox tackled him to the ground, but that didn't stop him from fighting for his life. The ShadowCrystal was no help, its voices silent and its presence cold to the touch when he tried connecting with it. Gritting his teeth, he pummeled Ferox's ribs with tight left hooks as he worked to bring his legs closer to his chest. The dark lord raised a knee to block Malcolm's punches, but that put him off balance. Rays of crimson light from Malcolm's totem ring streaked all over the cave's walls and floor as they rolled as one, clutching each other as they vied for control. Malcolm got a waft of decomposing flesh and fought against his gag reflex; he was grateful that his stomach was empty. A lucky punch slipped around Malcolm's middle block and connected with his jaw, sending sparks shimmering all across his field of vision. Warmth flowed into his mouth and he quickly tasted iron.

His strength was beginning to wane, and Ferox noticed it. With both hands, he began prying the ShadowCrystal gauntlet from Malcolm's forearm. Malcolm stifled a scream; it felt like his tendons were being pulled out of his wrist. A feral laugh slithered from the mouth of the man who looked like Draconex; his eyes locked on the shard that he'd once possessed fifteen hundred years ago. Clarity was returning to Malcolm's mind, possibly because of the pain in his right arm as Ferox tried to take his gauntlet. He set his teeth (the ones that weren't chipped) and used terramancy to heat the blood pooling in his mouth and, with a forceful blow, he spit the super-heated blood straight into Ferox's eyes.

Wailing, the dark lord let go of the gauntlet and grabbed his face. Malcolm slipped one boot in between him and Ferox and pushed, sending his assailant flying backward into the opposite wall of the cave.

Malcolm didn't care how loud his groan was as he rolled onto his chest (did he also whimper?). He was just thankful that the bout was over . . . for now. He counted to three before pushing himself up, firmly getting his feet underneath him. Panting, he worked his jaw a few times, spitting out more blood and bits of molar as he shone his ring's light across the tunnel at the unconscious body of his late master, now controlled by Lord Ferox.

Never meet your idols, Malcolm mused sourly.

From the mouth of the cave came a snort from Volcanor. His connection with telemancy had been severed when the Shadow-Crystal went silent, so he used what meager connection he still had with the crystal to channel animancy so he could speak with his dragon. In the tongue of the wyvern, he sent a low rumble back in Volcanor's direction telling it to wait.

He had this under control now.

Sighing, he slowly closed the distance between him and Ferox, trying to figure out how to win the approval of the man who, seconds before, had tried to kill him over the ShadowCrystal. Then it clicked.

Bingo.

This time around, he would voluntarily give Ferox the ShadowCrystal . . . if he could. Purple veins tattooed nearly every part of his body, and the crystal's power was a constant presence at the base of his very soul. Malcolm didn't know how strong their bond had become, but this was the only idea he could think of to not only avoid another brawl but potentially lay the foundation of mutual trust. Even though the ShadowCrystal granted him access to the other four Mancy planes, he had certainly noticed the toll it was taking on him: lapses in judgment, unpredictable emotional outbursts, less control over his body and mind . . .

And he *hated* not being in control. In *complete* control.

Malcolm went rigid, wincing as his jaw sent tendrils of pain across his face and down his spine. Without touching the left side of his face, he knew that it was swollen—maybe even fractured. It even hurt to curse out loud, an activity he greatly enjoyed.

Malcolm looked down, feeling a slight pull from his right gauntlet—almost like the ShadowCrystal was leading him toward Ferox; he was unsure if it was just his imagination or actually the crystal's power. Its whispers were too faint and jumbled for him to discern anything meaningful. Malcolm tried sliding the gauntlet off as pain traveled underneath his skin, emanating from the spot where his wrist touched the ShadowCrystal. Malcolm put the sole of his boot on the top half of Ferox's sternum and called out to the ShadowCrystal in his mind.

Heal me! Then I will release my part of our bond so you can be with Lord Ferox.

Malcolm waited, sliding his tongue gingerly along his chipped teeth and warm, inflamed gums. No voices came, but his jaw and mouth became numb as if a dentist had just injected him with novocaine. His eyes went to the ShadowCrystal and saw it pulsing, exerting its power to repair his busted face. In seconds, the numbness faded and Malcolm was relieved that no sensations of pain met his touch; his teeth were no longer chipped, their nerves exposed.

The crystal stopped pulsing and went dark, retracting its purple veins from his skin.

Malcolm scoffed. Returning his focus on the man under his boot, he put almost all of his weight on Ferox's chest until the dark lord wheezed awake. His eyes were puffy and barely able to flutter open as he regained consciousness.

"I've already killed the person whose body you are in," Malcolm began, cocking his head as he looked into the slits that were Ferox's eyes. The boiling blood had wreaked havoc on those eyes, and he was sure that Ferox was now blind. He continued,

"And I won't hesitate to do it again." He put more pressure on Ferox's chest before lifting his boot off and stepping aside. "Like I said before, I am not your enemy. We want the same thing: order across all realms." Malcolm played with his right gauntlet, twisting it on his wrist to make sure that the ShadowCrystal had disconnected from his skin. "Thousands of years have passed since you were free . . . A lot has changed. I therefore offer you more than merely my allegiance . . ."

Malcolm waited. The only response was Ferox's labored breathing.

"I can leave you here dumb and blind in a cave-in if I so choose." He was starting to become impatient, his mind reverting back to his plan of himself being the one to unite the realms.

But then Ferox started laughing.

"Clearly I underestimated you, terrramancer," Ferox said after he got his laughter under control. "And all this body-hopping is not doing me any favors. You can lead me back to Philip?"

Malcolm furrowed his brow as the pieces started to connect. "Philip . . . You mean Grand Mystra Cindergray?"

Ferox let out a weak chuckle. "Yes."

Malcolm was taking a huge chance, but he knelt beside Ferox and said, "If you make any sudden moves, your story ends here."

Ferox's breathing slowed, and when Malcolm felt confident that he wouldn't strike, he slid off his right gauntlet and rested it on the other sorcerer's chest so that the ShadowCrystal was facing downward. Almost immediately the crystal activated, sending forked veins of purple lightning across his chest, up his neck, over his face . . . the face that had once belonged to the master he'd spent years hating with his entire being: Draconex. Malcolm suppressed a knee-jerk reaction to skewer the recently healed throat a second time by taking a step back and clasping his hands behind his back, squeezing them together until the pressure brought a grimace to his face. Draconex's eyes became beacons of light as they started repairing themselves. In seconds, all swelling had left his face, the ocular capillaries reconstructed, and the repaired pupils dilated to accommodate the dark surroundings of the cave.

"You can keep the ShadowCrystal." Malcolm stood again. "Call it an olive branch. From me to you."

"How considerate," Ferox said sarcastically as he slid up into a sitting position. He cradled the gauntlet in his hands and, with more than a little effort, popped the ShadowCrystal shard from its housing. Tossing the gauntlet aside like day-old trash, he then turned the crystal over in his fingers until the sharper end was facing him, and he groaned when he plunged it into his chest.

Malcolm winced as he watched the crystal embed itself deeper into his sternum. Ferox went rigid as the dark energy coursed through the body he currently claimed dominion over. He inhaled like he'd never breathed in oxygen before, his fingers curling into fists as his nails scraped jagged lines in the cave floor. After he seemed to establish a baseline with the ShadowCrystal's energy, he exhaled.

"How fitting . . . the body of an animancer."

Ferox slowly stood up and faced Malcolm, who fought every nerve in his being to not back away. Lips pursed and chin held high, he stood strong and hoped that Ferox wouldn't turn on him. Tense seconds passed before Ferox spoke again.

"Now . . . prove your worth and take me back to my son."

CHAPTER TEN

Gavin stood rigid at the Light Bringer's place at the roundtable, his chair slid out behind him. He hovered over Merlin's journal, his arms locked straight as his thoughts swirled. Everyone had congregated back into the helioarch to wait for Jen's return. She had decided to drop off her foster family back on Earth before explaining what had transpired between her and Fuzanglong in the skies above Camelore. But waiting had never been Gavin's strong suit.

Mira was at his side, a delicate hand on top of his own while she gently rubbed his back with the other. She'd always been attuned to his emotions, and her being next to him allayed his impatience and anxiety, if only slightly. He'd been staring at the same page in the journal for the last several minutes; he'd almost gone blind to what the text was saying. Abruptly he flipped to the next page before he closed his eyes and pinched the bridge of his nose.

Something was amiss, he knew. This string of bad luck, punctuated by Fuzanglong's return, did not bode well. And Gavin had thought he'd witnessed the end of the fifteen-hundred-year war with Lord Ferox's demise shortly after his release from the Halostone. Gavin wanted to move on. He was ready to help rebuild the Sorcery Guild, spend more quality time with Mira, and finally earn the rank of mystra.

But as fate would have it, the discovery of the Halostone had created more problems than solutions.

Placing his hand back on the table, he rolled his neck and looked at his girlfriend, smiling. She returned the smile, hers softer and more hopeful. He leaned his head over and touched her forehead, hoping to receive some of that hope through osmosis; it didn't work, of course—neither of them was a telemancer—but at least he gave it a try. Exhaling, he turned his gaze toward Charles, still under the strong proxiomnimancic spell, fighting for his life, lying motionless in the center of the roundtable, right where he and Jen had placed him an hour before.

Sunlight from the clear afternoon sky continued to provide sufficient light to render the ornate designs from the helioarch's stenciling above onto the smooth, lacquered surface of the round-table. The current angle of the sun brought its rays closer to Charles's feet, the image now changing from the depiction of the MystiCrystals' creation to that of Excalibur, the sword legendarily associated with King Arthur, being pulled from an anvil.

The top priority was to free Charles from Cindergray's spell before they could discuss a plan to rescue Genevieve from Cindergray.

But first Jen needed to get back here. What was taking her so long?!

The journal pulled his eyes down like a magnet and the skin around them went taut when he saw what was sketched on the page he'd carelessly flipped to: a longsword with half its blade intricately filigreed. With renewed vigor, he looked back to the mural that was currently being cast on the table (a few inches of it were now showing on Charles's boots) and he squinted, thinking.

The same shadowed etchings were inside the light-painted Excalibur.

Gavin stifled a gasp and went back to the page on which Merlin had sketched Excalibur, his mood completely bereft of the languid dejection from moments before.

"Everything all right, Gav?" Mira asked. Still at his side, she squeezed his hand in concern.

"Yeah, I'm fine, babe," he said distractedly as his fingers followed along with what he read. He finished the passage about Excalibur on the following page, almost wishing he hadn't read it at all. If he understood what Merlin was saying, things just got a whole lot more complicated.

He looked up and locked eyes with Victor, who could read him better than anyone.

Before Gavin could bring attention to what he had just read, the helioarch's doors opened and in came Jen, out of breath with her mid-length obsidian curls slightly frazzled.

* * *

With all eyes on her, Jen froze. She didn't know what to say, let alone what to even start with. Her thoughts had been consumed with getting her parents and Tyler safely back home, and once that had been accomplished, they'd shifted to the vision Fuzanglong had shared with her and what his cryptic last words could mean (while she clung tightly to Skarmor as he rocketed back to Camelore—Jen had never seen her griffin fly so fast).

And now she found herself back inside the helioarch with every eye trained on her, waiting for her to explain.

Despite her best efforts, her breathing was still fast and shallow, her cheeks hot and flushed. One hand on her chest, she ran the other through her wind-tousled hair as she tried to center herself. Her gaze crisscrossed the chamber and eventually settled on her father, catatonic and unresponsive in the middle of the table. If any sight could immediately sober her, it was that one. Jen blinked away the onset of tears, slowly took in a breath, and forced herself to step closer to the table, all the while probing her nexus to ascertain her father's condition and focusing on where she'd placed the TeleCrystal.

She stopped at the edge of the table and decided to fall into her nexus and check on him. It didn't take long for her to find it again, and when she identified the chronomancy lock, her fears were confirmed. Energy was still gushing outward into the void, just as forcefully as before, and after a brief attempt at staunching its flow, she had to admit that she wasn't strong enough in chronomancy to reverse it. Despair fell upon her; she knew of no other chronomancers who could immediately help. She couldn't do anything with that lock. Jen then decided to divert her attention to Charles, and what she felt made her tense up: his heartbeat was slowing at the same pace as his oxygen intake was falling.

The release of the chronomancy energy had not only prevented her from breaking the omnimancy spell, but it was also having an adverse effect on her father physically.

No . . . no, please, no . . .

Jen felt as though she were spinning, and before it could get debilitating, she pulled herself out of her nexus. She kicked herself for not realizing it until now; she wondered how much time her father had lost while she went back to her childhood home in Pennsylvania. Her fingers ached and, looking down, she realized she'd been grabbing the table's lip so hard that her knuckles were hyperextended and had turned a throbbing white. She exhaled, letting go of the table just as her ears picked up Gavin's voice.

"Jen, tell us what's going on." It felt like more of a demand than a question; his tone had more than a hint of curt impatience. His crossed arms and set jaw matched the glare he was giving her.

Just come out with it.

"We can't connect to the omnimancy spell any longer. The outflow of chronomancy energy is too strong and seems to have locked down all of the other planes." Jen looked at Victor. He was holding on to Jocelyn while giving Jen a look like he knew she had more to say. Jen exhaled sharply and forced herself to continue: "And his heartbeat is slowing."

Her mother gasped, covering her mouth.

Gavin slammed Merlin's journal shut. "You made us wait to hear this?" he bit out.

Heat bloomed in her cheeks and ears as Jen became defensive.

"I *just* found out about his heartbeat." She tried to keep her voice from trembling, unprepared for Gavin's intensity.

"Well, what are we supposed to do, Jen? You've apparently turned that spell into a ticking time bomb for Charles." He started making his way over to her, leaving his post at the Light Bringer's chair.

"Gavin." Victor's stern voice tried to cut in between Gavin and Jen, but nothing would seem to stop the astromancer's advance.

Gavin's strides were long and purposeful, closing the distance between them in seconds. He pointed at Victor. "Stop coming to her rescue, Vic." He stopped inches from her, seething. "Let's hope your journey back to Earth didn't waste precious seconds that we can't get back."

Victor said another word of warning, but Gavin ignored it as he continued to leer at Jen. Meeting his gaze, she stood there silent as she formulated a response. Her heart was thumping in her chest, but she refused to relent.

Mira reached them before Jen could start. "That's enough, Gav." She put a hand on his chest.

Without breaking eye contact with Gavin, Jen said in as calm a voice as possible, "It's fine, Mira. I got this."

Reluctantly, Mira removed her hand. Gavin crossed his arms once again and waited.

"Stop projecting your anger at our situation onto me," Jen began. "Yes, it was my idea to band together to break Charles's spell, and yes, I couldn't control the chronomancy lock, but let's not forget who the actual enemy is, Gavin. Who was the one who put my father under this spell in the first place?" Jen let her rhetorical question hang in the air for a few seconds before continuing. "This is *exactly* what Cindergray—or whoever the hell he really is—wants to happen. The more we fight amongst ourselves, the harder he'll be to track down, further preventing us from rescuing Genevieve, *who we now need more than ever to save Charles.*

"As much as we all want, we cannot change the past, and I don't know about you, but I am doing everything I can to save Charles before it's too late." At this point, she let the tears break from her lower eyelids and dribble down her cheek. Her emotions weren't a result of Gavin confronting her, but more because of how badly she not only wanted to save Charles but keep everyone else as safe as possible so they wouldn't succumb to the same fate.

She didn't bother wiping away the air-chilled streaks of tears on her flushed cheeks. She took one step forward and poked a finger at him. "And don't *ever* devalue my brother and the parents who raised me. Their safety matters, too, and with the fallout from Cindergray's escape, Camelore wasn't safe for them any longer."

Suddenly, the image of her with black-as-soot eyes and clawed hands radiating lightning in the middle of an intense whirlwind made her catch her breath and take a few steps back. Jen placed a hand on her neck over the spot where the Ring of Lancaster had rested, looking at the others standing in silence. She needed to breathe.

Gavin let his arms fall to his sides, slack. "Jen, I—"

She barely shook her head as she held up her hand. "What I need from you now is some space." Jen's voice was low and controlled, no venom apparent, though she couldn't erase that vision of herself from her mind's eye. Right then she promised that no matter what happened, she would do everything in her power to prevent that vision from coming true. The first step was to not squander another second fighting with Gavin; she'd given him enough to chew on. Finally, she finished with: "I'm going to plan our next steps with those who remember what we're fighting for . . . with or without our Light Bringer."

CHAPTER ELEVEN

The storm had since passed by the time Malcolm landed Volcanor near the eastern edge of the remnants of Watercress Castle. As cracks of blue sky streamed through the shifting blanket of clouds, Malcolm no longer found himself leading Ferox; he was now on the heels of the dark lord, trying to keep up while simultaneously feeling the rush of excitement that had been building inside him for years.

Now it was finally time for its crescendo.

Across the rubble-strewn entrance hall they went. Philip's pegasus was still lying in the same spot, but Malcolm noticed his spell was wearing off. The winged equine was on its side, struggling to stand up because half its body was still frozen. The wing that could move was harmlessly splashing in a puddle as it snorted in frustration. Malcolm furrowed his brow, confused as to why Philip hadn't tended to his animal; he wouldn't have left it if he weren't still somewhere in the castle.

Out of the corner of his eye Malcolm caught Ferox and, without slowing his stride, extended his left hand in a blur of motion. A spell the color of a deep bruise crackled from his fingertips and struck the partially immobilized creature in the throat. Instantly, the spell sent it spinning across the wet marble; its body slammed into the wall next to the drawbridge and didn't move, limp. Not daring to let his steps falter, Malcolm continued on his way, the hallway's curved stone wall quickly blocking his view of the pegasus he now assumed was dead.

He had enough awareness to not react to what he'd just witnessed and stay a few paces behind Ferox, but Malcolm couldn't help but feel a twinge of pity toward the poor animal. In the back of his mind, Malcolm was waiting for the inevitable mad chatterings of the ShadowCrystal to subvert his thoughts with its own and drone on about how the realms were better off with one fewer pathetic creature, but he quickly righted his mind after he looked at his bare right forearm.

He could not properly put into words just how relieved he was to no longer be merged with the ShadowCrystal; it was Ferox's problem now, though he seemed to be better suited for its volatile power. Malcolm didn't care if he was just a terramancer once more; at least he was in complete control of his mind and powers. The kind of unpredictability that came with accessing the ShadowCrystal's powers had prevented Malcolm from ever completely lowering his guard; caution was constantly needed, otherwise he would have lost himself and been a pawn to the ShadowCrystal's irrational desires and machinations. Malcolm had to keep reminding himself of that, but he needed to exercise extreme vigilance; even though he'd convinced Ferox to spare his life back at the cave, he couldn't be caught unawares if and when that decision fell out of his favor.

Ferox seemed to lengthen his strides as he followed the curve of the hallway, forcing Malcolm to almost break into a light jog. Surprisingly, Ferox had quickly gotten used to controlling Draconex's body, but Malcolm had already spotted several differences in comportment. The dark lord walked with a completely different gait, and the presence he exuded was one of ominous hostility. It was almost palpable and ramped up an evolutionary instinct of self-preservation to not mess with the man—a far cry from how he had come to view his late master. Behind the carefully manufactured persona of the Dark Watcher tribe commander, Draconex had been nothing more than a fraud; a disingenuous sorcerer who had to leech off of exterior power sources such as the ShadowCrystal and the Throne of Dragons in order to maintain his fearsome and ruthless reputation. But when push came to shove, that façade cracked as easily as brittle, cracked glass.

And then it shattered into infinitesimal pieces.

The dark lord's purposeful stomping refocused Malcolm as they marched farther down the hallway, which eventually opened up to reveal the blown-in door to the Grand Mystra's office chambers. Lord Ferox seemed confident as to where his son might be; he didn't even hesitate as he entered the gaping hole that was the office's entranceway, grabbing his cape and pulling it in front of him so it wouldn't get caught on any loose, piled-up rubble.

But why would Philip be in the Sacrarium? Malcolm thought as he followed Ferox around the large office desk and down the built-in staircase that would eventually lead to their destination. Malcolm had to slide over the desk's polished edge to not lose sight of him.

CLACK—CLACK—CLACK—CLACK!

Malcolm followed Ferox's heavy footfalls as they echoed through the subterranean corridors. Long-dormant memories awakened within him as he walked the path every tenderfoot walked when they were old enough to undertake the test to see if they were the Light Bringer. Just another bitter memory of his first terramancy master, Victor Huxley, looking down on him with disappointment. Malcolm's lips curled downward in contempt.

Just another scar reminding him that he was never good enough . . .

But now that Malcolm stood at the side of Lord Ferox, he'd be the one passing judgment on Victor for his failings as a mentor and teacher.

Malcolm was pulled from his thoughts when he saw Ferox standing at the controls for the Sacrarium—useless, considering that Malcolm had blasted through the wall passageway on the night of the Sesquimillennial Jubilee as he chased after Jen and her friends. To his surprise, however, Ferox pulled the ShadowCrystal from his chest and touched it to the control's hub, which should have only fit the Grand Mystra's signet ring. The crystal's tip pulsated and morphed into an exact replica of the ring's design, allowing Ferox to turn it.

But Malcolm's awe reached its peak when Ferox turned it *clockwise*.

And with that, they both sank into the floor.

His eyes darted back and forth as the floor rolled over every inch of his body, and by the time it reached his throat Malcolm felt the claws of claustrophobia threaten to tighten. He closed his eyes and kept them shut as he became fully submerged in the floor, too busy focusing on not passing out to wonder where he was being taken.

Relief came when the tightness around him relaxed. Malcolm waited to open his eyes until he felt only air around him. The smell of musty leather and aged paper slid into his nostrils. Upon opening his eyes, he took in a room devoid of windows and doors; in their places were artifacts hung from walls, shelves full of ancient books, and more items of mystic legend splayed on a long table.

What is this place?

Slumped over next to the legs of the sturdy table was the man he now knew was Philip Lancaster II; "Cindergray" was nothing but an alias. Malcolm's heart skipped a beat when he noticed him cradling the MystiCrystals . . . all but one.

Philip didn't budge or acknowledge his or Ferox's presence, even though neither of them had been discreet about their entrance into this secret room, this . . . secondary Sacrarium.

"What a fool I've been . . ." Philip muttered, rolling the opalescent crystals in his palms. "I should have heeded Mother's warning . . ." He looked up at them with puffy, reddened eyes.

Ferox stopped a few paces from the old sorcerer.

Malcolm's eyes bounced between the two men, unsure of who would speak next.

"Was I with my mother at all? Or were you controlling her entire time, Father?"

Philip's eyes glimmered with hurtful tears.

Ferox sighed and knelt to meet his son's eyes at the same level. "When I was thrown into her body, her soul fell dormant. The same happened to her nexus." He slowly extended a hand to his son. His voice was soft . . . charismatic, even. "Son, I tried waking her but could not. I realized I needed an outside source to bring her back."

"You masqueraded as her," Philip accused, not even acknowledging the hand in front of him. "And tricked me . . . Lord Ferox."

There was a pause that let that name hang in the air for one too many seconds. Ferox slowly retracted his hand and propped his elbows on his knees.

"And when you realized you could not access her nexus, you feigned a fatal injury"—Philip stood stiffly and placed the Mysti-Crystals on the table, one by one—"to transfer your life force into my body and take over my nexus."

Malcolm started goading his nexus awake, expecting a fight to break out any second; he tucked his right hand behind his back so Philip wouldn't be alerted to his primed totem ring, its central ruby glowing like flecks of heated embers. Ferox slowly stood, the ends of his black cape sliding closer to his feet like an oil spill going in reverse.

"You are an extremely gifted omnimancer, my son," Ferox said. "I knew that you would be able to hold both of our souls until I found a suitable body to inhabit."

Philip's eyes were still tight with scorn. He shot a fleeting look at Malcolm before returning his gaze to his father, unimpressed. "I see you've found one such body. Why have you returned?"

"I can only achieve what I've set out to do with your help, my son," Ferox said. Malcolm detected a slight warmth to his tone. He wasn't sure if it was real or fake.

"I should strike you down now. You caused the near extinction of the omnimancer." The wrinkles on Philip's face deepened as he slowly slid a hand into his robes. "And if it wasn't for my mother, you'd have succeeded."

"History gets recorded by the victors . . ."

Ferox shook his head, sighing.

"Rarely does the virtuous side win. The five omnimancer clans —including the Lancasters—had all the power they could ever imagine, yet they dared not use it to its fullest extent. Look at your collection down here, Philip."

Ferox spread his arms out as he looked around the small, enclosed room.

"Relics that have been given the status of legendary and mythical, believed to have been lost—or, believe it or not, fabricated— from every civilization, current and extinct, across the eleven realms." He turned back toward Philip. "Lost because the oh-so-wise five omnimancer clans decided to afford sovereignty to each realm, letting their inhabitants run rampant without a collective sense of order and purpose . . ."

Philip's face relaxed slightly, but his hand was still hidden in the folds of his robes. Malcolm dared a glance around the room, making sure the Grand Mystra never left his peripherals. It was an impressive collection. He wondered how long it had taken Philip (it would take time for Malcolm to get used to Cindergray's actual name) to amass one so large . . . and so rare. Malcolm imagined what he could have actually done with the eleven realms as an immortal omnimancer. He could have—

Malcolm tensed, realization flooding his body. The hair on the nape of his neck stood straight out and his scalp tingled with a wave of alertness. If Ferox could convince his son to join him, then he would be hard-pressed to keep Malcolm around. Having an omnimancer at his disposal would be much preferred to a simple terramancer.

"And you thought you could do better?" Philip was as still as stone, his eyes searching Ferox's face.

Malcolm swallowed, his breath now shallow as he tensed his jaw and looked between the two men. He'd sacrificed, fought, and planned too much to be disposed of so frivolously.

"It's much more complicated than that, Philip." Ferox took a step closer to his son, who looked to be on edge. Any sudden movement—or noise—could set him off.

Malcolm pursed his lips and, while keeping his head still, extended his left pinkie finger toward a weathered bust of a serpent with a square jaw that was near the edge of the back table. Using terramancy, he sent a small, concentrated gust straight at it. Malcolm's eyes widened when it failed to move the heavy bust, instead flipping open a heavily faded book of some sort, causing it to accordion out and cascade to the ground. Its fall wasn't as loud as Malcolm had planned for, but it was enough to startle Philip.

What ensued made Malcolm want to wash his eyes out with battery acid.

* * *

Ferox was unsure if he was making any progress with Philip, but at least his son didn't pull away as he took a slow step forward. He needed Philip to lower his guard just enough so he could latch onto his nexus and swap bodies. Then he would be a true omnimancer, finally able to focus on the objective he'd been waiting years—and now, apparently, centuries—to attain. He could feel the ShadowCrystal's energy coursing beneath his skin, waiting patiently to be called upon.

Philip's shoulder muscles relaxed ever so slightly as Ferox inched closer and closer. It was so silent that Ferox thought he could hear the faint *tick-tock* of his son's pocket watch nestled deep inside the folds of his robes.

Just a little closer . . .

THUDD—

The tips of his fingers were about to touch Philip's right hand when something fell behind him, making Ferox freeze in confusion. Philip's reaction was the exact opposite. Startled, his son brandished his pocket-watch totem and pumped his nexus's energy into its clockface, turning the dials into streaks of blue-white light. Any progress, no matter how minuscule, that had worked its way through Philip had immediately been erased.

Ferox cursed. He didn't have time to look behind him at whatever had made that unwelcome noise. Instead, he lunged to the side just as a spear of white light streaked through the place where his chest had been moments before.

Philip was on the offensive, and Ferox was done trying to convince him further. He had no choice but to resort to a more brutish tactic. Using the table for balance, Ferox torqued his hips around and brought a strong roundhouse kick straight into the hand that held the pocket watch.

Philip winced as the heavy boot knocked his totem out of his grip. Its blue-white glow vanished as it exploded into shattered pieces of glass and busted coils that clattered and bounced harmlessly across the stone floor.

Following through, Ferox brought his kicking leg onto the table and used his momentum to continue his twist and, finding Philip again with his eyes, lifted his other foot off the ground and planted a forceful back-kick directly into his son's jaw.

Dazed, Philip slammed into the wall just behind him, jiggling Excalibur in its housing. The sword didn't fall, but still the omnimancer blindly felt for it above his head.

If Philip drew Excalibur during this brawl, Ferox knew he would be stricken down.

Still on the table, Ferox was about to lunge at his son when a molten-red spell knocked Philip's hand away from the legendary sword's hilt. Ferox stole a glance to his right and saw Malcolm, his right arm outstretched and his ring glowing the same color as the spell.

Before Ferox could acknowledge the well-timed help, Philip twisted around and grabbed the hilt a second time. He slid off the table and grabbed a handful of wiry, white hair with one hand and brought the other forearm down to break the hold his son had on Excalibur's hilt. Careful not to get too close to the enchanted sword, Ferox toppled Philip with a decisive kick to the back of his knees, put himself in between his son and Excalibur, and tugged on the long hair in his closed fist so that Philip could do nothing except look up at him.

The fear in his son's eyes didn't bring about any paternal

sympathy; he barely hesitated before he knelt down and clamped his free hand on Philip's throat, causing his eyes to bulge. The same eyes that had looked upon Ferox in a simpler time when he was just Philip I, holding his newborn heir who would carry on his namesake.

But that was in the past, and Ferox vowed to do whatever it took to bring about the prophecy.

Casting that memory aside, Ferox opened a channel to the nexus he now commanded and let the malicious energy of the ShadowCrystal ooze in to further corrupt—and augment—his power.

Rolling his neck while his son gasped for air, Ferox squeezed harder. The power inside him churned and roiled like the sea stirred by Poseidon's wrathful trident. He let a low whisper of a breath escape his cracked lips as he began the process of constructing the forbidden animancy spell.

The spell to harness life itself.

The ShadowCrystal was starving with lust as it wrapped its tendrils around Ferox's nexus, aiding in stabilizing the volatile spell. Ferox knew that if he mishandled the spell's execution, it would prove fatally drastic; but if it worked . . .

The feeling, akin to acid reflux but far stronger, caused him to lurch forward and touch his forehead to Philip's. Almost like it came from a dream, he heard his son wheeze, "I wish . . . I had more time . . . with Mother . . ."

His voice faded away as Ferox was sucked into a torrent of nothingness, latching on to the forbidden animancy spell he'd unleashed as it rolled toward his son's nexus. If his control were to be cut, he knew that the spell would blaze out of control and instantly devour him and Philip. Despite his son's weakened outward appearance, his nexus was a strong, fiery microcosm of all the Mancy planes.

And there it was: Philip's life force.

Ferox pushed his abilities to the edge, straining in effort as if trying to wrangle a herd of angry, hungry felsen. He managed to direct the spell away from the omnimancer's nexus and latch on to the life force. Philip clearly expected as much, for he countered with a strong burst of energy coated in every Mancy plane; his spell had an inherently impregnable shield around it that prevented Philip's defensive onslaught from affecting Ferox himself.

The spell continued to bore into Philip's life force as his nexus fought to extract the foreign spell like a swimmer would a leech found on an arm.

But it was working.

Even though Philip's counterattack was chipping away at Ferox's energy, he could sense that his son was losing more . . . and much quicker.

Then something changed.

Ferox's spell increased in strength and Philip withdrew the majority of his energy. Ferox let too many seconds pass before he realized what was happening: Philip had turned his onslaught onto himself, working *with* the spell, not *against* it, while also targeting his own nexus.

No!

Ferox was about to detach from the distended spell but realized with dread that if he did such a thing, there would be no vessel to direct the growing strength of its power.

It would eviscerate not only Philip but himself.

Ferox felt a peaceful acceptance emanate from his son as he diverted all his attention toward atrophying his own nexus. Self-sacrifice was his final choice.

Aghast, Ferox was rendered ineffective as Philip allowed his own nexus to cannibalize itself. The endless void seemed to envelop the beacon of his son's immense, bright power source before being promptly absorbed by the voracious maw of the near-untamable proxianimancic spell, which was only growing stronger.

The process was almost complete. Ferox needed to return to his own nexus before the spell ran its course to not only accept the energy that the spell had collected but ensure that he would not be devoured accidentally if he stayed much longer.

Though boiling with rage, Ferox didn't have to wait long for the spell to return. With it came an energy surge so brilliant that he momentarily forgot that his plan had failed. A light so bright blinded his mind's eye, and when the energy concentration subsided, his sight returned.

Ferox was left gasping for air seconds after he was thrown back into the physical world. He'd survived the forbidden animancy spell, but at what cost, he was afraid he already knew

Philip was nowhere to be found. Where he had been were once-gleaming ivory robes, now stained with a dusting of ash. His boy was gone, but his frustration at not acquiring access to Philip's nexus waged war with the undercurrent of loss.

Ferox flicked his eyes up at Malcolm, who stood in a fighting stance, his primed totem ring glowing ruby-red and his mouth agape in shock.

* * *

He killed him . . . Philip . . . his own son . . .

After being nearly blinded by Philip's sudden cremation, Malcolm thought his eyes were playing tricks on him. Ferox no longer had the visage of his late master, Draconex. No, not quite; there were still glimpses of the former Dark Watcher commander, but when the man stood up, Malcolm had to tilt his head an extra couple of inches to meet his gaze.

His skin was no longer sallow and pseudo-decayed; it had the coloring of life again, in some spots more than others. His normally sunken cheeks had filled out, accentuating a sharper jawline. Streaks of jet-black colored his titanium-white hair, which was still pulled back into a tight ponytail. And the scar . . . the scar that ran vertically down his left cheek—Malcolm touched his own —was healed.

Glancing down at the mound of ash that was once the Grand Mystra, now nothing more than soot atop the wrinkled robes he wore, Malcolm surmised that Ferox had sucked the life out of

Philip and, in the process, assumed what Philip Lancaster I must've looked like.

With a clenched jaw, Malcolm rolled the fingers in his closed fists, waiting for Ferox to attack; instead, however, he just stood there, breathing deeply. As he waited, Malcolm couldn't help but wonder . . .

If Ferox stole the life from an omnimancer, did that turn him into one?

Ferox's neck issued a blitz of cracks and pops as he rolled it from side to side.

"You."

Malcolm knew it. This was where his story would most likely end: dying at the hand of the realms' most feared dark sorcerer, most likely in the same way as Philip Lancaster II. After all, he was the one who made the noise that precipitated their whole duel.

"You didn't run," Ferox said, cocking his head in thought. The more words he spoke, the more Malcolm noticed that his voice had altered as well. It was lower, more gravelly.

Malcolm inhaled and hoped his voice was steady. "Like I said, I am not your enemy." He discreetly stretched out the stiffness in his back but didn't drop his stance. Malcolm looked back down at Philip's ashes for an instant before returning his gaze to Ferox. He didn't care if his next question would anger the sorcerer—he needed to know. "You killed your son. Why?"

Ferox's gaze didn't falter; his mouth went thin and turned into a sneer. "*That* . . . was not the *intention*," he said through clenched teeth. "His command over omnimancy was what I was after." He parted his son's ashes with a dirtied boot. "But he had other plans before I could swap our souls.

"It wasn't a full waste, I'll admit now," Ferox continued, seeming to drink in the new physical features he'd adopted. "I seem to be closer to my old self than ever before." He raised his hands and bunched them into fists while he plastered a wicked grin on his face.

So Ferox is still just an animancer.

"But the ShadowCrystal," Malcolm said aloud. "It grants you access to all of the Mancy planes."

Ferox snickered as he dusted some specs of ash from the lower portion of his chest plate. "Its power pales in comparison to wielding omnimancy in its basest, nascent form." He licked his lips lustfully. "Even the power afforded by holding all of the MystiCrystals isn't enough to supersede even the weakest of omnimancers."

He ran the fingertips of his right hand over the MystiCrystals on the table.

"But I still need them to fulfill the prophecy."

After a few more seconds of holding his fighting stance, Malcolm relaxed, though he still didn't dare get closer to Ferox. An idea began to form in his mind, one that would make him useful once more to Ferox.

"You know," he said matter-of-factly, spinning his totem ring around his finger, "there are two more omnimancers out there. At least."

Ferox's ears perked up with that news. "The Lancaster blood-line survives?"

"Yes." *But not for lack of trying,* Malcolm bitterly said to himself. "And there's a good chance I know where they might be."

Ferox momentarily forgot about the MystiCrystals and struck him with an intense look of surprise. "They were the ones who brought me to Camelore. Take me to them."

It was not a request.

Malcolm smiled wickedly. "I could, but they have a small contingency of sorcerers with them."

"Let it be them who will be surprised this time, not us." Ferox gestured to Excalibur hanging on the wall just behind his shoulder. "Take this weapon. The knight of my guard needs a weapon befitting his new station."

Pride swelled in Malcolm's chest; finally, someone recognized his value. He felt comfortable enough to walk just past Ferox and stand before the sword made legendary by the prophesied rightful King of England, Arthur Pendragon.

He looked at Ferox out of the corner of his eye until the man said, "Brandish it."

Malcolm exhaled and slid the sword free of its scabbard, which was set into the wall. The gleam from the room's warm lights traveled up the blade's immaculately straight edge as he righted it vertically in front of him. Inlaid on the bottom part of the blade was filigree so intricate that Malcolm almost got lost in its detail. It came to a peak about halfway up the blade, where it continued as a link up to its point. It felt about as heavy as he'd imagined Excalibur would feel. With utter wonder, he imagined how sluggish he'd be if he ever carried it into battle.

"Now, point it at me," Ferox said, cutting through his intense admiration of the sword. Malcolm did as he was told and held the blade's point a few inches away from his chest. "Good . . . Let it become an extension of yourself." His voice was an eerie whisper. Malcolm hadn't noticed he'd taken the ShadowCrystal out of his chest. He brought the crystal to the sword and touched its tip to Excalibur's point. Much like how a freshly lit match responds to a stream of gasoline, a purple flamelike trail traveled down toward its cross guard. The sword's weight changed, becoming not nearly as onerous as before.

"You should be able to handle anyone who dares to throw themselves—and their spells—at you." Ferox returned the ShadowCrystal to its place in his chest. Without another word he brushed past Malcolm to the other side of the room, leaving him to carefully detach the scabbard from its setting on the wall and attach it to his belt. He slid Excalibur back into the scabbard, feeling an intense swell of pride and determination as he turned to follow Ferox to the podium that would take them out of this secret chamber, but Malcolm cocked his head in surprise and paused.

Ferox had picked up the leather book that he'd blown to the ground with his terramancy spell. He gently let the stiff pages fall to the left as he looked through the book, entranced. "This is perfect . . ." he whispered to himself. Malcolm strode over to the dark lord's side, peering at the page that Ferox had turned to.

Malcolm noticed a distinct craftsmanship to the art in the folded, time-worn book. Its earthy colors of red, yellow, and orange interspersed with hints of greens and blues outlined a story that seemed to show an ancient people worshipping a flying serpent (much like one depicted as the bust) as it flew over their temples. Malcolm stayed silent, waiting for Ferox to expound on his previous statement.

Finally, Ferox said aloud, "I don't care much for your wyvern, Malcolm."

Malcolm stiffened. *He addressed me by name. Not* boy *or* you . . .

"I don't desire dragons this time around. New me, new beast." Ferox stopped flipping the pages and pointed at a menacing serpent with plumes adorning its head like a lion's mane. The picture showed it spitting out curved plumes of orange and yellow fire. "The closest portal to Oxhualta. Where?"

Again, this was no request, but a command.

CHAPTER TWELVE

Imagine what a fine young apprentice Philip would be . . . all the things I could teach him . . .

The maniacal taunting of Genevieve Lancaster's husband echoed inside her head as she trudged up a grassy knoll several kilometers south of the castle ruins she had found herself in. Genevieve couldn't remember how she had gotten here, but she needed to get to Camelore to see her son. She needed to make sure her Philip was safe. She channeled animancy through her nexus and began searching for the familiar presence of her griffin, Ciella, expecting to pinpoint where she'd left her: on Camelore. Furrowing her brow when she could not locate her, Genevieve tried again with mounting concern. She had sent Ciella to Camelore to ensure Philip's safety just before her husband had made his stand against her, intent on taking the final Mysti-Crystal—the one that her family had guarded for countless generations.

The TeleCrystal.

Where could she have gone? She'd given Ciella the order only a few hours ago . . .

Right as Genevieve crested the knoll, she toppled to the ground, having slipped on a patch of long, wet grass, slick from the recently departed rainstorm. She went limp and rolled down the small hill for a few meters until she came to a stop as the decline leveled out.

She winced, waiting for more pain to erupt on the side on which she'd fell, but luckily she felt nothing of the sort. She sat up and surveyed the untidy state of her gown. Its velvety beauty was ruined by the rain, and the bottom trim of the gown looked to have been haphazardly torn off, showing her bare ankles. Looking skyward, Genevieve knew she was on Azumar by the two suns that fought to break through the fading gray clouds still lurking in the sky. But she had never before seen those ruins—or the castle it had once been. And she'd traveled to Azumar quite often as she rose to the rank of mystra. Sighing from both mental and physical fatigue, she dropped her gaze to the landscape beyond, catching sight of a small stream that cut through the valley below. She traced it to her right, where it meandered toward a copse of trees. She needed to hydrate and rest against something, and those trees looked as good a resting place as any. Grimacing, she got up and was careful to not slip again as she made her way to the glade.

How could you, of all people, expect to defeat me?!

The light wind had dried her rain-soaked cheeks well enough to make fresh tears stand out. The first tears carved a path for others to follow, and with every step Genevieve took, the more she cried.

Cried for her husband.

Cried for her sister, Gwendolyn.

Cried for her baby boy, Philip.

Cried for not seeing the signs.

But how could she have? She was deeply in love with Philip Lancaster. Just a few months ago, they had welcomed their first child into their lives. He seemed completely normal then. Didn't he? Maybe her love—which had now grown to include their baby —had blinded her to what was actually eating at him underneath the surface.

Why did he keep that from her?

Genevieve's legs felt like lead, but she waited until she was at the streambank before she collapsed to her knees and cupped the cold, running water in her hands. She let the water flow into her mouth and down her throat, not realizing just how thirsty she'd been. Genevieve had never tasted anything better, and each time she went back for more water she seemed to grow thirstier still, until she had to stop drinking so she could catch her breath, wiping her mouth with her sleeve.

Something moved in her peripherals just then. To her right she found a wild stag on the opposite side of the stream, about ten meters from her, drinking just as she had been (but more silent; it was truly a wonder that she didn't scare it off).

She was mesmerized by its beauty. Its antlers were easily triple the size of a normal stag's, rising up from the sides of its head like wisps of white smoke. Genevieve easily counted thirty gleaming stines which comprised its magnificent set of antlers. Lean muscles bulged and rippled under a gorgeous, white undercoat of fur.

Genevieve was frozen in awe. She had never seen a coat so white or a stag so impressive. She momentarily forgot about her thirst and knelt there, next to the babbling stream, in rapture. A sense of both calmness and determination overcame Genevieve as she watched the stag lift its head, its cupped, pointed ears twitching, picking up sounds that she couldn't hear, and looked directly at her.

Realizing that she was smiling, Genevieve braced herself to get up and slowly make her way over to the majestic animal, when she saw its body tense.

"Oh, no, no . . . shhh. It's okay," she consoled, but she sensed it wasn't her that was stressing the stag.

It looked to the right, then slightly up before it bounded across the stream and into the glade of trees, shortly followed by the briefest of flashes that led almost immediately into rolling rumbles of thunder. Branches hanging from the first few rows of trees rustled and bent as the stag's antlers moved through them with astounding speed, deeper into the dense copse.

Odd, Genevieve thought. *The storm should have already passed above.* She decided to take the stag's lead and leave the streambank for safety. With the rumbling not fading away but increasing in volume, she quickened her pace until she hid behind the closest tree and, leaning to the side so she could see the sky, peered up. What she saw instantly made her mind go to her husband's dragon, but she quickly dismissed that since the one she now saw soaring overhead was a wyvern dragon, and a massive one at that. It was only about fifteen meters above the ground, still not far enough away to prevent her from feeling the heat it exuded.

Genevieve's eyes tracked the airborne beast as it continued its flight south, to where she hadn't a clue. She couldn't put her finger on it, but everything seemed slightly amiss, like she was lost inside a dream that was a mirror-image of her reality.

SNAPP.

Twigs breaking brought her back to the present and she looked deeper into the copse; the trees thinned into a glade, where she saw the white stag once again. It was in an area that opened up, just enough to let the fresh sunlight stream through the breaks in the tree canopy from above. Parts of the stag were illuminated, including its face. The eyes that she looked into were so pure, so genuine. Before she could make any advancements toward it, the stag pranced the opposite way.

Unable to explain it, Genevieve knew she had to follow that stag.

CHAPTER THIRTEEN

Malcolm had already fortified his body with an apt terramancy spell by the time Volcanor reached the portal that would take them to the Oxhualta realm. He slid a pair of goggles (ones he had lifted from one of the lower-level laboratories before leaving the Watercress Castle ruins) over his eyes and tightened the back strap with a final tug, just before his dragon broke the portal's barrier and entered into the most ferocious sandstorm Malcolm had ever experienced.

Almost immediately, the gale-force winds threatened to rip him off of Volcanor. He grabbed onto his dragon's craggy spine for dear life as he scrambled to make himself denser by channeling terramancy to turn his blood into liquid mercury. He let a slew of curses fly out into the swirling sand particles around him, berating himself for his lack of foresight. He felt more solid and sluggish, but at least the intense sandstorm no longer posed a threat. He spared a glance over his shoulder at Lord Ferox, who seemed to still be in control as he straddled Volcanor, his chest pulsing with the bruised-purple energy of the ShadowCrystal. Malcolm slowly turned back forward and set his sights—and Volcanor's flight path—for the nearest cyclone.

The near-inhospitable planet was an endless rolling mass of sand that had large, venous rivers of glass quadrisecting the planet. Ageless cyclones plowed over its shifting surface, either growing in size and speed or splitting into smaller cyclones as winds took them in all directions.

The part of the glass river that stretched along the equator boasted some of the belt's widest distances, measuring almost one hundred kilometers across in some areas. A trillion years ago, a deadly planetary earthquake split open Oxhualta's crust, causing molten lava from its iron core to ooze out, which quickly super-heated the sand that traveled above the fissures and almost instantly resealed them. Every so often the shifting of the sands would crack the glass and fire-lightning storms would erupt from Oxhualta's bowels. The severity and duration of those storms depended on how deep the cracks were . . .

. . . and if the demons below were warring.

The apex predators of Oxhualta were ophidites, gigantic feath-ered serpents that had evolved to live for short periods of time above the planet's surface so they could hunt. They would ride inside the sand cyclones and snatch up any smaller creatures that were unlucky enough to have been swept up by the powerful winds. Once they caught their prey, the ophidites would burrow under the sandy surface and return with their catches to their den communities.

There have been times, albeit very rarely, when cyclones carrying ophidites have strayed too close to Oxhualta's portals and thus send an ophidite or two into another realm. History would not remember those occurrences as pleasant, but one of the more notable instances was when one such ophidite was flung into the portal belonging to Earth. It would later be deified—worshipped and feared alike—by the now-extinct Aztec empire and dubbed Quetzalcōātl.

Nary a sorcerer in the history of the eleven realms had ever attempted to tame an ophidite as their riding beast. Their species was widely known to be ferocious, uncontrollable, and downright terrifying. What's more, their planet is the stuff of nightmares, and any creature which has evolved to survive in such a climate deserves to be feared and given a very wide berth.

Malcolm cursed again, this time for giving Ferox the idea to tame an ophidite; if he hadn't aimed his terramancy air spell at the codex back in the Grand Mystra's secret second Sacrarium, Malcolm was sure he'd have chosen a different—and far less deadly—creature.

The winds that were not yet claimed by a cyclone couldn't make up their minds on which direction to blow, shifting every which way and affording Volcanor enough visibility to track down the closest-moving cyclone instead of waiting for one to ram into it unawares.

Ferox hadn't provided a detailed plan on how he was going to subdue and eventually tame a wild ophidite, so Malcolm was left to hope that the dark lord wasn't suffering from any unnecessary delusions of grandeur and would take the lead when they found one.

Now only a score of meters separated them from an immense, roiling cyclone of sand. Malcolm could feel the winds strengthen and carry more in one direction. Volcanor was fighting to stay on course with every exerted flap of its wings, and once it reached the cyclone's eyewall, it took everything the wyvern dragon had to not get swept up in the torrent of blinding sand. Malcolm felt Volcanor's body vibrate, followed by the echo of a ferocious, jarring roar that swirled around his ears just as they broke through the eyewall and into the cyclone's epicenter.

Volcanor was now caught in a column of sinking air and, snarling in surprise, adjusted to the new conditions as Malcolm scanned his new surroundings for any ophidites. The wind speed had dropped dramatically; white light poured into the open eye of this cyclone, immensely aiding to improve visibility along with any and all airborne sand particles that were funneled into the eyewall and out.

He strained his eyes, but Malcolm didn't notice any flying serpents along the swirling eyewall, which made him wonder how easy it would be to find one . . . Would they need to hop from cyclone to cyclone until one appeared? Or—

A streak of green shot diagonally in front of Volcanor, barely missing the dragon's snout but spooking it nonetheless. Malcolm felt a shudder as Volcanor pulled back and, as it banked to the left, Malcolm tracked the green blur as it flew farther away in the opposite direction, revealing the first ophidite he had ever laid eyes upon.

It was smaller than he'd imagined, but its size, roughly ten meters in length, did not detract from its majestic form. An amalgamation of a viper and a dragon snake, its long, svelte body coiled and whipped like a ribbon kite sailing in the wind. Below its mane of countless long feathers ranging in color from blue to red to yellow were scales of different greenish hues that cascaded down its body, bending and conforming like a perfectly tailored set of armor as it used its two sets of red-plumed wings (which matched its feathered spine) to effortlessly twist, curl, and turn inside the cyclone's eye. Its tail, very reminiscent of an arrow's feathered fletching, helped stabilize its flight through the unrelenting gusts of wind. The massive, boxy head twitched from side to side, up and down. Its forked tongue flicked ever in and out of its lipless mouth, and its slits for nostrils sniffed in anticipation of a fresh kill.

A jolt of adrenaline raced up his spine when Malcolm saw the ophidite's marble eyes lock onto Volcanor, its slitted irises becoming thinner yet. This was the first time he regretted not having the ShadowCrystal: he would have liked to gain access to animancy and communicate with Volcanor, since the dragon would not be able to hear any of Malcolm's commands over the deafening winds. Having no plan whatsoever, Malcolm spared a glance at Ferox . . .

But the dark lord was no longer straddling Volcanor.

He was tight-rope walking on its tail, moving toward the tip.

What the hell is he doing?!

Trying not to panic, Malcolm twisted back around to see the gigantic, feathered serpent begin its deadly strike as it rose higher above him and the wyvern dragon. Before Malcolm could take another stifled breath, the ophidite contracted its body and sprang downward into a perfect nosedive. It pressed its two sets of wings close to its body, which went rigid, cutting through the air like a knife, and used the sinking, low-pressurized air inside the cyclone's epicenter to quickly accelerate to terminal velocity.

And it was headed straight for Volcanor's neck.

Malcolm unsheathed Excalibur, which gave off a sharp, vibrating *shing!* as it slid free from its scabbard. The etchings on its blade pulsed with the familiar purple energy of the ShadowCrystal. Malcolm gripped the mighty sword with his dominant hand; he didn't trust the legends enough (it was said that Excalibur granted impenetrability upon its wielder) to rely on, so with his right hand he slapped Volcanor's side as hard as possible so that it could evade the aerial attack in time.

But Volcanor didn't budge.

The veins in Malcolm's throat protruded as he yelled with as much power as his lungs could muster, all while continuing to maim his hand on his dragon's cracked, scaly hide. His palm streamed cool, slippery rivulets of liquid mercury. He didn't care; the only thing that concerned him was why Volcanor wasn't *moving out of the way!*

Until, out of sheer desperation, Malcolm looked back at Ferox just in time to see the dark lord launch into the air via a flick of Volcanor's tail—

—straight into the path of the downward-hurtling serpent.

CHAPTER FOURTEEN

Ever since Gavin had decided to leave the helioarch and cool off, Jen felt like a pressing weight had been lifted from her chest, but she still couldn't understand why he chose to confront her in the way that he did. She'd first realized Gavin Kingsland's impatient decisiveness back when they had freshly escaped from the Sesquimillennial Jubilee massacre, disagreeing on their immediate course of action. After they had resolved that issue, Jen had thought that they were beginning to understand each other better.

Apparently she was wrong.

Focusing on what needed her attention more, Jen sloughed off Gavin's behavior like a winter jacket in the middle of summer and wasted no time in telling everyone else about her interaction with Fuzanglong and all of her visions.

Well, all but one.

The vision in which she had turned evil: eyes as black as soot; fingers crackling with deadly currents of lightning; and body levitating in the middle of a powerful vortex, primed to strike down any who would dare to oppose her.

"So Fuzanglong came here to *help* us?" Mira asked after Jen had finished.

Jen bit her lip, mulling it over until she found the right words.

"More like . . . to tell us that he won't interfere any longer," she said.

"He didn't say anything about how to save Charles?" That was her mother. Jocelyn's eyes carried an unbearable amount of concern for her husband and fear for his unchanged state.

From across the roundtable, Jen shook her head, dipping her chin slightly in disappointment. "No, but he gave me another vision." Jen noticed Victor leaning forward. "It was dark, but I saw a stag with stark-white fur standing on a rocky bluff." Jen rolled on the balls of her feet, her arms locked and palms pressed on the smooth surface of the table.

"Those were the only visions you had, Jen. Right?"

Holding her breath, Jen slowly looked toward Victor.

Victor counted the three off on his hand. "Fuzanglong, Charles, and the white stag?"

Jen's heartbeat accelerated. "Yes," she lied. She pursed her lips in thought as she looked around the table at five pairs of unblinking eyes. She felt horrible omitting the last vision, but she wasn't comfortable sharing it—and what its implications may be —with anyone yet. She pushed off the table and cleared her throat, wanting to change the subject. She saw Victor's eyes narrow in skepticism, but before he could ask more questions, she said, "But I don't know how a white stag plays into any of this, or if it even relates to finding Genevieve or not." She swallowed and tried not to meet her uncle's gaze.

Rez cleared his throat and raised a finger. "If I may?"

Thankful that someone other than Victor spoke up, Jen quickly looked over at her telemancer friend. "Please," she said. A hint of relief blossomed deep in her chest. She loved it when Rez got on a roll.

"It just clicked fer me," he began, his eyes wide like he'd had an epiphany. "Fuzanglong told you, 'Change will present itself to you,' right?"

Jen nodded.

He scooted forward in his chair in excitement. "What if, in this instance, he used 'Change' as a name . . . of sorts." Rez, seeing the face Jen made, quickly said, "Hear me out: in Celtic mythology, seein' a white stag foretells the start of a new journey, a journey that will alter the way you view things . . . issue a *change*."

Next to Rez, Hephalon had his arms crossed and was doing his tell when he fell into a deep thought: massaging his biceps.

"Now, if he's half the clever dragon as the stories indicate, there's a high likelihood tha' Fuzanglong definitely and *intentionally* did just that. Could it be possible that the stag leads you to Genevieve?" Rez raised his hands in mock-surrender. "Or maybe he was making you aware of a different journey in the near future?"

Jen looked around the room, letting his rhetorical questions hang in the air as she gauged the looks on everyone's faces. A common thread of unsurety with a hint of "he might be on to something" seemed to ripple around the room, including inside herself. Rez had proven himself to be their foremost expert in history and legends when they were tracking down the Mysti-Crystals, so why doubt him now?

Victor unhooked his thumbs from his belt and walked toward Jen, saying, "Whether that's true or not, we need to start moving. All we know is that Cindergray escaped with Genevieve. He'd bring her to a place he feels safe." He stopped at her side.

She voiced the first place that came to mind. "Watercress?"

Victor shrugged, sighing. "Logic would indicate that, yes. As is tradition for every Grand Mystra, his personal chambers are at Watercress." He winced slightly, etching deep crows feet at the edges of his eyes. "*But* . . . in its current condition, he might go elsewhere."

"Maybe some place familiar to Genevieve?" Mira offered.

"Could very well be," Victor said, running a hand down his beard.

"Then I'd say we need to pay Watercress—or whatever is left of it—a visit," Jen said, "and if they aren't there, then maybe we'll find another clue to get us back on track."

Heads bobbed in agreement all around the table.

"You should lead this expedition, milady." That was the first time Hephalon had spoken in a long while. Jen smiled warmly, bowing her head in thanks as she received his nomination.

"But a discussion—and a quick one at that—needs to take place first. One that addresses who will embark with Jen and who will look after Charles here," Victor said before leaning toward Jen's ear. He lowered his voice so only she could hear: "Gavin should be included in this. I'll check in on him." He smiled reassuringly and squeezed her arm for added measure.

All Jen could do was smile tightly and nod her understanding. She wasn't in the mood for Gavin to come back unless he were to apologize, but her complicated feelings toward him needed to take a backseat in a time like this. She watched Victor's cloak bellow out behind him as he opened the helioarch's double doors, headed toward what, Jen assumed, would be Gavin's hut.

Jen clapped her hands and redirected her gaze and attention to the remaining sorcerers in the room, ending on her best friend. "Mira, you're good at tracking, right?"

* * *

Gavin was zipping up a small duffel bag when three knocks rapped on the door of his hut. He paused for half a moment, looking out of the corner of his eye before zipping the bag the rest of the way. He threw it over his shoulder as he made his way over to the door.

He needed to find Excalibur, especially after what he'd come across in Merlin's journal. He had a pretty good guess as to who was waiting for him outside, so Gavin wasn't surprised when he opened the door to see Victor Huxley.

"Gavin," Victor said.

"Now's not a good time, Vic," Gavin replied, brushing past him.

"We need to talk."

Gavin didn't slow down; he didn't even turn around to see if Victor was following him. "That's all we seem to do now: talk.

Well, doing more of it won't get us any closer to freeing Charles. We need to *act*."

There came a soft splitting sound rumbling behind him and his right foot caught on something. He tried to pull it up off the ground but couldn't. Looking down, he discovered his foot had been encased up to his ankle in hardened dirt. Gavin drew in a sharp breath, but before he could employ astromancy to release himself from this earthen shackle, Victor stepped in front of him.

Seething from frustration and mild embarrassment, Gavin said, "Since when do we cast spells on each other?"

Victor had his hands on his hips. His breathing was measured as he stared directly into Gavin's eyes. The two men were nearly identical in height, with the slight advantage going to Gavin. Victor clenched and unclenched his jaw a few times before he said in a low but very stern tone, "When one of our own decides to go AWOL."

Gavin matched his breathing to Victor's and scanned the clear midafternoon skies as the terramancy mystra continued.

"What's your game plan here, Gavin? Gonna hijack one of the griffins and track down Genevieve yourself?"

Gavin rolled the fingers of the hand that was holding his duffle bag's strap. "At least I'm acting, Vic. You know, showing some initiative instead of staying holed up"—he pointed in the direction of the helioarch—"and tossing out ideas." Gavin couldn't pretend to be held down by Victor's spell anymore. He spread his fingers and felt the dirt crumble around his foot, but before he could take another step Victor placed a wide hand on his chest.

"No, you are *re*acting, Gavin. Reacting to getting your ego bruised by Jen when she called you out. We all know what's at stake here, and I can guarantee you Jen is taking it harder than everyone else," he said. "Charles is her father, and she knows that she can't do this alone. *That* is why she is still in the helioarch.

"She knows there needs to be a clear objective so, as much as she wants to be on the back of Skarmor right now, flying through each realm until she finds Genevieve, she's working out the best plan of action that will exponentially increase our likelihood of succeeding—and *surviving*. *That* is why she is still in there . . . she wants to do it *right*. And you should be in there, helping."

Gavin let his hand slip from his bag's strap and, quietly scoffing at his own ineptitude, he looked into the clear midafternoon sky as he tried to string his feelings into words. When it came down to it, Gavin felt . . . embarrassed. Embarrassed that he had chosen to act bullish and accusatory toward Jen back in the helioarch; he had clearly lost sight of what it meant to be a part of a team, especially reflecting on his actions that had led up to this moment, Victor having to physically hold him back from storming off in a rage and taking matters into his own hands . . . which, admittedly, was mostly spurred on by his contempt for how Jen had made him feel. Humbled, Gavin knew she did nothing wrong; it was he who was impetuous, making him more of a hindrance than a help to the rest of the group.

"I flew off the handle again, didn't I?" Gavin finally said after gaining enough composure to look Victor squarely in the eye.

Victor gave him a kind smile. "In times like these"—he raised an index finger to punctuate the point he was about to make —"don't mistake prudent reflection for wasteful idleness." He winked and opened his hand, gesturing at the bag.

Gavin nodded and handed it over to him. Shouldering it himself, Victor ushered him toward the helioarch.

After a few paces, Gavin asked, "What do you know about Excalibur?"

To his right, Victor flashed him an inquisitive look. His mouth opened, then quickly shut as he suddenly stopped walking and looked skyward. "Do you hear that?"

Gavin frowned and turned around to look at Victor, who was now a few paces behind. "Hear what?"

As if in answer, a low hissing sound cut through the silence.

Gavin slowly turned in a circle, trying to pinpoint the true direction of the sound, but it seemed to be coming from everywhere at once—even below his feet. When he was about two-thirds of the way around, something slithered out of the bright circle of the sun. Blinking away the searing afterimage of looking at the sun straight on, Gavin reached for Victor and tapped him on the shoulder.

"Vic, look at the sun."

Victor obeyed. He squinted but clearly saw what Gavin meant. "Fuzanglong's back?"

Gavin had thought the same thing at first, but when he saw two sets of wings splay themselves out about one-third of the way down the dragon's body, he knew it wasn't Fuzanglong . . . or a dragon.

"That's not Fuzanglong," Gavin said, grabbing Victor's arm. "Come on—we gotta get inside the helioarch."

Victor was still gazing intensely at the figure that was getting closer, and fast. They stumbled into a run. Gavin let go of the older man's arm, and he didn't have to wait long for him to fall into step as they raced toward the helioarch.

"An ophidite. Here?" Victor asked, shocked.

"I know." Gavin didn't need to look back to confirm. He recalled what he'd been taught about ophidites: they were silent and fast. It was only a matter of time before it landed on Camelore.

And he was worried about who was riding on its back.

* * *

The sun had reached a point in the sky where its filtered rays from the stenciled helioarch cast a depiction of the Light Bringer—who now everyone knew to be Gavin—holding an open book above his head as beams of light shot forth from the open pages, symbolizing the path toward the rebalancing of good and evil throughout the realms.

Exhausted, Jen embraced her mother. Jocelyn wrapped her arms around her and whispered in her ear, "A pebble may make a splash at first, but it will turn into ripples that quickly fade away."

Jen nodded, realizing that she was talking about Gavin. Enough time had passed since she had initially reacted to his outburst; now, after calming down, she knew that amends needed to be made. Grimacing, Jen pulled away and found her mother's eyes waiting. Alongside sympathy, Jen could sense a similar expectation from Jocelyn.

"Be careful, honey," Jocelyn said. "I have faith you'll find Genevieve."

Jen thanked her mother and said, "I won't give up. Not until he's been freed." She refrained from looking behind her at Charles.

Mira was behind Jocelyn, absent-mindedly playing with her braid and waiting to speak. "I'll get Skarmor and Pernissa ready," she said, now with a determined look.

"Thanks. I'll check on Vic and Gavin." Jen gave her a warm smile.

Her best friend's eyes lit up before she turned around and, on her way toward the doors, passed Hephalon, who was standing over Rez with one hand on his shoulder.

Jen went the opposite way around to pick up the TeleCrystal and slide it into her side pocket again before she zipped it closed. She knew Victor wouldn't find any issue in their plan; what she was worried about was how Gavin would fit into it all. He was an integral part of the team, and their chances of succeeding would greatly diminish should his efforts not be in alignment with hers and the rest of the group's. Jen let her fingertips slide across the smooth surface of the ancient table as she wondered how their next interaction would go. Sparing a fleeting glance at her father at the table's center, Jen sent a message to him through a burst of telemancy. Even if it didn't end up getting through the omni-mancy spell, she still needed to try.

Hang on, Father. We'll get you free. Just . . . don't give up.

Grimacing, she pulled her gaze from her father and focused on the doors.

Mira had meticulously slid every chair she passed back toward the table, which allowed Jen to beat her to the doors. She reached for the handle of the left door when it turned on its own. At first she wondered if maybe she'd subconsciously channeled telemancy to open the door, but then Gavin burst through and she quickly dismissed the thought. He abruptly stopped his momentum so he wouldn't crash into Jen, but that only allowed Victor to run into his back, exclaiming with an "Oof!"

Gavin quickly apologized to Victor and slid to the side to let him through.

"We have an issue," Gavin said to Jen. "A big one."

Jen suddenly felt bile rising in her stomach. "Gavin, we've already come to an agreement on what—"

"No, it's not about that." He looked earnestly at her as he tried catching his breath. "There's an ophidite heading straight for Camelore."

"A what?" Jen asked in pure confusion.

"A big snake with wings."

Gavin popped his totem orb from the pendant on his necklace and rushed over to Mira. His tone was hushed, clearly only wanting his girlfriend to hear what he had to say.

Jen had never heard of an ophidite before, but Gavin's quick description didn't sound great. The bile rose to her throat.

Victor was by her side in seconds and hovered a hand behind her back, whispering in her ear, "Camelore isn't safe any longer."

Mira unraveled her bullwhip as she finished listening to Gavin, the metal strips of the handle already glowing with her animacy powers. "I'm headed for the stables," she announced decidedly after receiving a quick kiss from Gavin. She shot a look behind her at the young telemancer. "Rez, I need your help with Pernissa."

"Oi, I'm there," Rez said, pushing his seat back and righting his vest before loping around the table to follow Mira out of the helioarch.

Hephalon was the next person in motion, grabbing the round shield he'd hung on his chair's back. As he slid his brass knuckles on he said gruffly, "Let's see what this's all about. My wager's on that snot-nosed ruffian of a man-child." He detached an axe from the magnetic plate on his back before lumbering out of the helioarch.

Jen scrunched up her nose, trying to figure out who he was talking about. "Malcolm?" Before she could question it further, she caught sight of Charles's body rising from the table, courtesy of Gavin's astromancy. Jen ran to his side and grabbed his extended arm. She could already feel an aching tension returning to her shoulder muscles.

"Just what do you think you're doing?"

His totem's glow slightly lessened as he side-eyed her. "We need to protect Charles, and ironically the Cube is the best place to keep him safe on Camelore, even if it is busted."

Before Jen could react, her mother's hand appeared on Gavin's arm as well. She'd moved like a silent spirit to his other side. "Then let me take him, Gavin," she said. This was the first time since Jen had been reacquainted with her mother that she'd heard her use a forceful tone.

And Jen kind of liked it.

With both of the ladies' hands gripping his arm, combined with Jocelyn's tone, Gavin relented. Reluctantly he floated Charles over to Jocelyn, who removed her grip and cradled his limp form in her arms. Jocelyn was lean and did not show a lot of muscle, so Jen's eyebrows rose when her mother didn't buckle under Charles's six-foot frame. Being a vampire must afford one not only extreme speed but extraordinary strength, Jen surmised.

Blinking away her surprise, she felt Gavin tug at her hand, which was still firmly wrapped around his forearm. "Jen, let go."

After a few seconds of watching him squirm, she released her grip and waited for Gavin to look her in the eyes. That moment never came. What drew both of their attention instead was a deafening *CRASH!* at the western side of the ceremonial chambers. Splintered wood and torn metal burst into the helioarch. Once the dust settled, Jen saw Hephalon roll to his feet and steady himself against the table (which was now dented and heavily scratched).

"Some assistance would be greatly appreciated!" Hephalon said as he picked up the mace and round shield he'd dropped. "Oh, and you owe me a cask of ale. Malcolm is here with that bloody wyvern." He spun the mace's handle in his hand and charged back out through the hole, yelling at the top of his lungs.

Stunned silence fell over the chamber as loose chips and pieces of wall crumbled to the ground. Gavin looked back at Jen, slack-jawed. In unspoken agreement, both he and Jen forgot their personal issues and headed together for the door while Victor said, "Jocelyn and I will get Charles to the Cube. Go help Heph and your friends."

Gavin flung open both doors. "Jen and I will cover you," he said over his shoulder as he reactivated his totem.

Jen primed her nexus as she followed Gavin to the right, catching sight of Volcanor belching rolls of fire at Hephalon. The metallurgist knelt behind his shield to protect himself from being immolated as the flames licked over its edges. With urgency, Gavin immediately started lancing spell after spell at the hellish dragon, successfully distracting it and causing it to briefly cut off its built-in flamethrower while it homed in on its new prey.

"Yeah, that's right—you want some more?!" Gavin yelled as he ran headlong at the dragon that was still carrying Malcolm.

Jen stayed right on Gavin's heels, flicking terramancy spells of her own (those were her strongest) as Hephalon stood back up and began to fling throwing stars at Volcanor's eyes with the intention of blinding it. The brute of a dragon reared up, roaring in pain as some of the sharp projectiles nicked its exposed belly and neck while others found flesh into which to stick, but they all missed its eyes. It tucked its wings in front of its face and body before any further damage could be done.

Jen was about to destabilize Volcanor's footing with an opportune ground-shifting spell, but a different and much more horrifying scream rang out above her head. Looking skyward, Jen froze in abject terror at what she could only imagine was the aforementioned ophidite (and she had to admit, Gavin's description was apt). The massive, snakelike monster streamed through the sky, vibrant feathers circling its head like a mane and down its spine; it swirled powerful torrents of wind from its two sets of arching, bright-red avian wings that stemmed from high on its scaly back, close to where shoulder blades would have been, and deftly evaded spells from Mira and Rez, who were riding Skarmor and Pernissa respectively.

Jen's eyes were pulled back to ground level at the sound of Gavin cursing. Volcanor, still shielding itself behind its cracked, venous wings, had rushed Hephalon, connecting with his round shield and sending him flying backward. Thankfully the area they were fighting in was relatively open, so Hephalon landed with a grunt on manicured grass. The fall gave Malcolm enough time to jump off Volcanor's back and unleash a barrage of spells with each hand, one directed at Hephalon, the other at Gavin and Jen.

Jen's adrenaline sent an alert into her nexus, which responded by giving her the hyper-quick reflexes of the long-legged fly. Almost as if Jen had seen the future, she rolled out of the spell's path right as Malcolm aimed and fired. Her feet found ground again and she quickly threw a look over her shoulder to make sure Victor and Jocelyn were well on their way toward the Pentarena. They indeed were, with the help of Victor's equivol, Kuirhan. (Mira must've also let him out of the stables when she and Rez took off with the griffins.) Victor was running alongside the galloping Kuirhan, having just helped Jocelyn get Charles on his back. Once her mother was settled, Victor climbed on the equivol and urged it to run faster.

The brief relief Jen felt melted into regret when she turned back to see Malcolm, having followed her gaze, already focused on Victor and her parents. A distance of about forty meters now separated them, but Jen knew that meant nothing. Malcolm could cover that distance in mere seconds if he wanted to, and it looked like he was about to do just that.

Another fierce cry from the ophidite split the skies, leaving a loud ringing in Jen's ears as she, along with Gavin, altered their course to intercept Malcolm. Hephalon, having the same idea as he barely missed being squashed by a shuddering stomp from Volcanor, jumped into the air with his axe already arcing downward and at an angle that would cleave Malcolm's head clean from his shoulders.

That was when Malcolm brandished a long sword so radiant that it took Jen's breath away.

He brought it up just in time to block Hephalon's swing, causing purple sparks to fly from where the two blades met. Jen swore she felt an energy wave pass through her half a second later as an electrifying *shing!* rang out in every direction. Stunned, Hephalon instinctively parried a powerful strike from Malcolm, which sent him on his heels and falling to his back. Malcolm continued toward Victor and Jocelyn, dismissing Hephalon like he wasn't worth any more of his time. He seemed completely content in letting Volcanor occupy the large man once more as he broke into a steady sprint; clumps of dirt and grass flew in his wake as he exercised his terramancy to augment his own speed.

Jen's heart sank in fear as she reached into her nexus and channeled the speed of a cheetah. Tears slid into the crevices of her ears, she was running so fast, hoping that she could get to Malcolm before he fell upon her uncle and parents. The Arbor Sacré, the focal point of the Pentarena, quickly grew in size. Her heart felt like it wanted to run faster than her body, forcing her legs to work in overdrive, but she'd misjudged how fast Malcolm proved to be.

Jen wasn't going to make it in time . . .

She stifled a scream as her leg muscles started to burn in protest from Jen pushing her body to its limits. Victor spun around and, his totem rings glistening in the sun, shot missile-like spells from his fingertips straight at Malcolm, who was about ten meters behind and closing fast. The spells the Dark Watcher didn't block with his sword ricocheted off his armor, harmlessly sizzling away into the air. Either way, none of the spells were slowing him down any.

Five meters . . .

Another round of spells which barely affected Malcolm and his blood-thirsty charge. It was like the glowing sword in his hands afforded him extra protection, extra strength.

Two meters . . .

Jen was excruciatingly close to grabbing ahold of Malcolm's

cape when a gust of air whipped across her face and arms, sending her nerves astray. A steel-blue blur swept across her field of vision, striking Malcolm in his left side and carrying him off into the sky. Jen's heart blossomed with relief when she realized what the blur was.

Silvress, Charles's dragon.

Jen couldn't tell if Victor had halted Kuirhan or if the equivol had stopped of his own accord, but it allowed her to reach them in only three more quick but large strides. Steadying herself against the majestic creature's large frame, she didn't know what to say, and she was out of breath anyway, so she, along with Victor and Jocelyn, watched as Silvress brought Malcolm higher off the ground, banked to the left, and released him. Two seconds later there came a slapping *splash!* confirming that Silvress had left him to fend for himself in Camelore's one and only lake. Seemingly satisfied, she banked again and made her way back toward them.

But that didn't give them a whole lot of time, Jen knew. Volcanor was already rumbling through the air to pick up Malcolm.

Jen turned to Victor and Jocelyn, sitting on Kuirhan, and squeezed both of their legs. "I'm so glad you're okay," she said as Silvress landed next to them. "And thank you, Sil." Jen scratched the dragon's rough chin, and she closed her slender eyes in appreciation.

"We're just about there." Victor gestured to the Pentarena's entranceway, tightening his grip on his equivol's reins.

Her uncle was about to snap the reins when Silvress snorted and took off into the air, swirling Jen's hair around her face.

"Vic, wait!"

Jen reached out, but it was too late: her father's dragon clashed with the rampaging ophidite. That was when Jen noticed for the first time a vaguely familiar figure on its back. Skarmor and Pernissa, finding themselves outmatched in strategy and stamina, had fallen behind, struggling to catch up to the serpent; thankfully neither of them—nor Mira or Rez—looked to be heavily injured. The clanking of Hephalon's weapons grew louder as he lumbered toward her, but Jen didn't look at him. Instead, she kept her eyes on the flying serpent, watching helplessly as it slipped easily around Silvress and, with its fletching tail, struck Silvress across her exposed back. Jen watched as the dragon tried to reorient herself in freefall, but the hit was so quick and unexpected that Silvress was unable to fully recover in time. A small crater line formed as Silvress struck the grassy ground, sliding to a stop a few dozen meters away from Jen. Already the dragon was back up, shaking off crumbling bits of earth, as Hephalon and Gavin rushed in, making sure she wasn't internally hurt.

With no more obstacles in its way, the ophidite soared into the Arbor Sacré's canopy, eventually corkscrewing down its thick trunk like a gigantic auger. It stopped, keeping itself coiled around the tree as it stared at Jen and the others with its slitted, hungry eyes, its forked tongue flicking out to taste the air for any intruders. That shadowy figure Jen had glimpsed on its back detached from the ophidite's spinal feathers, landing with ease at the base of the Arbor Sacré.

"Victor, get Charles away from here," Jocelyn said, dismounting Kuirhan. She rushed over to her daughter and embraced her lovingly. "Stay with your uncle, Jennifer," she whispered, tucking a stray strand of wavy hair behind Jen's ear.

She morphed into an albino bat before Jen could process what her mother was doing; for the second time in as many minutes all she could do was watch in stunned paralysis. Jocelyn, in bat form, fluttered after Volcanor. The unknown figure had since touched something to the Arbor Sacré's exposed roots, causing the tree's effervescent rainbow shine to bleed a sickly purple, the leaves on its branches withering as if in a timelapse and turning into thorns.

"Jenny, *no!*" Victor steered Kuirhan to block Jen from running after her mother, deftly twisting off the large equivol to grab both of her arms, not in a constricting way, but enough to make it difficult for Jen to break free.

She was too stunned to even yell after her mother, her bat form getting smaller and smaller with every erratic flap. Volcanor's demonic frame was now rising above the lake, carrying a drenched Malcolm. Jen continued to fight against Victor's tightening grip as tears streamed down her face. She sucked in ragged breaths as she finally relented, which gave her uncle enough confidence to let her go.

"Okay, change of plans," Victor said quickly, whistling for Skarmor. He waited for his griffin to acknowledge with a crisp *caw!* before he continued, "We have to get out of here."

"Leave Camelore?" Jen protested.

"We'll be able to do more for Camelore if we regroup elsewhere." Victor nodded at what had become of the Arbor Sacré.

"We're not leaving my mother!" Jen shouted. A light breeze kicked up with the arrival of Skarmor and Pernissa.

"Don't let your mother's diversion be in vain."

How was Victor staying this calm?

"Jenny, do you trust me?" His eyes did not waver.

Jen closed her mouth, thinking back to every choice she'd made up to this point and how Victor supported her through it all, even if it meant splitting up to survive.

Sometimes the right choice is the hardest one of all.

Jen pulled her shoulders back, standing at attention just as an idea formed in her head. "Only if you trust me on where we should go," she said. Even though she internally still wrestled with the decision of leaving Jocelyn behind, she wholeheartedly trusted both her mother and Victor.

He thinned his lips, seeming to understand how difficult a decision this was. "I'll follow you to the frays of any realm, my dear." He swung himself back on Kuirhan, grabbing the reins and making sure Charles was balanced properly in front of him.

Jen hopped on Skarmor next to Mira and announced, "Everyone . . ." She waited for Silvress to bring Hephalon and Gavin closer to their group before she continued. "Huddle up!" As Pernissa, Kuirhan, and Silvress brought their riders around Jen, she extended her hands to her sides. With the aid of terramancy, she cooled the air around her entire group to its dew point. A dense fog quickly engulfed them, and that's when Jen got to work on the first step of her plan.

Camelore's lake was deeper than he'd thought. And much colder.

Drenched and shivering from a numbing windchill, Malcolm sheathed Excalibur and found his usual handhold along Volcanor's craggy spine. Frustration twisted his gut, and he suppressed a yell that he knew would induce a throbbing headache if he let it out.

He had come *so close* to taking his old master down and beating him to within an inch of his life. Malcolm wanted Victor barely conscious enough to watch (with bruised, swollen eyes, preferably) when he helped Ferox restore order to the unruly eleven realms. But the first step was to give Ferox the body of an omnimancer. So Charles—unconscious and limp for whatever reason—was the first target.

That was why he commanded Volcanor to start strafing the area where Victor and Charles were at that very moment once they flew closer.

Ferox had made it to the Arbor Sacré and, with the eerie powers of the ShadowCrystal, transformed the mystical tree into a nightmarish version of what it once had been. The freshly grown thorns on its knotted branches seemed so sharp that Malcolm winced with phantom pain from just looking at them. The rivulets of rainbows that had once coursed along the surface of its trunk and branches were now pumping sickly bluish-purple energy as if the tree were an amputated appendage of a corpse that had died from asphyxiation. Ferox's ophidite claimed dominion over the Pentarena, coiled tightly around the Arbor Sacré; Malcolm could hear its unnerving hissing as it licked the air and waited. He still couldn't believe how Ferox had been able to tame that ophidite while in the middle of a cyclone . . .

Malcolm shook his head, focusing on what needed to be done. The tempo of Volcanor's beating wings increased and more smoke spiraled from its large nostrils as it pushed its enormous mass through the air. Malcolm sneered at the sight of the old terramancer, now holding back Jen as the rest of her friends landed their griffins around her. She looked to be in pain.

You haven't felt true pain yet, Malcolm thought with a snicker.

The moment seemed too perfect. Every last person he considered to be the bane of his entire existence was in one spot, huddled together, a score of meters from the Pentarena's entrance. They looked to be in the midst of plotting.

It was high time Malcolm crashed their party once and for all.

With warped delight, he spurred Volcanor on, eager to feel his knuckles splitting from raining severe blows on Victor's crumbling face.

"Volcanor, light it up," Malcolm commanded, and his wyvern peeled off altitude to begin the strafing run. He didn't care if he was still just under one hundred meters away. He wanted their attention. He wanted to instill fear in them.

Malcolm waited to feel the intense heat from Volcanor's flames, but it never came. Instead, the dragon grunted and roared and began to shake its head viciously.

"Volcanor!" Malcolm tried to settle his dragon down, but it ignored him.

Volcanor had lost almost all its speed, its beating wings acting like a parachute against its hurtling momentum. Malcolm was at a loss. What was *happening*? Volcanor seemed to be trying to shake something off its face. When Malcolm leaned to the side to get a better angle, a small, furry, white wing flicked out in front of Volcanor's snout and retracted just as quickly.

He knew of only one albino vampire bat . . . and only one person who could transform into it: Madame Diaema.

Malcolm exploded with exasperation. Every second that was lost dealing with Diaema, the closer his enemies would get to escaping, scattering his plans into nothingness like fine sand sifting through his fingers. He felt the veins in his neck protrude as he surrendered to the yell that had been mounting deep inside.

In a huff, Malcolm maneuvered his way to Volcanor's other side in hopes of getting a better glimpse of what Diaema was actually doing to his dragon. He tensed when he saw her firmly attached to Volcanor's right eyelid, clawing away at its red cornea with her clawed wings and feet.

"That's it," Malcolm bit out.

He pumped his right fist, activating his totem ring. His nexus flooded its central ruby with a fiery red and orange glow as he trained his clenched fist at the albino bat. Diaema must've noticed; she unlatched and flew under Volcanor's belly and out of sight.

But Malcolm was mistaken to think Volcanor would just let that surprise attack go. Malcolm's strafing command now a distant memory, the dragon dove, twisting into the most nausea-inducing corkscrew of Malcolm's flying career. Volcanor was out for Diaema's blood—and what was so aggravating was that Malcolm had seen bigger creatures not receive half of the rampaging energy Volcanor was exhibiting as it tried to capture Diaema at that moment.

Malcolm hung onto Volcanor's back, wishing for the dizzying flight path to end, when he spotted a cloud of fog rising up near where Jen and Victor were. Something didn't feel right, and he tried to win control over Volcanor. Malcolm didn't know if it was his efforts or Volcanor's minuscule attention span, but the wyvern dragon plateaued out and began flying in the correct direction once more.

The fog had grown considerably in size, which worried Malcolm, and with a strained yell he commanded Volcanor to dive at the dense cloud of vapor. Using his mastery over terra-mancy, he shoved his hands out in front of him, sending a blast of swirling air directly into the center of the fog. A hole spiraled out from its center, revealing nothing but grass and depressions where feet had once stood.

Volcanor followed through with the dive, plateauing out and lifting back into the sky. Malcolm couldn't understand it. *How* could they have escaped? And where to?

Those damning questions plagued his mind as he pointed Volcanor toward the Arbor Sacré and his new master.

CHAPTER FIFTEEN

Several puffy cumulus clouds dotted the ceiling of the troposphere like ovoid saucers, acting as cover for Jen and her group as they flew away from Camelore. The sun was just beginning its descent in the west, changing the clouds' colors from white and light gray to salmon with wisps of lavender.

Jocelyn's diversion was the only reason they'd been able to escape. Jen had to trust Victor when he had said that her mother was a survivor, but that didn't mean she couldn't worry still. As Skarmor soared through the skies, miles above the earth's crust, Jen vowed to do everything in her power to not lose either of her parents. One trapped on Camelore, the other in the most dangerous spell Jen had ever seen. But she had to push forward. Decisions were made. *Hard* decisions.

And Jen had a sinking feeling that they would only get harder.

She brushed a tear from her cheek and decided to focus on the task at hand, grateful that she hadn't let her mother's sacrifice go in vain and was able to flee before she'd gotten her entire group captured. Considering how little time was given to her, the idea she'd had for the escape was quite brilliant: drop the dew point around her party to create a dense but hollow dome of fog; turn everyone invisible with the TeleCrystal; escape undetected without fear of being seen and followed.

A steady breeze carried Skarmor westward. Jen felt uneasy at how calm it was. Her heart was heavy with regret that she had left her mother to fend for herself against Volcanor and Malcolm, but everything had happened too fast.

Mother, I will return for you, Jen vowed. *And we'll take back Camelore together.*

Jen was brought out of her thoughts by Mira reaching back and squeezing her thigh supportively. Jen smiled faintly and leaned forward, resting her head on her friend's upper back. She'd most likely detected Jen's conflicted, melancholy demeanor through the mind meld she and Rez had created with their telemancy shortly after escaping Camelore. The connection would help if anything unforeseen should occur, but it also gave Jen a sense of relief, knowing that they were all there with her. That thought alone elevated her mood.

She smiled to herself and looked off to the side, seeing how effortlessly Kuirhan was keeping pace with Skarmor while Pernissa and Silvress took up the rear. The gorgeous equivol galloped smoothly through the air, propelled by its special connection with the earth's electromagnetic field. Jen still found it fascinating that equivols didn't need wings to fly. Its alicorn had gleaming spiral ridges, reminding her of some pearlescent seashells she'd found wading along the shorelines of beaches to which her parents' had taken her during family vacations. The horn narrowed to a sharp point as it drilled through the air with every one of Kuirhan's head thrusts, his galloping motion flowing seamlessly throughout his entire body, over sinewy muscle and glistening hide.

Draped across the equivol's neck was her father, Victor's hand placed firmly on his back so that he wouldn't slide off. Her uncle seemed to be lost in deep thought, staring straight ahead and not minding how the steady breeze played with his silvery locks. Jen clenched her jaw at the sight of her father limp and unresponsive. She knew Charles was living on borrowed time, and the longer she waited to search for the white stag from her vision the more she feared that he would fully succumb to Cindergray's spell.

Jen clamped her eyes shut, cutting off what seemed like a never-ending well of tears when it came to thinking about her father (and now her mother, whom she prayed was still alive back on Camelore), and let the brisk breeze cool her flushed cheeks, regulating both her body temperature and emotional state. She needed to be alert and prepared for what was to come.

After counting to twenty, Jen opened her eyes and checked her bearings. About four miles below and several hundred meters away was the massive basin that had once been the Eye of the Sahara, otherwise known as the Richat Structure and former location of the lost kingdom of Atlantis. As Jen and the rest flew closer, she saw a hive of activity in and around the basin's perimeter, no doubt investigators, vehicles, and equipment from the governments of Mauritania and several other countries, most likely to determine what had erased such an iconic landmark from the face of the earth. Jen would be interested in what kind of conclusion they would arrive at once this was all over.

But now, Jen needed Skarmor to rise.

With a quick command slipping from her lips, her trusty griffin *cawed!* in acknowledgment and alerted Pernissa, Kuirhan, and Silvress to follow. Skarmor smoothly angled his body away from the horizon just as his mighty wings flapped stronger and faster, making Jen's stomach drop as he began his ascent. He gained altitude like he was going up a spiral staircase, swirling closer and closer to where the troposphere ended and the stratosphere began. Whenever he turned upwind, he used the breeze to jump an extra few meters higher with every flap of his wings. Mira unexpectedly let out an exhilarated *whoop!* as his pace increased, causing Jen to involuntarily giggle in momentary glee as she held on to Skarmor's hide like he was a seat of a roller coaster. She looked below and wasn't expecting to have her breath taken away, but it couldn't be avoided when she saw the beautiful dance that the other griffin, equivol, and dragon had created by following Skarmor's path, one after the other, almost like they were connected with an invisible string. Jen briefly lost sight of them as Skarmor took her and Mira into a relatively stable cumulus cloud; she could feel the chill of water vapor collecting on her bare skin. There were a few unexpected gusts of shifty winds, but Skarmor adapted to the ephemeral conditions with ease, and after a few short seconds he blasted through the top of the cloud, spewing cloudy wisps in all directions. Jen used terramancy to comfortably dry off both Mira and herself as she drank in the amazing sight of the crystal clear skies of the mesosphere and below it a blanket of clouds that denoted the ceiling of the stratosphere.

Unlike both Jen and Mira, Skarmor was seemingly unaffected by the serene beauty of the new strata of atmosphere; if anything, he pushed his speed to new heights now that he had left behind the volatile innards of the cumulus cloud. Jen had to temper Skarmor's eagerness, patting his sides and asking him to slow down. He complied with a clack of his beak, and she quickly felt their speed drop to a safer level as Kuirhan slowly caught up with him. Jen turned and looked up at what started as a pinprick but quickly grew into a large disc, one that had the exact perimeter of a certain Saharan basin sitting over a dozen miles below.

Jen directed Skarmor toward its edge, forgetting just how truly immense Atlantis was, now that she was seeing it from below. With Kuirhan only a body-length below Skarmor, Jen looked down to ensure Pernissa and Silvress were not too far behind. Small bits of Earthly crust crumbled from the base that held Atlantis aloft; clearly it was still settling into its new home miles above the clouds. Half-buried roots the width of blue whales arced and weaved through the floating island's underside, belonging to the Arbor Atlanti, the central tree responsible for sustaining Atlantis's suspended levitation.

A piece of Dimitri . . .

Jen would forever be indebted to her leshy friend. He saved her life three times and never asked for anything in return. Yearning to see him again brought a light fluttering sensation to the front of her chest, and she bit the inside of her cheek to keep composed.

Her thoughts drifted back to her father. Jen didn't know where else to take him. Or who else could come close to helping him. She hoped that Queen P'tara would keep Charles safe while she searched for Genevieve . . . and hopefully, in the meantime, have her physicians try to stabilize his heart and prolong his chances of survival.

Then M'balo's face appeared in her mind's eye, reminding Jen of the steadfast faith he had in her . . . and how he had made her feel.

But as Skarmor broke above the city's edge wall seconds before Kuirhan, the sight that awaited Jen sent a frigid rush down her spine, shattering her thoughts about the elder Prince of Atlantis. She knew the city of Atlantis had sustained damage by Fuzanglong shortly before she and Charles had raised it, but she hadn't imagined the aftermath was *this* disastrous.

Then came several thin, white beams that split the air all around Skarmor, leaving seared after-images on Jen's retinas and clipping the tip of Skarmor's right wing. Screeching, the griffin tucked and dove out of the way of more beams, Kuirhan close behind with Victor's jolted yells sounding even closer. Mira gasped, Skarmor panicked, and in the half-second before he began evasive maneuvers, Jen sent a message into the group's mind meld to warn Rez, Hephalon, and Gavin.

Stay back! Don't show yourselves!

Skarmor dipped and rolled through the air as some of the beams followed him like heat-seeking missiles. Jen clung to Mira as Skarmor barrel-rolled, confusing four beams until their trajectories crossed. A sizzling explosion erupted a few meters behind them, though luckily the only thing Jen felt was the residual shock wave.

"Why are they *shooting* at us?!" Mira yelled between the sounds of streaking beams.

Jen reoriented herself and saw a pair of Atlantean sentinel guards on the walkway of the city's outer wall, firing straight at Skarmor and Kuirhan. More were racing toward their compatriots, bringing their own firearms to bear.

We can help, Jen! Rez sent back.

Jen didn't want to debate this, now of all times. *No, something's wrong . . . they've only seen us and Victor. Get to safety. We'll find you once we figure things out, I promise.* She dared a glance below and saw Pernissa and Silvress in a holding pattern just below the city's edge, out of sight and harm's way.

Victor's voice rang in her head next: *Gavin, go to my cottage on Azumar. Wait for us there.*

By that time, Mira had already brought her bullwhip to bear, her defensive spells traveling through the long-braided whip and releasing from its tip before she deftly recoiled it, bringing it around her head to strike again. The firing sentinels were forced to take cover behind the wall's merlons, the raised sections of the battlements. With a hand tightly holding onto Charles, Victor alternated his fair share of spells with Mira's; they weren't giving the sentinels even a second of relief in order to get off properly-aimed shots of their own; the guards tried in vain to squeeze off a shot or two before they were bombarded by blindingly bright spells which harmlessly sailed through empty air.

Jen was surprised when Gavin finally responded with, *Copy that.* She'd expected a rebuttal and a headstrong charge. But she couldn't linger on trying to figure out his reasoning; more pressing matters called for her undivided attention. Even though the efforts of Mira and Victor brought the barrage of beams down to sporadic, poorly aimed shots, Jen knew it wouldn't last much longer. In the distance, two chrome-plated, convertible-style patrol cars were speeding their way.

The sentinels had called in for reinforcements.

Jen peered below and thanked common sense when she saw the retreating forms of Pernissa and Silvress, the tightness in her heart partially slackening and the focus needed to survive this skirmish now brought to full force. She commanded Skarmor to fly in low and skim the outer wall just below the sentinels as she wrapped herself in her nexus. Like sliding her fingers down the keys of a piano, she activated each Mancy plane one by one until they were all primed to enforce her commands, trilling in harmony as she waited for the right moment. She could feel her charm bracelet spinning around her wrist, each charm brushing against her skin as they revolved in a clockwise fashion.

NOW!

Jen selected terramancy and, with lifted fingers, bent every barrel of the sentinels' firearms into right angles as she passed below them and back toward Kuirhan. The patrol cars, which Jen could see had the Queen's Guard insignia plastered on their hoods and side doors, were now close enough to send out their own volleys of shots. Patrol guards stood in the open-air cockpits, perching their advanced firearms on the rim of their windshield frames and firing madly at Skarmor and Kuirhan. Jen's instincts kicked in and, switching to telemancy, she wrapped Skarmor in a forcefield half a second before the beams arrived, ricocheting off her shield every which way. Next she reached out through animancy and called Kuirhan over so he could share in Jen's forcefield with Skarmor.

A guttural scream made Jen look back at the wall. One of the redirected beams had blown a hole in a section of the battlement wall just under one of the raised merlons, sending crumbled stone, mortar, and an unlucky sentinel off the edge of the floating city.

"Mira, hold on!" Jen tensed and leaned forward. "Dive, Skarmor!"

Skarmor, without hesitation, tucked his large eagle wings to his sides and pointed his beak at the falling sentinel. The Atlantean flailed wildly, surely thinking he would plummet to his death. The sentinels and patrol guards all halted their fire, waiting to see how this would end.

Jen would make sure it wouldn't end in tragedy.

As the rush of air dried out her eyes, she reverted back to terramancy and sent a curved current of air toward the Atlantean, one strong enough to be able to catch him and keep him afloat until Jen could swoop in and offer him her hand. The guard, bewildered, tensed until he saw her charm bracelet, which was slowly rotating around her wrist with the terramancy charm glowing a soft white-blue.

"Take my hand," Jen said to him.

He gulped and shakily grabbed her outstretched hand and was hauled onto Skarmor right behind Mira and Jen.

"Let's get him back on solid ground, Skar," Jen said as she patted her loyal griffin.

Skarmor obliged and, in a few short seconds, touched down on an open stretch of Atlantis's walled walkway.

More guards filed in on either side of Skarmor, their weapons drawn and eager to be used, as the pair of patrol cars hovered meters away, the lighted edges of their chassis blinking a harsh scarlet. The man who Jen had saved fell off the griffin's back, his armor clanking on the stone walkway before he found his footing and picked himself up. He turned to look back at Jen. His face, along with the ones of nearly every other guard, slackened as they watched her pull out the TeleCrystal.

"I am a friend!" Jen said in Atlantean, climbing from her mount and holding the crystal high above her head as Kuirhan landed behind Skarmor. She tried to catch her breath as she said, "I . . . am Jennifer Lancaster . . . and I seek an audience with Queen Pt'ara."

* * *

Jen and the half of her group were escorted in silence across the empty skies of Atlantis. The floating lanes of traffic that had entranced Jen when she'd first set foot on Atlantis were all but gone; only patrolling hovercars, Skarmor, and Kuirhan flew a hundred meters above street level. An ominous, dystopian sense permeated the streets, buildings, and roads as Skarmor and Kuirhan followed the two lead patrol cars toward the Queen's palace. Not a soul was out on the streets, but Jen could hear distant shouting and muffled sounds similar to the guards' firearms. She furrowed her brow, unable to process how different the city looked compared to just twenty-four hours ago. A few shell-shocked faces peered out of lit windows and cracked-open doors, just to drift behind walls, out of sight, as Jen's crew and their escort passed over their houses. Skarmor and Kuirhan painted their elongated shadows across the eastern walls of some of the taller buildings as the sun receded in the ever-darkening sky.

Abounding devastation seemed to spread into every corner and crevice of Atlantis. Charred remnants of city blocks—some fully leveled—were more commonplace than the untouched, and dotted across the cityscape were tufts of gray smoke silently curling higher into the air from where the disembodied shouting had come. The once-shimmering waterway that separated the four rings of the city no longer reflected tranquility, peace, and order; instead, in its currents, there carried an eerie silence that matched its dull hues as it meandered its way around debris that stuck out above the water's surface like splintered boulders at the base of an ocean cliff.

Had Jen been that myopic to not even realize how severe the aftermath of Fuzanglong's attack had been once she'd helped Charles raise Atlantis into the sky? Preoccupied entirely with rushing to the Eye of the Sahara to bargain for Gavin and Pernissa's lives? Still holding the TeleCrystal in her right hand, Jen tightened her grip, feeling remorse at what she had brought to this city's doorstep. She looked at the palace and Akt'aron in the distance, the former showing more signs of destruction than the latter. She hoped that M'balo was safe; her last memory was of him flying off with Gavin on the back of Pernissa moments before being dropped off at the outer wall to fight alongside his city's warriors.

The patrol cars brought them to the front steps of the palace, still standing regal amidst the still-settling squalor in the golden hues of the sunset. As they touched down, two tight lines of guards poured out of the palace's entrance and quickly surrounded Skarmor and Kuirhan. They drew their weapons but were pointing them outward, away from Jen and her group. The patrol guards quickly popped out of their vehicles and ordered Jen and her friends to dismount. Jen obeyed and told Mira and Victor what they were demanding. After helping Mira off Skarmor, Jen noticed that Victor had Charles over one shoulder. He was visibly strained from the ever-stacking amount of fatigue that he'd been racking up for days at this point (not to mention Charles's weight). Jen couldn't have that.

"May we get some type of gurney or cot to lay my father on?" she asked the group of patrol guards.

The guard who had ordered Jen to get off Skarmor—a bald, gruff man—barked an order at one of the palace guards stationed at the top of the steps. The man was startled into attention and stiffly jogged beneath the towering archway just as Kl'to, Head of the Queen's Guard (the official name of the Atlantean soldiers, Jen had learned from M'balo), emerged with a female guard on his right. They both took the stairs with purpose, and the closer the woman got, the more Jen recognized her as one of the guards who had taken her to see Queen Pt'ara for the first time. Beside her, Kl'to's countenance was solemn but commanding as he made eye contact with Jen; the female guard's was more enigmatic. His chrome-armored tunic was smudged and dusted but still reflected the rays of the setting sun; the shining red borders were just as noticeable as the first time she'd laid eyes on it back when she was being held in the palace's holding cell.

He stopped a few paces away from her and nodded curtly to the female guard at his side. She walked past Jen to take the reins of both Skarmor and Kuirhan. Both creatures resisted at first, but a raised hand from Victor calmed their minds.

The front two patrol guards stood at attention, their firearms held across their chest plates, and said in unison, "Sir." They backed away from Jen, Mira, Victor, and Charles once Kl'to saluted back at them.

"The King is ready to see you," the distinguished warrior said.

Jen stiffened. "The *King*?"

Kl'to pursed his lips and clasped his hands behind his back. He looked at the thin black band on his right upper arm before returning to her. "The King is expecting you," he repeated, "and Soi'raa will look after your creatures." He gave the faintest of nods to the female guard holding Skarmor and Kuirhan's reins.

Soi'raa nodded back and the line of guards parted, clearing a path for her to lead the griffin and equivol through and out, toward the tall, trimmed hedges of the palace's garden, which were surprisingly intact considering the state of this ring of the city.

Kl'to about-faced and ascended the steps without another word. The butt of a weapon pressed firmly between Jen's shoulder blades, forcing her to follow in the military commander's wake. Skarmor chirped protectively and, with a hint of dread creeping up inside, she decided to comfort him one last time before he left the wall of guards. She darted over to him and rubbed his beak.

"Jennifer Lancaster, please," Kl'to called out from behind her. "Your creatures will be properly looked after."

Jen looked at Soi'raa apologetically. "Sorry, but I just know how Skarmor can be sometimes." To her trusty griffin, she said in a softer tone, "It's okay, boy. We won't be long."

He clicked his tongue as she continued to rub his beak. Kuirhan whinnied and tugged at his reins, taking Soi'raa's eyes off Jen. A split second was all she needed. She then patted his head in a final goodbye before she was escorted back to Victor and Mira and walked alongside them up the steps. Jen slowly ascended, her gaze lingering on her griffin until he'd passed through the garden's hedged archway and out of sight.

Before Kl'to could lead them up the first interior staircase, the palace guard that had run inside earlier now emerged from a hallway off to the right, pushing a floating plank toward them, a plank that looked identical to the one that Charles was lying on, pale as porcelain, in her second vision. Jen fought the urge to scream as Victor laid Charles down on it now, fighting the urge to scream and take her father off of it, but she balled her fists so tight that she almost cracked her knuckles, and as the pressure in her hands subsided she reminded herself that she would not let that vision become reality. Instead, she stepped closer to Charles and took his hand, her stomach churning. She squeezed his limp hand and glanced at Victor worriedly before that same palace guard pushed it up the entranceway staircase.

Jen looked up and saw that Kl'to had already begun ascending the wide, azure-streaked, sandy marble staircase, one adorned with opulent balustrades and a purple velvet runner so dark that it almost looked black. Aside from endless immaculate staircases as they rose higher, the palace did show signs of wear, noticeable cracks in its foundation and subsequent levels; but these were apparently no cause for immediate concern, as the staff stood idle, up against walls and in corners like penitent statues as she passed. They wore black satin tunics with white trim and had their heads in a perpetual bow, ignoring the debris and untidiness surrounding them. They were ghostly shadows, bound to be seen in these halls but not heard.

Jen's sense of unease only grew as she climbed the final few steps that opened up to the large hallway that had only one door: the door to the royal throne room. The last time she was in there, she'd saved the queen and her other son, Sh'tam, and was given her blessing to raise her holy city of Atlantis. Two more guards were stationed on each side of the massive arched doorway, both wearing the same kind of black band on their right arms. The doors parted to reveal the throne room, awash in no other light than the golden-pink of the setting sun. Shards of the glass dome still cluttered the perimeter of the room. Up on the raised dais stood one person, his back to Jen—the one person from Atlantis who could make Jen's heart stir.

M'balo.

Jen breathed a sigh of relief; he'd survived . . . but she had a somber inkling that his mother did not. Kl'to and the other guards ushered Jen and the rest into the center of the room. Jen was waiting for the floor to rise until she was eye level with M'balo, but the floor remained still.

Kl'to saluted upward and said, *"Mah Roi'tus."*

The young Atlantean turned around and looked down at his visitors. Without a word, he spun in the opposite direction and disappeared from view as he headed for the stairs. Jen glanced behind her at Victor and Mira where they calmly waited next to the floating plank that held Charles. Mira's eyes widened and she slightly gestured for Jen to turn around. Emerging from the left archway next to the dais's base wasn't M'balo but Sh'tam, his twin brother. Jen stiffened. They looked identical, their only tells being their earrings, which were on opposite earlobes. And Sh'tam's eyes . . . they were less kind, not as curious. Doubt tightened her throat, now unsure if M'balo was truly alive and how this interaction would end. Her thoughts were interrupted by Sh'tam, speaking for the first time.

"Omnimancer Lancaster," Sh'tam began, "and friends!" He raised his hands in a welcoming gesture; the thick, white tunic with striations of purple that was wrapped around his left shoulder and arm swayed as his arms moved. He wore his mother's crown.

"Prince Sh'tam . . ." Jen's mouth went dry. "Th-thank you for agreeing to meet with us."

He clasped his hands together, his royal adornments jangling with the movement. "It's *King* Sh'tam, actually." He closed his mouth but still wore a tight smile. "My beloved mother sadly did not survive our city's . . . *relocation*." His tone came off as spiteful, with a dash of resentment.

"I am so sorry to hear that." Jen bowed her head, unable to get M'balo's safety from her mind. "And your brother?"

Sh'tam bowed back, distractedly glossing over her question with the callous response of "He sadly met our ancestors at the southern gate." He furrowed his brow as he focused on Victor and Mira to Jen's left. "Why do your friends not bow in respect for my mother's memory?"

Jen tried to fill her lungs back with air after hearing about M'balo's demise. She stammered, awkwardly looking between the new King and her uncle and friend as she tried to break the spell of speechlessness. Though her heart ripped in two, she still knew that Victor and Mira were completely lost, oblivious to what had just occurred.

"Um . . . they don't understand Atlantean."

Sh'tam made a *tsk*ing noise, then snapped his fingers. "They must show deference." The pattering of feet were heard and in seconds, a servant came out of the shadows with a tray, on it two chalices. Sh'tam plucked them from the tray and gave one each to Victor and Mira. "I know your native tongue, but I wouldn't debase myself in the palace of my fallen ancestors to speak any language other than my own."

That comment brought Jen back to the here and now. She fought the urge to roll her eyes, but the chalices piqued her curiosity.

"Drink." Sh'tam stepped away and waited, the fakest of smiles plastered on his lips.

Victor swirled the contents of the chalice in his hand, skeptically peering at the sloshing liquid before looking back at Sh'tam, unimpressed. Mira held the chalice's stem with both hands and looked at Jen, who could see the request for help in her eyes.

Jen didn't want to assume what this magical elixir was, so she asked warily, "My friends will understand Atlantean if they drink this?"

"Extraordinary, isn't it?" He leaned forward at the waist, his tunic hanging from his lithe, ebony frame. "The royal physician for my grandfather, King Quan'to, created the drink your friends now hold. He was an eccentric man, but he revolutionized the way we Atlanteans concoct and practice medicine." He reverted back to an upright stance and loosely clasped his hands in front of him. "I would like them to hear what I have to say." His eyes held a mischievous glint.

Fearing that the conversation would not progress until Victor and Mira obliged, Jen did her best to reassure them that it was safe and purely meant for them to understand Atlantean. Mira, ever trusting, took Jen's word and smoothly tipped back the chalice until she had drunk every last drop. Victor took some extra goading, but eventually put the chalice's lip to his mouth and swallowed.

"Mmm," Mira said, "tastes fruity."

Sh'tam's servant reappeared and received Mira's empty chalice, followed by Victor's. Neither of them fainted or looked to be ill or in pain, but Jen still held her breath and hoped until Sh'tam spoke.

"Can you understand me?"

Victor blinked then raised his eyebrows, a look of surprise on his face. "Yes."

Mira exhaled in wonderment. "Whoa . . . ditto."

"Good," Sh'tam said. His eyes focused behind them. "As I told Omnimancer Lancaster, my mother perished during the raising of my city."

"Our condolences," Victor said as Mira brought a hand to her chest.

"Please bow," Sh'tam said after a few tense seconds of silence, the patience on his face starting to crack.

They both bowed in unison and when they finished, Victor asked, "Why didn't you offer us that drink when we were here before?"

Sh'tam snorted derisively. "My mother thought you were nuisances rather than guests, but I do not think of you that way."

The skin behind Jen's ears grew slightly taut at the faint sounds of shuffling of padded feet and sliding of metal.

"No, you definitely are not nuisances." Sh'tam's voice increased in volume. "After what I witnessed during the attack on Atlantis and what Omnimancer Jennifer and her father"—he gestured to Charles, supine on the plank—"did to our great city . . . you are a *plague*. My mother was wrong to allow you to defile the Akt'aron and remove our city from the earth."

That last sentence was punctuated with his royal guards grabbing Jen, Victor, and Mira.

Fighting against the strong arms of the Atlanteans, Jen strained out, "What are you doing?! We saved you and your citizens from the attack!"

Sh'tam seemed to be done listening. "Our crystal you took, return it to me."

Jen felt as though she'd been rocked by a battering ram, her mind swirling and trying to process this unexpected turn of events. "Sh'tam—"

"It's *King* Sh'tam!" he bellowed before quickly composing himself and straightening out his tunic. "You will experience pain in ways you never thought possible if you do not hand over our sacred crystal. Search her!" he commanded.

Two guards rushed her, one grabbing her arm with a gloved hand that felt prickly. Instantly Jen stiffened as if she were a wax figure, and the other guard inspected her pockets, belt, and boots. Finding nothing, he grunted in disappointment. Jen's eyes darted as far left as they could, barely making out Victor and Mira as Sh'tam contorted in frustration. Jen's field of vision started to shake, but she could see her uncle and friend, stiff and rigid just like her, surrounded by several guards.

"Where is the crystal?!" the king shouted, stomping up to Jen. He clamped her cheeks with his hand, his forehead creased with bulging veins.

Jen wouldn't have given him the satisfaction of a response even if she still retained the ability to speak, but whatever was on the guard's glove had paralyzed her entire body except her eyes. All Jen could do was look into his beady little eyes as they darted all across her frozen face.

Like a spoiled child who didn't get the toy he wanted, Sh'tam huffed and retracted his hand from Jen's face. "Tactos Kl'to," he bellowed, "take them to the palace's lower dungeons. Separate each conspirator and give them one-eighth rations." He glared at her as the guards lifted her off the ground and carried her farther into the throne room toward the passageway to the left of the dais. "Let's see how long the *omnimancer* can survive before insanity sets in."

Sh'tam's threat echoed in the immense, barren room as Jen's eyes bounced around in their sockets; too many thoughts and emotions churned inside of her, and it was getting increasingly hard to control them. Hot tears dribbled from the edges of her eyes and despair racked her internally.

She was beginning to think her vision of Charles would indeed come to pass.

CHAPTER SIXTEEN

"Let them run," Lord Ferox said smugly. "We now have their stronghold." He gestured to the entirety of Camelore from where he sat on a throne carved into the central, hulking, mystical tree he'd transformed with the ShadowCrystal's infectious powers. His ophidite had stayed coiled around the trunk, its feathers and scales rippling as it breathed and stared down at Volcanor. His wyvern was resting by the entrance to the Pentarena, motionless but for its eyes, which, though normally roaming, now were locked in turn on the feathered serpent, almost like each creature was measuring up the other.

"You're not mad that they've escaped?" This behavior absolutely floored Malcolm; if Jen and the rest had escaped on Draconex's watch, there wouldn't be a blade of grass left on this floating island—only ashes.

"Malcolm, Malcolm, Malcolm . . ."

Ferox rose from the inlaid throne, his obsidian cape swallowing up his arms. The purple glow cast by the thick veins of ShadowCrystal magic in the tree above rolled over Ferox's tall frame and highlighted his dark, full head of hair. He breathed in deeply before continuing.

"The capture is only as good as the chase. The die has been cast. The prophecy is slowly but surely becoming reality."

Malcolm followed him with his eyes. He knew that look: the ShadowCrystal was speaking to Ferox.

He slowly passed behind Malcolm, continuing, "We've taken their stronghold, and soon they will return to reclaim it." Ferox reappeared on Malcolm's other side, finishing with, "They will try and fail . . . and I will make them watch as I take hold of one of the omnimancers' bodies."

Before Malcolm could respond, Ferox became a shadowy blur and launched into the tree's thicket of thorny branches. Malcolm tried to follow the dark lord, but in the twilight he lost sight of him almost immediately. A tight squeal was heard off to his right, and the ophidite hissed as Ferox landed about three meters away holding something white and squirming. In a rush, Volcanor rolled its shoulders and dug its clawed wings into the ground, aggressively snorting thick cords of smoke, which quickly traveled into Malcolm's nostrils, stinging his nasal cavity and producing tears on his lower eyelids. Malcolm held up an open palm toward his dragon in an effort to calm it down; Volcanor still seemed aggravated but did not charge (which Malcolm took as a success). He then looked back at Ferox, squinting in the growing darkness and through the waves of soft purple light to pinpoint what the dark lord had found.

"What do we have here?" Ferox said. He let the small animal struggle a few seconds more before he threw it to the ground. "An uninvited guest, perchance?"

In his voice there was a hint of devious playfulness as he placed a heavy boot on top of one of its albino wings. It squealed a bit more before it transformed into a woman with porcelain skin and bleached-blond hair, her arm still pinned to the ground. She hissed at him and bared her sharp, glimmering canine teeth.

"Ahh, a *vesperite* . . ." Ferox said in wonder, using the old English term for "vampire." He knelt down to get a closer look at her like one would a rare specimen under a microscope.

There was only one albino vampire Malcolm knew.

"Diaema . . ." he breathed.

The bile in his stomach began to foment, his feet already in motion. Malcolm was going to make her wish she'd never foiled his plans of capturing Jen and Charles Lancaster—

But then he came to a stop. He had an idea.

Changing his tone, he started toward her again, saying, "Madame Diaema, you *survived*?!"

Diaema stopped hissing and glared at Malcolm, partly in confusion. The pressure of Ferox's boot was still heavy on her arm, shown by a slight wince that she carried around her eyes and mouth.

"You know this vesperite?" Ferox asked with more than a little curiosity.

Malcolm almost second-guessed why he was even contemplating lying to Ferox.

Almost.

"Yes, I do," Malcolm said as he closed the distance, knowing full well that Ferox had the ShadowCrystal in his ear, potentially spinning its own narrative about Malcolm and how Ferox shouldn't trust a word he said. "She helped me overthrow Draconex."

"Draconex . . ." Ferox whispered, remembering the name of the man whose body he now inhabited. His head twitched a few times as he rolled it to the other side, his brow furrowed as if intently listening to someone only he could hear.

The ophidite was coiled in wait behind him, its slitted eyes burrowing into the subjugated form of Diaema as Volcanor rustled its brimstone shoulders at the mention of its previous master.

The ShadowCrystal wasted no time, Malcolm thought ruefully.

Aloud he said, "As my spy she gained Draconex's trust and, when the time was right, took the ShadowCrystal from him."

Malcolm spared a glance down at Diaema, hoping she would play along, or at least remain quiet. All she did was look between him and Draconex, waiting.

Ferox grabbed the sides of her face with an index finger and thumb and inspected it, slowly turning her head from one side to the other. Finally, he let go and looked at Malcolm. "Why?" His calculating eyes turned to slits.

Malcolm held up an index finger. "First, Draconex was overusing the ShadowCrystal—treating it like a crutch. It was pathetic." He spat for added emphasis, then straightened his middle finger. "Second, I wanted to ensure the ShadowCrystal returned to you once you'd been released. Draconex had developed a crippling affinity for it, one that made me unconvinced that he would part with it willingly."

Eyes still slitted, Ferox slowly stood but did not release Diaema's arm. "Your dragon seems . . . disconcerted about this vesperite. Hardly a mark of allegiance."

Malcolm held his body rigid, suppressing the involuntary response to flinch. "Volcanor never got along with Diaema. It doesn't understand how she can transform into something so much smaller and different." He waited in silence, nervously rubbing the gemstone set into the butt of Excalibur's handle, wondering if he would have to use it if his lie wasn't good enough.

"Spy, infiltrator, and"—Ferox surveyed Diaema once again —"most likely . . . seductress." He released her arm and rolled her onto her front with a quick flick of his boot. "She must be a cunning warrior as well, being a vesperite, yes?" He directed the question at Malcolm, as if he were the master and Diaema the slave.

Malcolm crossed his arms as Diaema slowly clambered up, not bothering to dust herself off. If she was trained by Ephram La Proutagne himself, she should be an adept fighter. "Why don't you ask her yourself?"

A smirk lifted one side of Ferox's face before he shifted his gaze back to Diaema.

And lunged.

The first few blows and blocks happened so quickly Malcolm's eyes had a hard time registering it, but when Diaema was able to gain an arm's length or two from the offensive strikes of the dark lord, he witnessed two masterful fighters in a duel that was as much brawn as it was brain.

The feathered serpent jutted its head out from behind the mangled tree trunk, showing its forked tongue and hissing in excitement. Volcanor seemed indifferent, almost content with watching Diaema being attacked. Malcolm could tell that Ferox's strategy was to stay close to Diaema and use his brute strength to subdue her and win the fight, but Diaema was unnaturally fast, her speed gifted by abilities only vampires possess.

Eerie silence pervaded the entire space as the two fought, the only sounds to be heard those of quick footfalls on dry dirt and the cushioned blows of knees or arms blocking the next jab or kick. Ferox had not cast a single spell yet, giving credence to his time period's display of skill; the mark of an expert sorcerer was measured by how quickly they could best their opponent before calling upon the added aid of sorcery.

Malcolm winced in surprise as Diama struck Ferox's face with a clawed hand, leaving bleeding scratches an instant after she threw a blindingly fast low roundhouse kick to his lower torso, dropping him to one knee. Diaema seemed to glide over the ground to add distance between them, barely evading a retaliatory swipe. Still kneeling, Ferox touched the side of his face that was scratched, chuckled as he stood, and changed tactics.

For a brief moment, the inside of the Pentarena blossomed in all different colors. Ferox lanced several spells with bare-fisted jabs at the shadowy figure of Diaema, missing her with milliseconds to spare. Energy exuded from the ShadowCrystal set deep into Ferox's chest, energy from every Mancy plane sent crackling up and down his pumping arms, Ferox uncaring where errant spells struck. A few spells ended up scoring the massive tree, sending splintered pieces of bark toward the ophidite's head; it hissed in annoyance, retracting around the back of the trunk to protect itself.

It looked like Diaema was dancing to the rhythm of Ferox's spells, cartwheeling, diving, and spinning as she crisscrossed the open atrium of the Pentarena and then rushed toward Ferox. He noticed suddenly that the bottom of her ears were glowing, and it took a second for Malcolm to realize she was wearing earrings.

Totem earrings.

Diaema's next step created three doppelgänger copies of her. They emerged from the ground like shadows and quickly spaced themselves out in a loose crescent as she continued her charge. Ferox hesitated his onslaught of spells, unsure which Diaema was the real one, eventually deciding to aim at the closest one first. Diaema jumped straight at him and disappeared in a cloud of smoke as a spell shot through her chest; the next Diaema cut behind Ferox and pushed him to his knees. He reached back and grabbed the back of her shirt, carrying her over to his other hand which had morphed into a jagged blade, and skewered her. That Diaema also evaporated into smoke.

Was Ferox slightly out of breath? And was Malcolm mistaken, or was Diaema using telemancy?

Diaema slowly walked toward Ferox, her footsteps measured. "Have I proven myself worthy to be spoken to, or does Malcolm still need to speak for me?"

Ferox let out a grunt and flicked two purple spits of fire at her. They converged on her head, turning her into wisps of harmless smoke. Before the curling, opaque tendrils could fully dissipate, she appeared out of thin air behind Ferox. He was vulnerable and Diaema, showing prowess and combat skills the likes of which Malcolm had never seen from her before, was in a position to end Ferox's life . . . and Malcolm's ambitions. Squeezing the armor over his biceps in tense anguish, he sharply inhaled as Diaema reached for the nape of Ferox's exposed neck—and bit through air. She stumbled and shuddered, clawing at her throat.

Ferox coalesced off to Diaema's side, holding her throat with a conceited smirk. "Two can play with telemancy, my dear." He easily lifted her off the ground, and purple crackles of lightning traveled from his fingers to Diaema's throat. Her scream was cut off and she seized up as neuropathic signals were blocked; her body was showing the telltale signs of shutting down.

"Are you not convinced?" Malcolm cut in.

He raised his voice, hoping his harsher volume would break Ferox's concentration on what he was doing to Diaema. He looked like he had no qualms about ending her life then and there. He didn't acknowledge Malcolm right away, but the crackling current lessened until no more traveled through Diaema. He cocked his head and stared at her now-unconscious form.

"A vesperite that's a telemancer . . . *Fascinating*."

Fascinating indeed. Malcolm remained silent, his mind racing as he realized just how mysterious Madame Diaema truly was. As a species, vampires did not possess a nexus; therefore, accessing the Mancy planes was supposed to be impossible. But Madame Diaema clearly could . . . and that led to the only possible conclusion: she wasn't born a vampire.

She must've been turned after learning telemancy.

Malcolm stiffened to attention when Ferox's voice invaded his thoughts.

"This one will be of great use to my plan." He released his grip and Diaema fell to the ground in a heap, out cold. "She will aid you in your mission, Malcolm." He picked something out from underneath a fingernail and started back toward his carved throne.

Malcolm slowly walked up to Diaema's limp form and knelt next to her face. There was an electrical burn ring around her neck, but aside from that she bore no outlandish signs of injury. When she woke, he would have some questions about her past . . . including why she'd stolen the ShadowCrystal, and why exactly she was found with Charles Lancaster in that cave on Azumar.

Malcolm blinked, tearing his gaze from the vampire as Ferox's words finally registered. "Mission? What mission?" He stood back up and took a few more steps closer to the dark lord.

"Come to me once she awakens. For now, leave me and see to your vesperite spy. I do not want to be disturbed."

Malcolm took another step forward, gesturing in confusion. "But my Lord—"

The ophidite slid down the tree trunk, cutting him off and

blocking his view of the seated Ferox with its massive head and colorful, feathered mane.

"Okay, all right, I get it . . ." His arms flung up defensively as he slowly stepped back toward Diaema. He slung one of her arms over his neck and picked her up, looking in the distance until he decided to take her to one of the huts in the living quarters.

As he left the Pentarena in his wake, Malcolm was bombarded with questions concerning this mission Ferox would be giving him . . . and what had compelled him to stick out his neck for a traitor to the Dark Watcher tribe such as Madame Diaema.

CHAPTER SEVENTEEN

On Azumar, Gavin opened the door to Victor's cottage, letting rays of bronzed twilight stretch out across the main room's hardwood floor. Small, steady flames grew from the evenly spaced torches set into the walls after he said with more than a hint of fatigue, "Rallumé." The remaining shadowy sections of the room were coated in a warm, flickering glow. He felt equal worry as he did exhaustion, but those feelings were pushed aside when his nose caught a putrid odor farther inside the cottage.

"Oi, get a load a that *stench!*" Rez waved a hand in front of his nose, stopping to the left of the door to let his father through.

Gavin started toward the kitchen door, thinking that something had spoiled in Victor's fridge, but a glance at Hephalon as he strode over to a blanket draped over something lying on the couch made him realize just what that putrid smell was.

A body.

Hephalon lifted the blanket to reveal the corpse of Mystra Simone Chen. A liquid that was a combination of blood and something else had started seeping from her nostrils and out the side of her open mouth, her bloodshot eyes distant and dried up, her hands contorted into claws from the rigor mortis.

"Bastard," Hephalon murmured as he let the blanket fall back over Simone's decaying face.

"What is Mystra Chen doing here?" Gavin asked, his eyes on the back of Hephalon's head, waiting for him to turn around.

Hephalon breathed in, slow and deep, letting it out steadily before he said, "She survived the Jubilee massacre, and I, alongside Victor and Cindergray, brought her here after discovering that she was Draconex's mole." He finally turned to face Gavin. "Cindergray volunteered to stay behind and question her while Victor and I embarked to find passage back to you and the rest on Camelore."

Gavin lowered his head. Out of the corner of his eye, he could still see Rez glued to the same spot next to the open door. Gavin ran his tongue over his front teeth, thinking. He couldn't understand it; nothing seemed to make sense anymore. Considering what he'd read in the journal before all hell broke loose on Camelore, he was no longer convinced that Lord Ferox had perished in the Sahara Desert. And now, to discover Mystra Chen was a Dark Watcher mole—and killed by a man who'd positioned himself as the headmaster of the entire Sorcery Guild? His mind was liquefying.

Gavin said, "I'll take care of her."

He lifted his left hand and, keeping his orb inside his necklace's golden pendant, he channeled astromancy. He felt a surge of controlled energy pass from deep within and gather at his fingertips. As his fingers slowly converged and touched, the blanket deflated against the cushions, nothing beneath except the couch itself. Simone's body had been fully atomized.

"We best make ourselves comfortable," he said with a tired shrug.

Hephalon slid a large hand down his face and absent-mindedly stroked his braided, ginger beard. "That'll be difficult, lad," he confessed, referring to their split from Jen, Victor, and Mira. "I can't even bring myself to clean out Victor's ale stash—which isn't a lot, mind you—I'm just so beside myself." He gathered the blanket and rolled it up. "But I can bring *this* to the hamper."

Rez, making a disgusted sound as the burly metallurgist shuffled past Gavin, closed the door and dropped into the closest seat

—an accented armchair—exhausted. "Do you think Jen and Mira are okay?"

Gavin sniffled, trying his best to lace his response with as much optimism as possible. "Of course they are." He walked over to his friend and placed a hand on a bony shoulder. "And don't forget about Victor."

It took Rez a few seconds to realize his mistake. "*Eejit*," he berated himself, shaking his head groggily. "Sorry, Gav. I didn't mean t—"

"Hey . . ." Gavin tried lightening his tone since he couldn't bring a disarming chuckle to surface. "I was just giving you a hard time." He patted his hand on Rez's shoulder a few times before continuing to pace around the room, temporarily allowing himself to worry about Mira. He knew she could handle anything that was thrown her way, but he desperately wished he could be there by her side, ready to help if she and Jen couldn't reach an agreement with the Atlanteans.

Hephalon returned and began dismantling the armory he wore. "If you lads are indeed as tired as you look, I'd reckon sleep is in order." He leaned his round shield on the wall next to him. The next weapons off were his twin battleaxes. "This is as safe a place as any right now, and once rest affords us better clarity of mind, we can discuss what will come."

Gavin stopped pacing, arms crossed and eyes on Hephalon. He knew he wouldn't be getting much sleep tonight. He still had to process the cautious warning Merlin had written in the journal . . . and how Malcolm had possession of Excalibur.

But Gavin didn't protest; he went through the motions of settling in as Hephalon finished removing all his weapons and armor and Rez found a small snack in Victor's cupboard to quell his teenage hunger. Gavin said his goodnights as Hephalon took Victor's bed and Rez returned to the cushioned armchair he had fallen into from the start. With the satchel containing Merlin's journal at his side, Gavin sat down on the main couch, not getting too comfortable, considering it was where Simone's body had begun to decay. And he wasn't planning on sitting for long, anyway.

His mind didn't slow as seconds dragged into minutes until finally his ears picked up the faint murmur of snores from Rez. Quietly, Gavin stood up and, carrying the journal with him, walked into the kitchen and sat at the table next to the sole window. He slid the pendant from his necklace and popped out the orb totem. After enlarging it to the size of an apple and supplying it with enough power from his nexus to give it a soft glow, he placed it atop the flat pendant and opened the journal. He quickly flipped through most of the pages until he reached the one he was looking for—the one that had Merlin's detailed sketch of Excalibur.

As the silver light from Azumar's binary moons draped along the windowsill next to his shoulder, Gavin closed his eyes and let his memory take him back to the moment on Camelore when Malcolm had dismounted his wyvern dragon and brandished Excalibur: He had held the sword out like he was flaunting a trophy, spinning it in his palms as Hephalon came rushing toward him.

Gavin was pulled back to the present, his ears picking up a rustling sound in the main room. He lifted off the chair and peered into the darkness to see, faintly, Rez shifting positions in the armchair. He soon fell silent and restarted his droning snores.

Gavin closed his eyes once more, eyebrows bunching in an intense scowl as he focused harder, allowing the memory to resume: Hephalon's axe on Malcolm's sword, a clash of formidable weapons that sent a shock wave in all directions, an electrified, metallic pulse that froze the very blood in Gavin's veins. He opened his eyes and unclenched his stiff jaw, sliding his fingers along the rough parchment that held the quilled strokes of one of the most illustrious mystras of all. Merlin's text, which edged up to the drawing of Excalibur, read:

Excalibur: a sword so mighty and pure. Only hands belonging to its equal may wield it. Arthur Pendragon, my most promising tenderfoot, was one such being; he was reviled by Philip Lancaster for being chosen as Excalibur's steward. When he drifted off to the shores of Avalon, Arthur had been bound by regret for failing to stop Philip, by then calling himself Lord Ferox, in his purging of the five omnimancer clans, all of whom will never sire any progeny henceforth, except for the sole surviving Lancaster clan. The only solace derived from this immense loss —a loss which will ripple for generations to come—is that the Halostone, along with the five MystiCrystals, have been lost as well.

But in my time spent traversing these eleven known realms, I fear that there will be those who seek to not only complete what Lord Ferox started, but even to go so far as to resurrect him. Therefore, it is I who shall be the reluctant steward of this fine and mystical sword until the Light Bringer, one as pure and resolute as Arthur himself, comes along, for I will not live forever—not even I have attained the level of mastery over the Mancy Planes to cast such a spell.

However, I am versed enough to enchant Excalibur with two spells of different effects. In the unlikely but not impossible event that Lord Ferox is freed and I am not around to prevent it, I have cast a protection spell over Excalibur, ensuring Lord Ferox will never be able to hold it. The other spell is one that will be the dark lord's permanent downfall if Excalibur were to be plunged into his heart . . .

" 'Plunged into his heart . . .' " Gavin read those last four words aloud, his voice barely a whisper. He lifted his eyes from the time-worn page and let his body sway back until his shoulder blades hit the chair's backrest, his mind unable to shake the image of Malcolm holding Excalibur and the purple aura that surrounded it.

Gavin couldn't fully understand it, but something deep from within was telling him that Lord Ferox had survived Genevieve's final spell and was in league with Malcolm. He massaged his tired eyes, feeling a dull ache in his head as if a myriad of thoughts were bouncing off the inside of his skull like rubber balls with no intention of slowing down. He stared off into the distance at nothing in particular as the light expelled from his orb totem faded away.

How was he going to explain this theory of his to Hephalon and Rez, let alone the rest when they arrived at the cottage (if they arrived at all)? No one else could read Merlin's journal to corroborate his interpretation of the text, though it seemed hard to ascertain anything different from what Merlin was trying to say.

Gavin had to take back Excalibur; there was no denying that fact. And what made his decision to leave Victor's cottage then and there was the fact that he knew exactly where Excalibur was: in Malcolm's hands. His loathing for that disgraced sorcerer knew no bounds, and the more he ruminated on confronting Malcolm again, the stronger his urge became to leave Victor's cottage and take Silvress back to Camelore and end this once and for all.

But then Victor's voice echoed in his head, reeling in his immediate emotional reaction: *In times like these, don't mistake prudent reflection for wasteful idleness.*

Inhaling deeply, Gavin closed the ancient tome and slid it toward the center of the small kitchen table. As a silent fatigue seeped into his bones, he let his breath slowly escape through his mouth and reminded himself that he was not alone, that his friends needed to know what he had just read before he went gallivanting off, taking on the realms by himself.

If Gavin did that, and failed, he might as well have gone and joined Malcolm's side.

"Thanks, Vic," Gavin said, thinking of his old mentor's wisdom and how he continued to make him feel like an impetuous tenderfoot. He smirked at the thought as he stood up and started back toward the couch, when his eyes, as they passed over the open windowpane, caught a barely perceptible movement. If he hadn't been looking out the window at that exact instant, he would've missed it.

And whatever was out there looked to be getting closer to the cottage, staying hidden in the shadows of the trees and pitched ridges of Azumar's rolling countryside.

Swiping his orb and pendant from the table, he rushed for the door, careful not to rouse Rez in his armchair or Hephalon in Victor's room. The dull groaning of the door's creaky hinges made him wince but didn't scare him away from opening the door; he didn't glance backward, hoping Rez didn't stir, and quickly shut the door behind him.

With his orb gripped firmly in hand, Gavin took to the right; if he had gone the other way, he would've had to find a way around Pernissa and Silvress without waking them. Hearing only the soft padding of his own footfalls, he hugged the outer edge of the cottage until he could once again view the tree line and moonlight-drenched hills. He did not illuminate his orb for fear of alerting whatever was skulking about, but he had to assume it knew of his presence as well (the light his orb was emanating while he read the journal wasn't exactly subtle).

Gavin split from the cottage's exterior wall and sprinted toward the closest glade of trees, careful to not crunch any fallen branches as he entered. Even in the still night, the smell of bark and soil floated around him, as did the rustling of small nocturnal animals meters above him in the trees.

But one rustling sound was at ear-level . . . and was loudening. Before Gavin could realize what it was, a light grayish blur collided with his shoulder and knocked him to the ground.

Gavin was out cold before his head hit the soft, mulched soil.

CHAPTER EIGHTEEN

Just as Jen was being dragged deeper into the bowels of the Atlantean palace, so were her spirits. Under some kind of neuro-blocking agent, she was completely helpless, her body a prison. That thought made her think of her father, also imprisoned in his own body but from a different cause. The floating plank where he rested took up the rear of the procession toward the dungeon, with Victor and Mira in the middle. The guards, flanking their sides in pairs, were laughing—joking, even—about what fools she and her group had to have been to willingly be brought before the king.

The stairwell was relatively well-lit and wide enough to accommodate four grown adults standing abreast. Crystalline light fixtures stuck out of the walls at even intervals, casting the enclosed tunnel in a dream-like sepia tone.

With Jen in the lead, she couldn't even count on one of Victor's looks, which always seemed to soothe her in times when her anxiety ran rampant. She desperately needed one of those looks right about now. All she could do to mitigate her emotional distress was to try and focus on getting out of this mess. If she didn't, her father would die in Sh'tam's dungeon and the search for Genevieve would be over before it even began.

Jen's entire body jolted uncomfortably as her left foot caught the edge of one of the steps. The guard on her left cursed and gained a better hold around her arms, then continued down the interminable staircase. A small landing appeared, and they passed a door set into the right side of the stairwell without so much as a glance from the guards.

I guess that was the middle dungeon, Jen thought sarcastically as the guards commenced descending another flight of stairs. By now Jen had lost count of the stairwell's crystalline light fixtures, and she wondered just how deep the innards of the royal palace truly went. The guards' chrome-plated boots rang out on the unforgiving marble stairs, echoing loudly all around Jen and inducing slight claustrophobia. The guards had by now replaced their joviality with ragged breaths, most likely feeling the muscle fatigue of carrying adult humans for several uninterrupted minutes.

"We're . . . almost there," huffed a right guard.

"I don't care if the king thinks that adding a lift shaft to his throne room is a sin. It needs to happen," said another.

"Maybe Sh'tam should try carrying a prisoner down these stairs . . ." a third chimed in.

"Quiet!" hushed a fourth, to Jen's left. "If you keep it up, we'll all be thrown in his dungeon."

Though the neurotoxin gave no hint of abating its powerful hold on her body, Jen took slight enjoyment in the guards' struggle and bickering as they slowly brought her down to the lower dungeon, each step heavier and more haphazardly placed.

Locked in place, Jen saw the stairwell curve left, and a second landing appeared ten steps down, except this one ended with a guard standing at attention before a locked door that looked to be hewn from the same quarry as the palace walls and floors.

Jen's guards greeted the watchman, and after exchanging some rude comments about Jen and the others, they pressed their wrist bracers to the wall. A strand of red light traveled through the wall and around the door, filling in its frame until it glowed a steady carmine. Muffled clangs emitted from the other side of the door as it unlocked, and then it slid open to reveal a waiting Kl'to.

"I will take the prisoners to their cells, S'rac," the commander stated, stepping closer to Jen.

The left guard, S'rac, looked to his counterpart and said hesitantly, "But the King ordered us to lock them up, sir."

Kl'to slightly lowered his chin to show S'rac a better angle of the tapered chrome headband that he wore. "Your assistance has been appreciated, corporal."

S'rac swallowed audibly and, with the opposite guard's help, set Jen down on a circular imprint in the floor. "Yes, sir." He took two paces backward as the other two sets of guards placed Victor and Mira down atop similar circles on either side of Jen. Behind her there came a light shuffling she assumed was Charles's prone form right behind the trio.

Kl'to tapped his bracer and the circular imprint below Jen detached from the ground, turning into a floating disc that lifted her into the air. The head guard tapped his bracer once more before about-facing and striding farther into the dungeon, breaking right as the floating discs and plank followed close in tow.

The place Jen now found herself in was surprisingly large with several rows of cubed, individual cells encased by what looked to be frosted glass walls. They were tightly packed together and stretched for scores of meters, giving the dungeon an abyssal sense. The majority of the cells by which Jen was passing were occupied, and Jen wondered what all these poor Atlanteans had done to be thrown into the King's dungeon. She could only discern the blurred silhouettes of the prisoners, but they seemed dejected and lonely.

In the background came the *whirring* of the entrance door's locks, and once they stopped, Kl'to brought a hand to his ear and whispered something that Jen couldn't pick up. He took two more strides before a string of *pops* rolled overhead, quickly followed by wisps of black smoke evenly spaced out across the carved ceiling. The sterile lighting switched to a pale red, and klaxon bells erupted in every direction. Jen smelled burning metal. The commander tapped his bracer, her disc suddenly stopping, and turned to face Jen.

"We do not have much time, Omnimancer Jennifer," Kl'to said as he touched her temples. A warm sensation cascaded down her body, freeing the stiffness she'd grown accustomed to. Her knees wobbled and Kl'to caught her as she stepped off the disc.

"What's happening?" Jen's voice was hoarse. She held her throat as she tried swallowing. The prisoners in the closest cells were animated, some pounding on the walls, others nervously pacing around their small confines.

Kl'to was already helping Victor off his disc, making sure his legs were stable before attending to Mira. "You are escaping." He tapped his ear once more and said, "They will be on the next lift."

Jen was at Victor's side in a flash, but one look from his steel blue eyes covered her worried heart with some relief. "Why are you helping us?" she asked, still trying to wrap her head around Kl'to's sudden change in demeanor.

Mira was safely on the ground, touching her forehead as Kl'to let her go. "Prince M'balo lives," he said.

The meaning of Kl'to's words sent a rush through Jen's system, causing her legs to nearly buckle. She'd already started making peace with M'balo's reported death, so this news blindsided her. Jen now knew better than to believe anything that came out of Sh'tam's mouth.

"Where is he?" Jen asked as Mira came up to her, giving her a quick hug.

"Deep within the city's catacombs." Kl'to looked back toward the entrance, where sudden, bright flashes cut into the lock, which was welded into the marble wall. He then shot a quick glance in the direction he had been taking them and pushed Charles's plank over to Jen. "We don't have much time," he said as Victor grabbed the plank's other end. "You somehow broke free of the Hold, destroyed our visual recording devices"—he gestured to the blackened dots in the ceiling where the smoke had since dissipated—"and knocked me unconscious before escaping through the guards' lift shaft."

Like a slap, it finally dawned on Jen what Kl'to was doing.

"That is what I will file in my report to King Sh'tam." He nodded sharply at her as he pointed at the far end of the walkway. "There is the guards' lift shaft."

It looked similar enough to an elevator framed by elaborate columns sculpted into the wall. The insignia of the King's Guard was centrally placed on the lift's curved double door.

"Take it," he said. "You will be met by Soi'raa. She will take you to the Akt'aron."

"What about Skarmor and Kuirhan?" Mira asked, stepping forward.

"Your beasts? You will be reunited with them at the Akt'aron."

As he spoke, he gently directed Mira and Victor toward the lift shaft, which was still a good twenty meters away. Victor seemed to move the plank easily, almost like it weighed a fraction of what Jen thought it would.

Kl'to held Jen back only for a second. "The true king will rise." He then winked and said, "Make it look good."

Jen turned toward her uncle and friend. "I'll meet you at the lift. *Go.*"

Mira helped Victor push Charles toward the lift shaft as Jen looked back at Kl'to, who had turned his back toward her.

"Thank you," she whispered.

Not waiting for a reply, she touched the nape of his neck, causing him to faint with a potent telemancy spell. She tried softening his fall, but the commander was almost a foot taller than her and his armor made him feel like he weighed three hundred pounds, making the landing rough; but Jen was able to support his head before taking off his headband and throwing it at the closest wall. She heard it shatter as she scorched his backplate with a dousing of flame, careful to not burn his skin.

Back at the entrance, the bright sparks had made their way through the majority of the melted lock; Jen's time was running out. Quickly, but in control, she channeled terramancy and split her disc in two. Moving on, she picked up a second one and drove it well into the ground next to Kl'to, the impact splintering the marble floor with hairline cracks before she sprinted toward Victor and Mira, tensely waiting at the lift.

Mira was motioning at Jen to hurry when the doors of the lift parted to reveal half a dozen guards with drawn blasters and lowered helmet visors. Victor pushed Charles off to the side, sending the plank gliding down the last row of cells before hiding behind the closest column. Mira did the same on her side as Jen skidded to a stop, still too far away to reach either of them. Without a second thought, Jen dove between the two closest rows of cells to the left, tucking into a shoulder roll. Stopping in a crouch, she whipped her head back toward the walkway and froze.

Exactly where she had been seconds before stood . . . herself.

Jen massaged her eyes, making sure they weren't playing any tricks on her. That was when she noticed the telemancy charm on her totem bracelet was glowing and floating above her wrist.

She watched as her copy yelled, "Hey!" and dashed back toward the dungeon's main entrance. A clamor of boots could be heard as the entire squadron of guards exited the lift and chased after Jen's retreating decoy. Silently thanking her nexus's instincts, Jen slinked back toward the walkway and hazarded a glance. The guards were fully focused on the other Jen, lining up in a defensive formation as she fell into a fighting stance, her eyes shimmering with energy.

Victor had already retrieved Charles and was in the empty lift alongside Mira, who held the doors open for Jen. Once she'd darted inside, the doors thankfully began to slide shut almost immediately. Just then, an explosion blew in the dungeon's entrance door, letting more guards pour in and flank Jen's decoy from the other side.

Gasping for breath, Jen hoped that her telemancy spell would distract the guards long enough so they could safely make it to the Akt'aron.

"That was close," Mira said, leaning on the lift's curved, chrome-plated interior wall. Strips of blue light streamed down the gaps in the plates, showing their rapid ascent toward the level on which Soi'raa, Kl'to's contact, would be waiting.

"Too close," Jen breathed, fighting to get her breathing regulated as she checked on her father. His outward appearance hadn't changed for the worse or better: his skin was still ashen, and his eyes were not roaming under his eyelids. Holding her breath, Jen checked for a pulse, and when she found one—faint though it was, showing itself once every ten seconds or so—she allowed herself to breathe once again.

Victor placed a hand on her shoulder and said proudly, "That was some quick thinking back there, Jenny."

Jen smiled wanly at him, removing her hand from her father's chest. "What I did was as much instinct as it was luck, like when I used the moltic spell above the Amaranthine Forest."

Victor raised his eyebrows, that same memory flashing in his eyes. "Regardless, that was very impressive."

"You sure fooled those guards," Mira said.

"Let's hope they stay that way long enough to get out of here," Jen agreed, reaching for her friend's hand. Grinning, Mira gladly took it. Jen looked down at her father and said, "He's getting worse. I don't think all this moving around is doing him any favors."

With worry in her eyes, she looked at Victor. Her uncle's face was forlorn as he too gazed upon Charles. Jen slid her hand into Victor's, interlocking their fingers. He let out a ragged breath that carried with it a deep worry.

Suddenly, Jen felt a slight decrease in the lift's speed. "I think we're slowing."

Mira pushed off the wall, a hand going for her whip. Victor let go of Jen's hand, rolling out his neck and flexing his fingers, ready for anything. And Jen put herself between the lift's doors and her father, hoping beyond hope that when the lift stopped, there'd stand a friend and not a garrison of more guards ready to foil their escape.

The lift came to a smooth stop and Jen's heart skipped a beat in anticipation as the doors retracted and someone rushed inside . . .

"Omnimancer Jennifer, I am here to take you to the Arbor Atlanti."

Jen sighed, releasing her hold on her nexus, Mira and Victor clearly just as relieved to see Soi'raa. Kl'to's second-in-command stepped over to the lift's controls and touched her bracer to the glossy console. Once its frame turned from carmine to chartreuse she deftly tapped on it, the pressure from her fingertips lighting the screen in white blips. A second later, the lift's doors closed.

Jen felt the lift go . . . back down? Her cheeks flushed; she shot a worried look at Victor as she stepped next to Soi'raa. "Where are we going?"

"To the Akt'aron by way of a defunct tunnel once used by the King's Guard." Soi'raa didn't spare Jen a look; she remained focused on the symbols scrolling over her bracer as she spoke. "Before the crystal was gifted to us by the gods, other kingdoms had attempted to invade. This tunnel was a part of an underground network created to mobilize Atlantis's soldiers efficiently, allowing them quick passage to any ring of the city or station on the outer walls. Queen Pt'ara decommissioned it years ago, confident the Akt'aron's crystal would keep Atlantis safe forever."

The lift paused before sliding horizontally, picking up speed once again. Soi'raa wore a blank expression, but Jen could see in her eyes how dejected she was—jaded, even—now that she knew just how wrong the late Queen had been.

"Won't the Guard know where the lift took us?" Victor asked, thumbs resting in his belt loops.

Soi'raa looked Victor in the eye and raised her bracer, pointing at the highlighted symbols, then at the lift's console, which flashed the same exact symbols. "I overrode the controls. The console log will not reflect this stop."

Victor shrugged, apparently satisfied with this.

The doors retracted, and a strong scent of stagnant mildew and stale air assaulted Jen's olfactory senses. Pitch black seemed to seep into the lift. The entire front coverings of Soi'raa's bracers lit up, eating through the thick darkness.

"Take the plank or I will," she said, unfazed by the smell, and she waited as Jen grabbed the edge closest to her father's head. Soi'raa nodded and strode into the tunnel, lighting the way.

"I'll take the rear," Victor said.

"Thanks, Vic," Jen said, pushing Charles out into the tunnel with Mira right behind.

They quickly caught up with Soi'raa, her bracers illuminating the way as they forged deeper into the abandoned tunnel. A restless eeriness fell over Jen as she pushed the stone plank in Soi'raa's wake. The only things that were heard were grainy footfalls and echoed breathing as she mentally mapped their possible current location relative to the city above. Atlantis had four concentric rings that were separated by water, three of those being habitable. The Akt'aron was at the epicenter of the entire kingdom, and the royal palace was housed in the southern part of the next ring. Considering the purpose of the tunnel they trudged through, they should reach the Akt'aron in relatively short order.

Their Atlantean guide brought them to four paths that forked from the current tunnel that they were in, one presumably for each quadrant of the city. Soi'raa didn't slow; she took the second prong from the left, one that deviated the least from the main tunnel's direction. The thick blanket of stale air and damp vegetation was even more prevalent in this part of the tunnel. They were only a few paces in when the sound of flowing water made Jen look toward the tunnel's arched ceiling.

"We are now passing under the waterway separating the Royal Ring and the Center of Worship," Soi'raa said, almost like she had heard Jen's thoughts.

The rush of water became louder the farther in they walked, accompanied by the rhythmic *plop* of lonely water droplets. And just as quickly as the sound had arisen, it weakened and eventually faded back into the Stygian darkness. Jen and Mira exchanged looks that were a mixture of awe and caution—they were now counted among the few people to see Atlantis like this, which would have been so much cooler if they weren't technically fugitives at this point, with the King and his loyal guards after them.

A few minutes passed. Jen, who'd been thinking about everything from her father's condition to where Genevieve could possibly be, squinted in the thick darkness. She wondered if her eyes were playing tricks on her or if she was actually seeing, probably fifty meters ahead, floating strands of shimmering light.

"We're almost there," Soi'raa announced, again as if she'd read Jen's mind.

It didn't take long for Jen to realize that those strands of light were the colorful veins of the Arbor Atlanti, the tree that Jen and Charles had infused with omnimancy so that it held the power to raise Atlantis into the sky.

CAW-CAWW!

A familiar eagle's cry perked Jen's ears and sent jolts of relief through her heart.

Skarmor!

It took every ounce of her being to not run Soi'raa over with Charles's plank. Due to the layout of the subterranean tunnel system, the thick, gnarled roots of the Arbor Atlanti blocked a little more than half of the tunnel, so Jen couldn't yet see the griffin.

The sight of this part of the Arbor Atlanti brought an efflux of memories to the front of Jen's mind; a tear welled along her lower eyelid from reliving those tense moments when the tree had sprouted from the Akt'aron's floor, guided by Dimitri, the leshy sent by Merlin to protect her. Jen thought she had lost him deep underneath the Antarctic ice after they'd retrieved the Terra- and AstroCrystal, but he had never truly left her side, his powers far greater than she would have ever imagined. The indebtedness she felt toward Dimitri was incalculable.

The stunning hues of blue and green swirled beautifully together, traveling up the roots and into the trunk and branches of the Arbor Atlanti far above the tunnel. Its own self-sustaining power reservoir.

By the time they'd closed the distance to less than five meters, Skarmor's cry echoed throughout the tunnel once again, leaving no doubt in Jen's mind that he could sense that she and Victor were close by. She wiped the tears from her eyes just in time to see her trusty griffin emerge from the blanketed darkness of the tunnel. An Atlantean soldier whom Jen had never seen before followed closely in his wake.

Jen called out the griffin's name and he answered with excited stomps, his wings fluttering in short bursts as he shook his feathered head in joy. He waited for Soi'raa to walk around him and the large roots before he cautiously stepped over some of the smaller offshoots of the roots that spread along the floor, eager to reunite with Jen.

"You better greet him now, or he'll just get more excited." Jen didn't realize Victor had caught up to her.

"Thanks, Vic," she said, sliding around the plank's corner and bounding over to Skarmor. She wrapped her arms around his strong neck and he placed his forehead on hers, thumping his lion tail on the hard-packed tunnel floor. Her heart melted from his soft, sweet coos and piping notes. "Hey, there, Skar." Jen scratched the front side of his neck affectionately before he opened his beak fully and, lifting his tongue, let the TeleCrystal fall into her hands.

"I knew I could count on you," Jen said with a smile. She unzipped her right cargo pocket and was about to slide the TeleCrystal inside when it suddenly emitted a soft, prismatic glow. She turned it in her hands just as the Arbor Alanti's veins began to match the TeleCrystal's colors.

Enraptured, Jen slowly stepped toward the massive roots. She touched its rough, soiled ridges and was immediately overcome with emotion. Her lower lip quivered; she didn't bother trying to stop it.

"Hey, Dimitri," she whispered when she could speak.

The soft, pastel rainbow colors seemed to speed up, almost as if her leshy friend was trying to communicate with her.

"It's me. Jen. I miss you . . . I—"

She stopped, noticing her hand that held the TeleCrystal: it

175

was not hers. The hand she saw was mottled gray-brown, cracked like old tree bark. Patches of moss grew around her knuckles and down to her wrist.

Very reminiscent of Dimitri's . . .

Instinctively, Jen let go of the crystal and let it roll down a large root and shoot past Skarmor, clattering farther into the tunnel where more shadows silently waited. She'd brought her affected hand to her chest as she watched it leave her sight, and when she gathered enough courage to look at her hand again, it had returned to its normal appearance. She ran the fingers of her other hand over her smooth skin, knuckles, and bare palm: there was nothing to indicate that her hand was anything other than her own.

She began looking for the TeleCrystal but didn't have to search long; an ebony hand appeared from out of the shadows and offered her the TeleCrystal. Following the hand came the accompanying arm and then the awaiting eyes of the Prince of Atlantis, presumed dead yet very much alive.

"M'balo!" Jen gasped, rushing toward him as her heart swelled with unbridled joy.

The glow from the Arbor Atlanti made his eyes twinkle before they went wide as she stumbled into his arms. She felt his muscles grow taut as he wrapped his arms around her in surprise, his sun-kissed musk reminding Jen of how badly she had missed his smell.

M'balo sucked in a sharp gasp of air as together they fell to the ground in a huff. Jen lifted her head and blew a strand of hair away from her face as she looked into M'balo's eyes. She could swim in those azure pools for eternity. Her chest heaving and adrenaline quickly dying, embarrassment soon came when she realized M'balo was frozen in disbelief. Hastily rolling off of him, Jen profusely apologized. M'balo groaned as he propped himself up on one elbow.

"I am so, so, *so* sorry," she said again as she helped him back to his feet.

M'balo tossed the TeleCrystal into his other hand, rotating his arm with care. "It is okay, Jennifer." He locked eyes with her. "Your embrace, no matter how rough, is worth the discomfort."

Jen tucked some curls behind an ear, hoping it was still dark enough to hide the rouge on her cheeks as she took the offered TeleCrystal. She couldn't break his gaze. "Thank y—"

Her breath was stolen when he stepped closer and hugged her, this embrace much softer than the last. She wrapped her arms around him and rested her head on his collarbone.

Just cresting over six feet, M'balo had a youthful, athletic build: lanky and spry but strong. Instead of wearing his traditional royal garb befitting of an Atlantean prince, he was sporting a slimmer, tighter top and pants, though he still wore his earring and clipped on his belt was his dagger—the same one he had once entrusted Jen with to prove that he was her ally.

"I am so relieved that you are safe and in good health," he said into her ear.

Maybe it was a result of her frayed nerves or the relief she felt after seeing M'balo alive with her own eyes, but Jen realized just how soothing the prince's voice was. Smiling, she pulled away and looked up at him.

"What brings you back to Atlantis?"

Jen's smile faltered as reality came crashing back down on her. Before she could respond, Soi'raa returned, the swaying lights of her bracers rolling over the tree's roots and the curved walls of the tunnel. "No signs of tampering with our trip wire at this end of the tunnel," she said. She dimmed her bracers' lights now that there was more visibility due to the magical roots.

Skarmor stepped closer to Jen and brushed his head and neck on her shoulder, which gave her further comfort. Behind Soi'raa came Kuirhan, eager to see what was happening past the roots on the other side of the tunnel. He strode toward Victor, softly snuffing and neighing in greeting.

The skin around M'balo's eyes tightened, but his gaze remained locked on her face. His head moved slightly in the direction of Soi'raa, addressing her: "Good. They're not onto us yet, but let's not overstay our welcome." He looked over Jen's shoulder at the rest of her group and noticed the plank and its passenger. "Your father . . . is he all right?"

"No . . ." Jen sighed, dreading even bringing up the question she'd been wanting to ask him since she escaped Camelore. "It's a long story, but basically my father's under a deep spell . . ."

Just spit it out!

"We're wondering if there's anything you can do to help him."

M'balo squeezed her arm sympathetically, his eyes roaming Charles's supine form. "Once we get back to Base, I'll have our medic see if he can do anything." He then looked at Jen. "Follow me."

* * *

Once they'd safely reached a large, recently excavated burrow about fifty meters below the defunct tunnel, M'balo offered Jen an open spot in a blanketed seating area before leaving to brief his commanders and get some rations. Next to Mira, she anxiously awaited Charles's diagnosis as one of the few triage medics inspected him. Victor stood a few steps away, contemplative, arms crossed and fingers stroking his beard. He, too, intently watched the preliminary tests that were being run on his brother-in-law, who remained still under powerfully bright lights that oversaturated his body in stark white light.

Skarmor and Kuirhan remained in the tunnel above with Soi'raa, their size too large for the shaft that led down and opened up into this burrow that M'balo had claimed as his base. Solely illuminated by the effervescent veins of the Arbor Atlanti's roots, the burrow was a result of a cave-in as the roots had quickly wormed through the desert crust below Atlantis. Several strands had split off from the main root as it had grown, which had now become the structure of M'balo's base, almost like the roots were the fingers of a giant's hand, clutching the burrow in its palm. It looked to comfortably hold over one hundred Atlanteans, those who fervently believed that M'balo was the true King of Atlantis.

Jen turned toward her friend after she heard Mira scoot closer and smiled weakly. No words were exchanged, but the sentiment was clear: don't give up. Jen needed that reminder now more than ever when doubt could easily cause her to falter. She looked back in the medic's direction: He was standing with his back toward her but looked to be mixing some sort of concoction. His medical bag was set on a corner of the plank, open to reveal an unrolled section that held gleaming instruments as he continued to work in solitary. Jen wanted nothing more than to be next to her father and to hold his hand, to have the medic explain what he was doing in great detail. But she knew she needed to resist the urge; she had to trust the medic to do his job, and she would only be a distraction.

But it was difficult . . . forced to sit idly by, waiting, clutching to this notion of hope—the same notion that had convinced her to come to Atlantis in an attempt to prolong her father's life, while Genevieve, the only omnimancer strong enough to break the spell under which he had fallen, had vanished. Yawning, Jen let her eyelids droop closed and wrapped her arms around her knees. She fell into her nexus, slowly rocking back and forth, hoping to receive the kind of serenity only meditation could offer; but her mind would not let the worry—and, conversely, the hope—go.

Hope was a strange but intriguing feeling—it could either be a great strength or a crippling weakness, decided by whether or not one acted upon it. Even still, action did not always guarantee success, but the possibility was enough to convince Jen to try anything and everything possible.

She would rather try and fail than not try at all and wonder what-if.

That was why she needed to meditate: so she could detach from her emotions and gain enlightenment during this troubling, stressful time.

"I apologize for keeping you waiting." M'balo's soothing voice knocked against the barrier of Jen's nexus, bringing her back into the physical world. She opened her eyes to see him holding out a cup. "You need to hydrate."

Jen uncrossed her arms, let her knees fall to the ground, and took the offered cup. Mira's cup was already empty by the time Jen started drinking, and once the water hit her lips her body was reminded of just how thirsty she was. Five gulps later and her cup was next to Mira's on the blanket.

"Thank you," Jen said.

He sat down beside her. "We all have to look out for one another," M'balo said as he looked around at his people.

Jen slid an inch closer to him and caught Victor looking at her out of the corner of his eye. One side of his mouth perked up before he went back to watching the medic. Jen blushed and quietly cleared her throat. "How many are down here?"

"Our ranks are at one hundred ten strong. Paltry, compared to my brother's numbers, but what we lack in size, we make up for in spirit." He brought a hand down to his side and started massaging his left oblique, covered by a bandage.

Jen looked at his injury with guilt. "I'm sorry we brought such destruction to your city." Her fingers ran over the indentations of the TeleCrystal in her pocket.

M'balo took a few seconds to respond. "If you ask me, it was destined to happen. It was foolish to think that our self-imposed isolation would last forever."

"I'm glad you made it through." Jen brought her eyes up to his. He was already looking at her, his gaze unwavering and sure.

"Me too," he said back. "Though I would be in much better shape if it weren't for my brother."

Jen cocked her head in confusion. "You weren't hurt by us raising Atlantis?"

"No, Jennifer," he said, his tone serious and melancholy. "Sh'tam arrived at the gate at which I was stationed and, in the turmoil, opened fire. Bo'atu and I were the only survivors out of twenty stationed guards." He gestured at a young man across the way sitting in a loose circle of people. He rose with effort, and Jen noticed he was missing his left arm, a fresh bandage covering the shoulder.

M'balo continued, "Sh'tam was quick to report my death as a

tragedy, blaming you and your father's actions. He eagerly took the crown while Bo'atu brought me to Kl'to."

"M'balo, I . . ." Jen shook her head, at a loss for words. She felt shame for ever believing a single hollow word uttered by Sh'tam.

"My brother ensured that all witnesses of his attack were loyalists. He doesn't know I am alive and the leader of this rebellion." He took a breath, his eyes shining with unshed tears as they roamed the burrow's dark ceiling. "I was raised to believe that blood was everything. I never could have imagined that my brother would value power and control over family." He closed his eyes.

Jen wouldn't begin to pretend that she knew any part of Atlantis's history, but outside of the bubble they'd placed themselves in, Earth's history had been rife with conflict within countless ruling families all over the world and during every era. If anything, power-hungry family members seemed to be the most dangerous thing for a ruler.

A pensive silence fell over the small group. M'balo kept his eyes shut. Jen looked back toward her father, though her thoughts still resided on M'balo. Her heart ached for what he must be going through; how his brother could betray him so decidedly. She wanted to say something . . . *anything* . . . but she couldn't seem to find the right words. Instead, she moved her hand, imperceptibly at first, but as more courage filled her up, she slid it closer to M'balo's own hand. Just before her fingertips could brush his knuckles, she heard her uncle.

"Jenny," he said, just loudly enough to catch her attention.

Jen flinched and quickly withdrew her hand just as M'balo's eyes fluttered open. She looked at Mira so as not to seem like she'd been focused on him. "I'll be right back," Jen said to her friend. She turned to her other side and repeated this to M'balo, who nodded his understanding but still seemed to show a sense of shaken betrayal. Wishing she could do more to better his spirits, Jen walked up to Victor.

"Hey," she said, curious why he'd called her over but hesitant to get her hopes up about Charles.

"My most heartfelt apologies for taking you away from M'ba-lo," he said, his fingers still supporting the base of his bearded chin.

Jen felt a sudden prick of embarrassment. She took her eyes off Victor and said, a little too quickly, "There's nothing to be sorry about. We were just sitting by each other."

When she brought her eyes back up to her uncle, he remained still as he scanned her shifting eyes. "Okay, okay," he said, then graciously changed the subject: "Look . . ." He cupped her shoulders in his hands, facing her directly. "When the medic finishes his examination, I want to be sure that you're ready for whatever he'll tell us. Good or bad."

Jen clenched her jaw as she let Victor's words sink in. "Yeah . . ." She nodded. "To be honest, I'm kind of not allowing myself to go there until it happens."

Victor pursed his lips in a tight grimace. "If your thoughts are anything like mine, then they have a habit of running away with your sanity whenever you are stressed." Jen nodded and relaxed slightly as he rubbed her arm. It was hard for her to imagine Victor panicking, but the thought was strangely reassuring. "But we have to be prepared for either outcome." He brushed a smear of dirt from her bare shoulder before letting her go.

Jen spared a glance over at her father's face before the medic blocked her view. "You're right. No matter what happens." She forced her dry eyes to blink and smiled wanly. "But it's tough not to focus on that silver lining . . ." She felt a rush of emotion welling up inside and looked down at her hands. Jen didn't know if it was her mind playing tricks on her, but her right hand felt sore. Flexing it a few times, she thought of that weird instance by the roots of the Arbor Atlanti when the hand holding the Tele-Crystal morphed into Dimitri's.

"Everything okay?" Victor said.

Her uncle always seemed to have a read on her. Jen took in a breath, then said, "This strange thing happened to me before we came down here . . ." She found his eyes once again. "I was holding the TeleCrystal, and as I got closer to the Arbor Atlanti, my hand . . ." She absent-mindedly flexed it again, then crossed her arms and lightly scoffed. "I was probably just imagining things."

"Jen, what's going on?" Victor was not giving up easily.

Biting her lip nervously, Jen looked all around his face, hoping that what she'd experienced wasn't a symptom of something greater . . . and far worse. After a few seconds, she drew up some extra courage and said, "My hand looked . . . *different*."

Victor's eyebrows moved closer together in concern.

"Like it wasn't mine at all. It looked more like Dimitri's," she finished, thinking of the leshy's arboreal appearance and bark-like skin.

Victor's eyes relaxed a touch and he raised his chin, inhaling. "This is the only time it's happened to you?"

Jen nodded. "First time. Hopefully the last."

Victor rested his chin on a forefinger knuckle and stroked his beard with his thumb. "I think this is another instance of your nexus's abilities preceding your knowledge of the Mancy planes."

"Should I be worried?" Jen needed to know. She realized she was nearly on her toes.

He shook his head and smiled softly. "No, not at all. I'm surprised you're already able to access the proxitelemancic spell, even if you did it solely by accident."

"Proxi*tele*mancic?"

He nodded. "It's the telemancy version of the proxiomnimancic spell." He looked at Charles across the way. "The one used on your father. It occurs when a telemancer has attained the highest level of connection to the telemancy plane. Those who reach this hallowed level have the special ability to conjure the most powerful spell from their respective plane. But it doesn't come without its dangers, which is why the Sorcery Guild has forbidden these spells."

Jen wasn't quite sure what to say. She was again humbled by how intricately complex each Mancy plane was.

Finally, she spoke: "So the proxitelemancic spell makes me . . . shapeshift?"

"Basically," Victor said. "It alters every part of you, down to your molecular structure. That's why your hand is sore. Your body is reacting to the change, however brief." He pointed to the TeleCrystal. "Holding the TeleCrystal only strengthens that connection."

Jen brought her right hand to eye level and worked her fingers and wrist. Her totem bracelet clinked as it dropped toward the middle of her forearm. Blinking in amazement, she asked, "What are the other proximancic spells?"

Victor squared his shoulders to her and his voice took a serious tone. "Jen, there's a reason why these spells are forbidden. They're too potent and volatile. The slightest error in the ritual will result in death. Do I make myself clear?"

Jen nodded, her excitement checked by the grave reality of what these spells actually meant.

Victor looked to be weighing the decision to tell her more, but finally he relented. "You've already experienced a glimpse of the proxitelemancic spell and, considering Cindergray's true age, you've seen what the proxichronomancic spell can do."

"Immortality . . ." Jen breathed as the realization dawned on her.

"Well, close enough anyway. That spell stagnates aging, it doesn't stop it entirely. I can guarantee you Cindergray looked a lot younger when he mastered that spell and used it on himself. The proxichronomancic spell can also be reversed to accelerate aging."

"Unreal . . ."

Victor continued, interlocking his fingers in illustration as he said, "The proxianimancic spell gives animancers the chance to absorb another being's life force, or"—he pulled his fingers apart —"give their own energy away. The proxiastromancic spell, if done correctly, can tear open a new dimensional rift, essentially changing the space-time continuum."

Jen gasped. "Don't tell me there was an astromancer who tried?"

"One. Way before my time. He settled on Earth on a little island called Bermuda."

Jen couldn't believe it. *The Bermuda Triangle?*

"His attempt went terribly awry, managing to scratch a dimensional wall. I can't count how many innocent people have been lost by the chance he took." Victor closed his eyes and shook his head before going on. "And, lastly, the proxiterramancic spell. That one . . ." He trailed off, suddenly alerted to movement from the triage area.

Jen turned ninety degrees to look at the medic directly, her heart rate doubling in seconds as she waited for him to speak.

"I have never before seen an ailment quite like this one," he began.

And, to Jen's everlasting dismay, he then proceeded to tell her and Victor that every approach he had taken had come up short against this mystery spell. He couldn't even identify the root cause in order to create an antidote.

Every word felt like a needle stabbing her in a thousand different places simultaneously. She felt cold all of a sudden as tingles danced across her arms and back. The medic's voice trailed off as Jen's thoughts ran rampant. Echoed muffles only remained by the time Jen dove into her nexus. She quickly searched the void until she found the driftless aura that was her father. She could identify bits and pieces of him, but she could tell that he was getting weaker . . . much weaker. He didn't have long and should not be moved—and Jen couldn't wait any longer. Bleakness seeped into her hope when she sensed chronomancy energy still bleeding profusely from the entire spell—the direct culprit for Charles's constant decreasing heart rate.

Genevieve needed to be found.

Now.

Just as her nexus was agitated, her breathing was fast and shallow as her senses brought her back to Victor's side. Nothing else the medic could say would ease her mind or help her father, so without so much as a wave, Jen darted toward the shaft that led back to the tunnel where Skarmor waited. She blew past

M'balo before he could reach her and heard Victor call out for Mira. Jen weaved around several shocked Atlanteans, only to find her friend standing in the way of the shaft's ladder.

"Mira, we need to start looking for Genevieve," Jen said as she tried to side-step around her.

Her friend slid in her way again, holding out her hands. "I know, but just . . . wait." Her eyes flicked behind Jen, then focused back on her. Her next word was spoken softly, but it seemed to fill the entire burrow. "Please."

Jen halted and let out a tight breath, crossing her arms. Quick footfalls from behind brought Victor and M'balo into view.

"Jenny—" Victor began.

"Vic, there's nothing they can do for Charles here. I—"

"I know, Jen," Victor cut her off. His hands were out and fingers spread in front of him, telling her to calm down without saying the words. "I agree with you, but we need to be smart about this. Remember that Gavin, Rez, and Hephalon are waiting for us at my cottage."

Immediately, some of the weight on her shoulders lifted. She'd thought she'd have to plead her case to Victor and hope that he could be convinced to leave. "Oh . . ." The rebuttal she'd had ready to dish out died on her tongue, now completely useless. Looking at M'balo, she took in a breath. "M'balo, thank you for trying. I meant no disrespect."

M'balo grimaced. "There was no disrespect in your tone, do not worry. I am sorry our medical practices could not help your father."

Jen blinked away tears, nodding in agreement. "It's okay. It was a long shot, but we needed to know for sure." She looked back at Victor and Mira. "How'd you guys want to go about this?"

Victor took in a steady breath through his nose, propping his fists on his hips and looking into the dark shaft above. "I'll take Kuirhan to my cottage and update the others. Jen, Mira, you two should take Skarmor and head straight for Watercress. Once I've rounded them all up we'll meet you there."

Considering how dire the circumstances were, Jen was still able to feel a slight hint of ease with Victor's plan; thankfully, all she'd wanted to hear from him was that they could leave this place. She peered between Victor and M'balo, resting her eyes on Charles. The lights the medic had shone on him had since been extinguished and rolled away. He blended into the triage area well, next to injured Atlanteans who were either being worked on by other medics or resting in their narrow cots.

Jen couldn't take her eyes off her father. "I like that plan. Mira and I will go with you to Azumar, then break off toward Watercress to see if Cindergray is holed up there with Genevieve."

"But be careful. We can't forget about Malcolm. I know him well enough to know that he holds grudges. He could be snooping around there," Victor said.

"Right." Jen focused on M'balo's steady, piercing, azure eyes. "I'm sorry we have to leave so soon."

"Don't be." His smile was warm and understanding. "Find the person who can help save your father." He looked behind him briefly before turning back toward her. "He should stay here with us while you are away. This is the safest place for him at the moment."

"Moving him more will only cause more damage," Jen agreed. Her emotions overtaking her, she grabbed his hand. "M'balo, thank you so very much." She didn't let go.

And neither did the prince of Atlantis.

He squeezed her hand and said, "Go. Your destiny is out there. Mine is to reclaim my kingdom."

Jen nodded, fighting back tears. Her appreciation for the person standing across from her was nothing short of limitless. She let go and let out a quick breath. She couldn't help but smile. Clearing her throat, she said, "Now that the current king is out for our heads . . ." She took out the TeleCrystal to show M'balo. "We'll return a lot stealthier."

M'balo looked at her with mouth slightly open and raised his eyebrows.

Jen chuckled. "I can have the TeleCrystal turn us temporarily invisible."

"Fascinating," he whispered in understanding. "Provided nothing major changes in this civil war, come to the Akt'aron. My people will alert me and I'll meet you there," he said, pointing upward.

"May your nexus protect you," Jen said.

"And yours as well," he replied, holding up a hand in goodbye.

Smiling wider now, Jen climbed the ladder and, in a few minutes, reunited with her griffin. It was well into the night by the time Soi'raa led them up into the central chamber of the Akt'aron, and after one last reminder of their plan, Jen imbued the TeleCrystal with her own telemancy powers, and in seconds everyone was invisible, reminiscent of their escape from Malcolm on Camelore.

Now with no need to worry about being seen, Skarmor and Kuirhan carried Jen and the others past Atlantis's northern gate, and when she was confident that they were well out of eyeshot, she removed the invisibility spell and let Skarmor take them to Azumar's closest portal.

As she waited to arrive at Watercress Castle, Jen sent a question to Victor over their mind meld: *You never got around to explaining the proxiterramancic spell.*

CHAPTER NINETEEN

Malcolm sat crosswise in a hammock across from the one that held the bound, sleeping form of Madame Diaema. After Lord Ferox gave the order to leave him, Malcolm had gone to the closest hut that wasn't completely destroyed—and with his streak of rotten luck, it turned out to be Jen's.

It was well past dusk now, and the soft, yellow light of a desk lamp illuminated the area around his hammock, Jen's journal splayed open next to him on the page with her last entry. It detailed her excitement for the Sesquimillennial Jubilee, the ceremony at Watercress Castle which became the battleground for the worst sorcery battle (led by him and the late Lord Draconex) since Ferox's Dark Purge exactly fifteen hundred years in the past.

Idly rocking the hammock back and forth with his legs, Malcolm debated forcing Diaema awake just so he could return to Ferox with her and find out what he was doing and why he needed to be alone to do it. But truthfully, this gave him the needed time to think. How could he effectively use Diaema to get to Jen (since they were both clearly on the same side)? Still amazed that Diaema could wield telemancy, Malcolm also couldn't wait to figure out who Diaema truly was and why she had defected to the League of Light.

Madame Diaema stirred, and he focused intently on her,

189

stilling his hammock. This whole time his totem ring had been primed, just in case Diaema was strong enough to break out of her restraints immediately after waking up. But she didn't; she didn't even turn back into an albino bat and flit out the slightly parted windowpanes.

"What happened to your fearsome armor?" she asked sarcastically, still not bothering to fight against her restraints.

Malcolm ignored the question. "Since when were you a telemancer?"

Diaema scoffed. She made no attempt to answer him.

Malcolm snickered and looked at the base of the armoire where his battle-scarred chest plate, shoulder pads, and gauntlets lay. "It was getting uncomfortable." He looked at her face more closely. It was pale and flawless aside from a minor cut above her right cheekbone and a bruised ring around her neck from Ferox's grip. She acted like her injuries didn't bother her. Her eyebrows were furrowed in deep concentration, and Malcolm could guess what she was trying to do. "It's no use," he interrupted her focus. "Not long after you revealed your powers, Lord Ferox placed a barrier spell around this entire floating island. No incoming or outgoing telepathic messages." He shrugged and puffed out his lower lip in a mock-pout.

His guess was right. Almost immediately, Diaema's facial muscles relaxed and she opened her eyes to look straight at him. After several seconds made it clear that Diaema would not answer his question, Malcolm tossed Jen's journal onto the nightstand, its momentum abruptly stopped by the base of the desk lamp, and quickly stood.

"All right." He raised a closed fist, his totem ring coming alive as he funneled his terramancy powers from his nexus to the inlaid ruby in the center of his ring. "Lord Ferox is expecting us, so if you're not going to answer my question, we'll go now."

All Diaema did was raise an eyebrow.

Malcolm clenched his jaw and raised his fist a little higher. Diaema's restraints glowed and lifted her hands and feet from the hammock until she was suspended a few feet above the ground.

"Don't make me ask again," he said tersely. "I could just as easily have let him kill you, traitor."

Diaema bared her thin, sharp fangs as she hung there, immobilized by the ultra-dense earthen shackles. Malcolm stared right back at her, waiting.

Finally, she spoke: "If I'm a traitor, why would you ever save me?"

"Because Draconex *would've* killed you!" Malcolm yelled. Even he didn't expect such an emotional outburst to that question. He swallowed hard, noticing his arm was shaking. "And I want that bastard to roll in his grave."

Diaema's eyes narrowed to slits as she surveyed him. "And now you follow a new master."

Malcolm's heavy breathing distracted him from his own flurry of thoughts. He couldn't help but remember his conversation with Diaema when he sat on the Throne of Dragons in Draconex's lair, plotting his then master's downfall.

And Diaema was the one who had given him that nudge.

Malcolm's eyes refocused as he came out of his reverie. "My vision lines up with Lord Ferox's."

"Until it changes . . ." Diaema said cryptically.

Now it was Malcolm's turn to slit his eyes. *What is she trying to get at?*

"The only thing that will change is who each and every realm will bow down to," he said gruffly before he powered down his ring, the invisible hold on Diaema's shackles now gone. She fell the short distance to the ground with a choked grunt.

"Whether you like it or not, I saved your life." Malcolm took two steps closer to Diaema. "*You're*"—he pointed a finger at her —"indebted"—he then jabbed a thumb at his chest—"to *me*."

Diaema sat up after a few ragged breaths and looked down at her shackled hands. She didn't have to say it for Malcolm to know that she agreed with his statement, but she was a lot more conniving than he had initially thought.

And he would not be fooled again.

Malcolm had to ensure Diaema's temporary loyalty, and he

almost laughed when a brilliant idea popped into his head. He crouched on the balls of his feet so their eyes were on the same level, and he waited patiently for her to meet his gaze.

"I am *not* Draconex," he said slowly, a phantom itch traveling across the vertical scar on the left side of his face (a scar he'd shared with Draconex). "So I'm going to make you a deal. And you're gonna take it."

A few minutes later, Malcolm was making his way back to Lord Ferox with Madame Diaema matching his stride. His experiences as a Dark Watcher had made him jaded to say the least, and he had been burned one too many times when he let his hubris and inflated confidence lead his emotions, but this time felt different.

He felt like things were finally going his way.

* * *

Jocelyn was surprised at how easily she was able to slip back into the persona of Madame Diaema; ever since her moment with Charles in that cave back on Azumar, and her reunion with her daughter, she thought it had melted away to reveal her true self. Diaema would always be a part of her, she surmised. She couldn't deny that it felt extremely comfortable and, as the infected Arbor Sacré filled more and more of her vision, essential for survival.

Jocelyn was still reeling from the knowledge that Lord Ferox had survived, somehow finding his way into Draconex's body, and was now determined to find her husband or daughter, two of the only omnimancers left across all the realms, to complete his quest for realm domination.

As much as she wanted to keep her time as the vampire warrior in the past, Jocelyn knew she needed Diaema's training and expertise to survive. Her brother and daughter stood a much better chance if she was able to return with this information.

Looking away from the pulsating purple canopy of the Arbor Sacré and off into the star-swept midnight sky, Jocelyn let her thoughts float to her husband. She hoped that Jen and Victor had gotten him to Atlantis in time and that there was something their physicians could do to stabilize him, if not fully cure him. She had just been given a second chance at a life with him, and she'd do anything to keep it for good this time.

She swiped away a tear before Malcolm could notice and reminded herself that she needed the ice-cold strength of Diaema, not the ever-present compassion of Jocelyn. She wasn't even sure if she should tell Malcolm who she really was, but after a few seconds of mulling that over, she realized he could use that information against her. She refused to let anything else be used against her; she already was indebted to Malcolm. She loathed that to her core, but he did save her life. And he was right: if it had been Draconex, he would not have spared her life, even with his perverse infatuation with her.

HSSSSSSSS . . .

The bone-vibrating hissing of Ferox's feathered serpent pulled her from her thoughts as she followed Malcolm through the destroyed Pentarena, closer and closer to the man who was responsible for fifteen hundred years of war and death.

Lord Ferox was sitting upright in the throne he'd hewn into the Arbor Sacre's gnarled trunk, eyes closed. She could see the ShadowCrystal firmly set into his upper chest. Next to the right leg of the throne was a wooden bowl holding a swirling liquid that glowed as if radioactive, its bubbles turning blood-red when they broke the surface and popped.

Every step that brought her closer to Ferox, his ophidite would slither farther down the trunk and bare its menacing fangs a bit more. Then Ferox opened his eyes. His monstrous creature was instantly calmed by a simple lift of his hand.

Ferox was the first to speak once Jocelyn and Malcolm stopped five meters from him. "Step closer."

Jocelyn followed Malcolm, but her gaze never left the mysterious bubbling liquid next to Ferox.

"Your names will forever be associated with the rise of Lord Ferox," the man of the same name declared. His smile had disappeared and his countenance turned icy. "Because I've allowed it. Never forget that."

Jocelyn saw Malcolm's shoulders tighten ever so slightly (now that he had discarded his bulky, pompous armor), though he remained still and made no intention to respond.

Ferox reached down to his side and picked up the wooden bowl, extending it to Malcolm.

"Drink."

Malcolm's Adam's apple twitched nervously. He remained motionless.

The skin around Ferox's eyes tightened. "I cannot overstate the importance of what I am about to task you with, so loyalty must be proven." He swayed the bowl like it was a metronome, the liquid sloshing around its edges but never lipping over.

Jocelyn held in a breath, watching Malcolm. When he showed no intention of taking the bowl, Ferox tilted his head slightly as if hearing something from afar. He forced out an exasperated breath before bringing the bowl to his own lips and tipping it back. Teeth slick with a fresh coat of the vibrant-green liquid were bared at Jocelyn and Malcolm as Ferox lowered the bowl to reveal the lower part of his face. He licked his lips and yelled, "I will *not* ask again!"

Malcolm's eyes flashed toward Jocelyn before he reluctantly closed the distance between him and Ferox and took the offered bowl. After one last moment's brief hesitation, he slowly took a sip of the bowl's contents.

Almost immediately, Ferox then demanded: "Now give it to *her*." He flicked an aloof finger in Jocelyn's direction.

Even though her outward appearance didn't seem affected by the unexpected demand, Jocelyn was reeling on the inside. She had absolutely no clue what effects that mystery drink would have on her body and mind, and quickly realized she was way in over her head. She didn't want to lose another twenty years . . .

But what would Diaema do?

Right away, Jocelyn inherently knew that the vampire inside

her wouldn't bat an eye at the request. In fact, she'd finish the rest of the bowl and throw it back at Ferox with spiteful authority.

So that's exactly what Jocelyn did.

Stepping up to Malcolm's side, she snatched the bowl from his hand and, without hesitation, downed the rest of its contents. Flavorless, its tepid temperature and slick, viscous texture induced a slight revulsion that made Jocelyn's throat muscles spasm. Choking down the remaining sip, she wiped her lower lip with her palm and tossed the empty bowl back to Ferox.

He caught it and, with an impressed look, spun the bowl in his hands. "So far you've not made me regret sparing your meager life, vesperite."

"You best refer to me as Madame Diaema or I'll start regretting that I went easy on you during our duel." She crossed her arms and jutted out her chin. Jocelyn hoped she wasn't overdoing it.

Ferox scoffed and tossed the bowl aside. He wasted no more time with snide remarks. "What you drank wasn't lethal . . ." There was a malicious glint in his eye. "Unless you deviate from the orders I'm about to give you."

Nausea immediately gripped Jocelyn's intestines, twisting them so viciously that she did everything in her power to not collapse to her knees and try vomiting up her stomach's contents. *Stay strong.* If she broke character now, she'd be as good as dead— and the information she needed to get to Jen and Victor would die along with her. She felt Malcolm's eyes on her, could feel his fear and shock.

They both had been played like a fiddle and were now Ferox's pawns to control.

Ferox gave a nasally chuckle. "What? Did you really think that a few hours would be enough time for me to trust you both? That I would immediately accept your promises of undying fealty without actual proof?" Ferox *tsk*ed with his tongue.

There was nothing that Jocelyn or Malcolm could say to that; even if they could, Ferox didn't give them any time to respond. "Which is why I will be keeping a watchful eye on you," the dark lord continued. He rested his elbows on his throne's armrests and tented his fingers. "The potion that you just drank is a mixture of two spells. The first one is a coordinate spell, one that tracks your location. Not only will I be privy to your whereabouts at all times, but should you stray from the path outlined by your assigned mission, it will also boil you from the inside. Slowly." His molars made a clacking sound as a devious smirk pulled up the right side of his mouth. "The second is a dormant proxiterramancic spell."

Jocelyn could not believe what she was hearing. She'd heard tales of how insane Ferox had become between his lust for realm domination and the concentrated exposure of the ShadowCrystal, but it was something else entirely to witness it firsthand. How was he able to not only successfully create the forbidden spell of a Mancy plane that he had not been born into, but also to then mollify it into dormancy? She clutched her stomach, unable to comprehend that such a spell coursed through her bloodstream.

"Don't look so worried." Was Jocelyn's façade cracking? She glanced at Malcolm's profile: he looked as shocked as she felt. "You both are merely its carriers, sent to prime each realm for its inevitable destruction in the event that neither of the last remaining omnimancers let me occupy their body."

Lord Ferox stood, strode forward, and began circling Jocelyn and Malcolm. "Curious how I, a telemancer at birth, could ever master that spell, one reserved only for terramancers?" A derisive laugh expelled through his nostrils as he moved behind Jocelyn. "You are now beginning to grasp the extent of my powers."

Lord Ferox suddenly overtook Jocelyn's entire field of vision as if he were the rolling, dark clouds preceding a fierce thunderstorm, bringing her out of her own mind and sending a cold, electric chill down her spine.

Lord Ferox, eyes dancing with starved fierceness, was growing more animated and impassioned, something to which his ophidite had quickly become attuned. The serpent beat its feathered wings together, knocking against the lowest thorned branches of the Arbor Sacré, as he continued, "Not one sorcerer, tenderfoot or mystra, was fully aware of how advanced I had become in each Mancy plane since I had unearthed the ShadowCrystal and learned its ways." He touched the pulsating crystal that was half-embedded into his sternum. "With its raw power, I began experimenting with terramancy, the foil to my telemancy. Once the ShadowCrystal had guided me to proficiency, I then transitioned to the remaining three Mancy planes until I had claimed control over them as well, becoming versed in them all and achieving a breadth of power second only to natural-born omnimancers. But even then—even then I could still best them." Ferox was almost salivating, as if he were about to devour Jocelyn's very soul. "Because I was more than willing to break the very rules those self-righteous omnimancers vowed to uphold . . . including the conjuring of the proximancic spells."

The dark lord closed his eyes and, lifting his chin into the air, drew a prolonged breath through his nose. He returned to his throne and tugged at his cloak, sending it whipping off to one side so that it would not get caught as he sat back down. "That's what made the other omnimancer clans so easy to dispatch." His fingernails dug into the carved throne as Ferox reminisced.

"Genevieve Lancaster still lives," Malcolm said.

Jocelyn watched as Ferox's visage hardened and the fingernails of his right hand carved deeper lines into his throne's armrest. Glowering, he said, "I will make sure that is rectified while you travel to the Qonehr realm and find fresh scarbeian larvae."

Ferox's voice faded away as Jocelyn was swept up in her own thoughts. The proxiterramancic spell . . . Qonehr's nearly indestructible species . . . Jocelyn knew exactly where this was going.

And she couldn't do anything to prevent it.

CHAPTER TWENTY

Once both Kuirhan and Skarmor had flown through the portal leading to Azumar, Victor said his goodbyes to Jen and Mira and they raced away toward the remains of Watercress Castle. Victor, meanwhile, set his sights on his remote cottage.

Dawn had yet to break the eastern horizon as Kuirhan took Victor northward. He had always liked the moments just before dawn arrived; being able to see the tapestry of countless stars fade away the closer the sun came to greet the day, adding radiant bands of gold to the cosmic black sky. These tender moments of solitude were when Victor found it the easiest to meditate, his thoughts the clearest when given the chance to reflect.

As he scanned the shadowy terrain below for his destination, Victor couldn't help but hope that Genevieve was at Watercress. That was the only solid lead they had . . . if you could even call it that. Victor didn't like the notion that it would take longer than he would think to find her; time was already not on their side. Though if she were there in those ruins, Jen and Mira would still have to contend with Cindergray; but he trusted Jen to reach out through telemancy if reinforcements were needed before Victor had time to pick up the others and meet up with her at the castle.

A soft glow of interior lights through his cottage's windows caught his attention, and he spurred Kuirhan to start his descent.

The dim light of dawn made the sleeping forms of Pernissa and Silvress easier to spot near the eastern side of the cottage. Kuirhan snorted in recognition as he too saw his friends, and thus did not need any extra coaxing from Victor to land near them. As Kuirhan touched down on lush, Azumarian grass, Pernissa lifted her head and fixed her gaze on the newcomers. Victor smoothly dismounted his trusty equivol and greeted Pernissa, who was already on her feet and striding over.

After patting Kuirhan's neck and thanking him, Victor ruffled Pernissa's feathers on the crest of her head. She clacked her beak, cocking her head to one side.

"Skarmor's not here yet, pretty girl," Victor explained. "He's with Jen. But you'll see him soon."

He smiled and scratched the side of her neck before his ears picked up Hephalon's voice seeping through the door and walls. It was faint but alarmed; he was speaking fast . . . and pacing. Victor hoped Rez and Gavin were heavy sleepers.

Telling Kuirhan to stay with Pernissa and Silvress, Victor started toward the door, only to be nearly plowed over by Hephalon as he rumbled out of the cottage, door swinging forcefully open right at Victor. He quickly stepped back just as Hephalon, now noticing his friend, abruptly stopped a string of grumblings.

"Merlin's Beard!" he exclaimed, stepping over to Victor and wrapping him in a big hug. "I knew you'd knock some sense into those trigger-happy Atlanteans!" He peered over Victor's shoulder, presumably to greet Jen next.

"Jen's gone to Watercress with Mira," Victor said.

Hephalon's shoulders slumped, no doubt catching the unsaid meaning behind that statement. "Bugger. They could not help Charles in the slightest?"

"They tried. So many tests were run, but even their advanced medicine had no effect on the proxiomnimancic spell." Victor rolled his shoulders back and straightened his posture. "Jen and Mira should be nearly at Watercress by now. Let's wake up Gavin and Rez and start heading that way."

Hephalon held out a large hand to stop Victor from entering his cottage. "Gavin's gone, Vic."

Victor first looked down at his friend's meaty hand, then followed his arm up to Hephalon's face, a mix of extreme disappointment and shock plastered on his face.

"He's *what*?"

"Gone. Vanished," Hephalon said, raising his hands to mimic rising smoke. "Silvress woke Rez and me up not too long ago to alert us, but by then he'd managed to put quite the distance between us and him."

It didn't make any sense. Victor thought his talk with Gavin back on Camelore had realigned the boy's priorities and made him see reason, for the good of the group. Victor shook his head as he tried to understand Gavin's motives for abandoning Hephalon and Rez. But why take off on foot and not on either Silvress or Pernissa? Victor looked up to see Rez stepping out of the cottage.

"I'm sorry . . . I should have woken up and stopped him as he was leaving," Rez apologized, dejected.

Hephalon faced his son. "You know this is not your fault, my boy. Gavin duped us both. Only he is to be blamed for his actions," the metallurgist said.

Still, Victor went into his cottage to check, all the while knowing that Gavin wouldn't just be sitting on his sofa.

Where could he have gone?

* * *

Gavin stirred awake. Grass blades and leaves tickled the base of his skull as he looked to his right, then left, unsure of where he was. Blurry dots of orange light seemed to float in the darkness surrounding him. He moaned, groggily rolling to one side as he blinked his eyes into focus.

"Arthur?"

His brain was too busy with survival to process what was said. Something moved in his peripherals, causing him to jump to his feet. Instinctually going for his orb totem, he tapped his pendant —and realized with growing concern that it wasn't there.

And the shadowy figure was slowly edging closer to him.

"Stand back!" Gavin yelled, crawling away from the figure and closer to the perimeter of what he now realized was a ring of floating cups of flame. If he had to, Gavin would do his best to funnel his astromancy through his hands, though he, a paladin, still needed a totem.

Anything to survive. And to get back to Hephalon and Rez.

A hollow chittering behind and above him invaded his hearing. He didn't need to look behind him to know that chilling sound. It was a serknid. A big one at that.

His breath caught in his chest when he realized that he was in the Amaranthine Forest.

"My perimeter spell will protect us, don't worry," a feminine voice said.

The bending of branches and rustling of leaves led Gavin to believe that the serknid was retreating. A thin bead of sweat trickled down his right temple as he clenched his jaw and brought his balled fists into a fighting pose. The voice sounded friendly, but that alone wouldn't make Gavin lower his guard.

"Who are you?" he said finally.

A white glow emanated from clasped hands a few meters away, revealing the face of a woman. A woman who looked astonishingly like Jen.

Gavin's knees locked as he looked upon the Lancaster of legend. His mouth suddenly went dry. "Genevieve Lancaster?" His astonishment didn't last for long; almost instantly he searched the vicinity for Cindergray. Nocturnal forest creatures rumbled and chittered in the opaque darkness, made thicker now that he was staring directly at a bright light.

A smile etched the woman's face. She nodded, her long curls sliding over her shoulders as she took two steps closer. "I'm relieved to have found you, my friend. Ever since my duel with Phi— . . . with Lord Ferox . . . ended, things seem . . . *different*."

"Is anyone else with you?" Gavin asked.

Genevieve frowned and looked over her shoulder; together, she and Gavin watched as a stag as white as freshly fallen snow trotted into the circle of flames. At first, Gavin took a step backward, but stopped, sensing that this animal meant no harm. The air around him seemed to alter. It was a stag like none Gavin had ever seen before: its antlers twisted and twirled toward the heavens, spinning a tale of its own with its countless stines; its large eyes glimmered without the need for any light source; its hooves held legs that looked as if they'd been sculpted from fine china but held strength underneath the ivory skin. The stag came to a stop in the middle of the ring and kneeled, dropping its head in a deferential bow.

At Gavin.

Gavin Kingsland.

The Light Bringer.

"Have you met this stag before, Arthur?" Genevieve asked, sheer surprise in her voice.

Gavin blinked, having a difficult time formulating words. His eyes were now moist with tears. "No," was all he could muster. He slowly dropped his fists, his fingers uncurling as his whole body relaxed. He then stammered, "A-and my name's not A-Arthur, it's . . . Gavin. Gavin Kingsland."

It was Genevieve's turn to stumble over her next words. "I—well . . . I-I beg your pardon?" She brought a hand to her chest and stepped closer to Gavin. "I'm terribly sorry. You look remarkably like our King Arthur . . ."

Gavin was distracted by the stag getting up off its haunches. He didn't want to alarm Genevieve with the news that she was no longer in the sixth century, but the sooner she was told the better. A path began to form in his mind.

"I am . . . related to him."

"Arthur never spoke of a sibling or cousin," she replied, a hint of wariness in her tone.

By now Gavin had fully disbanded the notion that he was in danger. Trying to collect his thoughts, he rubbed his forehead.

"No, sorry. What I mean is that he's my ancestor." He waited a few beats, surveying the elder Lancaster's face.

Expelling a breath of disbelief, Genevieve said, "I beg your pardon? I don't quite follow . . ."

Gavin swallowed. He could see Genevieve balancing on a thin wire. His next words would either guide her into understanding or push her off into an overwhelming maelstrom of confusion. "Your duel . . ." Gavin decided to use her experience to ground her, to lead her gently to the truth. "Your duel was preserved in the Halostone. I was there when you and Ferox were released. I watched as you overpowered him."

"For how long?" Genevieve asked.

By the look on her face, it was finally dawning on her. Gavin swallowed and slowly reached for her hand. He could see the side profile of the Ring of Lancaster glistening on her right hand from the flickering perimeter spell. "What you have to realize is—"

"Please, just . . ." Genevieve shook her head and pulled her other hand toward her chest. "Don't make me ask again." She sounded forlorn and looked defeated.

Gavin sighed. He dropped his outstretched hand, along with his eyes, and said, "Fifteen hundred years." He brought his gaze back up, unsure of the look he would find on Genevieve's face; but when he laid eyes on her, her expression hadn't changed. She seemed resigned. There was nothing more he could say, and he didn't wish to rush her to respond. In waiting for her, he was drawn back to the stag. It stood patiently next to Genevieve, its eyes following Gavin as he paced.

Slowly, Genevieve's eyes closed and she inhaled a shaky breath. Turning around, she carefully walked to the opposite edge of the ring of flames. Suddenly, the forest's ambient noises lessened until they ceased entirely, a brief reprieve in the nocturnal ecosystem . . . almost as if the woodland creatures gave Genevieve deference while she worked through her feelings. The stag remained resolute, intently meeting Gavin's gaze whenever he looked back upon it. He started toward Genevieve when the stag tilted its head toward him, letting one of its stines brush against his arm.

Gavin stiffened. A rush of energy traveled up his arm and blossomed when it reached his spine, roaming to the tips of every nerve in his body. Frozen, he let the feeling sink in, almost like he had heard a language in which he was unaware of ever being fluent. He saw nothing, heard nothing, but felt everything. Gavin was unable to describe the sensation precisely, but it gave him a new purpose.

He looked down at the stag. For the first time, its eyes were not on him. It was staring into the forest, almost as though it had nothing more to share with Gavin. He rolled his tongue, feeling the light crackling of a dry mouth, and accepted the calling that the stag had given him. With squared shoulders, he focused again on Genevieve, her head dipped forward as she held her face in her hands, and stepped up to her. Gavin risked placing a hand on her shoulder. She did not recoil.

"My son . . ." Gavin could tell Genevieve was suppressing her sadness, but it could be heard in the soft tremor in her voice. "What became of him?"

Gavin ran his thumb back and forth on her shoulder in sympathy as he thought hard about his response. "He grew old, never losing his love and admiration for you." He couldn't bear to tell her the full truth. Not right now, and not while she was still in the midst of processing this news. "He also made sure your family line continued."

Genevieve turned her head toward Gavin, the heart-shaped profile of her cheek shining in tracks of tears. "The Lancasters have survived?"

"Yes, and they need your help. I can take you to them," Gavin said. For the first time in what seemed like ages, hope filled his heart, providing additional energy and determination.

The early morning slivers of golden sunlight began to filter through the thinner parts of the forest's canopy, making it easier for him to read Genevieve's expression. She'd fully turned around to face him.

"What's happened?"

As Gavin began to explain, he let the white stag lead them out of the Amaranthine Forest, all the while silently praying that by the time he returned to Victor's cottage, Jen, Mira, and Victor would be there waiting.

CHAPTER TWENTY-ONE

On the plot of land overlooking Lac Cravath that once held Watercress Castle, Jen couldn't help but feel like she was trespassing through a haunted burial ground instead of walking through the fresh ruins of a once-bustling mecca that had consistently produced illustrious sorcerers from each of the five Mancy planes, including all of her ancestors, for hundreds of years.

After Mira pointed out the lifeless form of Cindergray's pegasus near the castle's destroyed drawbridge and the surprising remnants of a recent duel that scarred the length of the castle's main entranceway, Jen was on high alert, her nexus primed should anything unexpected happen. Did Genevieve fight back against Cindergray, or had there been an unwelcome visitor?

Like Malcolm?

Jen tried to hush her mind and focus on the mission at hand, which only further increased her anxiety. Deep down, she knew Cindergray was a good man who had been warped by an obsession that overtook his life and sanity; but if it came down to it, she would do what she must in order to convince Genevieve to come with her.

For her father's sake.

With Mira a step behind, Jen cautiously crept past the crumbling columns of the grand ballroom toward the Grand Mystra's main office chambers. Both had agreed that the Sacrarium was the most logical place for Cindergray to take Genevieve, but considering the mysterious demise of Soter and the castle's freshly battle-scarred ruins, it could very well be abandoned and possibly looted.

The arrival of early dawn brushed the air with an eerie veil of silence as Jen led Mira and Skarmor into a curved hallway. Jen wasn't prepared for her visceral reaction to seeing Watercress Castle in such dilapidated shape. For a place in which she'd only spent a short time, she was surprised at the toll her emotions were taking on her. When she was here last, her adrenaline had kept her focused on escaping not only with Merlin's journal and the ChronoCrystal but also her life, blurring everything else out. Now, with her senses heightened, Jen could almost feel the anguish and torment of the fallen sorcerers, their souls seeming to be tethered to the crumbling walls and chipped marble walkways, forever prisoners of a mark in history that Jen hoped would never occur again. That was the eventual goal, of course, but in order to get there, she needed the guidance and experience that only Charles Lancaster could offer.

"Skar, I need you to stay here and make sure no one sneaks up on us," Jen said to her loyal griffin. She was a few steps away from a gaping hole in the wall—one that used to be the door leading into Cindergray's office chambers.

Skarmor clicked his beak in understanding and turned around to face the hallway.

"Ready?" Jen looked at Mira, holding in a breath and out her hand.

Mira stepped closer to her and took her outstretched hand. "Ready."

Jen smiled, an unexpected flash of comfort warming her, and led her best friend into the dim chambers, the only light coming from the stained-glass window set above the Grand Mystra's desk. Jen looked at Mira the instant after she found the stairwell to the Sacrarium still open. Mira pursed her lips and nodded.

Jen came to the edge of the first step and stopped. Looking

back at Mira again, she found herself saying, "Mira, if Cindergray refuses to release Genevieve . . ." She found it hard to finish her thought.

But Mira knew what she meant. "I know." Her soft features belied the seriousness in her eyes. "I'll back you no matter what, girl." She squeezed Jen's hand reassuringly.

The edges of Jen's mouth lilted briefly in a quick smile before she turned her attention back to the spiraling, shadow-filled staircase. She let her hand slip from Mira's and steeled herself. The hardest step was the first, but after that, almost as if gravity gave her a helping hand, she descended the staircase with an intention to see this through.

They refrained from speaking as the stairs turned into a long corridor, bending at a right angle a few times to lead them deeper into the castle's bowels. Jen, like before, had completely lost her sense of direction, not knowing which way was true north. But the pathway to the Sacrarium had been etched into her mind, which was why she halted a few paces from the end of the corridor and held up a hand to catch Mira's attention. Straining her ears for any sound that might lay ahead, Jen waited in the silence until she felt comfortable in rounding the corner. Mira was on her heels, a hand hovering over the coiled bullwhip on her hip.

The Sacrarium's entrance was no longer hidden, just as Jen had surmised. The brick wall she had melded into at the Jubilee now had a gaping hole in it, rendering the wheel stand useless as the sole way to enter the sacred room that had once held the coveted ChronoCrystal and Merlin's journal, among other priceless artifacts. Now, anyone could freely enter and possibly loot the Sacrarium, turning it into just another normal room that contained nothing of note.

Stepping as light as if she were walking on crushed glass, Jen hugged the far left wall, her eyes never leaving the hole that led into the Sacrarium. Still no noise from inside, but she didn't want to take any chances.

A quick peer into the Sacrarium confirmed its emptiness, bringing a disheartened look to Jen's face. *Where could they be?* She relaxed her shoulders as well as the grip on her nexus, but that didn't help ease the mounting dread of what to do next. And where to go.

"Let's see what we can find," she said.

Together they stepped into the Sacrarium and began investigating. Mira was the most adept tracker Jen had ever known. She had an enviable connection to the world around her and, alongside her harmony with animancy, could detect where an ant had been just by looking at it. As Mira walked around the Sacrarium, hovering her hands over relics, down the sides of bookshelves, and across tables covered in stacks of tomes, Jen realized how much she still had to learn in not just animancy but the other four Mancy planes before she could be the omnimancer the realms needed.

Jen clenched her jaw and shook that thought from her mind. What she needed to be doing now was helping Mira search for any clue that might help them on their search for Genevieve. But what her friend said next stopped her cold.

"I'm picking up Cindergray, but not Genevieve," Mira said, bent at the knees and running her fingers along the dusty floor. "She hasn't set foot in here."

Jen's forehead muscles tightened in concern. She had too many thoughts bouncing around in her head to pick one to say aloud. Her eyes followed Mira as she walked past her and out of the Sacrarium, stopping to stand right in front of the wheel.

"But she was *here* . . ." Mira twirled in a circle, pointing at the path that had led them to the Sacrarium. ". . . and walked the same path we did." She hovered her hands over the wheel and looked down.

And that's when a memory hit Jen so hard she jumped. "Cindergray said to turn the wheel *counterclockwise* to enter the Sacrarium . . . but he specifically said to never turn it *clockwise*."

Mira took two steps back. "What'll happen if you turn the wheel clockwise?"

Jen shrugged. "I don't know."

"Another chamber, maybe?"

"I honestly didn't think much about his comment until now," Jen said. She took the spot Mira had just vacated and gripped the wheel with both hands, looking at the indent set in its center: it matched Cindergray's signet ring, a ring which was back in her hut on Camelore. Biting her lip, Jen thought of different ways to work the wheel. Her eyes bounced from the stand, briefly into the Sacrarium, back to the wheel, and finally fixated on her totem bracelet. With an idea firmly in mind, she gave Mira a hopeful look, saying, "I hope this works," and rotated the bracelet around her wrist until she found the terramancy charm. Its sleek teardrop design slid over the tips of her fingers as she momentarily admired the beautiful colorful stripes set in its center to symbolize each element of terramancy.

"Forgive me, Heph," Jen regretfully whispered as she touched her charm to the wheel's indentation.

Calling on terramancy, she liquified the charm and watched as its coruscating colors dissolved away. She waited for the metal to settle into every groove of the indentation before she willed it to harden. In seconds, she had created her own copy of Cindergray's signet ring. Holding her breath, she grabbed the wheel with her other hand and tugged it to the right.

At first she was met with slight resistance, but with no intention of acquiescing, she kept pulling, and a jolt of accomplishment rushed through her when the wheel finally obeyed and turned clockwise, lowering her and Mira into the floor as if it had turned into quicksand.

Jen clasped Mira's hand in solidarity as her feet disappeared into the floor, slowly followed by her legs and torso. The feeling was distinct but similar to what she had felt when entering the Sacrarium. By the time the floor had reached her throat, she instinctively held her breath and closed her eyes in preparation for being completely submerged. The tightness of the floor around her set off warning bells in her mind, but her firm grip on Mira's hand and her curiosity of where the wheel was taking them staved off any claustrophobic fear that was hungry to envelop her.

Calling on her nexus once more, Jen felt the floor free her feet, then her knees. In seconds, she came out of the floor (which had now become the ceiling of a room even smaller than the Sacrarium) and continued to be lowered into an empty chamber.

No Cindergray or Genevieve . . .

Where are they?

Once her feet felt firm ground, Jen let go of Mira's hand and she drank in the contents of a chamber that presumably only Cindergray had ever seen. It was smaller than the Sacrarium but filled with countless books, weapons, clothing, and artifacts of the ancient world.

"Yep, both of them were definitely here," Mira said, then stiffened after taking a couple steps toward the room's center.

A bad feeling crept into Jen's bones. "Mira? What is it?"

"Draconex's scent is also here." Mira looked at Jen with shock in her eyes. "Just as strong as Cindergray's and Genevieve's."

Meaning that he was here at the same time as them. "What? That doesn't make any sense. Draconex died before we'd even found the Halostone . . ."

"Creepy weird," Mira said, wheels turning in her head as she walked to a particularly dusty area of the floor near the opposite wall and knelt down.

"Maybe they brought Draconex's body here?" Jen spun around in a slow circle, taking in all that was stored in the chambers. "For . . . some reason?" Or did Malcolm lie that he'd killed Draconex?

Her thoughts trailed off as she saw a broken, chipped stone bust of an Aztec (or was it Mayan?) serpent head. She walked toward it and noticed a thin booklet next to the bust that had been haphazardly folded, almost like it was dropped. She picked it up carefully; the booklet felt brittle, but it held its shape surprisingly well. Gingerly turning the stiff pages, Jen realized this was an ancient codex of one of the Mexican civilizations from long ago. She came to a colorful representation of a giant winged serpent engulfing men with a spray of fire, but stopped when Mira gasped from across the room.

"Ew!" Mira exclaimed.

Jen shot up, eager to see what Mira had found. She placed the codex on the closest table before hurrying over to her friend. Mira stood transfixed, hands splayed out, and staring at a pile of dust in horror.

Then Jen realized it might not be dust.

"I found Cindergray . . ." Mira whispered, bringing a hand to cover her mouth.

Jen blinked in shock. "What?"

She looked down at the pile of ashes, then back up at Mira. A range of emotions battered her from every angle, vying for her outward expression. She had so many more memories of the Cindergray who was the mentor and sage sorcerer she had confided in than that of the man whose actual name was Philip Lancaster II, the duplicitous, delusional son of Genevieve Lancaster and Lord Ferox, who used his status and power as the Grand Mystra to affect the war for his own selfish gain. But to choose the former would be a blatant lie, pardoning Cindergray's horrific actions over the centuries, many of which Jen was still ignorant. Her heart sank, not because of his shocking demise, but because of the bloody legacy he left in his wake.

"No!" Jen yelled, slamming her open palms on the table next to her. The table's legs cracked from the abrupt strike, but didn't buckle.

"I'm sorry, Jen," Mira said.

"It's not like that." Jen turned away. She looked up in an effort to dry her tearful eyes. "He wasn't who we all thought him to be." She sniffled. Her hands had curled into tight fists, knuckles white, and her forearms soon ached from the tension. She realized she had activated terramancy in her emotional state, so with care she released that Mancy plane as she relaxed hands. "Is it . . . only Cindergray?"

Mira didn't need to double-check. "Yes." Her voice was barely a whisper, but it was confident.

Jen centered herself by counting out three breaths, then turned back toward her friend. "Are you all right?"

Mira tried to smile, a quick, half-hearted lift of the right edge of her lips; it came and went in the blink of an eye. "I'll be fine. It's just . . ." She looked at her feet. "He was supposed to be the best of us."

Jen took a step closer and hugged Mira. Eventually her friend brought her hands up to hug her back.

"Let's strive to be better, then," Jen whispered in her ear. She pulled away, smiling, and nodded encouragingly, both for Mira and for herself.

Mira nodded back while blotting her lower eyelids. Her countenance got stronger by the second. "Okay," she breathed. "Genevieve must have left this room the way we came in." She looked around as she walked back toward the wheel stand. "I don't see any other exit."

Jen looked around as well, nodding in agreement. "And since we didn't run into her on our way down here, she must be somewhere on Azumar." Jen reconsidered that and added, "Hopefully." She was thinking aloud at this point, hoping to find the right path.

Her mind pulled her focus back to the codex she'd placed on the table at the other end of the room: those ancient drawings; that terrifying, gigantic serpent . . . it looked somewhat like—

"The ophidite," Jen said, unable to make her voice louder than a whisper.

Mira followed her gaze and, seeing the codex, threw a look back at Jen. Picking it up, Mira said, "Is this what you were looking at before?"

"Yeah, but I didn't realize what it was until now," Jen said, walking up to Mira's side. "May I?"

Mira carefully passed it off to Jen, who only needed a second to get to the page on which she'd seen that winged serpent.

There.

"That's that flying snake we saw coiled around the Arbor Sacré. The ophidite." Jen pointed fervently at the serpent that belched flames at terrified humans.

Mira tilted her head slightly as she viewed the page. "Someone else touched this book," she said. "Malcolm."

Malcolm? *He* was here too?! How did he learn of this chamber?

Jen's mouth opened, but no sound came out. She could barely keep up with all the questions bouncing around in her mind as she tried to comprehend how he fit into all of this. Was Malcolm the one who killed Cindergray? Or was it Draconex? Her head pounded with confusion. It surprised Jen that Malcolm could have attained the power to defeat an omnimancer such as Cindergray, the Grand Mystra of the entire Sorcery Guild.

Jen and Mira exchanged awe-struck looks before Mira broke away and looked at the ceiling. "Whatever happened down here, Draconex, Malcolm, and Genevieve all left."

"Together?" Jen had to lean against the table as all of this information was thrown at her. If Genevieve had sided with Malcolm, then Jen's worst fears would have been realized. After all, he had been able to convince Fuzanglong, a legendary dragon, to attack Atlantis . . .

A soft ringing pervaded Jen's hearing, splitting her focus. She clamped her eyes shut as a familiar voice echoed in her mind.

Jen . . . Jen! Can you hear me?

It was Rez.

Jen's eyes popped open; in her excitement she almost dropped the codex. It wobbled in her hands as she announced to Mira: "Rez is reaching out!"

Jen? Rez asked again through the telemancy bond they shared.

Rez! Yeah, I can hear you.

You'll never guess who's with us.

But Jen already knew the answer. *I'm glad Vic got there safely.*

No—well, yeah, he's here and that's aces and all, but . . . Gavin found Genevieve!

If Jen hadn't been leaning on the table, she would have collapsed from the surprise. But she did let the codex slip from her fingers, which had gone limp, and the ancient book dropped to the floor beside her boot.

"Jen? You okay?" She heard Mira's voice, but she was too focused on communicating with Rez to acknowledge her friend.

Hold on, Rez . . . Genevieve is with you at the cottage?

You heard me right! Flippin' astounding, innit? Gavin, we lost him an'—

Rez, Mira and I'll be right there. You can fill us in then.

Ah, yeah, sorry . . . I'm bustin' with excitement and I have a tendency to ramble.

Of that Jen was well aware. *We have news to share on our end too. We'll be right over. Don't go anywhere.*

Trust me, Jen, we're stayin' put. Signin' off!

The white noise of the telemancy bond dissolved as Jen's other senses returned. Opening her eyes, she saw Mira right in front of her, nervously brushing her braid, their kneecaps a hair's breadth from touching.

"Jen, you're scaring me," Mira mustered once Jen made eye contact with her. She flipped her braid over her shoulder and was about to sit on the table's edge next to Jen when she sprung up. Mira searched Jen's face as if she couldn't decide which feature to look at.

Jen started toward the wheel stand. "Come on, we have to go. Genevieve's at Vic's cottage."

"What?!" Mira exclaimed. Instantly, she was next to Jen as she slid her terramancy charm into the wheel and turned it clockwise. The floor beneath them rose up as Jen explained her communication with Rez, reluctantly pausing as they melded into the ceiling and resuming once they were back in the main chamber above.

Mira expressed as much surprised excitement as Jen felt herself, and together they raced with the graceful speed of gazelles through the secret passage, up the spiral staircase, out of Cindergray's office, and onto Skarmor.

"Skarmor, to Vic's cottage," Jen said, out of breath, as Mira wrapped her arms around her midriff.

The griffin, seeming more than happy to do anything other than stand guard a second longer, stretched out his mighty wings and carried Jen and Mira into the air. The sun had broken above the horizon like the yolk of a cracked egg, covering the world with a golden light that mirrored Jen's resurgence of hope.

Mira squeezed Jen with a high-pitched squeal, and Jen couldn't help but smile and wiggle in response. She hadn't a clue how Gavin had done it, but thanks to him they were one step closer to saving Charles. The wind pulled happy tears over the apples of her cheeks that rolled into her ears, but Jen didn't care.

Skarmor coasted through the crisp morning breeze with expedience, and Jen threw a parting look back at the ruins of Watercress Castle. Now that she had personally seen Cindergray's private secret chamber, she made a mental note to return there and explore further after this was all over.

And her side had won.

There had to have been thousands of years of history stored in that secondary chamber that could possibly shed more light on who Cindergray was, not to mention the extinct cultures that spanned every realm.

"Jen, down there!"

Mira jostled Jen out of her swirling thoughts, and she looked along the castle's southern exposure atop the cliff overlooking Lac Cravath. At first she struggled to see what Mira was pointing at, but then a black form bounded out from a pile of rubble.

"What is that?"

She'd never seen that animal before. It was very lean, with large canine teeth curving out from both its upper and lower jaws, reminding Jen of a cross between a leopard and saber-toothed tiger, but it had a dark, slate-gray hide reminiscent of a rhinoceros. Its tail branched into two tips, one longer and sharper than the other, which swayed lazily behind its svelte body.

"A relicontus," Mira answered. "They never roam this far north. I wonder what it's doing here . . ."

CHAPTER TWENTY-TWO

Malcolm kept telling himself that his mind was playing tricks on him; that's why he was feeling off, not because Ferox's elixir, sloshing in his stomach right this very moment, was laced with a tracker and a fatal reaction should Ferox sense a deviation in his mission.

And don't forget that you're now a carrier of Ferox's proxiterramancic spell.

He needed to be at his best. The stakes had never been higher.

Sitting behind him was Madame Diaema, the other proxiterramancic spell carrier, as the massive wyvern dragon, Volcanor, hurtled to their first of eleven realms: Qonehr.

Qonehr was a realm that aged extremely fast, as did its species. Its tectonic plates took not millions of years to drift across its crust but rather hundreds, which, seeing as Qonehr was half land, half water, posed a significant issue for its indigenous life. The accelerated movement of its crust led to many cataclysmic natural disasters, triggering a mass extinction event every decamillennium, and like clockwork the next era of species would begin their own rapid evolution until the next apocalypse arrived to eradicate the majority of them.

Except for scarbeians.

Scarbeians, the apex predators of their realm, were gigantic, destructive, hard-shelled insects that, if they were ever to travel between realms, inevitably turned into an invasive species. Having a common ancestor with the much smaller scarab beetle found on Earth, Scarbeians were mantle-boring creatures; they dug hundreds of thousands of meters underneath a planet's crust, creating a vast network of tunnels for shelter, birthing, and quick and efficient hunting. It was this very same knack for boring deep underground that was the deciding factor of their survival on the volatile realm of Qonehr.

Many philosopher-sorcerers of the Guild had speculated that scarbeians were to blame for Qonehr's accelerated continental movement and eventual bioapocalypse every ten thousand years; others claimed that they simply adapted to survive. Either way, scarbeians were survivors, never-tiring.

Millennia ago, when the portals on Earth were far less moni-tored, scarbeians slipped through and in record time inhabited nearly every continent. One ancient East African civilization in particular began to revere them, associating the scarab with the cycle of birth, life, and regeneration. Sacred trinkets and amulets were made in their likeness and placed in sarcophagi of deceased, mummified rulers of Egypt.

Malcolm winced, torn from his thoughts by a few sharp tips of the MystiCrystals that dug into his thigh, jostled into particularly uncomfortable angles from their housings on his belt next to two burlap sacks he'd stolen from a Camelorean hut. He irritatedly flicked them aside so as to not cause any deeper scratches across his skin. The MystiCrystals, he hoped, wouldn't become a hindrance on his mission, since they were the final part in Ferox's plan to subjugate the eleven realms—provided that Malcolm would cross paths with Jen and take back the TeleCrystal, the final one needed to complete the set once again.

One step at a time, Malcolm had to remind himself. The first step of his mission hadn't even been achieved yet: collect eleven scarbeian larvae, inject them with his blood (which contained strains of the dormant proxiterramancic spell), and transport them to each realm and let them do what they did best: dig. Lord Ferox had realized that their accelerated growth would activate the spell, and as they would instinctively bore into the ground, the scarbeians would secrete the spell, thereby dissolving the mantle of every realm like acid.

The only way to stop the proxiterramancic spell from destroying each realm? For the sentient beings to recognize Lord Ferox as their leader.

Cunning, devious, ruthless . . . impressive. Malcolm wished he had thought of it on his own.

Volcanor snorted—its version of letting Malcolm know that they had arrived at the portal to Qonehr. Malcolm tightened his jaw and looked several hundred meters below at a large sinkhole located just off the coast of Belize. In the morning light it looked like the pupil of an eye that belonged to a colossal giant, staring at Malcolm, daring him to dive in.

And that's exactly what he was going to do—even though Malcolm despised the portals that were submerged in water, superheated by flames, or hidden in some form of toxic gas. The Qonehr portal below had two of those three.

And it was currently dormant.

Malcolm noticed Diaema's legs tightening around Volcanor's rib cage, no doubt preparing for the impending dive. "You ready?" he asked.

"Does it look like I have a choice?" she bit back rather tensely.

Malcolm looked back down at the sinkhole, not bothering with a response. He brought his totem ring to bear, flashing it with enough terramancy to make it glow like fresh embers.

Now or never . . .

He kicked Volcanor's side, commanding it to dive.

A raucous bellow rumbled from its throat, vibrating its whole body as it flapped one final time, its eyes locked on the sinkhole's epicenter. The hellish dragon dropped its smoky snout, its brimstone body following immediately. The memory of when Malcolm had entered the watery caldera of that dormant volcano in search of Fuzanglong hit him almost as hard as the wind from Volcanor's direct plummet toward the sinkhole.

Just like he had done in the caldera, Malcolm called upon terramancy and moved his hands in quick circles as he focused on the water molecules below. In short order, a small speck in the center of the sinkhole quickly grew and grew into a whirlpool so great that the rushing saltwater could be heard from a hundred meters away.

Malcolm didn't breathe in relief just yet; that was only the half of it. The last part was separating the layer of anoxic hydrogen sulfide three hundred meters below sea level so abruptly that a chemical reaction would form, activating the portal, all before Volcanor reached it (and with the dragon's unerring speed, it wasn't a matter of seconds but hundredths of a second). If Malcolm was too slow or didn't direct his spell accurately, the gas wouldn't part, and Malcolm, Diaema, and Volcanor would be swallowed by the ocean, never to return.

Just as Volcanor plummeted into the underwater cyclone of swirling waters, Malcolm thought he heard Diaema scream his name. He paid her no heed; he couldn't afford to be distracted. Before the smell of rotten eggs (courtesy of the hydrogen sulfide) had the chance to seep into his nostrils, Malcolm closed his eyes. Visualizing the bonds of the oxygen-depleted, murky layer of water, he proceeded to tear them apart so viciously that his eyes hurt.

BMM-BOOM BOOOMMM!

Malcolm, soaked from errant whirlpool cords of saltwater and eyes still closed, felt as if a slew of muffled fireworks had exploded around him. He risked opening his eyes just in time to witness a blinding light swallow them whole.

Then there was no sound. No wind. Not even a drop of water.

Then, a rush as if he were in a howling wind tunnel.

A second, larger rush like none other overcame Malcolm as Volcanor tore through the gateway from Earth to Qonehr. He held on to his dragon's rocky spine as it screamed out of a cliffside, high above an angry, foaming sea that seemed determined to engulf it with unending crashes of wave after forceful wave.

They needed to start their search over land, so Malcolm

tugged at Volcanor's spinal protrusion and forced it to ascend. Volcanor tucked one massive wing close to its body and reoriented itself before it became inverted. Malcolm was able to view the portal gateway now: on this side it was a crater inset into the cliffside. He caught the acrid odor of methane, or some flammable gas akin to it. In seconds, Volcanor had banked around in the opposite direction, and now only open land lay ahead.

The sky was covered in bands of hazy gray clouds, making it hard for sunlight to penetrate, and the land below Volcanor's venous wings seemed desolate for as far as the eye could see, but Malcolm knew that the mantle of Qonehr, deep below its crust, teemed with life.

"Now all we need to do is find a scarbeian hole," Malcolm said aloud, not caring if Diaema could hear him.

She did. "So is this a part of your *vision*? You realize how myopic and selfish Ferox's plan is?"

Malcolm kept his eyes forward, scouring the patchy grasslands for any entry point to a scarbeian tunnel. He just needed to find the entry, then he would let Volcanor sniff them out. His dragon was hungry, after all. The trick was to stop it from devouring every last larva. Malcolm only needed eleven.

Diaema was still pestering him. "You know that it's impossible to reverse any and all proximancic spells? The proxiterramancic spell will collapse each realm if you go through with this."

The salty air irritated Malcolm's eyes and the frequency of his blinking increased. Yet he did not acknowledge the vampire. The strong crashes of ceaseless waves could still be heard in the distance. He counted ten before she interrupted his focus once again.

"What happened to the Malcolm who sat on the Throne of Dragons? Hungry to step out of Draconex's shadow, thirsty for the power and control that only the Dark Watcher commander can possess?" Diaema paused. "And you achieved it." She laughed, almost derisively. "You killed Draconex and had an actual chance to mold the Dark Watcher tribe the way you saw fit, finally answering to no one but yourself."

Malcolm's left eye became extremely itchy. He used the side of his wrist to try to rub the irritation away as his right eye stayed glued to the barren, hay-like grass below. He was rubbing so hard spots of light danced across his vision.

"But now?" She scoffed. "Now you are nothing but a lackey whose only purpose is to run the errands of others." Diaema tsked in disappointment. "I'd call that a massive demotion."

"This is still the prophecy!" Malcolm yelled, twisting his upper torso so his eyes could skewer Diaema with daggers. "I've planned for this day for *years*, Diaema, as I was constantly cast aside, underestimated, and made to feel inconsequential . . . valued less than maggots." His jaw fiercely jutted out as he glared at Diaema, his breath fading back to normal. He then turned back around and resumed his search. "My time is *now*, and my legacy will be one of change," he said haughtily.

"Even if it means staining your hands with the blood of billions across each realm?"

"The realms are disjointed—they need the guidance only Ferox can provide. I will aid my lord in becoming an omnimancer, after which he will have even more power to reverse the proxiter-ramancic spells, and we will rule the entire coalition of realms with an iron fist. A firm proclamation is the only way to make them see reason, and collateral damage is to be expected."

Malcolm could no longer hear the waves, only the shifty winds that bent the strands of long grass in rolling angles.

"Ferox will never trust you," Diaema said, her voice resigned.

Malcolm's initial instinct was to backhand her, but something inside him resisted the urge. Diaema was right, as much as he told himself otherwise. If Ferox trusted Malcolm, then why did he trick him into taking an elixir that had both the ability to track his whereabouts and kill him on command if Ferox caught a whiff of disobedience?

That would also explain why he handed over the MystiCrys-tals so readily.

Malcolm's response stopped in his throat when he caught sight of a field of lines, formed by trampled grass, that connected several large holes. There seemed to be a certain method to where the holes were dug, as well as the shapes the lines themselves made, reminding Malcolm of the Nazca Lines in Peru.

"There they are," he said instead. Malcolm didn't know what Diaema was playing at; after all, she was in this as deep as he was. Their lives were now entwined together (as much as both of them resented that), and their survival relied on their mutual cooperation to follow Ferox's orders.

Malcolm commanded Volcanor to the nearest hole. As his dragon dropped in altitude, his doubts of whether or not Volcanor's hulking frame would fit evaporated as the tips of its wings cleared the edges safely. The hole looked to be twenty meters in diameter—a comfortable fit for Volcanor, even at its full wingspan.

A quick snort ignited yellow-orange flames that flicked out from the wyvern dragon's nostrils, casting the tunnel's surprisingly smooth walls in much-needed light as it descended deeper. The fire in its nostrils also aided in sniffing out its prey: there, in this instance, were fresh larvae. Malcolm had to channel terramancy to create a wedge of air in front of him so that Volcanor's smoke trail wouldn't assault his eyes, nose, and throat.

The tunnel led them farther into Qonehr's mantle; the temperature methodically dropped and the atmospheric pressure increased. Every so often Volcanor would have to alter his flight path, lazily banking right or left as it followed the path the adult scarbeians had dug in the distant past.

Every so often Volcanor would speed past intersecting, shadowy tunnels, and Malcolm would detect rumbles and deep clicking sounds from what he assumed was hordes of scarbeians in the other direction. Unsure of how close they were or how easily they would be alerted to a foreign presence in their passageways, Malcolm kept his breathing tight, staying focused on finding just enough larvae to get out of this highway to hell with as few bumps and scrapes as possible.

Without so much as a warning, Volcanor splayed its wings and abruptly shaved its speed down to practically nothing. Malcolm's inertia slammed his head and chest into the craggy spine of his dragon, sending pricks of sharp pain across his sternum and spine. Diaema let out a screech of surprise, and as he blinked away stars Malcolm caught sight of her falling deeper into the vertical tunnel. Volcanor, almost spitefully, snorted and flapped its wings again, beginning an ascent toward a tunnel intersection it had meant to take but had accidentally blown past.

Malcolm tossed a glance back down and watched Diaema disappear into the shadows eating away at the edges of Volcanor's firelight, only to see a small albino vampire bat flutter back into the light a second later, squeaking in frustration. With a smirk, he found a better grip on Volcanor's back and surveyed the new tunnel ahead, not bothering to wait for Diaema to catch up.

There were more slopes in this new tunnel, and its walls weren't as smooth as the previous one, with spindly roots becoming more prevalent the farther in Volcanor flew.

There came a flutter behind him, and then: "You chose to just stare at me as I fell?"

Diaema, it seemed, was nonplussed.

Still wearing a lopsided smirk, Malcolm said, "I knew you'd be fine."

The light from Volcanor's nostrils dispersed as the tunnel opened up into an enormous burrow filled with hundreds upon thousands of scarbeian larvae. They were separated in batches as they fed on outcroppings of decaying roots and plants. A large, hollowed-out cocoon had been plastered to the highest point of the burrow's ceiling; it emitted a soft, mint-green glow over the sea of squirming insects. Volcanor seemed overwhelmed by the number of larvae below, and its wet breathing indicated the current state of its hunger: starving.

The dragon took off before Malcolm could untie the sacks from his belt and dove headlong toward the closest batch of larvae. Volcanor spat out dripping balls of flame at the larvae before it landed, its talons sinking into the burnt, gelatinous bodies of its prey.

This close up, the larvae weren't much longer than Malcolm's forearm—a true wonder how they'd grow to be as large as Volcanor.

Malcolm yelled his dragon's name, but the beast was too fixated on its meal to listen. It roared in earnest and sank its teeth into the charred remnants of the larvae it had stomped on. Those still alive continued to mindlessly suck on the subterranean roots, completely oblivious to their impending fate as a quick meal for a wyvern dragon.

Malcolm finally worked the sack's knots from his belt, cursing in triumph, and slid onto a bed of undulating larvae. He almost lost his balance under the constantly shifting ground, but he kept from faceplanting into the oozing pile of larvae with two quick stutter-steps.

"Stay up there!" he shouted back at Diaema, not waiting for her verbal acknowledgment before he jutted his totem ring at a dozen larvae to his left. A tingling chill stiffened his fingers as his ring shot forth an icy blast of energy, flash-freezing every larva in its path. Mindful of Volcanor's beating wings while it slurped up more larvae into the bottomless pit that was its stomach, Malcolm flicked one of his sacks open and picked up the first larva of ten.

The first few frozen bodies stuck to his fingertips as he tried depositing them into the sack, but as his fingers became more numb it became easier to release them. He found an open area to stand in that Volcanor had just cleared of larvae; his dragon had since moved off to the right to feast on more helpings.

Five larvae fit snugly into each sack, and when both were filled, Malcolm drew the strings tight and looped them around his neck. He started after Volcanor to toss Diaema the sacks when the ground shook and he lost his footing, parting a clump of larvae as he slammed into the ground.

There was another shake, this time much more intense, and toward the middle of the burrow the mound of larvae grew like a tidal wave, ready to sweep Malcolm away. As the highest larvae began to roll down the mound, he realized with growing dread what was happening: a fully adult scarbeian was in the burrow with them.

And it was now awake.

Flailing as he tried to stand back up, Malcolm let out a string of curses. He picked up the squishy larvae that were impeding his progress and threw them aside. He managed to sit up, and there was Volcanor, still feasting, head down in gluttony, completely ignorant to the arrival of this latest threat.

"Volcanor!" Malcolm boomed, feeling the veins in his neck against the rough fabric of the sacks.

He finally got his feet under him and leapt, using terramancy to fling himself across the distance that separated him from Volcanor, and landed clumsily on its tail. With the full sacks pulling at his throat, he let out a prolonged grunt and crawled up to Diaema.

"I could've used some help!" he said.

"You told me to stay put!" she shot back.

A vibrating, cicada-like sound split his eardrums as the adult scarbeian stomped toward Volcanor and its riders. Malcolm rolled his eyes as Volcanor finally stopped eating and looked dumb-foundedly at the charging beetle. Larvae slid off the scarbeian's shell as it hurtled at Volcanor, the invader that threatened its offspring, releasing more bone-rattling noises.

Malcolm planted his heels firmly into Volcanor's sides and commanded it to fly. Volcanor didn't need to be told twice, and it lifted off the ground, still chewing the last morsels of its dinner. With its sights set on the tunnel it entered from, Volcanor beat its wings intensely to get its gargantuan body higher in the air. Malcolm, pressed up against Diaema's back in their hasty escape, looked behind him at the feral scarbeian and realized he had dras-tically underestimated the beetle's speed.

Its frontal spur shot out and sank into Volcanor's left leg, preventing it from escaping. The wyvern roared in sudden pain and arched around to unleash a beam of scalding flames at the scarbeian.

Malcolm shot a trio of spells at the insect's eyes, intending to blind it, when he stiffened. In his mad dash to Volcanor, he'd forgotten to inject one final larva with his blood, which would accelerate the larva's growth and activate the dormant proxiterra-mancic spell. He cursed.

"What could possibly be upsetting you now?" Diaema said sarcastically as she too tried to not slip off the thrashing Volcanor.

"I forgot to inject a larva for this realm," Malcolm bit out, furious at his own ineptitude.

Diaema rolled her neck and, without even a snide remark or rebuttal, morphed into her albino bat form. Malcolm traced her path as she erratically flew toward the scarbeian that was attacking Volcanor, dodging the wyvern dragon's incessant fire blasts and finding one of the last larva to still remain on its shell. She sank her sharp teeth into the larva's squishy flesh before it could fall into the rolling mass of its kin.

A particularly violent thrash almost made Malcolm fall off Volcanor's back. His dragon roared again, angered that the scarbeian showed no signs of letting its leg go. Righting himself, Malcolm then unsheathed Excalibur and swiped at the beetle's frontal spur, crown of its head, and roaming antennae . . . anything to get it to release Volcanor.

Eventually, between Malcolm's wild hacking and Volcanor's fire blasts, it became too much for the scarbeian to handle; it released the dragon, dropping to the ground, defeated and more than a little hurt.

Free at last, Volcanor took off as if shot from a catapult, hurtling into the tunnel with a new fervor to escape Qonehr's mantle as fast as possible. Diaema had wrapped herself around Volcanor's tail before the scarbeian released it, and now held on for dear life, not daring to move as it hurtled back up the tunnel, carelessly and rashly careening into the walls. Volcanor yearned for the surface, not caring if it alerted the entire colony of scarbeians with its riled-up bellows and realm-shaking collisions with tunnel walls. There were several times when Malcolm thought he would lose his grip on Volcanor's back, but somehow he held on, determined to see this mission through.

After a few more rough bounces and a white-knuckled turn, Volcanor miraculously brought them back into the main tunnel.

Malcolm could just make out a small pinprick of light far above. With relief knocking at the door, he adjusted the sacks' strings around his neck. The skin underneath the spun twine would be raw for days. He didn't care. They'd get out of this jam with enough larvae to drop into every realm.

He didn't worry about how he'd cross paths with Jen; he knew that he would think of something.

CHT-CHT-CHITITTTT . . .

The hair on the nape of Malcolm's neck bristled, and he fought the urge to look behind him. The droning chittering from the scores of scarbeians clawed at his ears, echoing in spirals off the tunnel's circular walls. Their speed and vastness was almost too much for Malcolm to fathom; he could feel them getting closer despite Volcanor's impressive pace. The surface was still too far away for comfort, but he would not look back.

"Malcolm, you need to see this," Diaema said, now right behind him. Her tone was clipped.

"We got this," Malcolm said, leaning forward as if to help his wyvern dragon go faster.

"Malcolm!"

"We have *got this!*" he repeated, still refusing to look over his shoulder.

The opening was getting bigger and bigger, and Malcolm could practically taste the salty breeze lapping over the cliffs of Qonehr. Just a little bit closer . . .

The entire tunnel shuddered. The anticipation was too much for Malcolm. He looked behind him and saw ravenous scarbeians clamoring over one another, the closest one only meters away from the tip of Volcanor's tail. Malcolm's curse was drowned out by the scarbeians' manic chittering. Darkness fell over them, which caused him to look back toward the opening. The blood froze in his veins.

The opening was blocked.

He, Diaema, and Volcanor were now drenched in claustro-phobic blackness. A mere second later, the scalding heat of Volcanor's breath lanced a stream of fire up toward the opening.

Yelling so loudly that his lungs felt like they were being crushed, Malcolm stared directly at what turned out to be the blockage: the ribbed abdomen of another scarbeian, most likely the obstacle into which he would crash and die. But Volcanor's flamethrower startled the massive beetle, causing it to flee . . . only it was too slow; Volcanor headbutted the cooked scarbeian as it shot out of the tunnel, sending the oversized insect cartwheeling into the air.

Malcolm filled his aching lungs with the fresh, salty air, whooping in triumph as his dragon carried him and Diaema away from the grassland that was now overflowing with scarbeians. Thankful that their evolution had taken away their ability to fly, Malcolm pointed back toward the sea and ordered, "Volcanor, take us back to the portal!"

He continued to holler as he turned toward Diaema, but suddenly went quiet as he looked upon her face: its features were stretched in a mix of sadness, anger, and shock. He quickly turned back around, hoping she did not catch him looking. Clearly this was not the same woman he had come to know on Feralot when she was Draconex's mistress. She seemed more . . . human. He heard her muttering something, and used terramancy to block out the rush of wind long enough to hear:

"Jen, my baby girl . . . I'm so sorry."

Malcolm fought the urge to turn back her way until his lower back cramped in agony. *Diaema is Jen's mother? Jocelyn?! How is that freaking possible?! Jocelyn died on Ocuul twenty years ago!*

He bared his teeth and let out another yell, this time spurred by the blatant, rage-fueled shock he now felt. How could this be? Diaema had been by Draconex's side since his rise to power as the commander of the Dark Watcher tribe. She'd come to him initially as a bodyguard after Draconex had caught wind of her impressive exploits as a vampire-assassin under Ephram La Proutagne on Vespre (at least that was what Draconex had told Malcolm). She had sat back and watched Draconex wage war against the Sorcery Guild *and* try to capture Jen when she was first discovered and again later as she gained more control over her omnimancy powers. Charles Lancaster had been locked up in Feralot's prison bay for decades. Had Diaema really let him languish there? Had she put her daughter in harm's way, too, all for the glory of Draconex?

It didn't make any sense.

But then Diaema stole the ShadowCrystal shard from Draconex, leading Malcolm and his master to confront Ephram on Vespre, where he'd revealed to Draconex that she'd remembered everything . . .

Malcolm's mind was putting the pieces together.

After Vespre, he and his former master had then gone to that one cave on Azumar, where Diaema had been with Charles. Only for Draconex to be thwarted by Victor rescuing them—

Malcolm seethed, letting the howling, swirling sea air tousle his slightly overgrown, dirty-blond hair. Volcanor was nearly to the portal, but Malcolm couldn't stop his current train of thought: Victor was Jocelyn's older brother . . . which meant that Diaema, the woman sitting behind him, was also related to his former master.

The revelations compounded, growing an elaborate web of connection whose tendrils all led back to Jen.

Malcolm's equilibrium shifted as Volcanor banked to the right, curving toward the portal, which was excreting natural gas.

Time to light it up.

Sparing half of his focus on activating the portal to Earth while he still worked on processing Diaema's real identity, Malcolm commanded his wyvern to blast the crater with its hottest flames. Searing white rolls of fire sprang out of Volcanor's massive maw (along with a rumbling roar, as always) and doused the crater, causing the flammable gas to ignite. Immediately, an otherworldly glow overtook the entire crater. The portal was now open on both sides, but waiting on the other end was three hundred meters of crushing ocean water.

Only two flaps of Volcanor's wings away from breaking the portal, Malcolm yelled behind him, "Hold your breath and hang on!" He had half a mind to not warn Diaema at all and see if she survived, but with what he knew now, he realized he might need her.

Because he knew now how he would find Jen.

Preemptively channeling terramancy, Malcolm barked an order at Volcanor the instant before they broke across the portal's barrier. Their surroundings instantly turned to whiteness, devoid of sound. Malcolm knew he had little to no time; quickly he flipped the larvae sacks onto his chest and lay down on Volcanor's spine as the dragon's wings fully covered him and Diaema. Their hop between realms was short-lived, and all at once there came the deafening sounds and hostile turbulence of a wall of deeply pressurized saltwater from the Pacific Ocean.

Volcanor's speed, incredibly, did not diminish as it torpedoed through the water, covering the three hundred meters to the surface in mere seconds. It unfurled its monstrous wings, sloughing off layers of water, to keep itself airborne.

Malcolm felt the heat from the cresting sun on his face; no clouds were present, and he had to look toward the shimmering ocean surface to give his eyes a moment to adjust to the brightness. A speed boat passed below, its few shocked passengers looking up at the dragon he rode with their mouths open in shock, only one of them having the presence of mind to point at Volcanor in terror.

Malcolm ignored the horror-stricken people below as he looked toward the closest landmass. "Take us to the Everworld Portal," he ordered his wyvern dragon.

Volcanor spewed steam from its snout, flushing out the last drops of saltwater, and flapped its heavy wings, pointing its brimstone-crusted body to the southeast. Malcolm peered into both sacks to confirm that the larvae were still frozen; it would take half an hour to reach the portal, and he could shoot them with another ice spell until they were needed.

* * *

Jocelyn couldn't believe what she had done. She was so lost in her thoughts that she didn't know where on Earth she was; frankly, she didn't care. At least not until she was able to process how she had been the one to seal the Qonehr realm's fate with the proxiterramancic spell.

Lord Ferox never mentioned how quickly the spell would work, only that it would give him the needed leverage to secure the obedience of every realm . . . lest they decide to not cooperate, in which case he would let the proxiterramancic spell completely disintegrate them.

And Jocelyn was to blame for infecting the first realm of eleven.

She tried justifying her actions. Ferox would have surely known if the spell wasn't activated on Qonehr, therefore triggering the part of the elixir she drank to kill her instantly for her insolence. In that split second between Malcolm confessing his forgetfulness and her decision to do it herself, Jocelyn had felt fear like never before. Fear that made her instinctively react and do something she would never normally do just so she could survive and hopefully find a way out of the bind she found herself in, and maybe even fix the damage she'd been privy to—complicit in— before it was too late.

But that was just an excuse. She shouldn't have come to Malcolm's aid. She should have just sat there. Or maybe even helped the scarbeian drag Volcanor to the ground and watch as it ate the dragon's heart out.

Jocelyn squeezed her eyes, hot and wet with fresh tears. She could hear the roar of blood inside her own head. She'd failed her entire family: Jen, Victor, Charles. She wished that she could tip Jen and Victor off through telemancy, tell them what was happening and how to prevent more realms from falling victim to the proxiterramancic spell; but she had a sinking feeling that Ferox would know if she did that and then go after them.

Her Diaema persona reprimanded her at that thought, telling her to snap out of it. There were many times in Diaema's checkered past when she had had to do things that she wasn't proud of in order to survive, either to win a battle or gain the upper hand politically. Jocelyn had to remind herself that she'd done what she thought was needed at that moment and, no matter how badly she wanted to, there was no going back. No amount of wallowing and self-blaming would rewrite the past. Diaema would own it, and Jocelyn had to own it as well, though she would make sure that, moving forward, she wouldn't let her actions go in vain. The end would justify the means, and the ultimate goal was to escape with her life and warn the others before Ferox held all of the realms in the palms of his hands.

You get one last self-pitying moment before you pull yourself together, or you might as well make Ferox kill you here and now, she told herself in Diaema's tone.

"I'm so sorry . . ." Jocelyn said, thinking of her family.

Her sobs were getting weaker; she'd been distraught ever since Volcanor had blasted out of the underground tunnels on Qonehr, and was running out of tears. She needed to pull herself together; Jen and Victor were out there, somewhere, doing everything to save her husband. She needed to save *herself* in order to help bring Ferox down. Jocelyn let a sigh escape her parted lips and along with it the tormented anguish she'd let fester deep in her heart. It was a cathartic moment, one that righted her focus and crystallized her intentions for what was to come. She sat up straighter and let the wind dry the tear stains on her porcelain cheeks as she looked around, gauging her bearings.

The midday sun and clear skies provided excellent visibility as Volcanor hurtled over the heart of Venezuela. Jocelyn realized Malcolm was taking them to the Everworld portal, set deep in a sinkhole near the summit of Auyán-tepui, one of Venezuela's many table-top mountains and the one that boasted the world's highest uninterrupted waterfall, Angel Falls.

Everworld, also known as the Gateway of Portals, was the gas giant realm. It consisted of barren islands that floated above a thousand-year-old storm. Among the countless islands, only eleven housed the portals to the other ten realms. Over the millennia, as Everworld had matured and its storms had fizzled out, before a newer and stronger one would start, the magnetic powers of the portals slowly drew those select eleven islands closer in proximity to each other. Nowadays, Everworld was the preferred realm to start in if a sorcerer wanted to realm-hop quickly and efficiently, and it was clear to Jocelyn that Malcolm's intention was to capitalize on that exact accessibility in order to deliver an injected larva to each realm so the proxiterramancic spells could start in quick succession of one another. Jocelyn would never call Malcolm an ally, but in this instance she could be convinced to call him smart.

Flying only several hundred meters above sea level they weren't exactly hiding their presence, making Jocelyn wonder how many people would end up seeing the gigantic wyvern dragon that was as black as volcanic soil soaring above their heads, and what their reactions would be.

Of course, seeing a dragon would be nothing compared to witnessing your entire planet crack apart and implode.

A quick glance below Volcanor's wings showed the transition from populous, semi-urban and rural areas to swaths of land still untouched by humans. Thick, verdant canopies of trees now covered the landscape below as winding rivers split into them like cracks in an old vase. Jocelyn lifted her gaze to look ahead and saw the flat-topped mountain.

From the air, Auyán-tepui was heart-shaped with a ravine that opened a wedge in its northwestern side. Volcanor looped around to face the ravine and its cliffs, revealing Angel Falls in all its splendor. Its cascading waters tumbled over a rocky gorge that dropped over eight hundred meters. Far below, its base hid behind rolling clouds of mist, from whose depths sprung half a rainbow.

Jocelyn's reverence for the majesty of the waterfall was dashed at the sight of Malcolm pulling out a frozen larva from one of the sacks strapped around his neck. He thawed it out and, as it squirmed into wakefulness, poked his palm with Excalibur's tip and held his closed fist over the larva's mouth. Drops of blood fell into the open, sucking hole, and without any fanfare, Malcolm tossed it over Volcanor's side. Jocelyn watched as the twirling grub disappeared into the mist at the base of Angel Falls.

Earth would be the second realm to fall victim to the proxiter-ramancic spell.

The eternal rumble of the plunging water reached its loudest volume as Volcanor flew straight above Angel Falls' edge, continuing on its path to the Everworld portal one kilometer to the west.

The majority of the sinkholes atop Auyán-tepui were the result of several erosive cave-ins, but the Everworld portal had been there long before the mountain plateau was even created. Unlike the Qonehr portal, this one was currently active, so there wouldn't be any extra stress while passing through. Volcanor was almost straight above the portal when it tilted its body downward and initiated its dive, startling some hawks, wrens, and swifts that were either perched atop the leafy canopy or flying directly underneath.

The humid rainforest was quickly replaced by a flash of white light as Volcanor disappeared through the portal. The familiar sense of intra-realm weightlessness overcame Jocelyn in that split second before gravity returned, albeit a little heavier, and the saline air of Everworld's atmosphere assaulted her nostrils.

The wyvern was spit out of the gateway from Earth, which was set into the side of a small, crescent-shaped volcanic plug that had broken off from a much larger floating island eons ago. Lava spillage from a distant eruption had created a ledge along the concave side of the crescent island, now completely smooth due to the battering it had sustained whenever the powerful storm from below would reach the island's high altitude.

Volcanor snorted and moaned as it landed heavily on the ledge, clearly fatigued from all the constant flying. It favored its right hind leg as it settled onto the smooth volcanic bedrock. Jocelyn didn't budge; she looked out of the crescent bay and noticed a few other islands off in the distance, hazy as they hung ominously in the air almost as if they were patiently waiting for her and the horror she would bring to their realms.

A gravelly sound caught her attention and she watched

Malcolm finish his slide down Volcanor's cracked hide, after which he made his way around to its injured leg. Jocelyn gave it a few seconds before she followed him, her thoughts racing. Their first conversation on their way to Qonehr made Jocelyn believe that Malcolm was trying to find ways to justify Ferox's actual plan for realm conquest. She remembered how she had played him back in Draconex's lair as he knelt in front of the Throne of Dragons. Back when she only knew herself as Diaema. He had eagerly taken a seat on the throne with a new motivation to take the initiative and do it his way.

Jocelyn put on Diaema's face and slid down, landing as soft as a trained assassin could, and walked underneath Volcanor's wing. She ran her fingertips along the underside of the wing as she said, "You seemed pretty apathetic when you dropped that larva and sealed the fate of the realm you grew up in."

Malcolm was finishing up a healing spell, his totem ring depressed into the laceration on Volcanor's leg, a faint red glow pulsing around his closed fist. He looked at her with a face of stone, but there was a glint in his eye that she had a hard time identifying. Without a word, he went back to tending his dragon's injury.

Jocelyn kept her distance at two steps away and leaned on Volcanor's side as she inspected her nails, trying to look as nonchalant as possible. She could feel the steady rise and fall of Volcanor's massive chest. As she waited, that look he'd given her made her feel more and more uneasy.

"I can't guarantee it will be that simple when we get to my home realm, Vespre," Jocelyn mentioned, flicking her gaze back at Malcolm. She hoped he would infer the hidden meaning.

He did. He exhaled derisively as he stood up, patted Volcanor's leg, and looked at her, dusting his hands. "Right," he said patronizingly. He pulled the sacks' straps over his head and tossed them at Jocelyn. "Here, take them for a second." He stepped over the dragon's tail and walked around to its other side, out of sight.

Jocelyn cocked her head, confused at his sudden change in

behavior. She looked at the lumpy sacks in her hands, still thinking about Malcolm. Something was different about him . . .

She followed his path and found him unstrapping the Mysti-Crystals from his belt. Before she could say anything, he spoke first.

"I was wrong about you, you know. Being a traitor and all." He held the four MystiCrystals in his hands and shrugged. "You're a survivor. Always were, always will be. You make sure you're on the side that wins."

Jocelyn stopped, heart racing. She leaned over and rested both sacks on the ground. What Malcolm said was untrue; she wanted to correct him, but she realized that if she did she'd be giving away her true identity. The last thing she wanted was for Malcolm to know that she was Jen's mother and Charles's wife.

Instead, she said, "What makes you so certain?"

Malcolm shrugged again, walking over to the base of the volcanic plug. "You did what needed to be done on Qonehr."

Jocelyn rested her head on Volcanor's hide, trying to maintain an air of indifference. "So you think Jennifer Lancaster and her friends don't stand a chance?"

As she watched, a small section of the volcano was pushed in by an unseen force. It was rectangular in shape, and as Malcolm began sliding the MystiCrystals in, she knew he was using terramancy to store the crystals.

"I'd bet my terramancy on Lord Ferox." Malcolm finished placing the last MystiCrystal in that small opening before he closed it back up with a wave of his ring hand. "Jen is way over her head." He was looking straight at her now. "She doesn't have the strength to do what's needed to take him down."

Jocelyn's blood began to boil. *You better watch it when you talk about my daughter . . .* She kept her outward appearance as unreadable as she could, but on the inside her maternal instinct to protect her only child was swiftly rising.

Suddenly, Jocelyn found herself in a stare-off with Malcolm, and the longer it persisted, the louder her internal warning bells blared. Without breaking eye contact, she took her silky-platinum hair out of its ponytail, letting it fall in straight strands over her shoulders, covering her totem earrings. Disregarding Diaema's insistence on keeping her true intentions suppressed, Jocelyn channeled telemancy and reached toward Malcolm's mind. Surgical precision and gentleness were needed when tapping into someone else's mind, lest they should be alerted, so with absolute attention, she parted the veil into his mind.

What she found stunned her so intensely that she gasped.

He knows who I really am.

With her mask lifted, Jocelyn needed to act. Baring her sharp canines, she pushed off the ground, intending to take Malcolm by surprise. She was always much better at close combat. But the instant her feet left the ground, the breath was ripped from her lungs as Volcanor's massive tail sent her sailing into the side of the volcano with enough force to shatter her left arm. She felt her body stiffen as volcanic rock rolled over and encased her entire body.

Malcolm strode up to her and before she could say anything, he struck her in the face, sending her into unconsciousness.

CHAPTER TWENTY-THREE

Amidst the backdrop of a roiling storm, Jen was levitating in the air. She looked at her fingers, hooked like claws. Purple lightning crackled over her knuckles and fingertips, sending an electrifying sensation up her palms. She scanned the ground far below her, seeing her friends and family.

Jen couldn't understand it, but all she felt was rage. Unbridled rage. Before she could stop herself she sent lightning streaming toward her friends and they disappeared in a blinding explosion. Then she set her sights on her family. Jen would never forget the terrified expression on her mother's face as she clung to the limp form of her father. Nor the blazing look of disappointment in Victor's eyes.

Without a word, not even a goodbye, Jen pointed her fingers at the people she trusted more than anyone else and willed more forked beams of lightning down upon them. Again a powerful explosion engulfed them, but before the storm could blow away the blast, Victor shot out of the fiery mushroom cloud straight at her. His survival was so unexpected and he was so fast that Jen only stared, helpless, as he tackled her—

And that's when she woke up in a cold sweat, screaming her uncle's name.

Hands grabbed hold of her upper arms. She attempted to tear

them off of her, but the more viciously she struggled, the harder they latched on. Opening her eyes, the first thing she noticed was rolling, green pastures zipping by below. The trees gave off short shadows, indicating that it was getting close to midday. Reality slowly sank in: Jen realized she was flying through Azumar's skies. Skarmor was chirping in concern.

And Mira was the one holding her.

Jen relaxed, though she felt embarrassed; she didn't even realize she'd fallen asleep. "I'm sorry."

Mira was behind her, so she couldn't directly look at her; she could only see her out of the corner of her eye.

"For what?" Her friend threw out a light chuckle as she rubbed Jen's arm. "I was dozing off, too, but you beat me to it."

"Thanks," Jen said, trying to rub the fatigue from her eyes. She couldn't remember the last time she had a deep, uninterrupted sleep.

"Don't mention it," Mira said kindly. "I'm just glad I caught you."

Jen laughed. "Yeah, that would've been bad." She tried her best not to show Mira how shaken she was from her dream—and it *was* a dream, not a vision. Jen couldn't quite explain it, but the sensations she felt while receiving a vision were completely different from dreaming.

She was stunned that her mind had latched onto her most feared vision and built upon it in such a way; she had willingly hurt the people she loved the most—done it so brutally as though they were nothing but pesky ants begging to be squished.

Jen was beside herself. Would the visions come to pass? As she stared up into the cream-blue sky brushed with wispy clouds, she doubted if it was even possible to alter her actions enough to stop them.

She decided that was too heavy of a topic to ruminate on. She needed to remain focused on saving her father and hope that the choices she made would lead to much better outcomes.

"Jen!" Mira rested her outstretched arm on Jen's shoulder, pointing straight ahead.

Perking up, Jen leaned forward in earnest and saw Victor's humble abode. Her heart sang, knowing Victor had safely arrived, when she saw Kuirhan standing next to Pernissa and Silvress. The latter two were sitting, Pernissa on her haunches and Silvress resting her head lazily on her curled tail. Skarmor cawed in excitement, catching Pernissa's attention. She stood up, chirping back and stomping her lion's tail in anticipation of seeing her friend. Light smoke lazily plumed from the cottage's lone chimney stack, making Jen realize just how badly she wanted to curl up next to that fire and melt away the chill inside her bones.

Jen waited for Skarmor to settle on the ground and then slid off his back. Mira quickly followed suit, catching up to Jen after she scratched her griffin's neck in thanks and made a beeline for the cottage's door. Skarmor went straight to Pernissa, rubbing the side of his head on hers as they exchanged soft cooing sounds, their wings fluttering in contentment.

Jen's heart raced, reaching a crescendo as she pushed in the door to see everyone in the main living room, huddled around a woman. A woman who bore a close resemblance to herself. Jen froze as Genevieve's purple-flecked eyes found hers. She felt like a complete oaf, standing there catatonic, unable to say anything like—

"Hey," Victor said softly, suddenly blocking her view of her ancestor.

Jen flinched, not realizing his approach. "Vic . . . she's really here."

His eyes grinned along with his mouth. "Right over there." He nodded.

"Have you—"

"Told her about Charles?" Victor finished her question. "We'd just started right before you arrived."

Jen let a breath escape her chest, one of relief; she couldn't quite believe her timing.

"But Jen . . . Lord Ferox is alive."

Her blood turned to ice in her veins. This new information threatened to shatter her confidence like sugar glass, the luck she had been feeling now crumbling into despair. She furrowed her brow as her mind went into overdrive. It just didn't seem possible.

"How? We saw Ferox get atomized by Genevieve's spell!"

"We saw his *body* get atomized. It turns out his soul entered Genevieve's body during her containment spell."

The shock coursing through her system started to take its toll. Her legs felt wobbly, so she locked her knees to prevent herself from passing out. She looked past Victor at Genevieve, who was sitting calmly on the sofa.

"Is he still *in* Genevieve?" Jen asked warily.

"No," Victor said, more forcefully than he intended. He took a small breath before continuing, "No, he—why don't you hear it from her." He waved her inside, draping an arm over her shoulders. Jen's mouth went dry as she fell in step with him.

"Mira," she heard Gavin say as he rushed into view, picking up his girlfriend in a sweeping hug that forced Mira to press up on her toes. Jen respectfully looked away just as they drew in for a kiss. In the armchair off to the right, Rez was tracking her, a smile on his face that showed happiness but really covered up a profound worry. Hephalon was standing in between the armchair and the sofa, arms crossed, appearing lost in his own thoughts; he didn't even greet Jen, which was uncharacteristic of the jovial metallurgist.

That's when dread filled her to the core; Jen didn't know if she was ready to hear how Ferox had survived, but she didn't have the luxury of blissful ignorance. The urgency to get back to her father in Atlantis was never more prevalent than it was now. Charles needed to be by her side to face and defeat Lord Ferox once and for all.

"Genevieve, let me introduce you to your youngest descendant, Jennifer Lancaster," Victor said, gesturing gracefully at Jen.

When Genevieve looked up and locked eyes with her, Jen became entranced, surprised at how similar their coloring was to her own: a striking violet, with golden flecks that danced around the pupil as if sprinkled by a higher power. Jen couldn't believe she was mere feet away from the legendary mystra, a distant relative from a bygone millennium, and she wondered if she was still lost inside a dream. All Jen could do was try to keep her knees from buckling as she smiled sheepishly.

"Jennifer, so wonderful to meet you," Genevieve said. She stood up and spread her arms warmly.

"Same," Jen mustered as she walked into her ancestor's embrace. "I can't believe you're actually here," she said after they had both sat down.

"I have your friend Gavin to thank for bringing me here," Genevieve said, looking appreciatively at the astromancer, who was standing off to the side with Mira. He nodded, raising a hand respectfully but remaining silent. He was letting Jen have her moment, and she silently thanked him for that.

In an effort to establish a deeper bond, Jen opened her cargo pant pocket and pulled out the TeleCrystal. "I've been told that our clan was—*is*—the guardian of the TeleCrystal." She handed it gingerly to Genevieve who had a look of astonishment plastered on her face.

Her ancestor took it as though it were sculpted from dried sand and the slightest of movements would cause it to crumble. "My goodness . . . I *thought* I had lost something that our family had cherished for ages." She looked up with tears in her eyes. "And you have brought it back to its rightful place. I thank you." Genevieve leaned forward and hugged Jen once more.

Jen gladly accepted the embrace, finding it hard not to get emotional; she had to wipe her left eye when they pulled apart. "It wasn't just me. It took a concerted effort from all of us here"—Jen looked around, going quiet as she struggled to finish her sentence—". . . and my parents, Charles and Jocelyn, who are not here."

"Yes, Victor mentioned your parents briefly," Genevieve said, repositioning herself on the sofa. "And that your father is an omnimancer as well."

"Yes, but I fear he doesn't have much time left. He's fallen under the proxiomnimancic"—Jen glanced at Victor, making sure she'd pronounced it right—"spell, and it's too strong for any one of us to break it." She took in a breath; she'd never really thought about how she was going to ask for Genevieve's help. There wasn't a strong kinship yet between them to guarantee that Genevieve would agree to helping Charles, but Jen had to be optimistic . . . just not blindly so. "Have you had any experience with that kind of spell?"

Genevieve leaned into the sofa's cushioned backrest. "Only the most adept of mystras are capable enough to learn the proximancic spell that relates to their Mancy plane, and only an omnimancer with mastery over each of the forbidden spells has the power sufficient enough to reverse one that's been activated." Her eyes went distant as if gazing upon memories still too raw for her to share. "They are deadlier than any known pestilence, though that didn't stop Ferox from using them on the other four omnimancer clans . . ."

Her eyes refocused and she cleared her throat, handing the TeleCrystal back to Jen. Accepting the crystal, Jen slid her thumbs over its smooth, linear surface as Genevieve continued.

"Jennifer, I need you to understand that a spell of this design is nearly impossible to stop once it's been cast." A shadow of sadness covered her features.

Jen's face went numb. A fearful tremor rolled its way to her extremities. Genevieve noticed and reached out, taking Jen's hands, which were now cold and trembling.

"Can you save him?"

Jen's question seemed pointless now, but she needed to ask it.

Genevieve heaved a deep sigh. "Omnimancer mystra though I may be, I did not have the chance to master all the proximancic spells. I fear I cannot lift this spell." Resolve burned in her eyes as she rubbed Jen's hands. "But I will try my utmost."

Jen looked at the Ring of Lancaster adorning her ancestor's right middle finger and sighed, adjusting her level of hope with this unexpected revelation. Tears welled in her eyes. All she could say was, "Thank you." Deciding that her father was a much higher priority than discussing Ferox's survival and Cindergray's unexpected death, Jen followed with, "I can take you to him. He's resting in Atlantis."

When Genevieve nodded in agreement, Jen stood and looked around the room. Everyone's face was pale and showed a look of either empathy or shock, but none of them stopped her from leading Genevieve straight to the door. She itched to be on Skarmor, winging her way to Atlantis to do everything they could. They had to *try*.

She opened the door, but before she could step foot outside Gavin intercepted her, partially blocking her path. "Hey, Jen . . . I'm going back to Camelore."

Jen set her teeth, shaking her head in disbelief. "What do you mean? We're all going to Atlantis."

That's when Victor appeared to her right. "This was something we'd discussed before you and Mira arrived," he said.

Gavin continued, "There was a white stag with Genevieve when I found her."

Jen immediately thought back to her vision of a white stag standing on a cliff, late in the night.

"And when it looked at me . . ."

Jen was held in rapture as Gavin explained how he had come across the stag and the unexpected connection that had been created between them while in the Amaranthine Forest. He further disclosed the calling he'd received from the stag to find and remove Excalibur from the hands of evil. As Jen began to realize that the sword with which Malcolm had fought Hephalon on Camelore was in fact the sword of legend, it all became less unbelievable.

If she hadn't had visions of her own, Jen would have found it difficult to relate to Gavin's decision; she would have tried to convince him to first accompany her back to Atlantis. But she sympathized with the look in his eyes; it mirrored how she felt about her need to save her father and prevent herself from falling into darkness. The more he told her, the more she knew that she had to let him go; he was doing what he thought would align with his destiny, just as she was. They just happened to be on separate paths. She turned solemn when Gavin told her that, after leading him and Genevieve out of the bowels of that forsaken forest, the stag had disappeared, entrusting Gavin alone to take Genevieve the rest of the way to Victor's cottage.

What fully convinced her was the way he described the final pages of Merlin's journal and how the renowned sorcerer had predicted Lord Ferox's survival and the best chance to end his destruction for good. Jen's emotions were further put to the test when her family, of blood and by association, decided on who would embark to Atlantis with her and return to Camelore with Gavin. Mira would go with Gavin, along with Hephalon and Rez, while Jen would have Victor and Genevieve by her side. The groupings made sense, but she was still overcome with sadness to see the group split up once again.

"We'll rescue your mother too, Jen. You have my word," Gavin said once he settled next to Mira atop Silvress's back. Pernissa was already standing, carrying Rez and Hephalon. Jen let Skarmor remain by Pernissa's side until she was ready to go.

"I know," Jen said, feeling her chin quiver. Victor pulled her to his side in a supportive embrace as they both watched Silvress and Pernissa take to the skies, following the sun's path in the sky toward the portal to Earth.

Skarmor stomped earnestly a few times as he watched Pernissa ascend; she looked longingly back at him, flapping a few times in midair until Hephalon softly urged her to follow Silvress. By the time she had committed to her new destination, Skarmor was slowly trotting over to Jen and Victor, whining plaintively.

Genevieve was off to the side, a pensive look etched on her face as she, too, watched the dragon and griffin shrink into the distance. Her profile reminded Jen of her own, astounding her even further considering that they were fifteen hundred years apart. She saw a little bit of her father in Genevieve, too, which helped Jen right her focus on their destination: Atlantis.

She was still staring at Genevieve when her ancestor looked at her. Jen didn't avert her eyes, just kept them steady, now fully on Genevieve's, and smiled sweetly. "Are you ready?"

With Victor already over by Skarmor, Genevieve extended a bent arm, saying as Jen hooked hers through it, "Entirely."

They walked in step to Skarmor as he knelt down to give them an easier climb. Jen let go of Genevieve, and Victor helped her onto Skarmor, then hopped on himself, leaving a space for Jen closest to Skarmor's neck. Victor told Kuirhan that he wanted him to stay on Azumar and that he would return for him. With a mission like this, it was better to have smaller numbers than not.

Silently, Jen mounted her trusty griffin and called to him.

It was time to free Charles.

CHAPTER TWENTY-FOUR

By the time Skarmor reached Earth's portal, Jen had told Genevieve and Victor about the plan for how they would enter the floating kingdom with a little help from the TeleCrystal. Both agreed to the plan, and before they went through the portal Genevieve fully briefed Jen on what had happened to her since being released from the Halostone. And who was controlling her until not long ago.

As they passed through the interrealm veil to Earth, Jen was mortified that Lord Ferox, once Genevieve's husband, had been thrown into her body, knocking her unconscious as he paraded around as her. Genevieve had been too weak from the battle to retake her own body, and she fell back into a coma-like state several times. While this was happening, she'd had no idea what Ferox was doing between being released from the Halostone to when she had regained control of her body in the ruins of an unknown castle, looking at an old man, soaking wet from a recent storm.

Genevieve's description of the old man led Jen to believe that it had been Cindergray. Upon hearing that Cindergray was actually her son, Philip II, Genevieve nearly fainted.

"Gavin didn't mention anything about my son still being alive," Genevieve said as Skarmor clipped through the skies.

"I'm sure he said what he thought was pertinent at the time," Jen said, trying to justify Gavin's words.

"He was right there in front of me," Genevieve said, eyes unfocused, seeing her first memory out of the Halostone in the ruins of Watercress Castle. "Reaching for me . . . and I abandoned him."

"You didn't know, Genevieve," Victor consoled.

"I need to see him after we help Charles," Genevieve said, a thin blip of anxious urgency in her tone.

Jen held her breath. With everything that had transpired since she'd arrived at Victor's cottage to the present moment, flying to Atlantis, she realized she hadn't told anyone about what she and Mira had found deep within Watercress Castle. She didn't even know how to start her explanation, but she felt it was time. She flipped around on Skarmor so she was facing Victor and Genevieve and just started speaking.

"My friend Mira and I started the search for you at Watercress Castle, which used to be the headquarters of the Sorcery Guild. We discovered a secret chamber that I assume was only known by Cindergray . . . sorry, *Philip*." Jen stared into Victor's eyes as the wind blew her curls to either side of her head. "A secondary chamber near the Sacrarium."

His eyes widened, but he said nothing.

Jen continued, "Down there, Mira was able to pick up fresh scents of your son and two other sorcerers . . ." She leaned to the side so she could see Genevieve. ". . . And you."

Genevieve shook her head. "I have no recollection of ever being down there."

"After Ferox left your body, I believe those two other sorcerers, Malcolm and Draconex, returned and found Philip in that chamber, and . . ." Jen was finding it hard to summon the courage to tell the woman that her son was murdered, so she said it in the only way she could: "That was where we found your son's ashes."

Genevieve's gasp was drowned out by the steady wind, and she closed her eyes with such force that her crow's feet were extremely pronounced.

Jen looked away, starting to turn her body back around when

249

Victor caught her arm. He looked at her with the eyes of a man who had been caring for her for much longer than she had known him, and he was terrified. He leaned forward, pulling Jen's ear to his mouth.

He said, "What if Ferox somehow found Draconex's body to possess?"

With the wind fluttering her curls over her ears, Jen could still hear her breathing; it had turned shallow. "Then that means . . ."

Jen's eyes went wide. She didn't even want to say it out loud. Gavin and his team certainly weren't expecting to face Lord Ferox on a mission that revolved around reclaiming Excalibur.

"We need to get to Charles *now*," Victor said through his teeth, careful to not agitate Genevieve further.

Jen nodded, blinking her eyes back into focus and looking again at her ancestor. "Genevieve, I am so sorry," she said, truly feeling horrible. Her perception of Philip, the man she'd known as Grand Mystra Cindergray, had been forever tarnished by his actions toward his own family, but seeing the torture in Genevieve's eyes was almost too much to bear.

Genevieve straightened up, letting the wind dry her tears. "It comes with the oath that I took as a mystra. My Philip understood that, too . . . I know it."

Jen could read between those lines, and a piece of her heart chipped off. Even though the woman's words were admirable, Jen knew they acted more like a protective wall for the pain Genevieve was feeling deep inside. When Jen closed her eyes, new tears were pushed out and streaked into her ears. She wished she could have that kind of external fortitude. Genevieve had been imprisoned knowing that her son was an infant, and to be released after what must have felt like mere seconds to her only to then learn that her son had aged dramatically and died before she could properly reunite with him . . .

It was truly tragic.

"It would be a disservice to my son's legacy if I did nothing to help our descendants now."

All Jen could do was smile sympathetically back. Maybe one

day, when the time was right, Jen would tell her the truth about her son and his true legacy of deception. Or maybe she wouldn't.

An instant later, Jen no longer felt the sun's rays on her neck and arms. At a quick *caw* from Skarmor, she repositioned herself forward and saw the underside of the floating city of Atlantis. With the mission pressing on her emotions and nerves, she took the TeleCrystal out of her pocket and watched as the crystal connected with her telemancy fronting in her nexus. Like a second layer of skin, a slight energy surge emitted from the TeleCrystal, rolling over her body, down onto Skarmor, and across to Victor and Genevieve. In seconds Skarmor and everyone riding him turned invisible as the griffin ascended over the outer gates of the city.

Not much had changed in the handful of hours since her last departure from Atlantis. Contained plumes of smoke still wafted skyward as patrol cruisers surveyed the city's roads, which were both vacant and in disarray.

Without Jen needing to remind him, Skarmor arced toward the center of the city where the Akt'aron stood, looming over the concentric rings of civilization and water like a crystal-encrusted tree.

Go to the Akt'aron. My people will alert me and I'll meet you there, M'balo's voice echoed in Jen's head. Her emotions were already high, but to be back with the person she had set out to find, who was just as eager to free Charles from the proxiomnimancic spell, made Jen feel the onset of nausea. At this moment, there was nothing she wanted to do more than hug her father and have him hug her back.

A set of guards were stationed at both of the Akt'aron's entrances. Unsure if the four of them were all in league with M'balo, Jen chose the eastern entrance and created a diversion by making the water underneath the closest bridge crest out in a mighty splash. The two guards leveled their spears in the direction of the harmless noise and slowly marched toward the bridge, eyes scanning their surroundings.

Skarmor deftly glided through the entrance and landed near

the southern side of the Arbor Atlanti, out of sight of both entrances. A roaming sentinel appeared from around the giant, glowing trunk, which precipitated Jen to reveal herself and her group.

"Kl'to!" Jen waved as his path brought them into sight.

His surprise only showed in the slight raising of his upper eyelids, and his pace never wavered. "Omnimancer Jennifer," he said once he was at Skarmor's side.

Jen dismounted her griffin, and as Victor and Genevieve followed suit, she said, "M'balo didn't say you'd be the one waiting for us."

Kl'to lifted the edge of his mouth in a restrained grin. "Sh'tam was none too pleased when he found out that you had escaped his dungeon prison under my watch, so he put me on guard duty here as punishment." He gestured toward her ancestor in question.

"Oh, I'm sorry," Jen said. She tried to lighten his mood, adding, "But if it's any consolation, I'm glad it's you who we're meeting."

He tightly nodded back, surprising Jen with his lack of response. She felt Victor and Genevieve's presence looming behind her, so she stepped aside and said, "Let me introduce you to my ancestor and fellow omnimancer, Genevieve Lancaster."

Kl'to bowed to her. "It is an honor, Omnimancer Genevieve." And without further preamble, he motioned toward a lift station set into the south wall. "Let me take you to our King."

The interior of the lift was spacious enough to accommodate everyone, including Skarmor (Jen assumed that this lift was the one they'd used to get Skarmor down below initially). Once in the lift, Kl'to waited a few seconds as it dropped them deeper into Atlantis's substrata before tapping in a code on the lift's console, similar to the one that Soi'raa had entered when she had taken Jen to the guards' defunct tunnel. The lift stalled, then pulled Jen to the right as it slid in the opposite direction, dipping momentarily down a small slope before stopping its descent.

The doors slid open and Jen was met with the familiar smell of mildew and stagnant air only a subterranean tunnel could produce. Wasting no time, she ushered Genevieve and Victor ahead of her and took up the rear of the single-file line. The soft *whoosh* of the lift's doors closing faded away as her footfalls joined the rest of the group's, bouncing off the damp tunnel walls. Her heart felt wedged high in her chest as she followed Victor around a soft turn that connected a larger but sparsely lit section of the tunnel where the roots of the Arbor Atlanti effused a hauntingly calm shimmer of blue and green hues.

"I will remain here with Skarmor while you tend to your father," Kl'to said as Jen stepped up to the shaft that abutted the knotted roots.

Jen thanked the Atlantean commander before beginning her downward climb into M'balo's burrowed base. Following above her first came Genevieve, followed by Victor. Halfway down, Jen's foot slipped out of the foothold, but her hands kept her from falling. She let out a breath and had to check herself; she was getting reckless, focusing on already being next to her father rather than the task at hand, which was dangerous, even if it was as simple as climbing down a ladder.

Faint lights below her feet caught her attention, and after she landed lightly on the ground she looked up at the others: Genevieve was still a few meters above. When she turned back to the burrow, Jen did a double take: the entire space was empty, save for M'balo and Charles. M'balo had his back to her as he looked over her father's floating plank.

The rustling of Genevieve's gown caused Jen to raise her hands to help guide her ancestor to the floor. Once she was safely on the ground, Victor jumped off the third-to-last rung, his cloak billowing as he absorbed his momentum with his knees. He too looked slightly confused at the empty space as he stood back up to his full height.

Jen shrugged, leading Genevieve toward her father. "M'balo!" she called out, ready to walk into his open arms.

But when he turned around, even though the man before her

wore M'balo's clothing and looked like him, he was not the prince she had grown fond of.

It was Sh'tam, his twin brother.

"So nice of you to return, Omnimancer Jennifer," Sh'tam said.

Just then, a piercing cry echoed from the top of the shaft.

"Skarmor," Jen breathed, looking at Victor. Her totem bracelet activated its glow just as his rings slid onto his fingers. She turned around to see several guards drop from the shaft, their blasters drawn.

Jen twirled around, putting herself between Genevieve and Sh'tam while Victor did the same toward the encroaching guards.

"What is happening?" her ancestor said, alarmed.

A low, haughty laugh emanated from Sh'tam's nostrils. "You must be the fabled Genevieve Lancaster. Another omnimancer." He wriggled his arms in front of him mockingly, his face contorted in melodramatic amazement, then dropped the act. "One much more powerful than Jennifer, I presume."

Genevieve placed her hand on Jen's shoulder, stepping out into the open. She looked at Sh'tam, seeming unimpressed. "I'm here to help Charles Lancaster. I *presume* he is behind you."

Sh'tam didn't spare a glance behind him; he just smugly shrugged his shoulders and said, "Indeed! And might I say, your Atlantean is perfect, Omnimancer Genevieve."

He lifted his hand, his demeanor changing from one of playfulness to glowering seriousness. Several more guards melted out of the shadows in between the glowing roots along the curved perimeter of the burrow.

"But you cannot touch him, for he is my prisoner."

Jen wanted to lash out, but she knew that any rash decision would only hurt her chances of getting to her father, so she refrained from anything more than balling her fists and staring down Sh'tam.

"What have you done with M'balo?" Jen tried to keep her voice steady.

Sh'tam's stare returned icicles. "We do not speak that treasonous heretic's name!" he yelled. Agitatedly, he repositioned the bangles and bracelets on his wrists before continuing in a much calmer tone, "I have plans for him. He will serve me one final time in the Atra'dyu."

Jen squinted in confusion, but she wouldn't deign to respond to this. Whatever *Atra'dyu* meant, it did not instill confidence.

On either side of Sh'tam, the guards drew silently closer; some brandished blasters while others twirled long strands of rope above their heads or off to their sides. She guessed Victor was seeing much of the same from the guards who had entered out of the shaft.

"You, on the other hand . . ." Sh'tam trailed off, but his meaning was clear as he slid a thumb across his neck.

Jen rolled her eyes, then reached toward Victor and Genevieve through telemancy.

Don't let them touch you—they have some kind of agent on their gloves that locks up your muscles.

Initially, surprise came from Genevieve, then understanding.

Victor replied, *Not fun. What's the plan here?*

The ropes that some of the guards were twirling started crackling with static electricity.

Staring at Sh'tam, Jen sent, *I don't know. Our odds look bleak, but we need to try to get to Charles.*

Two omnimancers and a terramancer against, what . . . a hundred or so Atlantean warriors?

I like those odds. That was Genevieve.

Jen smiled.

So do I, Victor sent.

Jen felt a surge in her nexus and cast her first spell at the same time as Victor and Genevieve, like they were of one mind. The immense, spherical burrow flashed in a myriad of colors as the brightness of Jen's spells blended with her relatives'. She made a break for her father, but he and Sh'tam were swallowed up in a mass of soldiers, ready to protect their king at all costs.

At least Charles will be protected, too, Jen thought, and she juked to the side, letting a sizzling net sail past her.

The ground shook and cracked as Victor knocked several

guards off their feet. Genevieve sent white streaks of chrono-mancy spells toward a different section of guards, freezing them in time as they tried in earnest to set up a defensive formation.

That was where Sh'tam and her father must be.

Jen hopped between terramancy and animancy as she focused her efforts alongside Genevieve, blasting searing flames at guards who chose to get a little too close for comfort and dodging blaster bolts and more electrified nets with the lightning-fast reflexes of a white-tailed mongoose. Against the backdrop of bright spells and flashing blaster barrels, Jen and Genevieve managed to collapse the guards' defensive barrier; but Sh'tam had slipped off deeper into the throng of his armored bodies.

Continuing to evade several more errant bolts and duck under a splayed net that barely caught her shoulder, Jen found herself at arm's length from an enormous warrior, his chrome plates a size too small for his bulging frame. Genevieve was nowhere to be seen as Jen arched her neck to look at her newest opponent. His lips parted and a growl emanated through clenched teeth as he ditched his blaster and started swiping at her with hands the size of baseball mitts.

Jen rolled under his wide stance and came out the other side in a crouch next to one of the dispatched electric nets. Careful to not activate the current, she twisted it into a rope and whipped it around the Atlantean behemoth's ankles. Once she felt the tip of the net reach her other hand, she channeled the strength of a silverback gorilla and yanked as hard as she could. The giant's feet slid out from underneath him and Jen swore she felt the ground rumble from his fall.

He did not stir.

Jen didn't have time to celebrate her victory. She stood back up and found her uncle and ancestor moving through a thinning pack of guards, the two of them fighting back-to-back; it looked as though they were old sparring partners, twisting and turning around each other to knock down guards at a satisfying and alarming rate.

From where Jen stood, her eyes couldn't get a read on Sh'tam's location so, as her spells continued to shoot forth from her finger-tips, she decided to use her ears. Channeling the echolocation of the common vampire bat, she welcomed an array of sounds ranging across almost every decibel level. Singling out Sh'tam's voice in the cacophony proved to be difficult, but once she detected his noticeable, fast-paced breathing, she looked confidently to her left in the direction of the shaft's opening.

Sh'tam is trying to escape with Charles at the shaft, Jen sent to her relatives. *I've got him.*

If either Victor or Genevieve sent anything in their telemancy bond, Jen was unaware of it. The only thing that mattered was getting to her father.

She kicked off the ground, checking guards to the ground and denting their chrome armor as she rammed into them with the brute force of a white rhinoceros that only animancy could gift, paired with hardened shoulders and arms courtesy of terramancy. The guards farther down the path toward Sh'tam must have seen Jen coming; they seemed less inclined to be trampled, so they opted to either step aside or at least look like they were trying to stop her with purposefully late tosses of their nets or poorly timed blaster shots.

Sh'tam's breathing was the only thing Jen could hear; she was dead set on stopping him before he could take her father away from her, no matter what. His breath crackled in her ears amidst his sudden outbursts at whichever guards were unlucky enough to be nearest him. Jen picked up her pace when she spotted her father's floating, stone plank between the last line of guards.

The spray of spells she threw at the guards' feet blinded them, and as they covered their eyes with their gloved hands, she soared high over their heads with a terramancy-enhanced leap.

Now, with no one between her and Sh'tam, Jen tore up the ground as she sprinted the final few meters, catching the so-called king by surprise.

But that only lasted for a split second.

His eyes became steel as he reached behind his back and drew two slender daggers. He spun them in his hands as he met Jen's rush, his smile a mischievous thing. The blades were so sharp that each thrust seemed to puncture the very air with a high-pitched *shing!*

Jen's nexus went into overdrive to save her from getting impaled in the throat and abdomen, but with every swing, Sh'tam seemed to get faster and anticipate further into the future. His next two counterstrikes sliced Jen on her upper arm and across her cheek. His form was so fast, the blade so sharp, that she didn't even feel them break skin until she noticed a hot, wet streak traveling down her cheek and her left hand slick with blood.

"Did I mention that I am the most advanced and complete combatant in all of Atlantis?" Sh'tam's conceited tone nearly made Jen gag. "I am also the head trainer of the entire King's Guard."

He launched himself at her, bringing his knee up to strike Jen directly on her forehead, but she rolled to the side, narrowly missing a brutal strike that would have cracked her skull wide open.

Jen pushed off the ground and, after making sure no other attackers were in her blind spots, let Sh'tam twist around and go on the offensive once more. Jen waited, her skin crawling with adrenaline, until he was two steps away before she raised her hands, sending a thick cloud of dust directly into his menacing eyes.

His rageful screams cut through the din of the fighting all around the burrow, but that gave her enough time to run straight for her father's plank, unguarded and pushed up against the closest wall.

Jen hadn't a clue what she would do once she got to Charles; she'd think of something once she was next to him. Her father's head was turned away from her, facing the burrow's wall, but seeing how sallow his skin was drove her to strain her muscles, letting her reach a dizzying speed. She slid into the side of the floating plank, the abrupt stop sucking all of the air out of her lungs and chipping the densely packed soil with the edges of the plank. She coughed as she sucked in more air, but she didn't care

—she was next to her father. She touched his wrist and that small contact caused her to start crying, but another emotion quickly took control when her knees suddenly buckled from behind: terror.

"Dirty play, Jennifer," Sh'tam admonished as he whacked the side of her head so hard that tiny stars exploded all across her vision. "I can play dirty too."

She crumpled to the ground, unable to move. Facing the interior of the burrow, she watched helplessly as Victor and Genevieve were overrun by waves of guards. She tried screaming, but all she could muster was a wheeze as her vocal cords quickly became numb. Her body's reflexive spasm from a harsh kick to her stomach caused her to curl up into the fetal position. Two more kicks landed with dull thuds to her sternum and, again, her stomach.

A thin but insanely strong hand grabbed her cheeks and forced her to watch as her relatives were taken down, Victor wrapped in an electrified net and Genevieve limp like Jen was; a lucky guard had touched her bare shoulders with a numbing glove, but not before that arm was sheared clean off by a spell.

With her stamina melting away too quickly to process, the last thing she heard before Stygian darkness overtook her was Sh'tam's sickening laughter.

CHAPTER TWENTY-FIVE

Gavin held Mira's hands, which were wrapped around his waist as she slept during the flight to Camelore. They had already traveled through the portal to Earth and were biding their time before their showdown on Camelore would commence. Gavin ran his hand along Silvress's tough, slate-blue-gray hide; he would have never gotten this far had it not been for the cooperation of Charles's dragon. She had grown on him, and he was debating if he should find his own dragon once this was all said and done, barring that he survived reclaiming Excalibur.

And killing Lord Ferox with it.

He jostled uncomfortably at the thought, threatening to wake Mira. Wincing, he looked over his shoulder and saw the side of her head planted on his back, her glossy, black hair shimmering in the sunlight. He got lucky—she was still fast asleep. Gavin caught her scent on the breeze, and it intoxicated him, taking him away from the horrors and burdens of war and this constant struggle to survive. Being next to her again on this longer journey made him realize he would do anything to survive so he could grow old with Mira. Maybe even wed her someday.

Gavin surprised himself at the thought. For as long as he could remember, all that had mattered was astromancy and his mastery over it. He'd been so focused on rising through the Sorcery Guild ranks, ever since he'd been given a second chance after Victor had saved him in the Pit, to earn the rank of mystra before he turned twenty-five; but the personal growth he'd experienced in the last couple months changed his perspective more than he'd thought. Or maybe he just needed some time alone with his thoughts to articulate what all these feelings really meant.

He let out a long, burdened breath and looked down at his girlfriend's hands in his own. He rubbed where they overlapped with a thumb, admiring her soft skin and her slender fingers. He would never stop admiring her natural beauty. He revisited his future plans, realizing that it was true: he wanted nothing more than to be with Mira.

And he would protect her at all costs. He would give his life for hers if it came down to it.

But first he needed to take back Excalibur and use it on Ferox. That was the prophecy—that was what the white stag had communicated to him back in the Amaranthine Forest, and what the Light Bringer was destined to do. Plain and simple.

But no, it wasn't simple. Not at all. Gavin, along with every tenderfoot that had passed through the halls of Watercress Castle, had been taught about Merlin's prophesied warrior who would restore balance to the eleven realms and end the thousand-year war with the Dark Watchers. He remembered revering the Light Bringer, this mysteriously mythic being, wishing that he would matter half as much. Little did he know that he was the person for whom the Sorcery Guild had searched for centuries.

Now, all grown up and the Sorcery Guild all but obliterated, Gavin had learned that the mantle of the Light Bringer was a heavy privilege, one only further compounded by his interaction with the white stag. It made him feel horribly guilty that his only desire was to be with the love of his life.

Maybe that desire would lead him to restore the needed balance.

Gavin, you're thinking in circles. And you're tired, he told himself, breaking his gaze from Mira's hands. He looked to the right to see Pernissa gliding a few meters from Silvress's wing, carrying more than her fair share of weight but looking as though it didn't affect her (which made sense, since Pernissa was Hephalon's griffin, and had flown his weight around for years). Rez was sitting in the front spot atop the griffin's back, twirling his card totem between his nimble fingers. Hephalon took the rear, unusually stalwart and silent, his long, braided beard a cascading auburn waterfall with streaks of gray that seemed to multiply with the passing of each day.

Gavin would never be able to fully express his gratitude to them for following him into this battle. And it *was* going to be a battle. Hephalon's distant gaze made it seem like he was already there, even though his body was still on Pernissa; Gavin imagined the metallurgist envisioning the confrontation and inevitable exchanging of spells and planning a path toward victory. Hephalon was as fiercely loyal as he was an adept terramancer, and Gavin knew the man wouldn't go down without a grisly fight. He hoped it wouldn't come to that.

But either way, Gavin knew it would end today. He could feel it in his bones.

It would've helped if Merlin could have been more specific as to exactly how the Light Bringer would bring balance to the realms. Excalibur wasn't won by the frightful or lost by the absent-minded; to wield such a legendary sword, you had to be not only worthy of its valor, but strong of body and spirit, to undertake the responsibility associated with it.

Malcolm was neither of those things, which made Gavin seethe all the more. It was a travesty in its purest form for someone of such foul repute to rest it on his hip. Gavin didn't even care how Malcolm had obtained it, only that he would soon lose claim of it.

Preferably losing his head in the process.

Afternoon clouds dissipated as both dragon and griffin broke into the stratosphere, alerting Gavin that Camelore was nearby. In an effort to keep their stealth intact, Gavin had them remain below the clouds for as long as possible. With as many times as

Malcolm had surprised him and the rest on Camelore, Gavin burned with the desire to finally return the favor.

Gavin signaled *Follow me* with his hands to Hephalon and Rez, directing Silvress underneath Camelore toward its eastern edge, where the slightly elevated terrain would grant them the best vantage point over the floating island.

The cracked underside of Camelore was heavily shadowed as it hung suspended in the air; the ease with which it floated belied its true size and tonnage. Gusts of wind whistled around its rocky outcroppings, sending Gavin back in time to when he, just a young tenderfoot, would practice drills and techniques with Mystra Mangstrom as they channeled astromancy to invert gravity and use the underside of Camelore as their training grounds.

He knew every inch on and under Camelore, so Gavin had no reason to suspect—or expect—that he was being watched. It started when Silvress stopped so abruptly that Gavin had to throw an arm out in front of him so he wouldn't slam into the dragon's neck. Unfortunately, his inability to absorb the loss of momentum caused Mira to wake up.

"What is it, girl?" Gavin asked, his efforts in trying to calm Silvress seeming to be futile.

Mira removed her arms from around his waist and groggily asked, "What's going on?"

Silvress snorted in short bursts while flapping her wings frantically, warily scanning the barren landscape of Camelore's underside. She would not fly any farther.

Hephalon brought Pernissa back around to meet Gavin. "Everything okay over there?"

"Not sure," Gavin said, an eerie feeling beginning to flood his nerves. "Something's spooking Silvress."

Just after he said that, Gavin saw a part of the landscape move. More like . . . *slither.*

Silvress bucked and let out an astonished roar as she began to turn herself around. Gavin's head swiveled to not lose sight of that part of Camelore's crust, his mind initially explaining it away as a trick of his eyes, since the shadows were so deep and dark; but he quickly discarded that thought when a row of feathers fanned out from the crust and a long body detached itself, changing its camouflaged coloring to its normal scaly green and emitting a hiss that tore through the air and clawed at his ears.

The ophidite.

"Babe, hold on!" Gavin looked over his shoulder at Mira, giving her a quick kiss on the cheek as she wrapped her arms around him again.

"Uh, fellas?" Rez said, pointing at the feral winged serpent. Pernissa cawed in fright and sped up, having the same idea as Silvress.

Cursing, Gavin urged Silvress to fly faster. In the corner of his eye he saw Pernissa dart away, beginning her own evasive aerial maneuvers. He could see the tip of Mira's whip trailing over Silvress's left side, and he knew his girlfriend was ready. He fumbled with his orb totem as adrenaline hit him like a freight train, causing his fingers to tremble slightly and lose their dexterity.

He groaned. "Come *on!*"

It didn't help that Silvress's flight path was fast and erratic, but the orb finally popped out of his pendant. He caught it in one hand as he tried to reorient himself in the chaos. Silvress was cutting through the air like a bullet, causing Gavin to combat the intense g-forces by putting a defensive astromancy spell around Mira and himself.

By the time Gavin secured his totem in his hand, the ophidite had disappeared. He glanced over in Pernissa's direction, noticing that she had turned back around and was racing toward Silvress. Hephalon shouted something that Gavin couldn't quite under- stand. Silvress was flying more smoothly but was still on high alert. Confused, Gavin looked around but couldn't locate the deadly serpent.

"Where did it go?" he said loud enough for Mira to hear.

A few seconds passed, then she said, "Watch out!"

Gavin flinched at the sudden warning but still didn't see

anything.

Almost as if he had thought it into existence, a sharp hiss hit his right ear. Before Silvress was dive-bombed by a creature five times her size, Gavin got her to dart to the left. The rigid body, plated with scales and outlined with spinal feathers, shot a couple of meters off to Silvress's side; like a good predator, the ophidite noticed its near miss and curled its sharp tail, slamming it across Silvress's back and tail in less than half a second, barely missing Mira.

Feeling as though he'd just been in a head-on collision with a semitruck, Gavin felt his hip socket pop and saw his totem fly out of his grip, down in the direction of the ophidite.

"I'm fine," Mira said, as if reading his thoughts. "Go after your totem!"

"Sil, there!" Gavin said without hesitating. He pointed, and by luck Silvress was still lucid enough to obey with a tight roar. She curled her svelte, aerodynamic body into a pike and with a forceful flap of her wings and a whip of her tail she sent herself into a headlong dive straight toward the ophidite.

Gavin straightened out his arm as Silvress gained on his falling totem, but he knew they wouldn't make it when the ophidite's head swiveled to look straight up at him. It unhinged its jaw, opening its mouth so wide that Gavin could see, bordered by its monstrous fangs, a tunnel of ribbed, pinky flesh set around a flicking, forked tongue.

Almost skinning his arm along the tough scales of the ophidite body, Gavin was about to have Silvress bail out when Mira's whip shot out from behind him and wrapped around his totem. A *caw!* split the air and Pernissa whizzed into Gavin's vision, flying above the ophidite's snout as Hephalon swung his mace with herculean strength, connecting solidly with the serpent's cheek bone. Without needing a command, Silvress rolled, missing the serpent's gigantic maw and blasting the other side of its head with a spout of condensed flames for added measure.

The ophidite made a sound akin to a roar as it writhed in pain, no doubt feeling an incendiary burn and a broken facial plate. Malcolm hoped that Silvress had blinded the damn thing.

Pernissa wasn't too far away now, and when Silvress caught up to her, Gavin said, "Let's get topside! Anywhere on Camelore is better than here."

The ophidite was even more agitated now. It hissed so loudly that Gavin felt his bones shake. The ophidite was gaining as Silvress and Pernissa charged for the closest edge of Camelore, but it clearly still felt the effects of their attacks: it rammed into the crust as it slithered in chase, sending chunks of dried dirt and sediment crumbling from the island's underside and falling toward the earth.

"We're almost there!" Gavin said.

He winced when he rested a fist on his right hip, remembering that it was still dislocated. Pressure on his left shoulder distracted him. Looking over, he realized it was Mira's arm—and in her hand rested his orb totem.

"Thanks, babe," he said as she dropped it into his waiting hand. "Now, lean to the right."

Immediately he reached behind him, pointed his orb at the wild ophidite, and fired off a few spells at the floating island's underside above its path. More chunks of sediment were blasted away, crashing into the serpent's face, only enraging it more.

"I don't think that's helping!" Mira said, holding his waist tightly with one hand and flicking her bullwhip totem to crack her own spells at the ophidite.

Gavin grunted and looked ahead, noting that Camelore's edge was still several hundred meters away. With the rate at which the ophidite was gaining, they wouldn't make it even at Silvress's top speed.

"Gav, what are you doing?" Mira asked as Gavin stood up, balancing on Silvress's back.

"The ophidite's too fast. Get topside with Heph and Rez, and I'll meet you there. Watch out for Malcolm."

He leaned down and gave her a kiss on her forehead before launching himself toward the island's underside. Channeling astromancy, Gavin grabbed ahold of the invisible fabric of gravity and charged his feet with his totem. He felt the pull of gravity take hold; quickly he drew his feet above his head and, steeling himself, he dropped onto the crust upside down. A thin ripple of white energy rolled across the rocky landscape from where he landed, securing his hold with astromancy.

Trusting that Mira had listened to him and wasn't waiting around, Gavin kicked off the crust with a solid push of his heels and began sprinting toward the incensed serpent. Its eyes were bedeviled with malicious intent and its wings had since drummed up a fierce headwind, but Gavin wasn't deterred; injecting his orb with energy, he let it float in front of him as his hands swirled in a pattern that would conjure a beam spell. Just as he completed the motion and a crisp, white beam of light shot out from his totem, the ophidite pointed its tail at him and sent feathered spurs his way. Some were instantly disintegrated by Gavin's spell while others seared past his head and legs, lodging themselves deep into Camelore's crust.

By the time his spell reached the ophidite it had swerved out of the way, rendering the beam harmless as it sailed through the air, eventually fizzling out. With a curse Gavin planted his right foot and lurched to the left, just in time to miss several more feathered projectiles. They struck in a tight grouping right where he'd been seconds before.

Gavin didn't look back, just ran, reaching his top speed and then some with the help of his powers. He hurtled over mounds and around outcroppings, hoping he was leading the ophidite away from Mira and the others. Then he felt the wind die down, and the constant, low hissing stopped. Skidding to a halt, he threw a look behind him and sucked in air.

The ophidite was nowhere to be seen.

"Oh, no . . ." Gavin breathed.

With an uneasy feeling in the pit of his stomach, he rushed in Silvress and Pernissa's direction. They too were out of eyeshot, which had to mean that they'd made it to the surface.

Now knowing the ophidite's lethal speed, Gavin prayed he

would beat it to Mira and the rest. He stumbled over the uneven terrain, having lost his focus, but recovered well enough to keep his feet moving. His eyes were glued to the edge of the island, but it seemed like no matter how fast he moved his legs he wasn't gaining any ground.

"Come on!" he yelled again, tears clouding his vision.

After the longest five seconds of his life, he reached the edge and, after scaling it with ease, released his gravity spell. With sweat stinging his eyes, Gavin peered across an open, grassy field. To the right, far in the distance, were the griffin stables, and in the distance directly ahead was the Arbor Sacré, looming over the entire island like a sick, rotting husk. The tree's bruised colors of purple and dark red coursed along its deadened bark and leafless, barbed boughs.

Gavin scrambled over the lip of the giant floating rock and sprinted toward the top of the grassy knoll. Releasing his grip on astromancy and placing his totem back in his pendant, he fell to his knees next to Hephalon, who lay on one side, his splintered round shield and scorched battleaxe barely out of his reach.

"Heph!" Gavin yelled, shaking the burly man roughly. After a few seconds with no response, he rolled him onto his back and checked for a pulse. Thankfully there was one, and it was steady enough, but Hephalon was out cold.

Working quickly, Gavin summoned astromancy once again. Gleaning sweat from his forehead, he isolated three hydrogen atoms while easily finding an atom of nitrogen in the air. He brought his fingers to the metallurgist's nose and, with the snap of his fingers, chemically bonded them together.

"Whew!" Hephalon reflexively shot up from the concentrated ammonia gas like he'd been launched from a trebuchet. "Merlin's Beard!" He swatted at his nose, but quickly grabbed his leg instead and moaned.

"Heph, what happened?" Gavin asked loudly, hoping to cut through the man's visible pain.

"He—he killed Silvress," Hephalon said, still clutching at his leg but looking down the other side of the knoll.

At the bottom was a fallen dogwood tree. Next to it, in a pool of blood soaking the grass, lay Silvress. One of her wings had been torn to shreds. A lazy breeze had blown a few white flower petals onto her body, some stuck where fresh blood stained her hide.

Gavin rocked back on his heels and sat next to Hephalon, trembling in shocked sadness. He didn't fight the tears, and the first one to fall trailed down the border of his nose and eventually stopped along his top lip.

"I shouldn't have stayed behind . . ." He dropped his chin to his chest.

Hephalon crawled over to his battleaxe. "Perny was still alive when I was rendered unconscious. And he took Rez and Mira."

Gavin snapped his head up so abruptly that his jaws clicked. "Who's 'he'? Malcolm?!" His blood began to boil.

Hephalon stuck the head of his axe into the ground and propped himself up with great effort. "No. The bastard resembled Draconex, but it wasn't him."

If Mira is dead . . .

Gavin clenched his teeth, containing the fury inside as he helped Hephalon stand. Both of them looked upon the body of Silvress, the breeze drying Gavin's tears until all that remained was a scowl, ready to unleash hell on Malcolm and whomever his twisted accomplice was.

"I'm willing to wager my entire armory that he's waiting for us under the Arbor Sacré," Hephalon said, a crack of fatigue in his voice.

Gavin inhaled and nodded, finding it hard to tear his gaze from a creature that had befriended him so willingly. He silently promised her death would not be in vain.

"Can you walk?" he asked Hephalon, unblinking.

Hephalon snickered, kicking the head of his axe and guiding it over his shoulder. "I can do more than that, lad. I can *fight*."

"Then it's time we go to work," Gavin said, pulling his gaze from the fallen dragon.

The long blades of grass brushed against his boots as he

started toward the spellbound Arbor Sacré, and every step became quicker until he was in a full sprint.

Not too long after, Hephalon matched his pace.

"You think this metallurgist is only good at whacking hot iron and drinking ale?" Hephalon huffed, and slowly he began to overtake Gavin.

With surprise written on his face, Gavin caught up with him, and together they hugged the southern shoreline of the island's small inland lake and set their sights on the Arbor Sacré, nestled in the center of Camelore. The grass in a fifty-meter radius of the tree was bereft of nutrients, and its usual healthy, verdant coloring had been replaced by brittle, hay-like stalks that crunched under both sorcerers' footfalls. The translucent invisibarrier walls of the Pentarena had been demolished, allowing them to cut through the animancy section. Gavin looked around the abandoned area, but not even the ophidite was coiled in the tree's branches.

Hephalon motioned to Gavin, signaling that they should separate and meet on the other end of the tree. Nodding, Gavin popped out his totem and felt it grow in his hands. If a trap was imminent, he would be ready.

Massive, curled dead leaves littered the purple-veined tree trunk, cracking like centuries-old pottery under his weight. Gavin's head was on a swivel, determined to not be taken unawares, when he heard a voice from Hephalon's side of their perimeter run. His adrenaline surged and he followed the curve of the gigantic trunk until he saw Hephalon. The terramancer mystra had his axe and mace angled in front of him in an attack stance, a sneer plastered on his face.

"Let them go! *Now!*"

A condescending laugh came from closer to the base of the Arbor Sacré, and when Gavin slid to a stop he noticed a tall, shrouded man standing at the foot of a throne that had been carved into the tree itself. He held Mira by the arm and Rez, limp and unconscious, by the throat. He was not Malcolm. Mira was the first to notice Gavin. She screamed his name, causing the man to look Gavin's way, and when his eyes fell on him, his laughter cut off and his eyes widened ever so slightly.

"My, you look *exactly* like Arthur . . ." the man said in an uncannily familiar voice. His face looked almost *too* similar to Lord Draconex's, but his skin was healthier, he held more muscle on his frame, and his pulled-back hair had more jet-black coloring than arctic white. In the middle of his chest glowed a deep-purple crystal.

The man caught Gavin's fleeting look at Mira.

"Ahh, is this your Guinevere, Arthur?"

Gavin had a comeback on his tongue but kept it to himself; he didn't want his emotions to cause him to unintentionally hurt Mira. Instead, he repeated Hephalon's order, this time much calmer but just as stern: "Let them go."

Gavin almost lost it when the tall figure pulled Mira closer and sniffed her hair before shaking Rez like a rag doll. "No, I think I'll keep them. I hear it's very hard to find good help in this millennium." He looked back at Gavin with an upturned nose. "And put away that bauble, boy. For if you use it, your friends will meet a horrific end."

Gavin looked at his totem, and the light encapsulating its entire surface winked out before it minimized to the size of a marble.

"And fret not, for your griffin is in the stead of my ophidite."

"I find that hard to believe, considering you killed my dragon," Gavin said coldly. It was difficult to not envision her bloodstained body and shredded wings.

"A reminder of your fate should you not heed what I say," the man responded callously. "After all, very soon I will be your heralded ruler."

Gavin's mouth slackened and he exchanged a glance with Hephalon. They had come to Camelore for Excalibur and instead got the most reviled sorcerer to ever live.

"But first," Ferox said, the ruthless cold in his eyes matching that of his tone, "you will get me Charles and Jennifer Lancaster."

CHAPTER TWENTY-SIX

Malcolm watched from atop Volcanor as the scarbeian larva, injected with the proxiterramancic spell, twisted and twirled in its descent toward a massive fault line near Ocuul's equator.

Once it disappeared into the dark fissure, he looked at his two sacks, one fully empty while the other held the final frozen larva: one last realm which he intended to visit.

He just needed Diaema to take the bait he'd left behind with her.

"Back to Everworld, Volcanor," Malcolm said indifferently. The wind at that altitude was extremely shifty and tousled his grown-out, sandy hair every which way.

His dragon huffed and, shaking his massive head, started back toward the portal through which they'd arrived.

The sepia tone of Ocuul's atmosphere surprisingly reduced its clarity, lending to Malcolm's decision to close his eyes and trust that his dragon would remember the way back as Diaema's words echoed in his mind.

"You know he will never trust you . . ."

An annoyingly sharp statement to which Malcolm had initially taken offense, but as he emptied the sacks of larvae, he'd begun to view it as a boon—an opportunity at redemption. Once he completed his mission and returned with Jen as his prisoner, Lord Ferox's trust would be more than earned. It had to, otherwise Diaema would have been right and all of this would have been for nothing.

Malcolm had devoted his life to Lord Ferox's vision, trusting that the history books and the Dark Watcher tribe's dogma had remembered it correctly as was passed on from generation to generation; and now that Malcolm was an integral part in its execution, there was no turning back.

That mentality was what separated Ferox from the likes of Draconex and every other Dark Watcher who had perished during the Sesquimillennial Jubilee massacre. The process might very well get messy, but what should never be lost was the end goal, and if the realms wouldn't bend a knee to Lord Ferox then they would die. There was no other alternative.

Malcolm's skin prickled as the interrealm veil passed over him, and when he opened his eyes, the sepia hue of Ocuul had been replaced with the monochromatic, overcast atmosphere of the Everworld realm. A fine mist coated his face as Volcanor rumbled past the portal islands of R'eath and Kkonthia, both of which he'd already visited. He heard the swirling winds and the thunder crashes of the ageless storm raging below. Out of curiosity, he glanced down and saw the fomenting clouds churning their way through the lower atmosphere strata, continuing their monotonous rampage across the gas giant with no intention of dissipating.

Looking back up, he smirked. There it was—the island that held the portal to the final realm for his last larva. Volcanor banked to the right, putting the island belonging to Nyzanth's portal directly in its flight path.

As they passed around the Vallei Mortic island, the one that held Earth's portal came into view. It was still several hundred meters away, but Malcolm could hear a loud cracking noise that echoed from its crescent bay. There in the distance was Diaema, her body encased in the layers of lava rock Malcolm had covered her in. She tucked her neck into her chest and her rocky prison exploded outward, sending chips and shards twirling off the island's edge to be quickly swallowed up by the top of foamy storm clouds.

"Volcanor, land on that mountainside," Malcolm snapped at his dragon, pointing back toward the Vallei Mortic island. He had no choice but to alter his plan.

Volcanor rumbled in obedience, circling back and latching onto the cracked mountain with its sharp claws. All the while Malcolm intently watched the small form of Diaema, dealing with his frustration over the fact that he would have to go to Nyzanth once he was finished with the vampire.

Errant, shifty gusts of the eternal storm below threatened to dislodge Volcanor from its perch, but the dragon was stubborn, slashing the air with its leathery wings to combat the buffeting winds.

Malcolm had wanted Diaema to escape, of course, knowing that whatever kind of bind he chose to put her in would be easily destroyed with her extreme strength. And from there she would surely take the MystiCrystals he'd purposefully left behind. It was too good for her to pass up. (After all, Malcolm knew that she'd been looking for a chance to escape ever since she'd reluctantly agreed to partner with him.)

Her body looked stiff, her eyes scanning all around her, until finally she shrank, taking on her albino bat form. She fluttered in the direction of Earth's portal gate.

"Take the MystiCrystals . . ." Malcolm muttered, watching intently.

As if Diaema had heard him, she bounced in midair as her flaps quickened and she reversed course, gliding back toward where Malcolm had hidden the MystiCrystals.

Diaema was back in human form in the blink of an eye, and she drove her hands into the base of the volcano, digging until she found them. Scooping them up, she then ran back toward the portal and jumped in, disappearing into the shining gateway back to Angel Falls, Venezuela.

"Good little Lancaster," Malcolm said. "Volcanor, follow Diaema!" His stealth all but gone, he pointed at Earth's portal gate.

Volcanor chomped at his command zealously, pushing off the mountainside with enough force to tear out chunks of rock and sediment.

The time was now. Jen would be his.

CHAPTER TWENTY-SEVEN

AAAAAAAAHHH!

The roar of a frenzied crowd brought Jen back from the dark void of unconsciousness. The smell of fire and sand filled her nostrils as her body slowly awoke. When she tried moving, a pain like nothing she'd experienced before shot through her abdomen, causing her to arch her back and slam her head against something smooth and hard. Crying out in pain, she pried her eyes open to find that her hands and feet were clamped to a plank; she couldn't even move her fingers and toes. Ahead of her was an immense, opaque wall, frosted with natural light. To her right a flaming basin rested atop a lone podium; from it came the wisps and breaths of a calm fire that didn't have to contend with any breeze. Jen stiffened at the sight of, to her left, the commander of the King's Guard, Kl'to. He was standing at attention, arm at a right angle holding a spear, facing forward like a good soldier.

"Kl'to, what's happening? You have to get me out of here," Jen whispered. The split skin on the right side of her face pulled uncomfortably.

At first she didn't think he'd heard her; he continued to stare ahead, but before she could repeat herself she heard him speak out of tight lips.

"I am sorry, Omnimancer Jennifer." Kl'to's eyes shone with remorse.

Just then the fresh memory of Victor and Genevieve struck her, and she relived the sight of them getting overtaken by countless guards as Sh'tam repeatedly drove his foot into her stomach.

"Where's Victor and Genevieve?"

Kl'to repeated, "I am sorry—"

"*Stop* saying that! Just tell me what's going on!" she said, her exasperation finally catching up with her. Her abdomen blazed again with pain, but she needed answers before she could focus on her injuries. The droning of thousands continued on the other side of the wall, a sea of volume that ebbed and flowed. "You watched Skarmor as you let us walk right into a trap." Her throat started to close from a wave of emotion. "Please tell me you weren't a part of it . . ."

Kl'to didn't move save for his lower jaw, which grinded imperceptibly from side to side. "The king has my family," he finally said. "He suspected cracks in my allegiance ever since your escape from the palace's prison. It wasn't long until he descended upon my wife and daughter, hiding them from me and threatening the kinds of torture devised for only the worst of our criminals . . . unless I helped him root out Prince M'balo's rebellion." He closed his eyes and dropped his head, finally letting the guilt and fear show on his usually stoic visage.

Jen bit her lip, swallowing a knee-jerk, reactive statement she knew would only make Kl'to feel worse. Instead she focused on what needed to be done to find her relatives and Skarmor. One issue at a time.

Resigned, she said, "I take it you won't release me."

That's when Kl'to finally looked at her. And that was all he needed to do: Sh'tam had trapped him. He might as well have been imprisoned alongside his family. He swallowed and, flicking his eyes down at her leg, whispered, "I returned what is yours. I am sorry I cannot do more."

Jen furrowed her brow and craned her neck to follow Kl'to's gaze, but the crowd roared again, distracting her. A chorus of horns blared outside and the frosted wall began to slide up, allowing the impatient sunlight to spread across the scuffed marble floor, closer and closer to Jen's bound feet. Kl'to straightened and looked ahead, sparing one last utterance before he escorted her out into the blinding sunlight.

"Your father has been placed in the King's Guard's detention center in Ring Two."

The harsh sunlight struck Jen's eyes and she winced, closing them briefly. When she opened them again, Kl'to was no longer by her side. She was alone as her floating plank took her to the center of what she now realized was an open-air stadium. Several columns dotted the base of the large arena, with limestone doors and chrome-latticed gates alternating the perimeter. Above the first level spanned many rows of stands, all of which were filled with bobbing heads and whipping arms as the crowd jeered louder. As the arena grew vertically in Jen's vision, unveiling more sun-drenched stands, arches, and staircases, she guessed, aghast, that this stadium could hold easily over fifty thousand spectators.

And it looked like every seat was taken.

Movement below snapped her sights back toward the arena's first level. Built into the curved stands directly ahead and set safely one story above the arena floor rested an elaborately decorated, covered viewing box. The figure standing front and center was Sh'tam. Jen's breath caught in her chest when she saw, draped in shadows off to the king's left, Genevieve. She searched for Victor, but he wasn't in the royal box. The king gestured to her with both hands, his layered tunic flowing with every movement. The crowd surged with both cheers and boos in response, and Sh'tam dropped his right hand; with his left he pointed in the direction of another frosted glass door.

Slowly it rose to reveal two guards pushing an ornate chrome sled, and on it was a cage that held an agitated griffin.

"Skarmor!" Jen called out, fighting against her restraints.

Her griffin heard her over the din of the riled bystanders, cocking his head before ramming his cage with a shoulder, only making it rock slightly. The two guards dropped their ropes, leaving the sled not even a quarter of the way into the arena. Jen was glad that Skarmor was still alive, but furious that they had caged him for some sick enjoyment.

"Citizens of the most glorious city on Earth," Sh'tam boomed, drawing Jen's attention, though only partially. He raised his hands, and as he held them higher the crowd swelled louder. He seemed to feed on their energy. "I call you to the Atra'dyu, today, to celebrate the start of my long and cherished rule as your rightful king. I bring to you the one responsible for Atlantis's misfortunes as of late."

Another roar. Sh'tam waited for the noise to die down.

"Jennifer Lancaster used her devious, unholy powers of wizardry to tear Atlantis asunder, thereby removing our beloved city from its hallowed grounds, left to drift aimlessly in the heavens."

At that point, it would have been futile to argue the veracity of Sh'tam's claims. Either the citizens believed every word he said in blind allegiance, or they were too scared of his wrath to oppose him publicly. Regardless, Jen couldn't stand Sh'tam's voice, and the longer he spoke the harder she found to listen.

Genevieve was surrounded by guards but wasn't shackled, leading Jen to believe she'd been immobilized by the King's Guard and paraded around as Sh'tam's trophy, to show that he could subdue an omnimancer.

Well, so far that's true for me too, Jen thought as she tested her hands and feet again; she was not going anywhere or casting any spells.

"It is time for her to pay for her crimes and see how she fares, no?" Sh'tam asked, his voice inflecting upward as if he was genuinely asking the throng of people.

Again, he soaked up the crowd's reactions, his eyes closed, and it looked like he was smelling something quite intoxicating. He clapped, and the limestone façade below his box opened.

"Let the festivities begin!"

Skarmor's cage unlocked with a sharp *clang*, allowing him to walk out warily as a massive lizard slithered out of the same opening he'd been dragged through. Skarmor cawed, giving Jen one last look before focusing on the muddy-green lizard as it roamed closer to him. Jen noticed for the first time that they had stuck his wings to his body with a leather harness; there would be no escaping to the skies today.

Someone strode out of the dark opening under Sh'tam's platform, and the sight of him startled her so badly that as the plank's shackles released, she collapsed to the coarse, sandy ground.

"M'balo . . . ?"

Confused, Jen looked at the man she'd grown to trust as he walked menacingly toward her, flipping his dagger in his hand. His demeanor was strange, and without a word he sent the dagger twirling straight at the bridge of her nose.

Jen struggled to find her legs, but she managed to dive to the side just fast enough to dodge the dagger, which embedded deeply into the plank. The coarse sand cut up her elbows and arms as she slid to a stop, but she refused to check her fresh injuries.

"M'balo, what's gotten into you? It's me, Jen," she said as she backed away, hands up in surrender.

He didn't say anything and continued his advance, which only added another layer to his odd behavior. Closer now, his eyes appeared extremely foggy, as if he'd developed severe cataracts. Without warning, M'balo launched into a full sprint and, before Jen could react, drove her into the ground.

The quick and hard takedown stole all the air from her lungs, and she felt a few pops in her rib cage as M'balo raised a fist at her. Grunting in effort, Jen managed to get her hands close to his chest and, with the backing of terramancy, shoved as hard as she could. The blast of air she'd channeled was so intense that M'balo's chin struck his chest and his legs kicked out as he flew ten meters in the air and landed back toward the open gate from which he'd entered.

The crowd buzzed with a mix of adulation and disapproval as Jen stood up, wiping blood from her chin and shaking the stiffness from her wrists. M'balo was slow to get up. Jen found it hard not to rush to his side and check on him; he clearly was under the influence of something. Cross-stepping to her right, she kept her hands out in front of her for the next charge as Sh'tam's voice rang out across the arena.

"Enough warming up!" Sh'tam clapped and M'balo backed away, head down and arms crossed over his chest, into the shadows of the opened gate under the royal box. "I will fight my brother to settle the royal ascendancy later."

Jen stole a glance back up toward Sh'tam and saw Kl'to standing on his right side, eyes staring unblinkingly into the packed stands on the opposite end of the arena. The crowd reacted to something, and Jen half-turned to see a suspended cloud of fine sand above a fallen Skarmor, the lizard creature whipping its tail and snapping its rows of crooked, sharp teeth in triumph. Skarmor awkwardly rolled to one side and, once he found his feet, pushed himself up. His wings still trapped, he roughly shook his entire body, sending streams of sand in all directions before he whacked his tail aggressively on the ground and went to reclaim the offensive. Jen started toward her griffin when Sh'tam's obnoxious tone assaulted her ears again.

"Are you ready for the fight of the century?!"

Atlanteans all around the immense, oval arena shook the stands in anticipation.

"It will be a feast for your eyes! I, Roi'tus Sh'tam, know how to entertain my people!"

Jen's heart rate accelerated as her eyes fell back into the darkness of the opening once more, unsure of what or who she would be forced to fight next. Another gargantuan warrior? A bloodthirsty predator? She anxiously swallowed as she returned to the stone plank in the arena's center, staring at M'balo's stuck dagger. She decided not to touch it and instead circled the plank, waiting to see which gate would open this time.

"Spellcaster versus spellcaster!"

The far gate to her left creaked open. Slowly.

"And they're related to each other!"

Out came her uncle, Victor Huxley.

The loudest eruption of the crowd made Jen temporarily deaf.

"No, no . . ." she whispered, flicking her gaze between Victor and Sh'tam.

But she couldn't stop it. Before she knew it, her nightmare began.

Not even two steps into the arena, Victor snapped his fists out in front of him, sending condensed fireballs screaming toward Jen, thin smoke trails following in their wake. With hardly any time to react, she spun the plank and hid behind its thick casing, covering her ears as the concussive blasts struck its front side. She felt the heat reach around the plank's edges for her and had the thought to jump. Seconds later a fan of flames sliced through the opening between the sand and the plank's bottom edge.

Jen looked at the flames as they licked only air below her feet, now hovering a safe several inches off the ground, and she was thankful she heeded her instincts.

She blinked away sweat, thinking. She needed to get to Victor. He must be under the same ailment as M'balo. If she could only give herself enough time to ascertain what could have possibly turned him into a mindless slave . . .

Prepping herself by taking three quick breaths, she leaned to the side, leaving the protection of the plank and levitating out into the open. She was shocked to see Victor less than a meter away, his eyes cloudy and upper lip turned upward in a scowl. Jen let out a sharp yelp as she dodged a crooked bolt of lightning and rotated her arm to draw a forcefield with her telemancy. A loud crash emanated behind her, but she couldn't look back to see what had happened, could only assume that was where the lightning bolt had struck.

Dropping to the ground, she repositioned her forcefield for a better angle of protection when she noticed that she couldn't see her arm. At all. Fear enveloped her, convincing her that Victor's last spell had cleaved it clean off, but the erratic movement of Victor's eyes made her realize that he couldn't see *any* of her.

She'd turned herself invisible.

Now conscious of the TeleCrystal's slight *thrum* in her pocket, she silently thanked Kl'to and used her invisibility to her advantage. She slowly followed Victor around the stone plank, holding her breath as she did so. All of a sudden, he stopped, his head the only part of him that moved as he tried to detect her.

Steps away, Jen raised her hand toward Victor, a firm grip now on astromancy, and hoped that was the correct plane to detect any foreign anomaly in or around her uncle. She used her palm like she would a detector wand, hovering it near his head and back, noticing that wherever she moved her hand, she could see Victor's internal organs, bones, muscles, arteries, veins, et cetera. She found a small dot of inflammation on his neck, the aftereffect of an injection, and soon thereafter Jen noticed a foreign fluid coursing through his bloodstream.

Her mind locked into diagnosis mode, toiling over how to flush the substance out of him. Jen was focused on thinking of possible antidotes when Victor abruptly spun around and grabbed hold of her throat.

Her nervous system, stunned, started to crash, eliminating her hold on both astromancy and telemancy, and her invisibility spell winked out. Victor wore a lazy smile as he lifted her off the ground to the resounding uproar of the entire stadium. Her time on Empyyr flashed before her eyes, when she had been in the Chimera Course and an evil Victor had choked the life out of her.

"Vic . . ."

Jen couldn't speak; every second felt as though Victor tightened his grip with more purpose. Pressure filled her eye sockets, which forced tears to muddle her vision. She clawed at his hand, but he wouldn't let go. Her oxygen levels were dangerously low; Jen knew that she'd pass out soon if Victor didn't snap out of it. She tried one last time to talk, but spluttered as she failed to fill her lungs, spitting directly at Victor and into his open mouth. Victor lurched his head to the side, bringing his free hand to wipe her saliva (*Why is it glowing?!*) from his face. With lips now shut, he worked his mouth around and spat over his shoulder. Above a curled snicker, his cloudy eyes were trained once more on her.

Then, suddenly, his smile left and his face went slack, quickly followed by his grip. Jen crumpled to the ground, sucking in much-needed air, her legs and arms turned to noodles. She used terramancy in a desperate attempt to allow in more oxygen to her lungs. Frantic, she looked up at Victor. He had a hand to his forehead, his eyes clamped shut.

Jen pulled herself to her feet, albeit shakily, and was about to send her uncle flying backward with a gust of wind when he opened his eyes. She stopped conjuring her spell.

She could see his pupils and irises.

Jen stifled a smile and grabbed her uncle's shoulders. "Grab me and pretend to struggle," she said.

Victor was clearly confused, but he did as he was told. Together, they kicked up sand as they pushed and pulled at each other. The crowd seemed to believe it—they were fully engaged, yelling out who they wanted to win; some cheered for both of their deaths.

"You were under some sort of trance," Jen said as they locked arms. "Sh'tam has Genevieve with him, and Charles is in the King's Guard's detention center." Privately she wondered if her saliva had somehow been the antidote. Had her nexus once again come to her aid and imbued her saliva with the necessary elements to free Victor, hence its supernatural glow? It was a mystery she resolved to bring to M'balo if they ever saw each other again.

"Jenny, how did we get here?" Victor looked as if he had a horrible migraine, closing one eye and breathing through clenched teeth.

"I'll explain later. Knock me to the ground." Jen searched her uncle's eyes, which seemed more and more lucid. "Trust me," she said with a barely perceptible wink.

Victor flashed a tiny smile, then pushed. Jen fell straight to the ground, clutching her throat as she crawled away on her back. Victor closed the distance, bringing his intertwined hands together in front of him and separating them dramatically.

The ground cracked, a deep, haunting sound, and Jen rolled to one side. Completing the roll, she looked at the small fissure Victor had just created: sand streamed over its edge in sheets. Getting up, she feigned being flung back by an air spell. She made the landing look too good, and it actually hurt her ankle when she struck the ground twenty yards away. She rolled to the edge of the arena and, looking up, saw that she was under Sh'tam's royal viewing box.

Victor stood over her seconds later and grabbed a fistful of her shirt. Lifting her up with ease, he mouthed, *What next?*

Jen hardened her skin and bones with terramancy, replicating the extreme durability of diamonds. Victor began to strain underneath Jen's denser body.

Throw me, Jen mouthed back.

She didn't have to explain further; Victor caught onto her plan. Nodding, he summoned his most concentrated air spell and released her. Jen couldn't breathe in the gale-force air tunnel as she was flung into the air, but it was over in less than a second when she slammed into the bottom of Sh'tam's suite, blasting through the ornate marble and limestone exterior. Jen managed to catch an edge of the opening her body had created, hanging onto it as large sections of the platform struck the arena floor several meters below.

The crowd's reaction was mixed, but excitement seemed to win out at this new development. Jen lifted herself over the edge and into the partially destroyed suite. Sh'tam used his elegant throne's armrest to slowly stand up, his ebony skin caked with fine marble dust as his eyes met hers. Farther into the suite, near the archway that led out into the stadium's back hallway, Kl'to ordered a contingent of guards to establish a perimeter around Genevieve.

"You insolent little—" Sh'tam began but was cut off by a tumultuous roar from his people. He, along with Jen, looked across the arena to find the lizard lying limp in blood-soaked sand, belly up. Steps away, Victor hopped on Skarmor's back and cut through the leather harness. He threw it to the ground as more cheers shook the entire arena.

"This is not supposed to happen!" Sh'tam screamed. Shaking, he lunged at Jen.

Jen still kept her terramancy spell active, so even though Sh'tam made contact with her, she barely felt it. She stumbled a few steps backward, Sh'tam's momentum completely gone. With more rageful screams he threw a punch into her fortified gut, which broke his hand in several places. Sh'tam's scream reached a higher pitch as his eyes went wide. He crumpled to the ground, holding his mangled hand close to his chest.

"Kl'to, slit her throat!" He pointed with his other hand at Genevieve.

Jen saw Kl'to's hesitation as every other guard drew their close-range daggers at her ancestor. Extending the arm that wore her totem bracelet, Jen closed her fist. The six guards, save for Kl'to, froze with a chronomancy spell. She then knocked Sh'tam flat on his back with a firmly planted kick to his sternum as Skarmor's familiar *caw!* pierced the air. The gust of wind that announced her griffin's arrival into the suite tousled Jen's hair, slick with sweat and crusted with sand, as she gazed at Kl'to.

"Do the right thing, Kl'to."

There came a stifled grunt from Sh'tam as Skarmor's right front paw pinned the manic king to the floor. "Tactos Kl'to, *kill that omnimancer!*" Sh'tam demanded. He screamed as Skarmor put more weight on his chest.

Jen didn't make a move toward Kl'to, just kept his gaze with her own, strong and uncompromising. Kl'to needed to make his own decision. She could infer that the commander was thinking about his family and their future safety. He reached for his sword and unsheathed it.

"Jen . . ." Victor said warily.

Jen didn't budge. She watched Kl'to intently as he raised his sword, the hammered steel reflecting like a mirror, and dropped it, letting it clatter on the polished marble ground. He then stepped up to Genevieve and touched her temples with gloved fingers. Instantly she relaxed, free from her invisible restraints.

Jen ran to Genevieve and gave her a hug as Kl'to stepped to

the side. She smiled and nodded at the commander before pulling away from her ancestor. After asking Genevieve if she was all right, Jen looked to Victor, who still sat atop Skarmor.

"We really need to get to Charles," she said.

Victor nodded, looking down at Sh'tam. "What should we do with him?"

Jen shrugged. "We're, what, five meters above the arena?"

Victor considered the hole in the platform's floor. "I'd say that's fair."

Jen turned to Kl'to. "Can you take me to the holding area below this suite?"

"Yes, indeed."

"Thank you." She turned back to Victor. "He'll survive."

Victor smirked and had Skarmor slide a wailing Sh'tam over the suite's edge.

"Let's go," Jen said to Kl'to, grabbing Genevieve's hand as she dashed out into the hallway and down a set of wide stairs to the ground floor. Turning immediately to the left, Kl'to led her and Genevieve through a set of thick drapes and into a dim, square room that looked identical to the one in which Jen had woken up not too long ago. M'balo stood off to one side, head slumped and arms dangling at his sides as if he were sleeping standing up. The noise of the three entering alerted him. His head slowly rose and his breathing quickened.

Without thinking, Jen ran up to him and pulled his head to hers, pressing her lips to his. His cloudy eyes went wide as he initially fought against her, but as she leaned deeper into the kiss, the prince stopped struggling and his eyelids flickered shut and for a moment, just a moment, only she and M'balo existed; everything else faded away, as if she were entering a previously undiscovered sixth Mancy plane. The butterflies in her stomach supercharged her heart with ecstasy as she slid a hand down his arm and entangled her fingers with his. Her whole body tingled in warmth, wanting their kiss to never end.

M'balo squeezed her hand, causing Jen to open her eyes in time to watch his reopen, this time revealing beautiful, azure-blue irises. With her eyes locked on M'balo's, Jen softly pulled away, slinking the hand that had been holding his head back to her side. The smile she wore was the biggest, most free smile she'd had in a long while.

"O-Omnimancer Jennifer—"

"It's just Jen," she said, tucking a loose curl behind her ear. "I think we're done with formalities."

His jaw was slack, but he raised one side of his mouth into a lopsided smile. "I guess you are right."

He held the side of her face in his hand and they both softly laughed. She nestled into his hand while he leaned forward and gingerly kissed the top of her head.

Then the arena crowd's commotion broke the spell of the moment. Jen straightened and took his hand from her face, looking through the open gate into the arena. Through it, she could see Skarmor watching over Sh'tam like a sheep dog would its flock.

"My brother," M'balo said, also looking out. Confusion was etched on his face until it dawned into understanding. "My brother used the Shadow Sleep on me." He looked back at Jen. "Did I hurt anyone?"

Avoiding the long story, Jen said, "No, thankfully. Your brother said that he was planning on fighting you for the throne, presumably while you were under the Shadow Sleep. But that won't happen now."

"He would win that duel, guaranteed, and claim the throne without contest." M'balo shook his head, fixing his brother with a look of contempt. "That would ensure no one would rebel against him ever again."

Jen grimaced and squeezed his hand. "I have to go. My father was moved to the Guard's detention center." She jutted a thumb behind her. "I brought Genevieve to help."

He smiled back at Jen, briefly looking over her shoulder at her ancestor. M'balo also noticed Kl'to and gave him an appreciative nod. "You look like her," he said, diving once more into her eyes. His countenance then grew gravely serious. "I need to settle this power struggle once and for all, before my brother causes Atlantis to fall even further into bedlam."

Nodding, Jen took M'balo's hand and matched his gait as they entered into the arena, Genevieve falling behind them. Victor alerted Skarmor and he stopped forming a small sandstorm around Sh'tam with his wings and bounded over to Jen.

"Good luck," Jen said to the prince, and leaned in for a final kiss.

"May your nexus protect you, Jen," he said back to her after they shared a quick but tender moment.

Jen waited for Genevieve to mount Skarmor before she got on herself, and in seconds he was in the air. As he flew to Ring Two, Jen saw Sh'tam crawling on his elbows as M'balo went to the floating plank in the middle of the arena and pried his dagger out of its center. The brothers began fighting just as the outer walls of the stadium blocked her view, leaving Jen to pray that M'balo would be the victor.

She turned forward and set her sights on the King's Guard station.

* * *

Due to the heightened state of unrest across all of Atlantis's rings, the King's Guard station was vacant save for one guard, who was dutifully watching the entrance to the detention center. Victor made quick work of him and used the guard's bracer to unlock the sliding doors, revealing an interior lit red from the glow of the four eerie head busts floating above. Charles's plank had been positioned in the room's center.

In her impatient dash to her father Jen clipped her shoulder on the edge of the door, which was still sliding into its casing in the wall. She choked back a gasp when she saw him—exactly as she had envisioned back on Camelore. A chill frosted the base of her spine as Victor and Genevieve flanked her sides.

Charles was dead.

Even before she checked on her father through her nexus, Jen knew it was too late. She went in anyway, trying everything she knew—even pleading with her own nexus—to bring her father back. But no answer came from the void; only silence. Dead silence.

Quiet sobs involuntarily squeaked out of her mouth as she turned her head into Victor's chest, devastated. The more breaths she took, the more forceful the sobs became. Victor's arms enveloped her, and she felt his bearded chin rest atop the crown of her head. They were too late. She'd found the one person who could dismantle the proxiomnimancic spell, but it had taken too long.

She had failed.

Quiet fell over the trio in the detention center. Jen felt drained beyond comprehension. Her brain reminded her of what Gavin, Mira, and the Hephalons were facing back on Camelore, but something inside her pushed that thought away. She needed to grieve in peace, even if for just one more second.

"Stand aside," she heard Genevieve say.

Jen rolled away from Victor, looking at her ancestor through puffy, soaked eyes. "Charles is gone, Genevieve. I'm sorry," she croaked, wiping her stinging eyes.

Genevieve had her eyes locked on Charles's face. "I can bring him back."

Jen tried her best to not be flooded with false hope. She covered her father's cold, clammy hand with her own, letting a sharp sob escape her lips.

Genevieve went on, "I can give him the energy of my life force through the proxianimancic spell."

"But you'll die, Genevieve," Victor said.

Genevieve flashed a weak smile, and her expression told Jen that she'd already made up her mind. "I am from another time. I sacrificed myself so my baby boy and the Sorcery Guild could survive." Her eyes glistened with tears of her own. "My Philip lived a long life, and I am just now realizing that my sacrifice was meant for this moment. This will ensure the Guild's—and the entire coalition of realms'—survival, I'm sure of it."

Jen looked up at Victor, knowing as well as he did that there would be no convincing Genevieve otherwise. She desperately wanted her father alive, but not at the expense of watching her ancestor perish.

A deep, resonating rumble came from outside. Jen looked up and saw the floating busts slow their macabre, spinning dance above her. "Is that from the arena?"

"No. Far below, and deep inside Earth," Victor said. Jen saw that his totem rings were glowing, and she knew he'd based his reply on what he felt through terramancy.

"We don't have much time," Genevieve said as she gently pushed them aside. "Please, let me do this."

Agreeing to Genevieve's final wish, Jen stood next to Victor as her ancestor, the woman who had saved the eleven realms from Lord Ferox fifteen hundred years ago and was prepared to give her life to do it a second time, laid her hands over Charles's heart and called upon the proxianimancic spell.

A wondrous light sprung forth from her hands, quickly enveloping Charles and herself. The light was brighter than anything Jen had ever seen, but somehow it didn't hurt her eyes. As she watched in awe, the light slowly faded and only Charles remained. Next to him, near the edge of the plank, was the Ring of Lancaster, and pooled on the spot where Genevieve had stood moments ago was her gown. Movement on the plank tore her attention back to her father, and in a heartbeat she was helping him sit upright.

"Jen?" he said groggily, looking first at her then her uncle as she helped him from the plank.

She slid the Ring of Lancaster into her pocket.

"We gotta go, Father."

He flailed in sudden panic, his memory returning. "Cindergray! Where is he?" Charles demanded, tense and trying to free his arm from Jen's grasp.

"Charles, *hey* . . . look at me," Victor said, now on his other side. "Calm down. We found him, and he won't be hurting anyone else."

Charles stopped his frantic movements and let out a shaky breath. "I'm sorry, I—" He looked around the holding cell quizzically. "Are we back on Atlantis?"

"Yes, but we need to get back to Camelore. Immediately," Jen said, helping Charles step over the unconscious guard and out of the detention center. "I promise we'll explain everything on the way, okay?"

Her father looked to be returning to his usual self. Jen was beyond relieved. "Okay," he said, proving he could also walk on his own.

Another dull but deep rumble shook the air.

Skarmor was pacing just below the station's steps when Jen whistled to him. He quickly cleared the entire set of stairs with one leap and a helpful flap of his mighty wings and landed perfectly in their path. All three of them hopped on Skarmor with Jen taking the front spot, and with haste she gave Skarmor his new heading: Camelore.

With Atlantis slowly receding into the distance, Jen peered in the direction of the stadium but was too far away to pick out what was happening inside. She could tell the stands were still full and still hear surges of cheers from the blood-thirsty crowd. Hoping beyond hope that M'balo was faring well, Jen found herself reminiscing about her first kiss with the prince. How perfect it made her feel. She wanted to chase that feeling again and, as Skarmor dove below Atlantis's outer gate toward Camelore, Jen made a promise to herself.

One that she intended to keep.

She exhaled and began to meditate so she could prepare for the intensity of what was to come. Only a few seconds into her trance, her mind's eye saw concentric circles of different colors propagate toward her.

Then came a ringing sound, and then:

Jen . . . Jenny, can you hear me?!

She tensed, forgetting about her meditation technique.

Mother? Are you all right?

She had a sinking feeling in the pit of her stomach. Her mother did not sound well.

I'm so sorry . . . It's all my fault. Through their telemancy bond, Jocelyn's voice seemed strained. Possibly even clipped, as if in pain.

Where are you? What's going on?

I thought I'd escaped, but he followed me. Jocelyn's thoughts seemed disjointed.

Who?

Malcolm.

Jen stiffened. Why wasn't Malcolm or her mother on Camelore?

"Vic," Jen said through her teeth.

She felt him lean closer to her back. "Everything okay, Jenny?"

Jen didn't have time to respond as her mother sent another message.

He has the remaining MystiCrystals, Jenny. He's left for Nyzanth.

But Jen's priority was not where Malcolm was going. *Mother, where are you?* she sent.

Near the portal to Everworld. Angel Falls. I-I'm trapped.

Then we'll come get you.

Jen had just gotten her father back. She would not lose her mother now. What had Malcolm done to her?

To Skarmor, she said, "Skar, fly to the Everworld portal as fast as you can."

Her griffin banked to the right without hesitation.

There were a few open seconds without anything from her mother. Victor asked again, "Jenny, what's up? You're scaring me."

"Jocelyn," was all Jen could say as she waited for her mother.

"Is she—?"

But Jocelyn's telemancy drowned Victor out.

No, there's not enough time! You need to go to Nyzanth and stop Malcolm.

By now tears were falling down Jen's cheeks. *No, I'm coming for you!*

He has the MystiCrystals. Stop him before he returns to Lord Ferox . . . or we are all doomed.

Then the bond was broken.

Jen opened her eyes; all she could do was stare ahead as Skarmor streaked through the sky. She wanted to answer Victor's repeated question of "What the hell is going on?" but couldn't bring herself to respond. She could feel an anxiety attack brewing when Skarmor's call crystallized her focus.

As he blasted through more cumulus clouds of the troposphere, a white equine with a silky, silver mane and a glistening, spiraled horn emerged out of a nearby wispy cloud, matching their speed and going in the same direction. On its back was a woman with hair that radiated all colors of the rainbow.

"Vic." Jen looked over her shoulder at her uncle. "Isn't that Kuirhan?"

Victor chuckled incredulously. "And Teska," he said.

"Your old classmate? The one who helped you track down Kuirhan?"

Jen slowed Skarmor down as Kuirhan glided closer to them, his strong legs gracefully riding the air. Teska looked to be shorter than Jen, but her build was very lean and athletic, reminiscent of an acrobat.

"That's the one," Victor said to Jen before addressing his old friend: "What brings you out of the Amaranthine Forest?"

Kuirhan greeted Skarmor with a snort, matching his speed as they soared miles above Earth.

"You lot," Teska replied. "My relicontus has been picking up movement in and around Watercress Castle as of late. To hear that it's been demolished . . . I can't idly stand by, frying serknid omelets, while you're out putting your lives at risk for the safety of these realms. So I took a field trip to your cottage and found this fine boy grazing by your front door." She put her hand on Kuirhan's side and gently patted him. "He told me everything I needed to know to come find you." She looked toward Skarmor and smiled. "Chuck, it's great to see you again. I'm so glad you're okay."

"Thanks, Teska," Charles said.

The woman's beautiful, flowing hair cast glimmering hues of every imaginable color. It was soothing, but only temporarily; Jen felt pulled to get to her mother as quickly as she could and then track down Malcolm. Then an idea struck.

"Jennifer Lancaster, I presume?" Teska smiled at Jen. "You look so much like your parents." Jen nodded, smiling wanly, and felt Victor's hand on her shoulder, but before she could comment herself, Teska said, "So . . . how can I help?"

Her timing couldn't have been more desirable. Before Teska showed up with Kuirhan, Skarmor was the only flying creature on which Jen, Victor, and Charles could travel. Jen had been prepared to prioritize saving her mother before going elsewhere, but now, with Teska's arrival with Kuirhan, they could divide and conquer.

After quickly relaying what Jocelyn had sent her over telemancy (and at Victor and Charles's urging), Jen settled on taking Skarmor directly to Nyzanth to confront Malcolm, while Victor, Charles, and Teska would take Kuirhan to Angel Falls. The goal was to make it to Camelore before it was too late to assist Gavin and the rest.

Victor already on Kuirhan, Charles swung his leg around so he no longer straddled Skarmor. Before he hopped onto the equivol, Jen grabbed his arm.

"Be careful, Father," she said. She fished out the Ring of Lancaster from her pocket and handed it to Charles. "This belongs to you now."

Charles cupped the ring in his hands and let his fingers cover it from the wind. He looked up, eyes glistening, and hugged her. Jen sighed and squeezed him tightly.

"You're my guiding star, Jennifer Mintaka. I'll see you soon." He pulled away and finished with: "I love you."

Jen's lower lip quivered. "I love you too."

She let go of her father, who then took Victor's hand and straddled Kuirhan. Jen cleared her throat and ran a finger underneath both tear-filled eyes. Victor winked—a small gesture, but one she had grown to cherish from her uncle—then

Kuirhan galloped on the air currents, headed west toward Jocelyn.

"Skar, to the Nyzanth portal," she said to her griffin, her thoughts still on her uncle. He trusted her to do what was right. That confidence helped her to focus on what she needed to do: confront Malcolm and retrieve the remaining MystiCrystals.

She just hoped that she would find the strength to succeed, no matter the cost.

CHAPTER TWENTY-EIGHT

The portal to Nyzanth, located atop the Rock of Gibraltar, the northern promontory of the Straits of Gibraltar, was much closer than Jen had expected. The energy from Nyzanth's portal made the site exceedingly unstable and mysterious, leading to the fascination of ancient philosophers and the creation of the Pillars of Hercules legend.

Soaring high above the strait itself with the Atlantic Ocean to her left and the Mediterranean Sea to her right, Jen felt forlorn. She suspected it was a culmination of everything, from being apart from everyone else to her mind further processing Genevieve's final sacrifice. And what was still unfinished.

Jen couldn't afford to have her mind divided when she faced Malcolm, so she let her feelings surface in hopes that they could work through her system before it was time to focus on retrieving the rest of the MystiCrystals. Relaxing, she opened her arms and let the warm wind swirl around her as she meditated. Letting each emotion and thought run its course, she dropped deeper into the calmness of her nexus. Sorrow, worry, anxiety, and hope flashed against the backdrop of her mind; she welcomed the onslaught and released them one at a time, slowly quieting her mind and reaching the pinnacle of clarity.

Skarmor angled downward, gravity accelerating his speed

enough to bring Jen out of her trance. The Rock of Gibraltar's peak was straight ahead, and Skarmor leaned further into his dive. Jen searched for the portal, but she couldn't find it. She was unsure of where precisely Skarmor was taking her. Then, electric sparks popped and zoomed past Skarmor's beak, growing in frequency as he looked to be on a collision course with the promontory's peak; but seconds before he ran directly into unforgiving rock, a blinding light fully eclipsed Jen's vision.

Something akin to static crackled in her ears, and seconds later Skarmor carried her through a portal that Jen realized was created by reaching a certain velocity. She was now under a black, star-dotted sky in an atmosphere that was both arid and bone-chilling. Below Skarmor's flight path ran a line of crater-like holes in the ruddy, cracked landscape, reminding Jen of the Sahara Desert back on Earth. Not too far in the distance, the terrain changed dramatically as a higher crust of gray stone wedged itself between the ruddy dirt and miles of a mineral so black that it blended seamlessly into the midnight sky. The closer Skarmor dropped to the surface, the more Jen noticed strange pockmarks set deep into the starving crust. Upon further examination, they looked to be footprints of something titanic. She followed the markings ahead of where Skarmor was taking her and saw a large black mass, steadily moving toward the focal point where those three types of crust wedged together. She could now clearly hear a deep, methodical *thumping* sound emanating from whatever lay ahead.

"Skar, what's that?" Jen pointed at what she thought was some kind of indigenous creature to Nyzanth, but as Skarmor soared closer it seemed less organic.

Thick, cylindrical legs slammed into the dead ground in a zombie-like monotony, metal creaking as rusted hydraulics carried the foreboding castle that rested atop the moving platform. Bony, thin stone towers the color of onyx jutted up from the corners of square castle and a much thicker, taller one held dominion in the center, the tops of which all ended in spiky spires. There weren't any lights inside the nomadic castle, and Jen wondered what horrors were waiting inside.

Then a familiar roar that prickled her skin preceded an intense, hot light from behind, and she yelled at Skarmor to dive once she saw a white-hot fireball blazing directly at them. Jen held onto his neck as the griffin corkscrewed, looping under the intense rocket of flames before leveling out and almost flying directly into Volcanor.

Grinding her teeth, Jen began launching spell after spell behind her as the dragon chased them toward the castle below. Skarmor filled the night air with caws and chirps as he tried to outfly the wyvern dragon. Jen couldn't make out if Malcolm was on its back or not, which didn't give her a good feeling as Skarmor flew around the weathered stone towers, almost catching a sharp tip of one of the spires as he tried to outfly the much larger dragon.

"Welcome to Feralot!" Malcolm's voice rang out, coming from all directions simultaneously.

Jen's stomach twisted into knots; so this was the actual fortress where her father had been held prisoner for twenty years . . . and where Malcolm had thrown her foster parents after he'd captured them. Ire bubbled deep inside Jen as she swiveled her head around, trying desperately to locate him, but with how fast Skarmor was flying, she'd become more disoriented than usual. She glanced over her shoulder to see Volcanor stop its chase and land in a barren but gated courtyard that framed the fortress's central tower. Skarmor stretched his wings and soared around the outer perimeter of Feralot and flew low between the two spires farthest away from Volcanor, when suddenly Jen was blinded and knocked off his back.

She rolled over the unforgiving surface, skinning her shoulder and elbow as her momentum died. With effort, Jen stood up and watched Skarmor evade a few colorful spells from a shadowy figure not too far from where she'd landed. The flashes illuminated Malcolm's face, and she was taken aback when a memory of them, back when they were dating and he'd called himself Alex, stuck in her mind: they were watching a movie in her living room with the lights turned off, and she would look at him every so often to trace his profile as the television's glow played across his face.

Jen pushed that forgotten memory aside and rushed at Malcolm with the speed of a cheetah, driving him to the ground. His spells were cut off at the source as they grappled on Feralot's hard rooftop.

"You're getting faster!" Malcolm grunted. Volcanor's roar shook the entire fortress and in a few massive flaps of its wings, the wyvern dragon took to the skies in pursuit of Skarmor.

Jen kneed Malcolm in the gut, rolling away to give her enough space to attack from a different angle. "Malcolm, this has got to stop!"

Out of breath, Malcolm agreed, "You're right, Jen . . . Hand over the TeleCrystal and I'll let you live."

Jen's hand instinctively grabbed her cargo pocket which held the crystal.

He laughed and wiped a trail of blood from his lips. "I know you have it." He extended a hand as an aerial melee of dragon versus griffin unfolded above the two sorcerers. "Toss it over and I'll call off Volcanor. You know Skarmor won't last much longer."

Jen looked upward at the streaks of wings and tails. Skarmor was quicker than Volcanor, but the hellish dragon was more powerful. It all would come down to stamina. Jen didn't want it to last longer than it had to. She let her eyes drop back on Malcolm, who was standing a handful of paces away, his hand still extended.

"Is this how you want to be remembered?" Jen asked, priming her nexus. She grabbed the zipper of her cargo pocket but didn't slide it open. Her patience for coming to a resolution through talking was becoming increasingly diminished.

"You need to think *bigger*, Jen!" Malcolm said, dropping his hand. "That's always been your problem: you lack vision." He drew his longsword, the famed Excalibur, and side-stepped in a wide circle. He pointed its sharp tip directly at her.

Jen mirrored his movements, not allowing him to get any closer. "Ferox will only leave death and destruction in his wake.

He has no care or thought for anyone else. Not even those who do his bidding," Jen said.

Feralot's steady rumbling made Jen feel off balance. In the distance, the cliffs of gray stone were getting closer as the castle continued traversing Nyzanth's cracked, rough terrain.

"So that he can blaze a future distilled from a single vision." Malcolm's eyes had a hunger in them that couldn't be sated.

Nyzanth suddenly trembled, causing Feralot to buckle and tilt to one side. Jen began sliding down the roof until she quickly channeled astromancy to suction her feet to the stone with an extra bit of gravity. Malcolm stuck Excalibur into the stone beneath his feet; it slid into the hard surface like a knife through butter. He waited until Feralot corrected itself and leveled back out, then extracted his sword from the rooftop and looked far off into the distance.

"It's starting," he said.

"What have you done?" Jen's body ached with a terrible feeling, revolted by Malcolm's devious smile.

"I've used a planet-boring insect to distribute Lord Ferox's proxiterramancic spell throughout Nyzanth . . . and every other realm," Malcolm said, shrugging, "including Earth. And if Ferox gets what he wants"—he pointed at Jen—"he promises to save the realms."

Jen felt as though she'd been struck by an anvil, her lungs devoid of air, but somehow she found words. "Malcolm, Ferox is a *liar*! Only an omnimancer can reverse a proximancic spell, and he's no omnimancer. Even if he was, he would be nowhere near powerful enough. You need to master each one in order to even have a chance!" She saw his composure slightly crack, and she kept talking. "And a proxiterramancic spell of *this* magnitude . . . there isn't an omnimancer alive who we can turn to. He's played you!"

"No, no, you're wrong! You have no clue what you're talking about!"

Jen set her teeth and, with telemancy, took a glimpse into his mind in time to hear his current thought: *Ferox told me that he'd learned how to control each proximancic spell . . . yes.*

Malcolm's ring erupted in crimson light as he jutted Excalibur at Jen. Like a match thrown on a trail of gasoline, the crimson light bled onto the sword's hilt and traveled up its blade, casting it in a vibrant red that shimmered in the stark night sky. Then his eyes widened, and Excalibur's tip dropped slightly, and Jen read his thoughts once more.

Wait—he didn't do it on his own. He had help from the Shadow-Crystal.

Jen released her telemancy hold at that moment, deciding to drive home her point. "I've seen what the proxiomnimancic spell can do to one single person—the hold it has on their nexus and life force . . ." Her mind flashed back to Genevieve's ultimate sacrifice. "Think of how irreversible the proxiterramancic spell would be on eleven separate realms, much less one!"

Jen could feel the fortress becoming more unstable with every passing second. Feralot's rumbling was matched and quickly superseded by a tremor so powerful it snapped the roaming castle's feet from their housings. Feralot lurched, wobbling from side to side with such intensity that Jen became nauseous.

In the skies, the contest between Skarmor and Volcanor had turned into a close-quarter brawl. Skarmor had managed to jump onto Volcanor's back and was clawing at its neck. The dragon belched smoke as it issued a pained roar, trying to shake the griffin from its back without avail. The two grappled in the air, spinning as one, and right before Volcanor struck the stone spire closest to Malcom, Skarmor unlatched, flying to safety as the dragon split the spire in two and sent debris of all sizes hurtling toward Malcolm.

He somersaulted away from being crushed to death by the body of his wyvern dragon, but one of its wings side-swiped him, knocking Excalibur from his hand and sending him flying straight into the base of Feralot's main central spire.

Malcolm slumped to the ground and fell to his side. He imme-diately started crawling toward his dropped sword, but Jen beat him to it. She picked Excalibur up as Skarmor landed next to her. Its hilt was heavy and was built for a much bigger hand, but she was able to quickly adapt to its heft and presence.

Malcolm's head dropped to the ground, his outstretched hand turning into a tight fist and pounding the trembling rooftop in frustration. He rolled himself back toward the spire's wall and leaned up on it. "How do you keep besting me?"

Jen looked down at his belt and noticed it held the four other MystiCrystals. "Malcolm, it's over. You can be remembered for something much better if you help me stop Ferox from destroying every realm! No one will remember you if there are no survivors. We're running out of time."

Malcolm's focus left her face as he stared at something behind her. Holding Excalibur's point to his neck, Jen turned and saw, near the edge of the stone cliff, underneath a star-swept sky, a white stag. Its fur swayed lazily in a light breeze, and the trembling of Nyzanth made it look blurry.

Another one of her visions had come to pass.

An idea came to her. She looked back at Malcolm and the MystiCrystals he wore, but before she could say anything, Malcolm knocked Excalibur aside and jumped up.

CHAPTER TWENTY-NINE

Gavin wiped a mix of blood and sweat from his eyes, his entire body pushed to the brink of failure, as he forced himself to get back up. He couldn't leave Hephalon to duel Ferox all by himself. Hephalon was holding the last weapons he had on him: two tomahawk axes. Every other spear, axe, shield, and dagger lay bent, broken, or disintegrated around the battleground that was once the Pentarena.

Gavin knew Ferox to be mad, but his scheme to possess either Jen or her father so he could become a true omnimancer was psychotic. Not to mention the part where he would see each realm fall if he didn't get what he desired. It hadn't taken much else for Gavin or Hephalon to begin their attack on the dark lord, but the longer it continued, Gavin could see Ferox claiming victory if back up didn't arrive soon.

Standing on wobbly legs, Gavin mustered enough strength to power up his cracked orb totem once again. Mira was pinned up against the massive tree trunk, unconscious alongside Rez, gnarled bark crisscrossed over their bodies, leaving only their heads free. He charged, limping as he went to double-team the sinister sorcerer, when a bolt of lightning struck at the feet of Ferox, sending the dark lord careening toward the Arbor Sacré and knocking both Gavin and Hephalon down.

To his right, Kuirhan touched down with Victor, Charles, and another woman he'd never seen before on his back. Victor slid off and helped Gavin up.

Hephalon flipped his feet underneath him with a powerful kip-up and picked up his tomahawks, ready for more action. "About time you joined us!" he said, his eyes still trained on Ferox. His normally immaculate beard was disheveled and charred in certain areas, the braids frayed and mostly pulled free. Even counting all of that, Hephalon still looked in better shape than Gavin. His head angled sharply upward when a familiar cry split the air.

Pernissa flew into view, visibly injured and struggling to stay aloft as the ophidite chased her. Off kilter, her left wing was stiffer than the right but still usable enough to keep her airborne. But the feathered serpent was closing in, its mouth fully unhinged and awaiting its injured meal.

"Stay away from my GRIFFIN!" bellowed Hephalon.

He took two massive steps, windmilling his arms, and sent both tomahawks, now glowing with a fierce spell, flying. They cut through the air, and Pernissa tucked in her wings as the axes twirled past her, barely missing the tips of her feathers, and disappeared into the ophidite's open mouth. Pernissa splayed her wings out again and tumbled to the ground, her chest heaving in ragged breaths.

A choked gurgle escaped from the ophidite's angled nostrils as its scaly body went rigid in the air, and a second later, Hephalon's terramancy-charged weapons burst from the serpent's feathered tail, ejecting dark fluid and bits of organs as a fatal wake.

Without so much as another sound, the enormous flying serpent nose-dived into the ground, tearing a massive rut into Camelore's surface that ran for nearly fifty meters before the serpentine corpse rumbled to a stop.

Pulling out his brass knuckles totem, Hephalon yelled at Pernissa to find cover. At the tree's base near the carved throne, though still shaken from the blast, Ferox unleashed a hoarse scream at the demise of his ophidite. Chunks of dirt rolled off the dark lord's cloak as he slid his knees underneath his hunched form, faintly chuckling like a madman.

"Be careful . . . He has Rez and Mira," Gavin said, groaning as he tested the strength of his ankles. He pointed at the Arbor Sacré.

"Jocelyn's already on it," Victor said out of the side of his mouth, rolling his knuckles in anticipation of a fight.

Gavin's eyebrows shot up, trying not to seem obvious as he looked in the skies for a vampire bat.

Ferox slowly stood up and brushed his cloak off to the side. "Ah . . . your reinforcements." He rolled his neck, snickering. "They're much quicker than Genevieve's." He inhaled deeply and pointed a long finger at Charles, still on Kuirhan. "And I smell an *omnimancer*." He licked his lips and bolted at them.

Off to the side, Hephalon charged straight at Ferox, yelling with all his might.

"We'll take it from here," Victor told Gavin as Charles dismounted Kuirhan alongside the female sorcerer. The terra-mancer raised his hands, his fingers glistening with four nexus-activated totem rings. Before Gavin could argue, Victor, Charles, and the female sorcerer dashed in sync, meeting up with Hephalon as they unleashed a torrent of spells on Ferox.

Then he had an idea. He jumped up onto the strapping equivol and said, pointing at his girlfriend, "Kuirhan, head for Mira." The equivol neighed and galloped straight for her, surprising Gavin with his acceleration. He was even faster on the ground than in the skies, and in seconds, Kuirhan delivered him steps away from Mira.

Rushing up to her, Gavin grabbed the thick strips of bark but, strain as he might, couldn't even crack them. Bringing his glowing totem forth, he touched it to the bark and cast a spell that liquified all that covered Mira. He caught her in his hands and turned to Kuirhan. The top of the equivol's back was the same height as Gavin, so gently, he draped Mira across his back and jumped right behind her. He looked over at Rez to find an albino bat streaking down from the thorny branches and then morph into, of course, a human.

"Jocelyn!" he yelled, starting toward her, but was stopped when the female sorcerer he didn't know came crashing into the tree's trunk. Her flowing, rainbow-highlighted hair was slicked back with the help of a metallic headband. She bounced back up almost immediately, raised a hand to tell him she was okay before brushing herself off and running headlong into the melee, her headband totem shining brilliantly with animancy.

Spells shot every which way as Ferox deflected, parried, and countered everything that Hephalon and the three fresh sorcerers doled out. Ferox seemed to be in peak form, not giving any ground as he immediately readjusted to the woman's returned presence and quickly rendered her spells ineffectual. After kicking her aside for a second time, Ferox flipped Victor to the ground and grabbed Charles by the throat as he single-handedly blocked Hephalon's herculean swings.

Ferox unhinged his jaw, much like a python would as it prepared to swallow its prey whole. He angled his head as he went in for Charles, but the omnimancer brought his forearms down on Ferox's outstretched arm, dropping to the ground as the dark lord's grip was broken. Charles deftly fell to his haunches and, on the ball of his right foot, extended his left leg fully and toppled Ferox with a forceful sweep of the legs.

The sound of cracking bark drew Gavin back to Jocelyn. With her brute strength, she tore the thick straps from Rez as Kuirhan brought Gavin over to her side.

"Ferox has primed every realm to implode," Jocelyn said, working on the last bit of bark over Rez's ankles.

"I know," Gavin said, glaring at Ferox, who had managed to get back up and was staring straight at Jocelyn.

"I should have trusted my instincts." Ferox foamed at the mouth as he glared at her. "Now you will experience my wrath!"

The crystal which was embedded in his chest swirled with striations of purple, pulsing out bruised veins across his chest, throat, and face. His eyes turned an even deeper shade of black, never leaving Jocelyn. Ferox's hands curled into claws as he extended both arms to his sides and, with a raspy yell that carried behind it a thousand voices, dropped them toward the ground. Suddenly, Gavin felt an intense shift in gravity and Kuirhan buckled, rolling to his side and spilling Gavin and Mira off his back.

Plastered to the ground, Gavin thought of his encounter with the AstroCrystal's power beneath Antarctica; but this wasn't true astromancy—he couldn't negate it. He tracked Ferox as he sauntered over to Jocelyn, knelt down, and brushed the side of her head.

"You duped me, vesperite. Commendable, but foolish." Ferox grabbed her head and repeated in a deadly whisper, "*So . . . very . . . foolishhhhhh.*"

Jocelyn screamed, but her face and body, frozen by Ferox's spell much like Gavin's, didn't match the noise she was making. It unsettled Gavin deeply, and he tried to break out of the control the spell had over him, but he couldn't. The person who eventually stopped Ferox's torture was someone Gavin had begun to suspect he'd never see again.

"THIS ENDS NOW!"

Jen's voice boomed all around, distracting Ferox. He looked over his shoulder and into the skies; Jen was on Skarmor, and in her hands was Excalibur. Ferox withdrew his hands from Jocelyn's head, her screams instantly dying out, and spun around to face this new arrival.

"You must be Jennifer Lancaster. I was hoping you'd reveal yourself to me." He clasped his hands together and raised them at Excalibur. "And I see you've bested my knight." His head twitched to the side and harshly whispered, "Quiet! You'll be released in due time."

What was the ShadowCrystal saying to Ferox? Gavin wondered.

Jen didn't respond; she kept Skarmor hovering in the air. Gavin didn't know if it was the certain angle of Excalibur against the rays of the setting sun, or its inherent energy, but the longsword dazzled in Jen's grip.

Gobsmacked, Gavin hadn't a clue as to how she'd defeated Malcolm, who'd had the additional power of Excalibur backing him, let alone how she'd successfully taken it, but he didn't care. It did make him wonder if Jen was the actual Light Bringer, and if for centuries the Sorcery Guild had misinterpreted the role of the person who was able to read Merlin's journal.

If he wasn't the Light Bringer, so be it. He didn't care, as long as Ferox was vanquished.

"Let my friends and family go, Ferox," Jen said. Skarmor touched down, and she set foot on the dead grass of the battle-ground, her face gravely serious.

Jen and Ferox were locked in a stare-down, until the dark lord spoke.

"These paltry few won't mean much once the realms collapse in on themselves."

He started walking toward her.

Jen twirled Excalibur in her palm and started toward the dark lord as well. "Malcolm told me what you've done to each realm." She aimed the legendary sword's tip at Ferox's throat. "Reverse their proxiterramancic spells before it gets out of control."

"You are in no position to bargain, young one," Ferox lightly berated. He cupped his hands and held them up, passing Charles and the female animancer. "Your fate, along with all these miscreants', rests in my hands." He stopped and pointed at Victor, lying on the ground. "You feel the most connected with this man?"

Jen stopped walking and slid her other hand on Excalibur's hilt, keeping it pointed at Ferox.

He bent and picked Victor up by his collar, using him as a shield. "Now, now . . . let's not get hasty."

A rolling rumble split the skies, and Ferox looked into the darkening heavens.

"Right on cue. Do you know what that is, Jennifer? The sound of Earth's mantle crumbling from the inside."

Jen's eyes flicked between Ferox and Victor, then rested meaningfully on Gavin. She wanted him to be ready. "What will it take for you to stop the proxiterramancic spells?"

Ferox didn't let Victor go. He slowed his pace but drew ever closer to Jen. Gavin looked at his hands and willed them to move, but they might as well have been sculpted from marble; they refused to comply. He could only move his eyes, which he brought back on Ferox. Only a few paces separated the dark lord from Jen.

"Give me control over your body and nexus. *Then* I will save the realms," Ferox said with zeal. "You have my word."

A tense second passed.

"What about my friends and family?" Jen did not lower Excalibur.

"Their lives will be spared," he said breathlessly, as if he was on the precipice of receiving all that which he had dreamed.

Confused, Gavin caught Jen's gaze once more. Why did she keep looking at him and no one else?

Jen lowered Excalibur and, with a flick of her wrist, tossed it aside. She then proceeded to kneel down, her head bowed.

Skarmor cried out and began to race toward her, but Jen raised a hand to him and the griffin slowed to a stop, softly chirping in concern. Sparing a glance at the sword, Gavin noticed that Jen had thrown it in his direction. Screaming silence could be felt as Gavin's vocal cords (and he assumed nearly everyone else's) refused to work, to beg Jen to not sacrifice herself.

There had to be another way . . .

Ferox let Victor drop uselessly to his side and, resting an open hand on the crown of Jen's head, recited something in a hushed tone. Her head began to glow, a light that then cascaded over her entire body while also surging up through Ferox's. The blinding light overtook them both and in a second winked out, revealing only Jen, her body slumped forward in a kneeling pose.

All of a sudden, Gavin felt the pressure on his body dissipate and he could breathe easier. His eyesight tunneled after he forced himself to stand too quickly, but he pushed through it as he stumbled toward Jen. Vision in his peripherals returned, catching the moving forms of Victor, Charles, and Kuihran, but he remained focused on getting to Jen, who hadn't moved since Ferox had disappeared.

Gavin reached the spot where Excalibur lay when Jen threw

her head back, her body going rigid, and screamed. The noise she produced was so shrill and jolting, it froze Gavin in place. She then lurched forward in a convulsive fit just as a forceful wind started brewing. It emanated from Jen and rolled outward, buffeting Gavin before extending toward the Arbor Sacré.

Before he knew it, the wind had built into a tornado and he, Jen, and everyone else were in its eye. Victor and Charles rushed over.

"Jenny, hold on, I'm coming!" Victor yelled.

Over the raucous wind, Jen yelled back, "Don't come any closer—*please!*" She was in massive pain, her body seizing as she rose higher in the air. "Gavin . . . Excalibur . . ." She pointed to his right.

He looked down and saw the longsword that he'd been after for what seemed like ages but was only several hours. Its elegance was a stark contrast to the dead, prickly grass that surrounded it. Gavin didn't even realize that he had picked it up until its hilt seemed to accept his grip and an energy unlike any other traveled through him, healing his wounds and sharpening his mind. He looked up at Jen: crooked streaks of purple lightning bounced along her knuckles and fingertips while a mask of pain tormented her face.

"I won't . . . be able to . . . hold Ferox off for . . . much longer . . ."

Jen fought to get the words out as the ever-widening tornado sent catastrophic winds directly at the huts and the griffin stables, disintegrating them and picking up its mulched pieces, adding to the maelstrom that already included the remains of the shattered Pentarena compound.

"Now's your chance . . . to use Excalibur!"

Behind him, Hephalon had come to his son's aid. He had Rez wrapped in his arms as Jocelyn protected Mira, both of them still unconscious. Gavin re-gripped Excalibur, looking back toward Victor and Charles for advice. But no one could tell him what the right thing to do was this time. He looked back up, falling into a deeper stance so the wind wouldn't push him over, and saw Jen's eyes open. They were as black as soot, and she no longer looked like the girl he'd gotten to know over the past few months.

"I'm sorry," Gavin said to Victor and Charles.

He placed his other hand on Excalibur's hilt and, yelling at the top of his lungs while tears streaked his face, gathered enough astromancy energy to launch himself straight at Jen.

Without hesitating, he plunged the sword straight through her chest.

Jen's face wore a look of shock as her mouth opened and only a small whimper escaped. Gavin's diaphragm spasmed and he too found it hard to breathe. Suspended in midair with her, he looked into her eyes as the black drained from them. The tornado was still swirling around them, but he could feel its strength waning. His chin began to quiver uncontrollably as he looked down at her blood-soaked shirt and the small bit of blade that hadn't entered her chest. A trail of blood ran down the blade's thin, middle groove and pooled at the top of the hilt, his hands warm with her blood.

Together they slowly descended to the ground, and as he lay Jen's head on the charred grass, dark orbs of light expelled from her mouth. Gavin ducked out of the way and watched as they dissolved into the dusky sky, the clouds parting straight above in a growing circle. The wind was no more, and a reverent silence fell over Camelore. Gavin slowly withdrew Excalibur from his friend's chest and watched, horror-stricken, as she transformed.

Jen's likeness melted away to reveal Malcolm; he shared the same look that had scrawled Jen's face. Gavin let Excalibur slip from his hand, lurching up in shock just as Victor and Charles rushed to his side.

"*Malcolm?!*" Victor said, his voice scratchy.

Malcolm coughed up blood and smirked weakly. His neck strained to keep his head from the ground, but he was too injured to muster enough strength to completely sit up. "Ferox is gone."

"Where's Jen?!" Charles demanded.

Malcolm let his head fall back to the ground. He looked up into the darkening sky that was now clear of clouds. "Restoring the realms . . ." His eyes flicked to his former master. "I was misled, Victor. I hope I made up for it all."

His chest fell with a final exhale and his eyes rolled into his skull.

The rumbling from the earth below was still prevalent but an ancillary worry at the moment; Gavin still couldn't believe what had just happened. He looked down at his crimson-slicked palms as Victor knelt over Malcolm and recited the Sorcerer's Oath through light sobs and Malcolm evaporated into a halo of glowing orbs. They rose in serene silence, disappearing into the burgeoning night.

Moans from Mira and Rez caused Gavin to turn around. Together Victor and Charles, he walked toward Jocelyn and Hephalon, who were gently helping them out of their forced sleep.

No words were exchanged as Pernissa emerged from her hiding place to gather around everyone alongside Skarmor and Kuirhan. Gavin shared the unspoken sentiment that was on everyone's minds: nothing more could be done except pray that Jen—wherever she was—would save them . . .

CHAPTER THIRTY

Jen stumbled onto the sandy terrain of the Atra'dyu, wondering why Empyyr looked exactly like Atlantis's stadium. She stood up and dusted herself off, watching the MystiCrystal wink out and the roar of the crowd reach a fever pitch around her. Across the arena stood M'balo and Sh'tam, trading blows to see who would be the last brother standing and the rightful king of Atlantis.

Jen knew that this was just a projection, that the M'balo she watched at that moment was not the real M'balo. But she still ran toward him, looking around to see if there was a clue to how she could save the eleven realms. This was a huge gamble, she knew, and the closer she got to M'balo and Sh'tam, the more she realized that if her plan was going to work, she needed help.

From a being who called this realm home.

"Fuzanglong!" Jen yelled, turning around in a circle.

The crowd erupted shortly after, their cacophonous buzz seemingly swallowing her first, second, and third attempts at calling for the dragon. Finally, channeling animancy to attain the vocal intensity of one hundred howler monkeys, Jen slammed her eyes shut and called out his name one more time.

"FUZANGLONG!"

Everyone froze. The thousands of bystanders uncharacteristically went silent and the Atlantean brothers were stuck in their poses, their eyes glued on each other, Sh'tam's radiating fomenting anger and M'balo's grave responsibility.

Who dares disturb Empyyr?

A deep, judgmental voice rang out, collapsing the scene around Jen to reveal a shadowy expanse that seemed to stretch out into infinity. It was so dark that she couldn't even see her hands when she placed them inches from her face. A shuddering growl crashed down on her from all sides, and straight ahead could be seen two sources of light which quickly grew in size until they formed into a pair of shining eyes set into a menacing face that resembled Fuzanglong's but was not.

How does a mortal enter our holy domain?

Blinded by the dragon's eyes, Jen threw up a hand to shade her own as the massive dragon swirled around her, its scales shimmering as it floated in the expanse they both shared.

"I've come seeking Fuzanglong."

The dragon startled Jen by rushing toward her, its thick whiskers coiling and straightening as its glowing, yellow eyes bored into hers. *I am Zhulong, his brother,* the dragon boomed. He sounded almost annoyed.

"The eleven realms are collapsing," Jen started to explain. "They—"

Like a mist, Zhulong disappeared, leaving Jen alone and floating in the pitch-black expanse without a single word as to where he was going. She called his name, but like in a dream, she questioned if she actually said it out loud. Seeing nothing but Stygian darkness, Jen calmed her mind, unwilling to accept defeat. If Fuzanglong wasn't coming, then she had to find another way to reverse the proxiterramancic spells before they damaged realms beyond repair.

Willing her nexus awake, Jen began tapping into all the Mancy planes at once, trying everything to locate the MystiCrystal portal that she knew was still connected to Nyzanth. Though the last time she was in Empyyr, grabbing the Halostone was what sent her back to Earth. Did she have to look for something other than the portal to return?

Even though it was still too dark to see anything, Jen felt as if she was hurtling through the expanse at a speed so intense that it threatened to tear her apart. Moved by a force unknown, she let it happen, unsure of how much time had passed since Zhulong's abrupt departure. Suddenly, a thin streak of light cut through the infinite darkness like a gleaming knife cutting through thick, black fabric. She didn't know if it was inches from her face or a thousand miles away, but she looked down and saw that a translucent bridge had formed underneath her feet, one that meandered back to the rift.

Thinking this to be the pathway to the portal and nothing else, Jen started running toward the light and with every step she took, she noticed that the expanse surrounding the immense rift began to change, coalescing into a canvas of stars, galaxies, and nebulae. A cracking sound emanated from behind her; it was very soft and muffled at first but as the seconds passed it rose in volume until she had to look over her shoulder. When she finally did, Jen saw the bridge splintering into pieces as deep fissures traveled toward her, sending tremors along the bridge as a premonition of what was going to overtake Jen if she didn't pick up her pace.

She looked ahead, her heart dropping when she saw the length of the bridge she still needed to cover. But with no other options, she fired her legs into a sprint, quickly accelerating to match the speed of a cheetah with help from animancy.

Jen was making noticeable progress, but the fissures were just as fast, if not faster, and quickly overtook her. Her right foot slipped into a fresh crack, causing Jen to lose her balance. With the amount of speed she was carrying, her slight falter lurched her forward, sending her sprawling onto the bridge. She looked ahead: she was only a few dozen meters away from the base of the shining rift. Jen tried to stand, but the bridge was shaking so badly she couldn't remain upright for long.

Then the bridge started to buckle as sections broke off; some sank into the cosmic landscape below while others continued to crumble into countless specs of dust, left to float in the cold expanse. Luckily, the piece of bridge that Jen had fallen onto remained intact as it carried her closer to the rift, which had grown in length and width.

Jen set her feet in a wide stance and her arms bent at her sides. Every Mancy plane was primed for her touch; she wanted to be ready for anything. She was close enough now to the rift to see its jagged outline shining against the star-dotted backdrop as the floating section slowed to a stop.

Silence surrounded her as the light from the other side of the rift fought to overcome the darkness of the cosmos, pumping like a massive artery; but it was kept at bay. A voice inside of Jen's mind warned her about the rift, that it might not be the portal she was seeking. Before she could answer her own conscience, a familiar presence streaked between her and the rift as her entire field of vision was covered in cascading scales of every color from yellow to dark maroon.

Fuzanglong swirled above her, coiling and bending like a ribbon on a windy day before diving down to face her, his whiskers tense and straightened in agitation as his jade eyes bored down on her form, minuscule compared to his titanic size.

I thought I made myself clear to you when I said I will no longer interfere in mortal affairs, Jennifer Lancaster.

Jen's heart raced. "I didn't know where else to turn. The realms are disintegrating . . . I fear I'm too late."

Then why risk getting lost in the realm of deities to find me?

"Because I have to try!" Jen's emotions were getting the better of her. "I refuse to give up as long as I'm still breathing!" Hot tears coursed down her cheeks, blurring her vision. Her chest heaved as forceful breaths racked her body while she stared right back at the dragon of old.

You do remind me of Gwendolyn. Pure of heart and altruistic to a fault. Fuzanglong sounded almost patronizing. *The realms have been to the brink of annihilation before. It will certainly not be the last should they be saved.* He severed his gaze from Jen's as he slowly turned away. *It is inevitable.*

Quickly thinking, Jen said, "What about all of the treasure you've amassed?"

He stopped.

"It will all be lost." She swallowed, forcing herself to calm down. "How long have you spent collecting it all?"

My trove . . . A large pupil turned toward her out of the corner of an eye. Surprisingly, it seemed Fuzanglong hadn't realized that the destruction of the realms meant the demise of his beloved stores of gold and jewelry and artifacts. *There will be more to find in another dimension. Always is.*

He continued his exit.

"You said I remind you of Gwendolyn," Jen said, stepping to the edge of her broken section of bridge. She extended a hand toward him, and Fuzanglong waited. He didn't turn back around, but he was listening. "She died to protect the Halostone's location. She saved the realms then. Let me save them *now*."

The dragon remained suspended in front of her, intricately patterned scales slowly undulating as he breathed. Without warning, he shot off, disappearing into the cosmic tapestry of cloudy nebulae and pinpricks of stars.

Ripped of speech, Jen dropped her hand to her side, defeated. Her eyes found the rift again and she reached into her nexus to awaken astromancy. As her totem bracelet spun around her wrist and the astral powers surged through her, Jen's concentration was broken by Fuzanglong's return. This time, one of his front claws gripped a boulder-sized pearl that had iridescent flames dripping along its top.

This pearl is my most prized possession, Fuzanglong started. *I do not keep it deep inside the Earth's mantle like all my other treasures, for it has been stolen by other deities throughout the ages. It has given me wisdom to exceed all, prosperity beyond compare, and harmony with my inner spirit.*

He presented the pearl to Jen and dropped his chin so his jade-green eyes could be easily seen.

But it also takes. This rift behind me. You notice that it is getting bigger, yes?

Jen nodded. Her extremities were starting to tingle. She was scared as she met Fuzanglong's stare, but just as stalwart.

The closer the realms get to annihilation, the larger it gets. It is a tear in our dimensional fabric, and the only way to sew it up is from the inside. The dragon paused, and Jen knew he was waiting for her to say something.

"What do I need to do?" she asked, thinking about her friends and family. How she hadn't properly said goodbye.

Give yourself up to the pearl. Let it take your powers . . . and more if need be.

When Jen didn't move, Fuzanglong said, *You wanted to save the entire string of realms. This is your best chance!*

Jen took a half-step closer to the pearl. "Will I survive?"

Fuzanglong's whiskers twitched. *That all depends on how badly you want it.*

Jen took another step closer, this one bigger than the last.

She had just begun to feel comfortable in her new skin as an omnimancer . . . but the feelings she felt for the ones she'd met ever since the night of her twenty-first birthday were more powerful than any omnimancy spell.

Another step.

And if Jen could give them just one more day to live, she would. Even if she wasn't there to experience it with them, just the thought that she had made it possible was enough to take this risk. If she didn't, the fate of the realms was dust anyway.

She placed one hand on the smooth pearl, then the other, and opened up her nexus.

Instantly, Fuzanglong was gone—it was just her and the pearl.

And the rift before her.

There was a weird, magnetic attraction that her hands had on the pearl as she felt her power wax and wane, flickering as the pearl connected with her life source.

And she began to push. Push the pearl directly into the rift.

And as the pearl entered the ethereal light of the rift, Jen yelled and welcomed the stunning energy. She threw herself at the pearl, feeling her powers drain and nexus wink out until she was one with the light.

The last image in her mind was of her uncle, Victor Huxley, sitting next to her on his cot, the soft lights of his cottage bedroom casting a warm glow on his salt-and-pepper beard, as he explained the difference between wizards and sorcerers.

EPILOGUE

Atlantis
  Six years later

M'balo watched from the royal gardens atop his palatial estate as the latest Earthen aircraft left his kingdom's newly constructed landing pad, further strengthening the connections between Atlantis and the world below.

The sun was shining its radiance down upon the entire city, and he could hear laughter in the streets of the second ring across the waterway. Children were kicking balls around the streets, right next to an open-air food market. The smell of freshly roasted vegetables and meat spiced the air.

M'balo took in a long breath, a soft smile creasing his face. He brought his arms from behind his back and looked at his right prosthetic forearm and hand. He'd adapted to life as an amputee ever since Sh'tam took that portion of his arm during their duel for the kingship of Atlantis. The loss of half of his right arm was a small price to pay for his victory—something that his brother would trade his imprisonment for in a heartbeat. In an act of mercy and good faith that M'balo would reign justly and progressively, he had spared his brother's life, but he'd been banished to the lowest level of the royal palace's dungeon, to which only a select few had clearance.

Since then, M'balo had led the charge to modernize Atlantis and make its presence known to the rest of the world, trusting that an allegiance with every other country would be mutually beneficial to all. And he couldn't be more proud of his kingdom and the relations that had followed with the people of Earth. He ran his fingers down his prosthetic forearm, following the inlaid striations of crystalline veins in a carbon fiber exoskeleton toward his palm and watched as the artificial fingers contracted under his own will. His physicians and scientists had been hard at work ever since his incident to perfect the advancement of prostheses so that they could establish a connection with severed nerve clusters and grant the person full control over their new limb. The science was still in its infancy, but they'd come a long way in six years; M'balo could slowly make a fist thanks to Atlantis's brightest minds and his rigorous rehabilitation regimen.

A bright light caught his attention and he looked toward the center of the city, thinking it to be a glare from the landing pad's watchtower, but his body stiffened when he saw that the light emanated from the Akt'aron. No sound came with it, and in an instant it faded away and life on Atlantis continued on, but M'balo was already on his way there.

It took M'balo slightly longer than expected to reach the Akt'aron; he got caught up conversing with the citizens he had passed along the way. Now at the foot of the Akt'aron's outer staircase, he took the steps two at a time, eager to see what could have caused his sentinels to flock inside. At first it was difficult to see over his guards' visored helmets, but once word of the king's appearance trickled through the ranks, a path parted for him.

He stopped, suddenly out of breath, to look at the one person whom he never thought he'd see again.

Asleep, Jennifer Lancaster lay on her side, her back to the mystical tree that kept Atlantis afloat in the skies and her black waves of hair draped gingerly around her serene face. Her head rested on a straightened arm, and she wore the exact clothing she'd had on the day that M'balo had beaten his brother.

The day he'd shared a kiss with Jennifer.

A hush fell over the circle of guards around him. M'balo stepped closer to her as if he were treading on thin ice, and as he knelt down, Jennifer's eyes fluttered open, showing off her marvelously radiant violet eyes. They'd entranced him ever since the first time he saw her when he was just a prince and she a mistaken prisoner of his mother, the late Queen P'tara.

Jennifer smiled up at him, almost like she was expecting to see him, but it quickly turned into a frown when he laid a hand on her shoulder. She pushed herself up and rested on the Arbor Atlanti as M'balo stood up, dumbfounded.

"I am sorry if I have alarmed you," he said.

Jen blinked, shaking her head in quick bursts. Her eyebrows were furrowed when she said, "No . . . I—I thought you were another dream." She looked around the Akt'aron, then looked down at her hands. Her bracelet slid farther up her forearm. "I'm really on Atlantis," she said quietly, more to herself than anyone else.

"Yes." M'balo's heart was pounding incessantly. "To be frank, I thought I would never see you again," he said as he extended his actual hand to her.

Slack-jawed, Jen took it and stood up, eyes trained on his prosthesis. "What happened?"

M'balo waved his guards off. They turned around and exited to stand watch outside before he said, "The price of becoming king." He pressed his lips into a smile as Jennifer returned one of hers. "Where were you all these years, Omnimancer Jennifer?"

Jennifer's smile faltered. "I'm no longer an omnimancer." She touched her bracelet and rotated it around her wrist as she bit her lip, her eyes becoming distant. "I've been lost in Empyyr, the twelfth realm, trying to return home," she said, bringing her slender fingers up to the side of her face to tuck a stray curl behind her ear. "It's hard to explain." Her eyes returned to his and she smiled coyly. "And I told you: call me *Jen*. I'm just Jen now."

M'balo found it hard not to avert his gaze. He had never forgotten how stunning she looked.

"How long was I away?"

"Six years," M'balo said, watching her mouth it back in awe. "A lot has happened in the meantime." He offered his arm to her and gestured with his prosthetic hand toward the Akt'aron's exit.

"Wow," Jen said, falling in step with him. "It felt so much longer than that." She placed her other hand on his forearm and smiled at him.

M'balo grinned. "I would very much like to fill you in, if you have time?"

Still smiling, Jen said, "I can stay for a bit." She squeezed his arm as they made their way out of the Akt'aron. After a few seconds of silence, she continued, "Do you know anything about the whereabouts of my friends and family? And if they're all right?"

M'balo smiled. "Yes. I see them frequently, actually. Your father took over as Grand Mystra of a new sorcery university on Azumar, and your mother, uncle, and friends helped him construct a new castle there."

Jen was beaming with pride as they glided down the marble staircase toward the bridge that led to his palace in the second ring.

"Mintaka Castle, they called it," M'balo said.

Jen chuckled.

"What?" He looked over at her, noticing she was tearing up.

"Oh, nothing . . ." Jen shook her head and looked at her feet. "Mintaka is my middle name, that's all."

ABOUT THE AUTHOR

Gregory Heal is an independent author who is always trying to find creative outlets to express himself. He has countless more ideas that will become future books so stay tuned!

Having grown up in Southeastern Wisconsin, he enjoys outdoor activities in every season the Midwest offers from downhill skiing to sailing. He is also a first degree black belt in Tae Kwon Do and enjoys playing his drum set and painting when he is not working as a mortgage advisor.

www.ingramcontent.com/pod-product-compliance
Lightning Source LLC
Chambersburg PA
CBHW020218260626
47156CB00002B/433